One Heartbeat

The Hana Du Rose Mysteries

K T BOWES

Would you like to be part of it?

I'm a believer in 'try before you buy.'
There's nothing worse than forking out your hard earned cash
on a doozy and regretting it.
I don't want stinky reviews. I want you to love my work and feel
like you got value for money.

If you'd like 4 free eBooks to enjoy, you can join my mailing list
at ktbowes.com
The novels will arrive in your inbox.

Acknowledgements

For Andy, my technical guru and kindest critic.

Chapter 1

A crowd gathered in a fast-food restaurant on Greenwood Street in Hamilton, loud, hungry and covered in slick brown mud. The staff looked unhappy, descended upon without notice by the group of twenty.

"Amazing win!" a thick-set man beamed, slapping the back of a spindly blonde male who almost fell over. "I love this team. We might win the staff and old boys' league."

The blonde man grimaced and moved away from another debilitating slap to the back. His tracksuit pants dripped mud onto the tiled floor. "That hurt," he grumbled to the dumpy man standing next to him. "Pete, did you see him sit on my head during the game?"

"Shut up or he'll do it again just for the hell of it." Pete gave the thick-set man the side eye. "He isn't safe outside the chemistry lab. A Bunsen burner is the only thing he should be allowed to play with."

"And even then only under supervision." They smirked with a sense of shared conspiracy and Pete stepped up to the counter to take his turn. He shot a glance over his shoulder and scanned the queue. Then he leaned forward and whispered his order.

"What, sorry?" The teenage boy behind the counter leaned closer. "Was that a supersize burger or normal?"

A shriek sounded from behind Pete and his eyes rolled heavenward. "Damn it!" he cursed.

"Peter North!" a woman yelled, jumping the queue to slap the top of his head. "Have you forgotten our diet?" She ordered him a chicken salad with a fruit bag and he came away from the counter with a frown on his face.

"I ran around for ninety minutes, Henrietta," he whined. "I've burnt the calories in advance."

She shook her blonde curls and put her arm around Pete's shoulder. Chunky fingers ruffled his sandy hair and disturbed the parting at the back of his head. "Let's sit and share your fruit bag," she soothed, dragging him away from the promise of a cheeseburger.

The team gathered at one long table where they continued their excited conversation. The players resembled swamp creatures and the unpleasant brand of orange soil on their clothes and skin carried a rank smell. Other customers wrinkled their noses and moved away. Pete sniffed an armpit. "Do I stink, Henri?" he demanded, forcing his armpit into her face. "They need to look at the drainage on our home pitch."

"You smell of rose petals, my love," Henrietta lied. She turned her face aside and pushed a finger underneath her nose.

"It used to be a flax swamp." The chemistry teacher sat next to Pete and gave him a back slap which made him choke on a grape. "Our school is the oldest in the city and started when the first settlers came from the garrison. This rain isn't helping though. The water table is too high. I'm sorry they called the game off before full time. It's a good job we got ahead enough for the other team to concede the win."

"I'm not sorry the referee called it off," Pete grumbled. He lifted a piece of apple to his lips and the chemistry teacher jabbed his elbow, sending the fruit skittering across the table. Pete wrinkled his nose and looked at Henrietta for help.

"Here come the Du Roses." Her attention remained fixed on the sliding doors and her blue irises sparkled. "Hana looks soaked to the bone." She stood up and waved to the woman dashing through the doors and her hip banged into Pete's shoulder. Another grape left his fingers and rolled away. "We're over here, Hana!" she yelled, deafening everyone in close range.

Hana Du Rose's auburn hair reached her waist and flickered under the harsh strip lights. Thin and elegant despite the waterproof jacket burying her under layers of warmth, she waved in return. Her eyes sparkled with enough green to contain a hint of emerald. The baby girl in her arms looked dry, observing the lights and bustle with interest. Her Māori genes dictated a healthy olive skin, but some ancient European influence gifted her unusual grey eyes which glittered and shone as she studied her surroundings.

Henrietta hollered, bouncing on the balls of her feet. "Get your food and come over!"

Hana smiled as the whole restaurant winced at her companion's volume. "Okay," she mouthed. "Logan's just parking the car."

Appearing through the sliding doors came a giant of a man of six foot three or four. He carried an authoritative presence which caused several other customers to stop eating their burgers and stare. Ruggedly handsome with dark hair and features, his impressive physique betrayed a man not afraid of physical labour. His Māori heritage translated into confidence and satisfaction; his mana grounding him in an ethereal reassurance. He shook his dark head and rain droplets scattered around him in an arc. The baby laughed, her rosebud lips parting to show tiny front teeth. Logan Du Rose wore the same soccer strip as the others. Black shorts with a black-and-white striped shirt displayed the letters of his team, '*WPSB Staff and Old Boys.*' A round red insignia graced the front left while the back of his shirt read 'Du Rose' and a number four.

"You're soaked." Hana reached up and wiped the water from his brow. Her English accent differed from the cacophony of

New Zealand vowel sounds. "Pity Larry didn't turn up to open the changing rooms. You all needed a good shower."

"Yep. Dunno where he is." Logan turned a hundred-watt smile on Hana. He leaned closer to her and pressed a kiss against her forehead. "Shall I just order drinks? I don't want to eat fast food." His hand strayed to pat his muscular stomach and he wrinkled his nose.

"Good idea." Hana left him to order at the counter and drifted across to sit with the raucous crowd.

"Hana, did you see my goal?" a young man shouted from next to Pete.

She smothered a laugh and nodded. "Yes Tama, it looked spectacular. I didn't know you'd been practicing scoring with your bum!"

Everyone on the table laughed and spoke at once.

"Did you see Pete's goal?" cried Henrietta, patting him on the head with a meaty hand and dunking his face into his salad.

"That was an own goal!" Tama jeered and Pete pinked with embarrassment, muttering into his lettuce leaves.

Henrietta bridled in her boyfriend's defence. "Well, really!" she huffed. "My Pete only covered for the groundsman not showing up. Don't be so ungrateful!"

Murmuring began as the team conceded their muted thanks to Pete for standing in as a defender. Curiosity surrounded the mystery of Larry Collins' absence. "He might have forgotten," someone suggested.

"Or had too much wacky baccy last night," Pete snorted.

Tama kicked him under the table and shot a nervous look at Logan as he put the cups of fizzy drink on the table next to Hana. "Shut up, Pete!" he hissed. "Uncle Logan hates drugs."

"Maybe he's somewhere on the school grounds measuring the height of the grass and yelling at everyone to get off it!" shouted a huge man with a streak of orange mud across the bridge of his nose. He performed a superb impression of the groundsman, standing up and yelling in his best Larry Collins voice, "Get off that bloody crease!"

"Drama teachers," Logan whispered in Hana's ear. She clamped her teeth over her lower lip and smirked.

The gathered crowd laughed and moved on to other topics. Tama rose and stole the baby from Hana, cuddling her into his broad chest. She smiled up at him and made a gurgling noise. "Come on Phoenix, let's have some fun away from the rents." He returned to his seat and ate one-handed, feeding her ice-cream sundae in secret and snorting at the dreadful face she made against the coldness. Despite the faces, she waved her little arms and opened her mouth for more. Hana gave a sigh and leaned sideways against her husband, her fingers reaching out and twirling the wedding band on his finger.

"Did you enjoy your secret deodorant shower, Logan Du Rose?" She smiled up at him, scenting the strong maleness hidden beneath the haze of spray.

He shrugged and his gaze flicked to her lips and back to her eyes. He released a frustrated sigh. "No. The truck stinks now, so don't hurry your drink." His eyes flickered shut as he pressed his lips over hers. He released a groan. "Having Tama living on the sofa is killing me." His lips traced a line along her jaw and he sighed into her hair. "He's like a human contraceptive."

Hana laughed and her fingers coasted across the tattoo peeking from his sleeve. It ended above his elbow with italic script swirling through it like a lace fringe. Mud stained his face and neck, but he smelled good.

"Sorry we're late." A man with Indian heritage slotted himself onto the bench opposite and faced Hana. "Hey, Mum." He turned to help a tousled haired boy lift a laden tray onto the table. The child seized a packet of fries and plonked himself on Logan's knee without invitation. He swung lime green soccer boots back and forth under the table.

Logan nodded to his stepson. "Bodie." He turned his attention to the child in his lap. "You don't want to eat that crap, Jas," he said. He winced at the grease coating the boy's fingers.

"It's tasty." Jas dangled a bunch of fries in front of Logan's face and grinned when he jerked backwards. "You played great,

Poppa Logan." He reached up and kissed the underside of Logan's rough chin. He wrinkled his nose at the feel of stubble. "Daddy didn't play so good though." He looked sideways at his father. Small fingers stuffed another handful of chips between his lips despite the limited space. "You're not s'posed to let goals in Dad."

Hana leaned across to run a hand through her son's dark hair. "But Jas, he kept heaps out. He only let one in!" She gave Bodie a conspiratorial smile.

"Yeah, thanks Mum. I'm glad someone appreciated my efforts." He eyed his wrapped burger. "This won't help my game much though."

Hana looked along the table, shaking her head as she saw Tama still feeding ice-cream to her baby. "Stop it," she mouthed, seeing him bite his lip and carry on. With a cross exhale, Hana excused herself from the table, heading to the toilets near the back of the restaurant.

"Wait for me, Hanny!" Jas hopped off Logan's knee and followed, grappling at his crotch and sliding on his tiny boot sprigs. She waited at the door and held her hand out. "I don't need it," Jas reassured her, though he didn't let go of the front of his shorts.

"You obviously do," Hana retorted. She pushed the door open and gave a shake of her head as the child opened his mouth to protest. "No, I'm not going in the men's toilets. It's this or nothing, mate."

Logan sipped soda through a straw and stared around the restaurant. He missed nothing, his watchfulness a lifelong habit born of necessity. As Hana and Jas disappeared through the toilet door, a couple in their late-seventies arrived. They ordered at the counter before sitting nearby. The woman limped and the man carried the tray containing coffees and a muffin each.

"Tourists," Bodie said, nodding towards them. He moved with Hana's slender grace, but shared his features with her late husband.

"Yeah." Logan observed them with interest. "Poor buggers. Do you think their travel agent forgot to tell them autumn is wet and winter is cold?"

Bodie rolled his eyes. "Probably. Everyone in the northern hemisphere assumes New Zealand is hot all year around."

"Where do you think they're from?" Logan slipped his straw between his lips and took another sip of his drink.

"Policeman's intuition," Bodie said with a smug grin. "Their clothes look European. Not expensive, but different."

Logan's eyes narrowed. "I can see that. I wanted specifics."

Bodie snorted. "No idea, mate." He blinked. "Why, what do you think?"

"English." Logan jerked his head upwards. He pointed his straw towards the woman's coat. She'd taken it off and let it fall backwards over the chair while she leaned forward to sip her coffee. Her hand shook. "Look at the tag in the back of her coat. Marks and Spencer. That's an English brand."

Bodie's lips parted and his brow furrowed. "Oh." He swallowed. "You're good, man. You'd make a good cop if you weren't so dodgy." He smirked at Logan and the other man ignored his veiled insult.

He concentrated on the elderly couple, perplexed by something. A familiarity in the man's movements made him doubt himself. Thin and distinguished looking, the man sat as though the crowded restaurant didn't faze him. His calm contained a hidden authority which Logan recognised as one leader to another. His grey hair ran to white in a gentle, even way, cropped and neat above bifocal glasses.

"Do you know him?" Bodie asked. He reached across and snagged one of Jas' chicken nuggets. "You look like you do."

Logan shook his head and paused. "No. But yes. The man seems familiar." The sense of déjà vu rippled through him like a warning bell.

Bodie shrugged and helped himself to more of Jas' abandoned food. "They look harmless enough."

Logan nodded and went back to his drink, shuttering his eyelashes so he could watch the woman without detection. She looked delicate boned and seemed more uptight, jerky movements betraying her anxiety. She'd pulled her greying hair into a severe bun and she flapped and fidgeted while her companion perused the free newspaper.

"Hana's a long time." He shot the comment sideways, reluctant to remove his attention from the couple. "I might send Henrietta in after her."

"She's got Jas with her," Bodie replied. He rolled his eyes. "He's fascinated with the hand dryer. The motor blew up at the one in the cinema when I let him go in alone."

"Then don't let him go in alone." A darkness infused Logan's grey irises and he risked a sideways glance in Bodie's direction. "You need to rein him in, man. He's getting unmanageable."

Bodie shrugged. "I can't. Amy won't let me." He grinned as sauce dribbled off his chin.

Logan shook his head. "Don't leave it too late. He's a good kid, but he needs boundaries." He turned away, his gaze flicking towards the elderly couple and then the toilet door. Hana's absence sent a prickle of unease up his spine and he pushed his drink away.

In the toilet, Hana struggled with Jas. "Everyone's waiting, mate. We need to go," she argued.

"But it's eaten Action Man's hair!" he wailed. "He just wanted to see inside and it's stolen his hair!"

Hana poked her hand in the dryer and it activated itself, the powerful mechanism devouring the rest of the black mop. "It's sucked it into the filter," she said. "It won't come back out." She tried to fit her finger into the drain hole and failed.

"He doesn't like being bald!" Jas wailed and Hana fought her growing irritation.

"Then you shouldn't have stuck his face inside the dryer," she replied. It took a mammoth effort to keep her tone even. "Look," she hunkered down next to him, "why don't we get help? The staff might know how to get the filter out. I'm sure Daddy can speak to them."

Jas allowed Hana to lead him into the restaurant. She kept hold of his hand, noting how he pushed his Action Man inside his coat. Pale plastic legs protruded from a naked bottom but his bald head remained hidden. "Now?" Jas pleaded. "Can Daddy get it back now? He can arrest them if they won't help, can't he?"

Hana saw Logan's face light up with the special smile he kept only for her. She rolled her eyes and tried not to betray her inner annoyance as the grumbling child trailed after her. She stopped so fast, Jas ran up her heels and Action Man escaped his coat and skittered across the tiles. Jas yanked his hand free and went after him.

The sight hit her like a physical blow, taking her breath away so she froze on the spot. The colour drained from her face and her body refused to obey the simple instruction to run. Her legs trembled beneath her as the realisation struck her like a vehicle collision. Logan moved in her peripheral vision, rising from the bench and picking his way towards her. But he wasn't the only one.

The male tourist rose from his chair, his eyelashes fluttering over vibrant blue eyes. He lifted his glasses up and sat them on his head. He peered at her and Hana shook her head. "No," she gasped. "No." Her brain did mental somersaults as it tried to offer reassurance. She'd spent a lifetime imagining the moment only to discover it would never happen. Her mouth opened and closed as though she gulped for air and her gaze flicked towards the doorway as a family entered and brought in a breeze from outside. Hana craved the fresh air like a healing balm, promising herself if she could just get outside she'd be okay.

"No, Daddy! Ask them now!" Jas protested. Action Man's backside mooned to the restaurant as oblivious, Jas covered the bald head with his fingers.

"Mum?" Bodie ignored him, rising and watching Logan's journey through the scattered seating. "What's wrong?"

The tourist struggled with the extra chairs near his table, his face ashen and unreadable.

Hana's lips moved as she murmured to herself. "This isn't happening, Hana. Get a grip. It's a coincidence."

Logan reached her. "Hana, babe, what's wrong?" The anxiety in his eyes hiked her panic and words failed her. She gripped his hand to reassure herself. The bizarre hallucination would end if she could just hold on to him. "Hana?" He looked down at their joined fingers, seeing her knuckles showing white through the skin. The tourist kept coming, picking his route with determination as a new spring entered his step.

Hana's eyes widened, imploring Logan for help. His other hand closed over her shoulder and he squeezed life into her frozen bones. "I'm sorry," she breathed. She'd gone before he could catch her, fleeing the restaurant with her jacket billowing out behind her. She put her hands over her ears and focussed on the doors sliding open and closed before her, picking up enough speed to make it through the narrow gap. They hissed closed behind her and she dodged moving vehicles, drawing an angry horn blast in her wake. She became the broken teenager of almost three decades ago and shame washed over her. Panic made her abandon her baby and guilt mingled with terror. But she couldn't go back. Fear pinned her to the gritty floor of the car park.

Logan found her crouched next to their truck with her face in her hands. Rain fell on her head in sheets and soaked her hair. "What's wrong, babe. Tell me?" he begged.

Hana opened her mouth and then closed it, knowing she sounded crazy. He'd never believe she had just looked into the face of her dead father.

Chapter 2

Hana tasted the fresh winter air, gasping as though denied oxygen. She felt the sour taste of vomit in her mouth, but the feeble retches wrought nothing. She muttered to herself and fought the knot in her throat. Shame joined misery as Hana remembered Phoenix and she turned, ready to brave anything to retrieve her child. Anything. Even her father's doppelgänger.

Hana ran into Logan's broad chest, hearing him grunt. Phoenix giggled and made a grab for Hana's curly red hair. Tama righted her as she swayed with the impact. "I didn't finish my burger," he grumbled. "Where's the fire?"

"Hana?" Logan's grey eyes filled with suspicion and unanswered questions. Hana opened her mouth, but nothing came out. She had no words to describe what happened or how she felt about it. Instead, she took her baby and mopped at the dribble of ice-cream sick on her chin.

"When she gets diarrhoea, you're changing her nappies," she bit, accompanying her threat with a glare at Tama.

"What did I do?" he groaned. The men watched Hana stomp around the car, her wellies making a rubbery, clumping sound on the concrete. Her eyes darted to the sliding doors of the restaurant and then back to Logan.

"Get in!" she hissed, her body language oozing discomfort. She grappled with the door handle and her eyes radiated pure panic as she found it locked. Logan pressed the key fob and the lock sprung open. Hana bolted inside, taking the baby with her. She pressed the switch to lock her door and inserted Phoenix into her seat from inside the car.

Logan gave Tama a nudge and sent him round to the passenger side. Seconds passed as they both climbed in and settled. Hana let out a sigh of frustration. "I want to go, now, please," she begged, urgency making her sound petulant as she struggled with the straps of the car seat.

"Maybe you've got diarrhoea," Tama commented. He turned to face her, his lips widening in a grin. Seeing her frightened expression, he turned around and raised an eyebrow at Logan. He opened his mouth to speak and Logan gave a shallow shake of his head.

Hana dabbed sick from the baby's chin and complained to herself. She kept glancing through the side windows and her eyes widened as Logan drove past the restaurant's front doors to get to the road behind. He fumbled with his seatbelt as the elderly male tourist emerged and hobbled towards the car park on wavering legs.

The old man's face looked pale and ghostlike as he raked the parked cars with wide, blinking eyes. The woman emerged after him, putting her hand to her mouth before wrenching on his arm. She pointed at the departing Honda as Logan joined the main traffic flow. He watched in the rear-view mirror as the old man bent double, his shoulders heaving. A passing customer leaned towards him in concern, her head nodding as she asked if he needed help.

At the traffic lights, Logan turned to view Hana and her appearance made him swallow a ball of fear with an audible gulp. The stiffness of her body looked painful and her teeth worried at her lower lip until it bled. He reached behind and offered his hand, gratified when shaking fingers took it and squeezed. "It's okay, Hana," he soothed. "Lots of people have panic attacks; it's nothing to worry about."

Tama opened his mouth and Logan wasn't quick enough to still his tactless observation. "You don't."

"How would you know?" Logan growled and Tama pressed himself back into his seat. The traffic crawled onto Greenwood Street and passed the restaurant. Graffiti on the front wall invited him to do something explicit with himself. Logan spotted the tourists as the cars ahead stilled again. The man sat on a low wall by the play area and the woman hovered around him like a bumble bee. Logan took in the old man's military bearing but as he pressed the gas pedal and rolled the truck forward, he recognised something unexpected blossoming in the rheumy eyes. It took his breath away. Hope.

Something from Hana's past had come back to bite her and she hadn't anticipated its arrival. The man's physique gave Logan a clue, but it raised more questions than it answered. Hana told him her parents died decades ago. Logan frowned, wondering why she'd lie. Another glance at the devastation on her pretty face reassured him she didn't. He saw her trying to collect herself, her fingers patting the baby's chest in a gentle, frantic movement. The old man's appearance had traumatised her and she looked like she wanted to run. Logan stroked his fingers over her knee and her body temperature felt cold to the touch.

Hana closed her eyes and drowned in her silent agony. Her lips moved over words without a sound. "He's dead. He's dead. He's dead." The visions she'd buried moved through her mind, her father and brother slinging her Indian boyfriend onto the street for getting her pregnant. Logan's hand felt hot against her knee, thawing a section of the ice which ran through her veins. She saw her father's face in her mind, older, sadder, bent double by life and circumstance. She'd needed his help and instead he'd thrown insults and punches. The words returned to torture her, the sting not dulled by time but as fresh as the day he'd spoken them. Slut. Whore. Disgusting.

Hana squeezed her eyes closed and a tear tumbled free and crashed onto the rise of her cheek before plunging onto her coat. The waterproof material repelled it and Hana watched through her eyelashes as it pooled in her lap, joined by another and then another. She forced her wringing hands around her, hugging her stomach to keep them still. What did he want? Why was he here? Hana acknowledged the bitterest blow of all in that split second as she recognised him. Because she'd looked for her mother out of habit and not found her. She couldn't find her. Not ever. Jude McIntyre died months after the fight which detonated her family. Hana's brother banned her from the funeral and she didn't get to say goodbye. They took even that from her in their final punishment for her one catastrophic mistake.

Hana leaned forward and heaved out a long breath. The seatbelt cut into her neck and she held onto the pain and let it disperse the numbness. When it didn't feel enough, she clamped the fingers of her right hand over the scar on her left wrist and squeezed. A searing pain shot up her arm and into her shoulder. She relaxed and leaned into it. "I'm alive," her mind told her. "I'm alive."

Logan made the turn onto a side street and cut back onto the main road in front of the restaurant car park. The traffic crawled towards a busy intersection and Logan watched the elderly couple walk towards their vehicle. The woman talked with animation, holding onto the man's arm though his shoulders slumped like someone who'd been kicked in the head. Their smart white sedan looked like a rental and Logan glanced in the mirror again at Hana. He saw her wipe her eyes on her sleeve and pursed his lips. His quick brain memorised the registration number of the car. The woman opened the passenger door and Logan saw the Hertz logo in the corner of the windscreen. Possibilities flew through his mind. He needed to solve the mystery without upsetting Hana further. His fingers tapped a beat on the steering wheel as he planned.

The Hakarimata Ranges came into view and Hana's silence felt eerie as though she waited for a hatchet to fall on her head. She smothered the occasional sniff and stared at her knees. Logan withdrew his hand before the city limits, but he doubted she noticed.

"Are you back at the school boarding house on Monday?" Tama asked, his question jarring in the silence.

Logan nodded. "Yeah. It's better than it was. Less night duties now someone else pulls their weight. We don't stay on site during my free weekends because they can't resist calling me to sort out some disaster. We'll drive back on Sunday night or Monday morning before school." He watched Hana in the rear-view mirror again. She took a deep, fortifying breath and ran a hand over her face. "When do you go back to college?" Logan made the turn towards the Waipa Bridge and missed his nephew's look of misery. "I'm proud of how well you're doing."

Tama had inherited the Du Rose good looks and the ego to match, but his colour faded as the blanched look overtook his handsome Māori features. "Next week," he answered. Logan nodded. Keen to change the subject, Tama turned to look at Hana. Concern lined his forehead. "You okay, Ma?" Hana nodded, the motion shallow and non-committal. Tama turned around again, worry etched into his face. His instincts screamed of impending disaster and he dreaded it. "You sure?" He risked the challenge as the metal security gates at the bottom of the steep driveway rolled aside. He turned his body so he could get eye contact with her, saddened by the way she moved her head to avoid his gaze.

"Stop asking me, please." Hana shook her head from side to side, her voice sounding wooden and laden with doom.

Tama reached his long, muscular arm around the seat behind him and took her hand in his. Her fingers felt freezing against his skin. She'd given him more love in the last six months than he'd ever known and her pain drove a stake through his heart. He narrowed his eyes and sought to make it better. "I love you, Ma," he whispered. "Please be okay."

Tama felt Logan's sideways glance and stiffened, sensing mistrust cross the centre of the vehicle. Logan said nothing but Tama removed his hand and sat round, seeing his uncle's gritted jaw press through his cheek. As Logan made a tight turn on the incline, Tama saw his own name inscribed into his uncle's bicep. Nestled next to Phoenix in a cursive script, it offered a flush of pleasure but also warning. Someone loved him. He couldn't afford another screw up.

Tama peered behind him and caught Hana's attention, receiving a tentative smile through eyes filled with tears and a face which wobbled beneath his scrutiny. He felt an irrational anger for whoever caused her anguish, balling his fists in childish loyalty.

Logan halted the truck at the top of the driveway and Culver's Cottage loomed before them. It overlooked the mighty Waikato River at its convergence with the clay filled Waipa, restored to its former 1900s magnificence. Behind it soared native bush, the green hues rising to meet the angry grey sky with confidence.

Hana forced herself from the vehicle and sighed as she breathed fresh air. Rain pattered again and she watched Tama as he lifted Phoenix in her car seat and covered her with his jacket. "Ugh!" he grunted at the sugary vomit scent rising from her clothes.

"You can sort her out when she wakes up with a belly-ache," Logan muttered. His scarred fingers unlocked the front door and pressed buttons to deactivate the burglar alarm.

"Whatever," Tama grunted. "You love pacing the floor with your precious daughter. She's the only one who smiles at you when you're in a bad mood."

Hana kicked off her boots and stalked to the master bedroom, throwing herself face down on the four poster bed. She snuggled into the clean duvet, feeling the lead weight of grief in her breast. Questions without answers piled into the forefront of her mind. Should she have stayed? Would he listen to twenty-eight years of anger and regret? Hana pressed her face into the pillow until she couldn't breathe. The old Robert McIntyre listened to nobody, least of all his daughter. She allowed herself to gulp a breath and sighed it out. He'd stood metres away from his own flesh and blood and didn't realise. The baby he rejected sat nearby and his great grandson made a fuss about a doll's lost hair right under his nose. He didn't know. He couldn't know. "You missed it all," she whispered to the empty room. "Life and death and I did it without you."

Hana curled into a tight ball and pressed the images away. Her mother's silent tears played on a loop in her mind and she blamed herself. She should have gone back and explained. Her deaf mother had jumped in fright as the McIntyre men launched themselves at Vik. Hana meant to write to her but didn't, assuming her father would destroy the letter. The next contact with her family came in the form of Judith's funeral notice with a handwritten note. "Don't come. We don't want you there."

A fleeting image of her perfect older brother with his perfect wife and perfect children drifted across her inner vision. Hana shuddered and pulled the pillow over her head. Losing her mother hit her again like peas removed from the freezer, as fresh as the day an unkind hand froze them in time. She forced herself not to cry, pressing her fingers over the scar on her wrist to distract her ragged thoughts. They sought to suck her further into the abyss and she doubted she possessed the energy to climb the ladder back up. She heard Logan put Phoenix into her cot, his footsteps treading along the hallway to the kitchen. Then she heard the gentle strum of his guitar, soothing strains crossing the house as he waited for the kettle to boil. She recognised the tune, an old Māori song he often played. She imagined him standing in the kitchen with his foot on the seat of a chair, balancing the guitar across his thigh as he played left handed. The song made her feel grounded. Logan sang of Pokarekare Ana and her lover's yearning for reunion. "E hine e hoki mai ra. Ka mate ahau I te aroha e." He repeated the lyrics in English and Hana listened to his gentle baritone. "Oh, girl return to me, I could die of love for you."

Hana slipped off the bed and her jacket rustled. She chose her place beside Logan, not her bigoted father whose homage to forgiveness and grace proved nothing more than lip service.

"Nga iwi e! Nga iwi e!" Logan changed the song to one he said Reuben taught him as a boy. "All you people! All you people!" He sang many other songs but avoided those invoking strong memories of his father and his mother's deceit. Hana reached the kitchen door as he finished. She lingered there, watching her husband's long fingers stroking the strings. His brow furrowed and his mind strayed as he created a bridge of music before launching into anything else.

"Did you know Poppa Reuben could play?" Tama stood at the sink and pressed bread into the hole in his face, eating on the run as though his security might disappear without warning.

Logan nodded. "Yep. Get a plate and sit down."

"I didn't know you could play. You sound like him." Tama grabbed a clean plate from the draining board and added two more slices to the one in his hand. Plain bread, no butter. As though he didn't have time for niceties. He spoke with his mouth full. "He sang that song."

"Yeah, he gave me this guitar." Logan hefted the instrument against his thigh, but his fingers didn't still their strumming.

"For real? Where did you hide it all these years?"

"Alfred hid it in the storeroom next to the kitchen. Ma took me to Reuben for lessons as a kid. I thought he was my guitar teacher." Logan's jaw flexed against the bitter truth and Tama's face creased in disgust.

"That's sick!"

"Yep." Logan struck a bung note and the guitar reverberated as he leaned it against the wall. Hana ground her teeth, the jarring sound deliberate. He turned towards the kettle and yanked a mug from the cupboard above.

Hana picked her moment to intervene as Tama's lips parted with another ill-advised comment. "Sorry about before." She clasped her arms around Logan's waist from behind and held on, anchoring herself in this life and not the one long since passed. He relaxed and ran his long fingers over hers, feeling the dead coldness of her skin.

"I'm making you a drink, babe," he replied, dumping a tea bag into the mug and lifting the kettle.

Hana shook her head against his back. "I thought I'd walk over to see Maihi," she replied. "Phoenix will sleep for a while." Logan turned on the spot and hauled her into his chest. Hana sniffed his shirt, calmed by the summer sweet meadow scent of him; hay, horses and sunshine. "I'll take my phone. Text me if you need me to come back earlier."

Logan nodded, knowing he couldn't rush her. Pressing and cajoling forced her to run. Instead, he smiled and kissed the top of her head, infusing her with his love.

Hana wrinkled her nose at Tama, disturbed by the way he gobbled the bread. "Sorry you lost your burger."

He shrugged in reply. "Nah, the fat's bad for me, anyway." He waved a floppy slice of bread and waggled his eyebrows. "Uncle Logan can pump more weight than me. Need to beat him somehow."

Hana nodded, assuming they'd train together in the room next to the garage where Logan kept his exercise equipment. "You might as well work out before you get a shower. I'll see you later."

Hana closed the front door and chased her wellies around the porch. The heaviness in her heart matched the greyness of the day and the oppressive clouds. With a sigh, she stepped off the porch and skirted the house. Her jacket flapped in the cold breeze and she pulled her hood up to cover her hair. The rain eased as she climbed the fence into the paddock and began her long uphill climb.

Chapter 3

"What's going on?" Tama brushed crumbs from the downy hair coating his chin. His fingers lingered with pride over the first flush of a beard.

Logan raised a finger and shook his head. "Wait!" he hissed. He watched from the long kitchen window as Hana walked around the side of the house and climbed the fence into the paddock. Then he turned and leaned his neat backside against the sink.

"Wanna train for a while?" Tama licked his index finger and picked up the crumbs from his plate. "I didn't want to admit to Hana that I'm on the kid weights."

"Go for your life." Logan sounded distracted. "I've got stuff to do."

"Oh." Tama slouched in disappointment. "Stuff without me?"

Logan gave himself a visible shake and wiped an olive-skinned hand across the back of his mouth. "Did you not see the state of my wife?"

"Yes, but what can we do to change it? She went to pieces in a public place. You said it was a panic attack. I gave her a hug."

Logan sighed. "It wasn't a panic attack, Tama. She saw someone she didn't expect and it knocked her sideways."

"Who?" Tama spoke with his head inside the pantry and a bread wrapper rustled. He popped his face out. "Who did she see?"

Logan's eyes narrowed as he replayed the scene in his mind. "That old tourist. He's someone she knows. He'd already got my attention because he seemed familiar. I need to find out who he is."

"Who do you think he is?" Tama stuck his head in the fridge and the plate tipped. He held the slice of bread in place with his thumb. "Can I have jam on this?"

"I think it's her father."

"What?" Tama banged his head on the fridge door and let go of the bread. It slipped onto the tiles and he bounced forward to retrieve it. "Three second rule," he said, blowing at it and sending crumbs fluttering to the floor. "Oops."

"Yeah." Logan ground his teeth. "Oops."

"What are you gonna do?" Tama's eyes sparked with interest and he sat down at the table. The plate clanked against the wood. "You could take a hit out on him. You still know people." He shrugged. "Didn't look much like she wanted him here."

"No, I can't take a hit out on him." Exasperation leaked into Logan's words. "It's too late for Reuben to answer my questions, but maybe there's still time for Hana."

Tama gasped. "You can't bring him here. She'll go mental."

"Maybe not," Logan mused. "But it's worth the risk." He pulled his phone from the charger plugged in near the kettle and dialled. His eyes glazed over as the call connected and he bit down on his tongue.

"No man, no way!" Bodie spat the words. "I can't check registration plates without good cause. There are laws to protect *innocent* members of the public." He put a stress on the word, 'innocent.'

"It's important," Logan replied. "And please don't mention it to Hana." He figured if she wanted Bodie to know he'd sat within spitting distance of his grandfather, she'd have told him herself.

"Sorry and all that," Bodie said. He sounded smug and not at all apologetic. "But I've passed my next lot of exams and I've made the list for a vacancy. I won't get promoted for flouting the rules, so find another way. You nearly got me fired last year and I can't risk it again."

"Okay," Logan replied, sounding disappointed.

"What was wrong with Mum?" Bodie demanded and he invented an excuse.

"She forgot something important. We needed to leave."

"Cool, is that all you wanted?" Pique crept into Bodie's voice.

"Yep. Thanks." Logan killed the call with a wince. "Dick!" he whispered as the screen went black.

Tama screwed up his face. "Can you believe Hana gave birth to that guy? Just seeing his smug grin makes me want to slap him into next week."

Logan groaned. "Well, don't. If I can't then neither can you."

Tama finished the bread and pulled the fabric of his soccer strip up to his nose. "I stink," he announced. "Bummer about the changing rooms being locked. Can I have first shower?"

"Yep." Logan nodded and Tama left the room. He abandoned the plate on the table surrounded in a sea of crumbs. Logan went through the motions of clearing up after him, his brain enjoying the mindless activity while he ran through alternate scenarios. He could still see Hana through the window, her slender frame growing smaller the higher she climbed. Reaching the top of the property, she turned left and disappeared into the gully. His heart ached for her. The idea came as he knew it would and a slow smile drifted across his lips. "That should work," he breathed. "Good one, Du Rose. Follow the money."

Chapter 4

Hana made the twenty-minute walk next door in good time and only fell twice in the thick mud. The morning's rain had widened the gully, but she scrambled across without missing her footing. She knew the way but stopped to examine the hidden markers she and Maihi planted the year before as an escape route. The cloth strips looked stained and tatty, blending into the rustic fence as though part of it. Hana wiped her filthy hands on the grass and wrinkled her nose, hoping it was mud and not cow dung.

Maihi's husband grazed steers on the back blocks of Hana's land in return for meat every time they killed a beast. The bulk of the beef herd grazed the higher slopes and Hana edged around their paddock as brown eyes with designer lashes turned to follow her progress. Chewing mouths continued their circular action. A city girl at heart, she sighed with relief when she put a fence between her and the herd before starting the treacherous descent to Maihi's welcoming cedar wood house. The last rays of the late sun dipped below the range, leaving greyness in its wake. Hana dreaded a nightmare stumble home in the dark and knew Logan would be worried if she left it too late. She'd seen the concern in his face and felt grateful to him for not pushing. The quizzical look in his eyes told her he'd guessed already. "I didn't lie," she pleaded aloud, startling a nearby falcon feeding on a rabbit carcass. "I thought my father died years ago."

Maihi responded to the tentative knock on her back door with a hug and barrage of kisses. "Kōtiro," she cried, her brown face crinkling in pleasure. The word meant *girl* in Māori, but to Hana, it meant daughter.

"Hello, Maihi," Hana responded, kicking off her wellies on the porch. She allowed herself to be coddled and loved, fed tea and soup and given sympathy. The craving for maternal affection ate at a raw spot in her heart and the older woman kept it at bay with her ferocious love. Maihi warbled on with the latest news about her son's family, chatting away as she buttered bread and pushed it towards Hana.

"Eat some kai," she demanded. "You look real skinny."

Hana ignored the comment, not wanting to admit what she saw on the bathroom scales. Her weight had plummeted since Phoenix's birth and she hadn't yet worked out why. The approaching black and white cat distracted her. "Tiger!" Hana exclaimed. She reached down to stroke his soft coat and he wrapped his body around her legs, pressing close and purring. "How are you doing, old man? I miss you." He rubbed his head against her hand but the second she bent to pick him up, he fled. "Oh," she said, her voice laced with pain. "He thinks I want to take him home."

Maihi chuckled. "You do."

"Yeah, I do," Hana admitted. "It feels like we broke up." She watched Maihi's lavender female lick Tiger's tattered ears and face with a rasping tongue.

"Eat!" Maihi insisted, jerking her head towards the plate in front of Hana. She obeyed, though anxiety made the food roil in her stomach afterwards.

The visit spared Hana fretting for a while and her panic receded to a distant ache. Until the older woman zapped her as usual. "So, my love," Maihi said, plonking another cup of tea in front of Hana. "What's eating you then? Tell me." She peered at her over her glasses, her fingers deftly chopping kumara and taro and dropping it into a roasting tin.

"I saw my dead father this morning," Hana said, keeping her voice matter-of-fact. "In one of the fast-food places on Greenwood Street."

"A shock then?" Maihi said, not missing a beat.

Hana nodded. "I feel angry, frightened and disappointed."

Maihi cocked her head and diced a carrot. "Disappointed in him?"

"No." Hana pursed her lips. "In myself. He tried to talk and instead of saying the things I've spent twenty-six years bottling up, I ran." She clapped a hand over her mouth. "Oh, no!" she groaned, "I forgot something important. Please could I use your land line for a moment?"

Maihi frowned at the randomness of Hana's conversation with the manager of the restaurant. Hana rolled her eyes with embarrassment. "It's probably a fire hazard," she apologised. "Yes, it's a piece of tufty black fabric. It's meant to be hair. Hair. No, hair. No, not a person's hair. A doll's." She sighed. "It's Action Man's hair and it fell off in the dryer. Somehow it got sucked into the vent at the bottom." Laughter erupted through the handset and Hana jerked the phone away from her ear. When the voice resumed, it sounded strangled. Hana tipped her head and her unseeing gaze raked the blank ceiling as though searching for answers. "Ah, I see. Yes. Thanks."

Hana climbed back onto her stool and watched Maihi's wrinkled brown hands chop a carrot with surgical precision. "Apparently an angry Indian gentleman hauled a small boy kicking and screaming from the restaurant. A service repair man is trying to free the wig now. Bodie gave them Jas' address and they've promised to post what's left."

"Will you get the bill?" Maihi worked hard to control the escaping smirk.

"He said there'd be no charge but insisted Jas didn't stick Action Man's head in the dryer again. Oh Maihi, don't laugh!"

Maihi struggled to contain her snorts, contrary to Hana who could see no funny side. "What will you do?" Maihi asked, wiping the tears from her face with the hem of her apron.

"Write and thank them," Hana mused. "Or make Jas do it. They only laughed a little."

"No!" Maihi replied, her expression growing serious, "About your matua, your papa?"

"Oh, nothing." Hana voice dropped. "I ran away from the only opportunity I'll ever get to tell him how he made me feel. I went to him for help after I messed up and he discarded me like an imperfect blotch on his pristine landscape. There's nothing I can do. He isn't still sitting in the restaurant. I've missed my big moment." Hana sighed and bit her lip. Her voice became soft. "He'd aged so much I hardly recognised him. I have to let it go; let him go."

"Seems a shame." Maihi's chopping slowed. "All these years you thought he'd died. But he isn't. You shouldn't miss out on your chance to release all those emotions. They've stained your heart for too long."

"I don't have a stained heart!" Hana snapped. Her voice rose at the end. "I forgave him years ago. Dada held onto grudges and offences, not me. I dealt with it."

"Dada? Is that what you call him?"

Hana gave a slow nod. "Mother was Irish and my father is Scottish. Yes. He liked me calling him that."

"So how come you ran then?" Maihi asked. "If you dealt with it before your God, you'd have given your matua a hug and told him you were pleased to see him."

Hana's mouth opened but nothing emerged. She gaped and swallowed, speechless at Maihi's accusation. Injustice made way for recrimination and Hana felt un-forgiveness and bitterness steal back into her heart. "I thought I forgave him," she stammered." She sulked in silence, isolating those emotions which surfaced with such force in the restaurant and turning them over in her mind's eye, examining them for flaws. Maihi continued with her food preparation, humming the same song Logan played in the kitchen a few hours ago.

Hana jumped up in alarm, noticing the darkening sky and disappearing afternoon. "Oh gosh, it's getting dark. I should go home." Her eyes widened at the thought of making the bush walk alone.

The unmistakable sound of a motorbike climbing Maihi's steep driveway made the house rumble as reflected headlights bounced around the room. "It's your tahu," Maihi commented, drying her hands on her apron. "He's come for you."

Logan unfolded his tall frame from the motorbike and removed his helmet, running strong fingers through his messy fringe. Hana melted at his thoughtfulness, overridden by the realisation she'd have to ride pillion. "Oh, no!" she groaned. "Last time he took me on the bike, I melted my wellie-boot on the exhaust pipe."

Maihi ignored her and let Logan into the kitchen, closing the door to keep in the heat. He stood on the mat in his cowboy boots and accepted her hug, trying not to clout her with the helmet in his hand. "Your carriage awaits, my lady." He raised his eyebrows and she rose from the stool with obvious reluctance. "Come on," Logan said with a smirk. "It can't be worse than last time. Get a move on, wahine."

Maihi cuddled her, fortifying her for the bracing cold and the ride down the breakneck driveway. Hana tried not to think about it too hard as she grappled around on the deck outside for her wellies. Maihi's arm slipped around her shoulders, her mouth close to Hana's ear. "Don't you think it's time you trusted your man?" she asked, raising an eyebrow flecked with grey. "You need to let go sometime, Hana Du Rose." Maihi closed the back door with a wave over her shoulder.

Hana griped at her words, knowing she spoke of trust on more levels than just the bike ride home. She sighed, tensing as Logan settled her on the pillion behind him. He fired it up and Hana cringed as he handed her the spare helmet. It fitted better than last time and a scent of newness rose around her face.

"Keep your feet here," Logan mouthed over the sound of the engine. He leaned down to place her feet onto the rests, hoping to avoid a repeat of last time.

Logan's neat bum looked good on the wide seat and Hana afforded herself a longer stare as he righted the machine. He kicked away the stand and brought it upright. As she felt the powerful surge of the engine, her confidence failed her and she snatched at the back of his leather jacket. "Use the handrail," Logan called, his voice muffled inside the helmet and dulled by the powerful engine. When she shook her head so hard the helmet wobbled, he grappled for her hands and placed them over his chest. Hana gripped the leather of his jacket and clung on, reminding herself to breathe. The bike rolled forward and Logan kept his feet near the ground as it pitched and tossed over the rough driveway. Hana fought the urge to lean the opposite way to the turn, forcing herself to relax and follow the graceful movements of her husband's body. She put all her trust in him as Maihi suggested, finding an eroticism about the release of pent up terror.

Hana began by shutting her eyes but opened them half way down the mountain. The stomach lurching seemed less of a fairground ride if she could see the road. The headlights picked out bush and trees as the bike descended. Hana concentrated on her posture, conscious of not slumping forward as a dead weight against Logan's spine. At the bottom of the driveway, Logan checked the winding road and eased the bike left. He got up to speed before the first bend and Hana turned her face and leaned her head against his back. She snuggled in as close as the helmet allowed. The gear changes reverberated through the chassis and Hana felt the movement of Logan's body as he depressed the clutch and swayed with the bike. An experienced rider, he accounted for the extra passenger and how it altered the bike's handling. Hana felt trust blossoming in her gut and relaxed her fingers around Logan's chest.

Logan took the full force of the air buffeting them as they rode towards home and Hana experienced a budding sense of exhilaration cutting through the fear. She saw the last bend before their driveway as they hurtled around it, feeling a stab of disappointment. But Logan blasted past and onto the open road, increasing speed along the straights and handling the sharp bends with precision. Hana felt a strange peace as though something blew from her soul that shouldn't have been there. A tickle rose in her stomach as they sped forward and it bubbled up inside her helmet as a giggle. A yearning to go faster woke in the back of her brain, but she couldn't communicate with Logan. She satisfied herself with the brilliant night sky above and the glint of starlight on the Waikato River to her right. The Milky Way spread out before her, the same view from Logan's mountain where Phoenix burst into the world amidst leaves and dust. Hana grinned into her helmet, glad no one could witness her momentary lunacy.

They sped as far as Parker Road and Logan indicated left and made the turn, travelling the gravel road with care to avoid damaging his bike. At the small car park for the reserve he pulled in and parked, kicking the stand to support the bike. Only one other vehicle shared the space, a dark silhouette with a hunting dog's crate open in the back. Logan switched off the engine and lifted his leg over the massive chassis, but when he removed his helmet Hana remained still. Logan released her chin strap with gentle fingers and lifted her helmet off, brushing her red curls away from her face. She smiled at him in the darkness, not wanting to spoil the moment with words.

Hana perched on the bike as Logan put his arms around her and pressed his lips over hers. It felt private and safe, just the two of them. No fathers intruded, jumping from the woodwork like crazy jack-in-the-boxes to destroy everything. Logan's hand snaked beneath Hana's jacket and his fingers pushed her shirt up. His kiss deepened, searching for something in her soul. His touch against her ribs made her shiver. "Here?" she whispered and felt his nod against her cheek.

Logan lifted her from the bike and led her metres away. He spread his leather jacket on the ground between crowded punga trees. The unexpected exhilaration of the bike ride left a blush of risk on Hana's psyche and made her daring enough to undo Logan's jeans and expose him to the night. He moaned in pleasure and the sound induced a flicker of recklessness in her stomach.

Logan's kiss robbed her of air and his skin felt fiery to the touch. The cold licked at the fringes of Hana's nakedness as she stripped, winter nipping at her soft flesh. Passion dulled her awareness of the night noises as she sank to the ground, but they crept back into her consciousness as the pleasure passed and sanity returned. The creases of the jacket dug into her left hip and she jumped and squealed as a red eyed possum took a short cut next to her foot. Logan laughed, his deep melodious tones spreading through the darkness as he kept Hana beneath him. He kissed her again, nipping at her lower lip. "I should get you home," he whispered into her ear. "I left the boy taking care of our daughter. Anything could happen."

Hana put her arms around his strong neck and wished she could stay in the moment. He hadn't asked about her scene in the restaurant, but she owed him an explanation. Maihi was right. She needed to trust him. "That man," she began. A gulp swallowed her words and she struggled to continue. "In the restaurant. He's my father."

Logan nodded. "I guessed." He didn't press, waiting while she wrangled her thoughts into order. He spun slow, sensuous circles against her ribs with his finger.

"I don't know what to do," she whispered. The agony in her voice produced a low whine. Hana snatched at Logan's fingers, twisting them in hers and threading them backwards and forwards in agitation. "I thought I dealt with my feelings." She sounded petulant, like a child. "Why does my past keep coming back and messing things up?"

"Kōkau," Logan whispered. "Because it's unfinished." He pushed his free hand through her hair at the back of her neck. Hana closed her eyes, allowing the soothing movement to touch her soul. She sighed and sat up, feeling a familiar tingle in her breasts. "I need to get back to Phoe."

Logan studied the pale glint of Hana's breasts in the moonlight. He reached out a hand to touch their fullness. He felt the dampness of milk on her nipple and his eyes flashed.

"No, we need to go." Hana stood and replaced her clothing.

"If you're sure," Logan replied, his voice seductive. Hana bit her lip at the sight of his long olive body shrouded by leaves and ferns.

"I'm never sure of anything relating to you." Hana smirked, pushing her swollen breasts into her bra and buttoning her blouse askew in the dim light.

Back at the bike, Logan settled the helmet over her head and Hana smirked at how he made even the simplest task into a seductive gesture. He put his thumb into the space at the front of the helmet and brushed her cheek before snapping the visor down over her inappropriate remark. He winked, fitted his helmet over his dark hair and swung his long leg over the saddle, careful not to swipe her off the pillion with his boot. Hana stiffened as he started the engine and the machine boomed to life, disturbing sleeping birds in the native trees. They cruised home and even the steep driveway didn't seem as frightening as Hana remembered. Logan swung the bike down the slope and under the garage door as it opened, killing the engine and dismounting. He turned to Hana, looking at her in expectation as she stayed seated. Her fingers twisted her sleeve and she examined a clinging fern.

"Come on, Mrs Du Rose." Logan smiled and his grey eyes sparkled as he removed Hana's helmet. She pouted, wanting him to kiss her again and disappointed when he didn't. Instead, he held his hand out to help her dismount. In rebellion, she ignored him and cocked her leg over the front instead. The bike tipped with her uneven weight and Hana inhaled a frightened breath. "Idiot!" Logan caught her in his strong arms and set her down on the concrete floor. Hana breathed in his essence, torn between wanting her daughter and needing her husband. She pressed her face against his chest and heard herself groan.

"What can I do, Hana?" His voice sounded gentle and he made rubbing motions against her back. "Tell me how to help."

"I don't know." She sighed. "I'll tell you as soon as I work it out."

"You do that." Logan kissed the top of her head. "I love you," he whispered. "Don't ever doubt it."

"Thank you." Hana felt her chest hitch and held her breath, not wanting the misery to gain a foothold again. She let Logan remove her boots, enjoying his gentle touch against her feet. She moaned as he rubbed her toes and clapped a hand across her mouth to suppress the sound. "I fancied you from the first moment I saw you." The words slipped free and Logan looked up at her, setting her boots to one side.

"Really?" His brow furrowed. "Did you?"

"Yeah." Hana dropped her hand and twisted the cord from her jacket in agonised fingers. "How long did it take you to pluck up the courage to speak to me?"

"Weeks." Logan rose and his lips quirked. "But you already know that story."

"The-girl-on-the-train," Hana murmured. "The-Circle-Line-girl." She pulled the plastic toggle off the end of the cord, seeming surprised once it sat loose in her palm. "We were just kids on that tube train. It was a lifetime ago." She looked at her husband with a sigh. Her fingers stroked the handlebar next to her, feeling the rubber grips underneath as though reading braille. "Do you ever wish we could go back and do things differently?"

Logan took her hand and pressed her fingers to his lips, sensing she probed their shared history because the day's events had left her too afraid to go forward. He gathered her into him and Hana enjoyed the abandon of the moment, wrenching at the zipper of his jacket with naked hunger. "No," he breathed. "I don't. Because there's no guarantee I'd still end up here with you."

The clearing of a male throat cut through the tender moment. Hana looked towards the staircase and saw Tama standing on the top step holding Phoenix. He covered her eyes with one hand and she frantically rooted for his fingers with her rosebud lips, believing her food would somehow materialise there. Tama looked embarrassed. "Hey, old people getting it on in the garage; don't mind us." He indicated with his head towards the helmets nestled together next to the bike. "So, you finally got to use your new helmet?"

Hana heard Logan give a sharp intake of breath. "Oh, sorry," Tama said, noticing his uncle's flash of irritation. "I didn't mean to spoil things." He fixed his gaze on Hana. "Can you feed your daughter please, Ma? She's eaten a whole bowl of baby rice and is still hungry." He turned and headed back up the stairs to the hallway above, carrying the baby who let out a wail of angry denial.

"You bought the helmet for me?" Hana asked.

Logan shrugged and nodded. "Yeah. A while ago."

She breathed out a sigh of relief. "I assumed it was Caroline's," she said. She knew she poked the wasps' nest but couldn't control her mouth.

"Hana, stop." Logan gritted his teeth at the reference to his destructive ex fiancé. "I know you're hurting, but don't punish me."

"Sorry." Hana lowered her eyes in contrition. "I enjoyed the ride though," she conceded. "Maybe we could do it again soon?"

Logan's lips broke into a smile as though she'd handed him the missing puzzle piece. It formed a milestone, another hurdle in their young marriage tackled and defeated. "Okay. Deal."

Hana fed the baby in the kitchen, feeling the pressure from her swollen breasts lessen. Phoenix played hidey boo, wrenching the woolly jumper from over her face and displaying smiling grey almond eyes. Her right arm rested against Hana's waist and her tiny, smooth palm ran up and down her mother's bare skin. Her slate grey eyes, olive face and dark hair matched the other two people in the room. Hana sat her up to pat her back. "You're just mucking around now, baby," she said with a smile in her voice.

"She scoffed the baby rice." Tama flicked at the pages of the telephone directory on the table. "She's definitely a Du Rose."

Hana wrinkled her nose. "Why is the telephone book out? Were you looking for something?"

"Yes. No." Tama stopped and looked across at his uncle. Logan's face darkened and became unreadable. Tama felt the grey eyes boring into the side of his face and cringed.

Hana grew silent as the awkwardness stretched on, knowing she would never get a straight answer. Her mind flipped elsewhere, to an old fashioned living room in a mock Tudor house and a mixed up, psychotic man with a grudge against her husband's family. She stared at the red mark on her wrist where a crystal glass shattered and its ragged shard penetrated her vein. The surgical wound rose pink against her pale, delicate skin. "A woman at the baby clinic thought I'd tried to kill myself." Her voice broke the silence and Logan let out a gasp of horror.

"What?"

Hana's voice sounded low and her brow furrowed in a mix of emotions. "She handed me a leaflet and called me selfish."

"Then she's an idiot. She doesn't know what happened, Hana. Don't listen to people like that." Logan crossed the room in two strides and dropped to his haunches before her. He retrieved Phoenix and handed her off to Tama. "Why are you thinking about that now?" he demanded, his eyes the colour of grit. He scowled at the phone book as though holding it responsible for Hana's wandering thoughts.

"Because of what happened this morning." Her voice wavered. "He'd probably think that too."

"Who?" Tama bounced Phoenix on his knee and feigned innocence. Logan rolled his eyes and Tama silenced.

"The court case is coming up," Hana said. "The detective said I have to give evidence even though I don't want to. He's afraid Laval will get off the charges."

Logan squeezed her and kissed the side of her face, unable to argue with fact. Tama played with Phoenix and couldn't look at either of them. "We've been here before," Logan said, his lips against her hair. "And you pray about stuff, so it's up to your God. We all know you're a praying woman, so if He can't sort it, it sucks to be Him, aye?"

Hana smiled at her husband's simplistic way of viewing her faith. Logan's philosophies were refreshing, if sometimes a little skewed. She laid her head against him and relaxed, thinking of the exhilaration of the bike ride. Tama sat the baby's butt on the table edge and supported her with his big hands. He played a stupid game considering she'd just fed. He pushed his head into her tummy and wiggled it around, his hair flopping like a mop. She squealed and laughed, wrapping her keen fingers through the curls and tugging.

"Oh crap!" he exclaimed as Phoenix leaned forward and vomited over the back of his head. She kept him pinned in place with her fingers trapped in his hair.

Logan laughed and delayed rescue, wanting his nephew to suffer. "That's for the ice cream she's not supposed to have," he said with a smirk. "I might leave you there."

Hana kicked him under the table and he reluctantly stood, dumping a tea towel on the back of Tama's head and peeling Phoenix free. She kept handfuls of black hair in her tiny fists and whimpered sad squeaking noises of misery. Logan managed to get a napkin to her face as she barfed up more. "Bloody hell!" he exclaimed. "We told you this would happen!"

Tama headed from the kitchen with the tea towel wrapped around his face. Logan jerked his head towards his retreating back. "It's Mary, mother of God," he said, injecting sarcasm into his tone. Tama kept walking and a few seconds later, Hana heard the shower running. "Two in one day," Logan said, grinning at her. "Do you think he's growing up?"

Hana shook her head. "Na, he just knows he stinks for a change. Phoe should puke on him more often."

Logan continued to grumble, patting the baby's mouth with the napkin. "What can I do? The kid won't listen."

"Phoenix or Tama?" Hana yawned. "Don't be so hard on him." She lowered her voice. "He's still a child. He opens his mouth without thinking and his brains roll out." Logan raised his eyebrows but didn't comment. "He's trying, Loge, give him a chance," Hana implored. "He's desperate to please you."

"Yeah, he's very trying!" Logan commented under his breath and Hana sighed. He disappeared with Phoenix to their bedroom to wash and change her, returning with a clean daughter all ready for bed. In a sleep suit adorned with monkeys, Phoenix beamed at Hana and cuddled into Logan's shoulder.

"I'm not sure I should feed her again," Hana muttered, worried about the state of the child's stomach. But Phoenix seemed keen to replace what she lost on the back of her cousin's head and fed greedily. Logan picked up the guitar and strummed long, dark fingers over its strings, producing a low note. He fiddled with the tuning pegs to tighten the strings, dissatisfied with the sound. Hana watched in silence. Apart from Reuben's striking looks and the ability to play, the instrument represented his only legacy to his son.

No longer feeling the music, Logan put the guitar against the pantry door and sat down. Phoenix saw him from an upside down position and smiled, a cheeky, conspiratorial beam. He grinned back and stroked her downy head. The baby head-butted Hana's breast and carried on feeding, her lids growing heavy with sleep.

"Can I use the car for church in the morning?" Hana asked. "Or do you need it?"

Logan pulled a face. "I need to go out with Tama. Can I drop you off and fetch you afterwards?"

Hana nodded. "Yep. I'll keep Phoenix with me. The older ladies adore her. I hardly see her for the entire service."

Logan exhaled as though relieved. Hana eyed him sideways with suspicion. Experience taught her not to ask, suspecting she wouldn't like the answer.

Hana tidied the kitchen while Logan put his daughter to bed. She fingered the phone directory on the kitchen table, her eyes narrowed with irritation. "Am I the only person who puts anything away?" she asked the empty room. With a shrug, she returned it to the hall cupboard.

Tama appeared from the shower grumpy and uncommunicative. His wet hair stuck up at odd angles as he stalked into the lounge, his track pants riding low over his boxer shorts. He slumped onto the sofa and switched on the television, losing himself in a mindless movie with the volume up loud.

"Bedtime," Logan growled in Hana's ear, slapping her backside and pushing her towards the bedroom. "We've unfinished business, wahine." He locked the bedroom door and unbuttoned his shirt with slow, calculating movements. His eyes glimmered, dark and sultry.

Hana stirred around midnight in the throes of an awful dream. Michael Laval stood over her. He held Phoenix in his arms and laughed at Hana's distress. Her wrist spurted a rainbow of crimson shades but she only cared about getting her baby back. She took the whisky glass and smashed it into his face over and over again, feeling anguish as he dropped the baby.

Hana woke with sweat streaming from her body and her nightdress soaked. She'd tangled herself in the covers with her thrashing and reaching out, she discovered Logan's side of the bed empty. Her right hand brushed her left wrist expecting blood but felt only tenderness. The terror of the nightmare subsided to leave confusion.

Hana left the bed and padded across the room on shaking legs, the floorboards cold beneath her bare feet. She checked on Phoenix, putting her head inside the bedroom door and listening for her daughter's comforting snuffles. No sound came from the room. Hana walked to the travel cot, pressing her hands over the sides. Her fingers touched the cold empty mattress and she panicked. She ran, drawn by the light under the lounge door and the baritone hum of male voices.

Logan spun to face her as she blasted into the room. He half rose and his gaze searched the empty hallway behind her. "What's happened?" His voice sounded jerky and strange. The fire gave off an eerie glow behind him, outlining him with a yellow haze.

"She's gone!" Hana heard the terror in her voice. "He's taken her. He's taken my baby!"

Tama turned and Hana saw Phoenix snuggled against his bare chest. She put her palms up to her face and tried to breathe as light-headedness overwhelmed her. Her body struggled to understand the message to stand down and blood rushed past her eardrums. Tama winced. "You said I had to take care of her if she cried. Because of the ice cream." He sent a nervous glance towards Logan but his uncle had already reached Hana. He put his arms around her, stroking her hair and speaking soothing words over the top of her head.

Hana wore an old shirt of Logan's from the hotel. It clung to her skin with damp patches evidence of her nightmare. "You had a bad dream," Logan reassured her. "Phoe's here, look. She woke around eleven with stomach ache but I was just debating putting her back in her cot." He omitted his discussion with Tama over Hana's father, raising an eyebrow at his nephew in a shared acknowledgement of how close Hana had come to uncovering their plan. A second earlier and she would have heard more than he wanted her to.

Logan helped Hana into the wide bed, recognising her veiled terror as she struggled at the fringes of consciousness. "I'll get you a drink of water," he whispered, kissing her forehead and pulling her right hand away from its death grip over the scar on her wrist.

Logan passed Tama in the hallway and the younger man indicated the baby's room with his head and put his left thumb up. Logan narrowed his eyes and nodded. "Thanks."

Tama returned to the lounge and a mindless documentary about penguins. His hormones raged at the sight of Hana's slender legs and he tried to block all inappropriate thoughts from his mind. Anka's face swam in front of his vision, her body supple and athletic. The older woman had become his drug of choice. They both needed more and then more still. Until more was never enough.

One accidental fumble became a full-blown affair, a broken marriage, myriad destroyed friendships and a furious Logan. Anka lost her job at the school and narrowly avoided prosecution for sex with a student. Tama found himself expelled, but only after he punched Anka's son. "Trust me to bed Hana's best friend," he growled, shifting on the sofa in discomfort. He struggled to banish the image of Anka's rounded breasts and the way she spoke his name, knowing the difference between love and lust but sensing them blend into one. He touched the hard corners of the phone in his pocket and groaned. "No! Don't do it," he warned himself. His fingers fluttered in disobedience, drawing out the device and seeking her name in his contacts. Even reading it on the screen heightened his sexual appetite.

Hearing Logan in the kitchen running cold water into a glass brought Tama to his senses. He'd promised himself a new start with the acquisition of the Du Rose name, knowing Logan hadn't given it with ease. Tama's birth certificate still showed, '*father unknown*,' testament to his unwanted status. "Dude, you've got bigger problems than a quick shag," he reminded himself. He shook his head to clear his thoughts and forced himself to focus on the television, involving himself in the plight of the penguins and calming the loneliness in his soul.

"Lay down, babe." Back in the bedroom Logan patted his chest and Hana snuggled close, holding onto a clump of his shorts' fabric like a lifeline. It bunched the garment uncomfortably around his hip, but he put up with it as Hana stilled.

Logan stayed awake until he felt her dive off the cliff into sleep though she seemed fitful and unsettled for hours. He mulled over the difficult meeting taking place while Hana was at church the next day. The tourist sounded keen. Very keen. It pricked Logan's curiosity.

The crackly voice which spoke his name over the phone had a broad Scots lilt, confirming his identity. Hana's father. "The car hire company said you found my wallet," the old man said. "But I haven't lost it. They gave me this number." Logan held his nerve during the call, giving very little away. But the Scotsman proved cannier than he gave him credit for. "I've found the school logo you wore on your sports shirts. It's on the internet. I was going to call first thing on Monday morning. I want to see my daughter."

"Not yet." Logan considered his options. He needed answers first. "Why is she afraid of you?"

The old man's gravelly throat cleared as though with an effort. "Can we meet?" he asked. "I need to explain."

Logan agreed. He recognised Hana's natural instinct to run, but he'd seen regret in her eyes afterwards. She had questions that burned her soul. He knew because he wrestled with the same ones, desperate to ask Reuben why. *Why didn't you fight for me?*

Logan pulled Hana closer, brushing the damp curls away from her face and kissing her forehead. He couldn't shield her from life but he intended to deflect the blows as best he could.

Chapter 5

Hana arrived at church late and in a panic. "I wish I'd driven myself," she complained, lifting Phoenix from the car. "This is ridiculous!"

"I'm sorry," Logan said, sounding sincere as he kissed her soft forehead.

"Try not to be late fetching us!" Hana bit, feeling second rate and unimportant. "The car is mine in case you've forgotten."

"Yeah, I know," Logan called after her as she headed towards the main door of the church. He turned to Tama, his grey eyes flashing. "Why do you always let me down?" he demanded.

"I didn't wake up," Tama griped and Logan shook his head, slamming the driver's door. He started the engine and gritted his teeth.

"I woke you twice! Then when I'd already decided to go alone, you stumbled out of your pit demanding breakfast. I ask you for nothing, Tama. You let me down at every opportunity!" The unspoken word *thankless* hung between them. They'd reached the main road into Hamilton before Logan glanced into the back seat and realised in her panic, Hana had left the car seat. He slapped the steering wheel with his hand. "Great! Now she has to hold the baby the whole time. It also means we can't get caught up and arrive back late."

"I'm not sure we should do this at all." Tama pursed his lips and revealed the reasoning behind his reticence.

Logan blew out an angry breath and ignored him. The time for objections had passed long ago. He focused on the road, ostracising Tama with his stony silence. The name Tama meant 'son' in Māori, a paradox in the light of the boy's turbulent childhood. It's possible only Reuben and Logan ever thought of him as anything but a pain in the ass.

"I'm sorry," Tama muttered, his voice low and wracked with guilt. "I feel bad about betraying Hana."

"Yeah, whatever," Logan replied without grace. He detested lateness and Tama was the king of it. He glared sideways at his nephew, who avoided his gaze. Instead, Tama stared through the window and analysed his strange impulse which made him push people to their limit.

Logan cruised into the motel car park and slammed the driver's door behind him. Tama followed at a safe distance, stopping as Logan turned towards him at the entrance and put his finger to his lips. He leaned over the teen in a threatening stance. "You keep that waha papā of yours shut! The last thing I need is you shooting your mouth off and giving information that's not yours to give. Get it?"

Tama nodded once to show he understood, recognising the *loud mouth* insult. Inside the lobby, they approached a woman behind a wide reception desk. Middle aged with a large nose, she wore her mousy hair streaked with blonde highlights. Logan didn't bother asking for the tourist's room number, knowing she wouldn't give it. "Logan Du Rose. I'm here to see Robert McIntyre."

She'd begun the exchange with her hands clasped on the counter, but withdrew them in response to the waves of aggression oozing from Logan. Her attitude became stiff and unyielding. "Is he expecting you?" she demanded, her tone obstructive.

Logan's eyes narrowed and Tama elbowed him to the side. He replaced Logan's powerful authoritarian stance with a slippery flirtatiousness. "Yes, he asked us to visit." Tama's smile could have replaced the sun on its day off. The woman's features softened. "Can we wait in there?" Tama pointed towards a lounge set out for residents. The sound of glasses clinking through the open doorway gave testimony to the presence of a bar. Tama leaned on the counter until he'd drawn a reluctant smile from the receptionist. His seductive wink gained them access to the elite space.

"See, that's how it's done," Tama whispered. He stood back for Logan to go first and gave his uncle a sanctimonious smirk as he passed. Logan ground his teeth and Tama dodged a covert jab in the ribs, making his uncle bang his hand against the doorframe. "Not everyone hates me," he dared to mutter at Logan's rigid back.

"Who told you that?" Logan hissed under his breath.

Robert McIntyre and his female companion sat in a far corner of the lounge. They wore similar clothes to the day before. Logan saw Robert check and recheck his watch. He strode across and stilled before them, watching as the Scotsman hauled himself to his feet with difficulty to meet the challenge. "Robert McIntyre," the old man stuttered, holding out an age spotted hand. His eyes raked Logan's appearance, taking in the smart shirt and cufflinks, the cowboy boots and attitude. A set of eyebrows dusted with grey knitted at the sight of Logan's olive skin, dark features and piercing grey eyes. Robert McIntyre's bowed spine straightened as he attempted to match Logan's intimidating height. He might have managed it once, but age had robbed him. Logan clasped the wizened hand and shook it, sensing the other man's resignation. "I dared to hope Hana might come," Robert said, hope fading from his voice.

"Not today." Logan pulled out a chair and sat, gratified by the unity of Tama's sleeve brushing against his.

"She doesn't want to see me?" The old man's shoulders slumped and Logan leaned forward, resting his elbows on his thighs.

"She doesn't know I'm here," he replied. "I might not tell her."

Robert McIntyre nodded slowly, uncertainty in his face. "I don't have money," he said, "if that's what you want."

Tama let out a harsh gasp and Logan caught his arm, preventing the explosion of anger he sensed brewing. "I don't need your money," he said and shrugged, the expensive cut of his white shirt demonstrating his affluence. He saw Robert's eyes flick to the gold and paua of his watch face and shook his head. "Say what you came all the way from England to say." His tone sounded more abrupt than he intended.

"What do you want from us?" The old woman's voice wavered as she interrupted. An Irish brogue penetrated every syllable.

Logan spread his hands and made himself comfortable in the lounge chair. "Nothing. I want to know why you're here," he replied. "And that's all."

Hana's father sat back against the cushions and indicated the woman at his side. "First, I'd like to introduce my wife, Elaine," he said, making it sound like a formal tea party. "We've been married for ten years this week." The couple shared an intimate smile and Tama winced, shooting Logan a look of incomprehension. Logan inclined his head and waited. With a wobble in his voice, Robert continued, "I'm not sure what you know about me."

Logan fiddled with his watch strap as the awkward moment arrived. "Sir," he said with exaggerated politeness, "I know very little about you. Hana thought you were dead."

The old woman gasped and Robert's shoulders slumped further. His chest held a concave quality which betrayed muscle wastage attributable to more than just age. "Oh," he said. "That explains her reaction."

Logan frowned. "Maybe. But perhaps not. I know my wife came to see you many years ago, pregnant and needing your help. You threw her out and made it clear you never wanted to see her again. You banned her from her own mother's funeral and made no attempt to contact her. That's what I know about you."

Robert slumped in his seat and covered his eyes with one hand. The life went out of him and he appeared ancient and broken. Elaine tutted with concern and rested her hand on his thigh beneath the table. The pair's fragility communicated something beyond their years. "I have no excuses," Robert offered. "My behaviour that day was unforgiveable. Nothing justifies what I said or how I acted. I've never experienced anger like it at the sight of my beautiful daughter, pregnant. We had such high hopes for her and she offered no justification for her behaviour. I've gone over that scene a million times in my head and rewritten it as often. It was the worst day of my life, only equalled by the death of my wife some months later." He took a white handkerchief from his smart jacket pocket and mopped at his brow, the strain adding a grey tinge to his complexion. "Please forgive me?" he asked. "I treated you terribly."

"Oh." Logan shifted in his seat. "Not me. I met Hana after that." Tama eyed him sideways with curiosity, as though seeing Logan wrong-footed amused him. Logan spread his hands. "Hana's husband died ten years ago. He's the man you abused."

Robert blinked and his jaw hung slack. "Oh dear," he breathed. He glanced sideways at Elaine and did the calculation in his head. As they celebrated their union, Hana's was prematurely severed.

"She stayed at the same university," Logan said. The urge to recreate Hana as a heroine in her father's eyes dictated his speech. He realised his reason for visiting without her then; to go ahead of her and paint a different picture of her life. One in which she emerged vindicated and sainted. "She married the baby's father and graduated with her degree. You could have found her anytime you wanted."

Robert nodded, conceding regret in the slight movement. "She finished her degree," he breathed. "Despite everything." Logan ground his teeth together, getting no satisfaction from twisting a knife in the old man's hollow chest. "The child," Robert said. Logan saw the naked hunger flare behind his rheumy eyes. "What happened to the child?"

Logan swallowed. "He sat opposite you in the restaurant yesterday. Hana came from the bathroom holding your grandson's hand."

Elaine turned in her seat and her green eyes widened. "The little boy who was crying?"

Logan nodded and hid a smirk behind his hand. Action Man's wig-saga wasn't over yet. Robert rubbed his handkerchief across his forehead and eyes. "How did the Indian boy die?" His breath came in short huffs.

"Car accident." Logan didn't want to vindicate Vik. He tamped down the urge to drag the man's name through the mud as an adulterer and a fake, everything Robert had predicted. He couldn't do it, but he wanted the conversation to move on. Bitterness rose into his throat, hating that Vik enjoyed any of Hana when he didn't deserve her. Logan pushed away the memory of Vik's neutral face on the train. He'd worried about himself while Hana broke her tender heart on the seat next to him.

Tama looked at him in alarm, recognising the danger signs. He picked up Hana's story. "She had another child, a daughter who lives in the South Island. They emigrated here when the kids were small and Hana raised them alone until last year."

Elaine sighed. "The poor wee girl." Her green eyes darted to Robert, filled with anguish. "We should have done this years ago."

Robert dismissed the notion with a shake of his head. He extended his arm to include Tama. "Are you her son?"

Tama winced and looked to Logan for assistance. The answer threatened to lay bare his own turbulent history. Logan answered for him. "I'm her husband," he said. "We married last year. Tama's my nephew but he belongs to us. He's our whānau."

Tama cast his eyes down, hearing Logan's vote of confidence and knowing he didn't deserve it. He couldn't cope with the promise of Hana's rejection when she found out he'd gone along with the ruse. They'd both disown him soon, anyway. Once they found out about the other thing which kept him awake at night.

"What is this whānau you mentioned?" Robert asked, mangling the Māori word.

"It means *family* in Māori," Logan said. "In my experience, a family can take many forms. It's not always about blood."

The old man nodded in agreement, turning to Tama and proving he'd observed more than Logan gave him credit for. "Was that your baby you held at the restaurant? She's bonny. Is she yours?"

Logan felt a flush of apprehension. Tama glanced at him before answering and mistook Logan's discomfort as permission. "No," he answered. "She's yours. Your granddaughter."

Tiredness washed over Robert McIntyre like a rip tide. His face appeared even greyer and his head sank on his neck. He waved a hand in Logan's direction. "You'd better tell me everything," he said, a plea in his voice. "I want to know how you met my daughter. Tell me what I've missed."

Logan took a breath, feeling the weight of the explanation even before his lips parted. "I met Hana the last time she visited you. We travelled opposite each other on a London tube train. She cried all the way from Epping Forest until my stop. I was fourteen years old, but I never got her out of my head. I moved to Hamilton last year and met her again. We married a few months later and Phoenix is our daughter."

Tama looked sideways at Logan's face as a whole new concept opened up before him. Hana's relationship with his uncle took on divine origins he hadn't seen before. Understanding dawned. Logan married her so fast. As though he'd loved her forever. He pushed his thumb into his mouth and worried at the nail. What if he'd missed recognising his soul mate? How could he find her?

Logan's answer satisfied Robert and he processed the information with great care. He looked frail and weak though his voice still held a resonance of steel. Logan recognised the leader in him, Robert's mana hiding in a shallow grave beneath the surface. Resting, but not dead.

Logan sent Tama to the bar to buy coffees and gave him cash to pay for them. Then he tried to turn the conversation to lighter matters. "Are you still a vicar?" he asked. "Hana mentioned growing up in a vicarage."

The man's face sagged further and Logan regretted his question. "No," he replied. "After Judith died, I went through a difficult time and lost my faith for a while. I retrained as a primary school teacher and taught for the final twenty years of my working life. I retired five years ago, having worked much longer than I should. But the school struggled to replace me as the headmaster of Hana's old primary school. It's not a big village. Not somewhere the young dynamite teachers want to trap themselves."

"Hana spoke about a brother once," Logan said.

Elaine's face broke into a wide smile. "Oh, yes. Mark. He adores his little sister. He's missed her very much."

Logan's brow furrowed. "I don't think so. She seems to hold him responsible for what happened."

"Oh!" Both Robert and Elaine seemed shocked, sitting up straighter and looking at each other in confusion. "But Mark is the reason we're here!" Robert exclaimed. "He telephoned us a few months ago to say he'd found Hana. He paid for our flights and begged us to come."

Elaine's head bobbed in agreement. "Yes, he found her and then she disappeared again."

"Found her? How?" Logan's expression darkened and he braced his feet, ready to stand. A fight reaction flooded his senses despite the two elderly opponents.

"She slashed her wrists." Robert's blue eyes swam with tears. "He couldn't get to the bottom of why."

Logan sat back in his chair and shook his head in disbelief. "Her wrist!" His voice rose and Tama shot him a nervous look from his position at the bar. "One wrist, not both! An accident! Be careful what you infer." His tone sounded threatening. "Who's saying this crap?" he demanded. "How would her brother know anything?"

"He's a doctor," Robert said. His face creased into a beam of pride. "Mark saved Hana's life."

Chapter 6

Tama carried a tray of coffee to the table. He didn't like what he saw in Logan's eyes, a brooding anger hovering near the surface. He struggled to catch up with the conversation which had taken an alarming tone.

"Of course, she's stable!" Logan snarled as Tama settled into his seat. "He kidnapped her! Her injuries happened defending herself!" His eyes flashed a livid grey and Tama cringed at the warning signs. "Your hotshot son must have access to her address, phone number, everything. And the cops were crawling all over the case. Why bother to see me? And why not contact her before now?" His scarred hands balled into fists.

"Let's go," Tama said. He watched the vein beneath Logan's jaw tick as blood fired through. He glared at Robert. "We're done here."

Robert's eyes filled with tears and devastation bowed his spine in half. His wife rubbed her hand along his thigh as he spoke in wavering speech. "There are things you don't know. I had radiotherapy for lung cancer. My oncologist forced me to finish my treatment before allowing me to fly out here. It's been a dreadful few months of wondering what happened to her. Mark was called in as an emergency surgeon. Imagine his shock at finding his sister on the operating table." Robert paused and Logan's eyes narrowed, catching him out in a misdirection. "One of the nurses promised to call him when Hana woke up and she did, but he'd gone into another surgery. He went to see her afterwards, but she'd discharged herself. Then she didn't return to the address she gave the hospital and nobody answers the phone number there. He's driven over a few times but it's a house behind a locked gate in the middle of nowhere. Mark rang us in great distress. Nothing has gone in our favour and I'm sure you feel little sympathy. But I really want to see my daughter before I die."

Logan experienced a stab of guilt and controlled his temper with an effort of will. "Hana gave our address in Ngaruawahia. But then we went north for her to recover. I work at the school and we live there most of the time, apart from the odd weekend at home." He shook his head, relieved Hana hadn't been there if her reaction in the restaurant had been any indication of how she felt.

Tama whistled. "She'd freak out if she answered the door to her brother! I don't think she ever wants to see him again."

Robert's complexion paled. "Why? She loved Mark."

Logan peered at Hana's father with a furrowed brow. "She doesn't have great memories of any of you. Apart from her mother. She misses her."

"But it was one day!" Elaine protested. "They were a happy family until then. Perfect."

"Yeah, really sounds like it," Tama scoffed. "At least mine didn't hide what they were."

Logan ran a hand through his hair and checked his watch. "We need to leave. Just explain why your son ended up as Hana's surgeon. There's something not right about it."

"Mark is here on a temporary contract," Robert replied. "A colleague called him in one night for an emergency surgery and on his way home he saw an ambulance bringing in a woman with an arterial bleed. He recognised Hana and pushed himself into the situation, treating her in the resuscitation area and then volunteering to operate. He has extensive experience with this type of delicate surgery." Robert gulped and gave his wife a cautious look. "He said she's the image of her mother. She looks like my Judith. He noticed her hair first and couldn't believe his eyes."

Logan imagined Mark's shock at finding his sister bleeding out on an ambulance trolley. The effort of remaining detached and not letting personal difficulties affect his skill level in the operating theatre must have been exhausting. He'd broken countless rules performing the operation. Phoning his sick father and breaking confidentiality risked his job. Logan recognised desperation in the man's actions.

"It's the two degrees of separation," Tama offered. "Everyone in this country knows everyone else. You can't go five paces without bumping into a cousin. They've all got the same dad and he only had a bike." He caught Logan's eye and choked on the rest of the unspoken sentence.

"Your son informed Hana of her mother's death," Logan said, hearing his own unkindness but wanting to take the shine off the sainted son a little. "He sent a note via the university, telling her she wasn't wanted at the funeral."

The old man put a shaking hand up to his mouth. He looked grey and ill. "I didn't know," Robert whispered, tears filling his eyes and causing them to shimmer in the light. "She just didn't turn up. I thought she didn't care."

Logan looked away, knowing he'd caused damage for the sake of it and regretting it. Robert folded in on himself like a crushed paper bag. For all the wrong reasons, Logan wanted Hana to get closure with her father while she still had the chance. "I'll talk to her," he promised, craving the paternal love he saw in Robert's eyes. He wanted to have a conversation with Reuben more than anything he'd ever desired. He couldn't. And it squeezed his heart like a physical pain.

The group shook hands and the Du Roses left. Both men remained silent as Logan started the car. But Tama couldn't help himself. "Uncle Logan," he began, his tone wary. "What if Hana doesn't want this?"

"Don't!" Logan raised a hand in warning and Tama shook his head, dreading the argument later when Hana found out about his betrayal. Logan huffed and puffed, watching the digital display on the dashboard clock tick through its accusation of their lateness. Traffic built as an accident blocked the road to Horsham Downs and police diverted them in the opposite direction to the one they needed to go.

Hana sat on the church steps relieved the rain held off. The porch sheltered her from the cool wind as she worried about Logan. Phoenix nestled in her arms and blinked at the sky. Only the pastor's car remained in the car park and Phoenix started fretting, forcing Hana to lean against the wide front door and shove her under her blouse. "It's not the holy look I was going for," she grumbled. "Getting my boobs out on the church steps isn't a great way to make godly friends."

A click behind her warned Hana to shift to one side to avoid falling backwards through the opening door. Pastor Allen emerged, his brow furrowing as he saw her. "I didn't realise anyone stayed," he said. He closed the door behind him and jangled the key in the lock. "I think it might rain."

"Fantastic," Hana replied with sarcasm, putting Phoenix over her shoulder and patting her back. The baby burped and rubbed her eyes on her tiny fists.

"Want to tell me what's wrong?" Allen ran a hand over his face and sat down on the steps next to her.

"Not really," Hana replied. "You look like you've got your own problems."

"Nothing a good night's sleep can't cure." Allen smiled. "Stop deflecting, Hana. We're both too old for games."

Hana sighed and pushed the sentence around her head before speaking it out loud. "I read my father's obituary in a Baptist newspaper someone brought from England years ago. It detailed his work with the poorer churches in Birmingham and said how much they'd miss him. Then I saw him yesterday standing right in front of me."

Pastor Allen let out a slow whistle. "Wow! A resurrection story. I don't hear too many of those."

Hana groaned. "It's not funny, Allen. I thought he died."

"What did he say?" Allen turned his knees towards her, hanging on to every word. "Was it mistaken identity? Did he wake up in a morgue? Come on, Hana, get to the exciting bit!"

Hana cringed. "He didn't say anything."

"Nothing?" Shock rode across Allen's face leaving his eyes wide and his mouth open. "He said nothing?"

"I didn't give him a chance. I did what I always do when there's a problem and ran away."

Allen screwed up his features. "That's disappointing, Hana. I want to know the ending now."

"Sorry!" Hana's chest tightened. "I've missed out. I won't find him again now. But what should I have said to him? Oh hi, Dada, hope life's gone well for you since you called me a slut and threw me out of the house when I got knocked up at eighteen?" Hana drew Phoenix closer and the baby resisted with a series of wiggles and a wail.

Allen shook his head. "Maybe don't start that way. It's a bit of a conversation stopper. Interesting back story though. I always thought you were perfect."

"Don't look at me like that," Hana said, her face pulled into a pout. "I never told you because it's private. Do you tell everyone about your worst sins?"

"Every Sunday," Allen replied with a wistful smile. "It helps me stay real for all the other people who make mistakes."

"Well, aren't you the perfect Christian," Hana bit. She half turned her body away from him and patted Phoenix's back.

Allen snorted and jabbed her ribs. "What do you want, Hana?" he asked. "If you could have your meeting again, what would be the best outcome?"

"For him to say sorry," Hana snapped, surprised by the vehemence she heard in her own words. "But I know he won't.

He never admitted getting anything wrong and I can't imagine he's changed. He always made it someone else's fault, never his. I felt terrified of seeing him that day and confessing my mistake. We endured a six-hour journey on the train and then travelled another five after that. Vik was petrified yet he still came with me. They threw him out and my perfect brother beat him up. Vik never forgave me for putting him in that position. It always hung there between us like an accusation." Hana felt the tear roll down her cheek, snatching it away with her free hand and leaving a long, raised scratch behind.

"Ah," Allen said. He held his palms out to catch the first drops of rain. "So, you got pregnant by yourself and he had nothing to do with it. Amazing."

"You know what I mean," Hana bit. "You know what I mean!"

Allen slipped an arm around Hana's rigid shoulders, jerking in surprise at the feel of the bones close beneath her skin. He pressed a kiss to her temple. "I find when I look for an apology, it often doesn't come. How will you cope if that's the case?"

"It's academic because he's gone. I'm just hurt," Hana replied, her lips curving downwards.

"No, I'd say you're raging actually," Allen said with a knowing smirk. "Ropeable. Fit to be tied."

"I am not!" Hana sat up straighter and shucked off his arm with a flounce. "I forgave him years ago. What are you saying? That I'm bitter and twisted? You're meant to make me feel better." She waved a free hand and balanced Phoenix across her shoulder. "See, this is why I didn't tell you."

"No." Allen shook his head and eyed Hana sideways. "You didn't tell me because you knew what I'd say. For what it's worth, here's my ten cents of wisdom. I find it's better to give an apology than to expect one. Then at least fifty percent of the people walk away happy. I'd take those odds."

Hana looked at him sideways. Fury flashed in her green eyes. "He's the adult! I needed his help and I got his disgust and dismissal. He was in the wrong, not me!" Her voice rose to a screech.

"Fair enough," said Allen and leaned back against the door. He folded his arms and offered nothing else.

Hana's brain worked overtime. He'd set doubt growing in her heart and she tried to process it. She lost her way in the former certainty of her swirling righteous indignation. "I shouldn't have got pregnant, I guess," she conceded. "Mum and Dada taught me better. They had high hopes for me and I disappointed them."

Allen smiled and turned his head to meet her gaze. "What if Izzie had come home at eighteen, pregnant and dragging some spotty teenage kid behind her? Just as you thought you'd got her to safety and were about to give yourself a medal for a job well done." He nodded his head towards the baby dozing across Hana's shoulder. "Or Phoenix? Can you imagine Logan's reaction?"

Hana shuddered. "I'd rather not." She pushed the baby's dark hair back from her forehead and Phoenix lifted her head. Smoke grey eyes stared up at Hana. Her daddy's eyes. Hana sighed.

"I'd always seen the situation from my viewpoint," she admitted. "I stood there in the kitchen with my best yellow dress straining at the seams. I should've written or phoned first. It must have been a dreadful shock." She frowned. "I don't want to think about my father's pain and disappointment because then I have to take responsibility for causing it."

Allen nodded and picked at a flake of loose paint on the steps. "Justifiable anger and self-pity make wonderful crutches at the time. But later they become cricket bats to beat ourselves over the head with."

Hana nodded. A strange longing called from deep within her, wanting to feel her father's arms wrapped around her. "He wasn't all bad," she admitted, letting the illusion of his unkindness fall to the ground. "I painted him into a role over the years. We had good times. I loved him once."

Allen sighed. "And you both lost out. You could have benefitted from your parents' help many times. And imagine what they missed. I'm guessing the baby was Bodie?" Hana nodded. "Then they've missed his entire life and Izzie's too. There are no winners here Hana, only losers."

"Mum died," Hana said, her eyes beginning to leak. The steady drips increased to a flow and she brushed the tears away. "She passed away a few months later and I never got to explain."

Allen gave her shoulder a comforting squeeze with his large fingers. "I don't have any answers to your pain, sweetheart," he whispered. "But I think you do."

Hana wiped her eyes on her sleeve and struggled to collect herself. "Logan promised he wouldn't be late," she said with a sniff.

"Why don't you come back to ours?" Allen asked, his irises a soft, gentle blue.

"I can't," Hana replied. "Logan has the car seat and he isn't answering his phone." The temperature continued to drop as the rain began in earnest. Hana shivered.

The Honda screeched around the bend up to the church and skidded to a halt in front of the steps. Logan couldn't look Hana in the eye as he jumped from the driver's side. Her radar went on high alert. Tama remained in the car and made a show of fiddling with the radio. "Where did you go?" Hana demanded. She looked from one to the other.

Logan shrugged. "Nowhere important," he lied.

Chapter 7

Hana hugged Allen as Logan loaded Phoenix into her car seat. She remained quiet on the way home, processing her dark thoughts in the back seat while Logan shot covert glances at her through the rear-view mirror. He bit his lip and worried.

Logan slowed down on Hakarimata Road and eased onto their driveway. Hana gasped as the car slid to a halt on the gravel. Tama sat up straight. "Did you open the gate?" he hissed.

"No." Logan shook his head as the heavy metal slid closed before them.

"Is it faulty?" Tama lowered his voice but Hana disconnected her seat belt and leaned forward to listen.

"What's happening?" Dread laced her voice.

Logan held up his hand to silence them. He depressed the button for his window and it rolled down, revealing the sound of a car labouring up the driveway out of sight.

"What should we do?" Tama demanded and Logan shook his head.

"I don't know. Who else has the gate code?"

Hana pressed herself back against the seat. "Nobody nasty," she replied. "Anyone wanting to hurt me is behind bars." Her brow creased as she studied Logan's reflection in the rear-view mirror. "What about you, Logan?"

Logan didn't reply. He buzzed the gate and climbed the driveway with caution, the Honda's engine straining against the incline. He nudged Tama before the final bend.

"Be ready," he whispered, the jerk of his head indicating his seriousness.

Tama peered round at Hana. She stared at her hands, worrying at a plaster on her index finger. Her lips twitched as her mind ran over something more pressing than the unexpected visitor.

At the top of the driveway, Logan heaved a sigh of relief at the sight of Bodie's police car at the bottom of the steps. His stepson knocked on the front door and peered through the side windows, his navy uniform matching the painted porch.

Logan slammed the driver's door and ran up the porch steps. "What's wrong?" he demanded. His tone sounded aggressive and Bodie took a calculated step back.

"Mr Du Rose." Odering emerged from the passenger door of the police car, running a careful hand over the crease in his suit trousers.

"Odering!" Logan spat the detective's name and shot Bodie a dirty look. "Thanks for the warning," he snarled.

Hana stepped from the car and gave Odering a sideways glance. The memory of their last meeting still burned from his single-minded execution of his duty. Hana's heart hurried its thudding in her chest, instinct warning her he'd come with news of the imminent court date. Once in the kitchen, Bodie filled the kettle and flicked the switch.

"That's not a good sign," Hana breathed. "A policeman making tea?" Her mind forced her to relive the memory of a policewoman making tea in her kitchen at Achilles Rise. She'd just asked Hana to identify her husband's mangled body. "Will I need lots of sugar for my nerves?" she joked, her voice wavering.

Bodie's eyes flashed a coded message which Hana felt too rattled to interpret. She saw the detective in her peripheral vision and swallowed anxiety as she gave her son a tight smile. "Maybe," he whispered. "Maybe not."

Tama took the baby into the living room, laying the seat near the hearth rug and raking the fire with short, jabbing movements. He fantasised about prodding the poker through the detective's chest and satisfied himself with adding another log to revive the flames. "Guy's a dick!" he spat into the empty room.

Phoenix slept, her tiny cheeks a healthy pink and dusted by her quivering dark lashes. Tama listened to the rumble of voices in the kitchen and hesitated, wanting a drink but holding out. "The less time I spend around that jerk, the better!" he decided, pulling the car seat towards him. He settled on the rug and flicked the television on before falling asleep.

Tension built as Bodie fussed over drinks, plonking a teapot on the table and clanking around with cups, milk and sugar. Hana's nervous anticipation built to a frenzy and sensing it, Logan sat next to her, fitting his arm around her shoulder.

Odering drew his infamous notebook from his inside jacket pocket and sighed. With a glance at Bodie, he opened his lips and spouted formality. "I've brought news," he said and Hana winced, holding her breath until the room swam. "Michel L'Huillier also known as Michael Laval, died yesterday at the secure remand unit in Waitakere Prison."

Logan exhaled and Hana shook her head. "No," she breathed, "he can't have."

Bodie poured tea into Hana's favourite china mug and pushed it towards her. "Sorry, Mum," he said.

Hana traced a shaking finger along a line of strawberries on the mug's painted surface, not registering the sting of heat against her skin. "No." She shook her head with vigour. "No. He doesn't get to do that. It's not fair!"

Her mind recalled Laval's handsome, clean-shaven face as he gripped her around the waist and forced her to study his school photographs. His sixteen-year-old image sat alongside Logan's boyish body in the photo. Laval seemed so vibrant, crazy and dangerous. He couldn't be dead.

"How did he die?" Logan demanded and Hana squeezed her eyes closed. She sought to shut down the memory of Laval's alluring menace as he punished Logan through her. She fought to stay in the present, the nightmare threatening to drag her back into its spiky clutches. The dreams would come again, real and terrifying, robbing her of sleep and sanity.

"The press officer is speaking to the media this evening." Odering eyed Hana with wary concern. "The post mortem stated he died of self-inflicted injury, but other information suggests he ran across someone in prison with a grievance." Odering raised an eyebrow. "Someone he upset on the outside who seized their moment."

Hana held her breath too long and exhaled in a rush. Logan's arm tightened around her shoulders until he'd tucked her into his side. "Shame," he murmured, though he didn't sound sorry.

"How could this happen in prison?" Hana demanded. "It's not possible."

Odering shrugged. "I don't know, Hana," he said. The hand holding his notebook tipped so he could rub his eyes. He used her first name with a familiar ease and Hana felt Logan's body twitch in irritation. "The prison authorities will investigate it. The coroner plans to rule it a death by misadventure."

"There's a plus side," Bodie said, ever the optimist. Hana searched his face to find it. "You don't need to give evidence against him. It's over."

Odering gritted his teeth and exhaled. His tone carried pure bar., "Yeah and two years of work and resources just went down the toilet."

All eyes turned to him and shame crossed Odering's sharp features. "Sorry," he said "Please don't repeat that. I worked for justice and it's been a waste. I could have taken a hit out on him in the first place and saved a fortune in tax payer dollars."

Logan released a snort of laughter but Bodie reeled back in shock. He opened his mouth and then closed it again, deciding to keep his thoughts to himself. Logan leaned back in his chair and his body relaxed. "Don't expect me to feel sorry," he announced, his voice sounding loud in the quiet kitchen. "I'm glad."

"Better than feeling cheated," Odering confessed, dropping the notebook onto the table along with his promised promotion. "I've nothing to show for endless late nights and countless attempts to corner one of Auckland's slipperiest criminals." He waved a hand. "Unless you include divorce papers and children who don't recognise me when I turn up at home." His glance at Logan contained a flash of jealousy as Hana nestled against her husband's side.

"So, it's over?" Hana sat up straighter. "No court case, no giving evidence, no justice. He escaped."

Odering sighed. "Looks that way, Hana."

A spark of pleasure flitted across Logan's handsome features and he locked eyes with the detective. Odering stared back, emptiness replacing the age-old battle between the two strong men. Their history stretched further than anyone else at the table guessed. Odering sized up Logan as he'd done many times before. The man possessed undeniable mana, an aura of inner influence and authority which money couldn't buy. Logan always had it, even as a teenager. He met Odering's gaze with courage and a hidden smugness which made the other man's eyes flare with doubt. A sneaking suspicion crept into the moment.

"I couldn't care less about Laval, L'Huillier, whatever he called himself," Bodie said into the silence. "It's a good result and I'm glad we won't waste tax payer's money putting him on trial, watching him nobble a jury and then walk free on a technicality."

Hana wondered when her son became so cynical. He sounded like his father. Bodie flicked at a speck of dust on his uniform trousers and looked forward to returning to traffic duties instead of babysitting Odering because of his connection with the Du Roses.

After an awkward silence, the detective finished his drink and rose to leave. It felt like the end of an era. He reached his hand out to Logan. "All the best," he said, though he didn't sound sincere.

Logan nodded. "Likewise. I hope we don't meet again." He smirked and Odering's lips twitched.

"Bye, Hana," he said. He dipped his head and pressed a kiss to her cheek. The sparkle in his eyes showed how much he enjoyed riling her husband.

"What about the old man?" she asked. "Will I still need to give evidence against Laval senior?"

Odering shook his head. "I doubt it. The cancer will get him before his case reaches trial. Don't worry about it. It's over."

Bodie wrapped his arms around Hana and held her. She closed her eyes and breathed in his scent. His uniform shirt crinkled beneath her fingers. "I'll pop by after soccer training next week," he said, his voice low.

"Sure. Stay for dinner," Hana offered. "We'll go back to the unit tomorrow before Logan starts work." Bodie nodded and shook Logan's hand. The two men squared their shoulders and Hana tried to ignore the flare of testosterone beneath the guise of cordiality.

Logan shut the front door and leaned against it. He appeared lost in thought as the police car fired up and Bodie executed an awkward three-point turn. Hana collected mugs from the kitchen table and dumped them in the dishwasher. She pursed her lips and waited until Logan roused himself and took a step towards the hallway. "Logan, what do you think happened to Laval?"

His grey irises glittered and he shrugged. "Don't know, Hana. Definitely don't care." He padded down the back steps to the garage and she heard him clattering around with his motorbike.

He left for work early the next morning, rushing to get to a staff briefing with Angus. "What time will you get to the unit?" he asked Hana as he pushed his arms into his leather jacket.

"Lunchtime?" She framed her reply as a question, suggesting she'd rather not go back there at all.

Logan frowned. "Please, Hana. For me."

She pouted and rested her forehead against his shoulder as he ran his hands across the small of her back with tender fingers. "If I must," she whispered.

"Just for this year." Logan breathed into her hair and the warmth made her shiver. "School site during the week and home on my free weekends."

"Yeah, I know," she grumbled. "But I never promised to like it."

Logan tickled her ribs and Hana squeaked. He left her shaking her head at his underhanded tactics and acknowledging they'd worked. But she moved with deliberate slowness, packing their belongings and feeding the baby as though dragging her feet might put off the inevitable. Phoenix seemed extra tired and Hana let her snooze in the cot while she cleaned the house and filled a suitcase. Tama showered and while he splashed in the bathroom, Hana stripped his bed and dumped his sheets in the washing machine.

"Will you call to see Logan before you leave?" she asked when he returned to his room. One of his tee shirts dangled from her hand and she folded it with care.

Tama's fingers worried at the towel strung around his waist and he shrugged. "Maybe."

Hana nodded and turned to leave but the leaden atmosphere made her halt in the doorway. "Is everything okay?"

He slumped on the bare mattress, his shoulders rounding beneath the weight of an unseen burden. He swiped a shaking hand across his mouth and Hana tensed at the sight of uncharacteristic tears glittering in his grey eyes. She held her breath and waited. "I don't want to go back," he gushed. "College isn't for me. It's not what I want."

"Oh." Hana sighed and pondered the irony of having the same conversation twice in one decade. Last time with Bodie led to arguments and he quit university and joined the police force, anyway. Hana allowed the fraught memory to guide her towards a different interaction with Tama.

"I'm trapped," he began, nervousness lacing his sentence with halts and stammers. "Logan's paid for everything, the halls are great, I have an awesome room and made good friends. The work is easy, but I hate it." Tama worried at his thumbnail. "Ma, I'm not interested in soil maintenance, stock health and milk yields. I can't imagine myself farming for the rest of my life."

Hana gave herself a shake. "Yet you get amazing grades. The dean sent a letter of commendation to Logan saying what a model student you are."

Tama's shoulders sagged further. "That's why I'm trapped. I'm stuck between gratitude and misery. Logan wants me to prove myself, so I need to succeed, but it's killing me. He's so generous, Ma. I can't let him down again. I thought I could manage for the full two years, but it's hard."

Hana nodded. "Hard because you know he'll give you a job afterwards and you must take it."

Tama pressed the heels of his hands into his eyes. "Impossible. I'm gonna end up disappointing him whatever I do. He doesn't deserve it. Not again. I'm a fraud."

"Oh, Tama." Hana slipped an arm around his shoulders. "I get it," she sighed. "You need to speak to Logan. He'll understand." She prayed she hadn't overestimated her husband's sense of compassion, aware he only ever showed it to her. "We'll talk to him together," she offered and saw a tear plop onto Tama's hand. His fingers writhed in his lap. He'd come so far from the bullet proof teenager she'd first met and loathed.

"You need a plan though," she cautioned. "He won't just let you quit with nothing else to do."

Tama sat up straighter. He wiped the back of his hand across his eyes and sniffed.

"I applied to the fire service a while ago. I heard nothing so started college and tried to settle. But then they contacted me. Poppa Alfie forwarded a letter from the hotel last month and I drove up to Auckland for the physical exam. My doctor did the medical test and I passed everything. They invited me to a formal interview next Friday."

"What? Wow!" Hana floundered. She tightened her grip around his broad shoulders. "I'm so proud of you, Tama Du Rose."

He turned his face towards her and she saw gratitude in his eyes. "You've been a lifeline for me," he whispered. "You make me want to do better, to be a better person."

"It's mutual," Hana admitted, stroking his wet hair away from his face. "There's a good plan for your life, Tama. There's a bible verse which says, *'Whatever your hand finds to do, do it with all your might.'* You'll make an awesome fireman." She'd half-quoted scripture but hoped God wouldn't mind.

Tama gnawed on his lower lip. "I didn't know how to tell you," he whispered. "I thought you'd get mad."

"We both love you, you know," Hana replied. "We want you to feel fulfilled in whatever you do." She felt Tama sag against her. "All Logan wants is to equip you with the skills to provide for your own family one day. He means well."

"He wanted me to take over the farm and hotel, didn't he?" Tama asked and Hana cringed.

"That's between you and him, sweetheart." She resisted making half informed guesses about Logan's motivation in sending Tama to an agricultural college. "You need to speak to him."

"I'm waiting," Tama whispered. He sounded wistful.

"For what?" The subject change confused her. Hana blinked.

"For my soul mate," Tama replied. "Uncle Logan settled for Caroline when he really wanted you. I'm waiting like Logan wished he did."

Hana stiffened at the mention of Caroline, but he'd piqued her curiosity. "Why are you mentioning this now?" she asked. "And what makes you think Logan wished he'd waited?"

"He kinda said so to that old man."

"What old man?" Hana jerked her head back in confusion. "You're talking in riddles. An old man at the college or somewhere else?"

"Oh, crap! Nowhere!" Tama leaned over to grab a stray sock from the floor. He bristled with irritation and Hana struggled to comprehend the strangeness of the conversation. "Forget I said anything," he muttered. "He'll double kill me."

Hana narrowed her eyes and watchfulness stilled her body like a statue. "Tama," she said, her tone firm. "You know you have to tell me now, don't you?"

"Nope. Nope. Not gonna happen." He stood and dug around in his bag, searching for clean clothes and ignoring her.

"Fine then!" Hana rose and slapped her thighs. "I'll ring Logan and ask him myself." She stamped along the hallway and picked up the house phone. Her brow furrowed and she paused, deciding whether to ring Logan's cell phone or the direct line to his office. It wasn't important and he wouldn't understand her urgency. A spark ignited in Hana's breast. She wanted to know who Logan had discussed old girlfriends with and why Caroline's name had come up at all. She stared at the handset and decided. "Mobile," she murmured and dialled the first few digits.

"Don't!" Tama skidded along the hallway in his boxer shorts, one leg in his jeans and the other bare. "Don't, please don't!" he begged. He snatched the phone from Hana's hand and held it above his head so she couldn't reach it.

Hana stood on tiptoes and grappled for it. "Give it back!" she hissed. The dial tone whirred and the cord pulled taut. "You're breaking it!"

"Please, Hana!" Tama whined. "Don't ring him."

"We're waking the baby." Hana took a step back and cocked her head. Tama swallowed and his gaze darted to the phone and then back to her face.

"I'll tell you." He waved the handset and the cord swayed from side to side. "But you must promise not to go crazy."

Hana narrowed her eyes and her body stiffened. "Why would I go crazy?" she demanded. A thousand thoughts travelled through her mind, each one worse than the last. Caroline's name drifted in and out of the picture like a veiled threat. She took a step back and her hand clapped over her mouth. "He's cheating, isn't he? Logan's cheating with Caroline."

"No!" Tama dropped the phone with a clunk and lurched for her arms. His fingers skimmed her painful left wrist and she cried out. "I promise it's not that, Hana," he soothed. He hauled her into his chest and wrapped his arms around her with ferocity. Her face mashed against his sternum. "Logan adores you. You're forgetting how this conversation started." He kissed the top of her head.

"With you quitting college?" Hana extracted herself enough to breathe.

"No, with me saying I want what you guys have. He wishes he waited for you. I heard it in his voice."

"When?" Hana wrestled herself free. "When did he say it? Who did he say it to?"

Tama dropped the phone back in its cradle and pushed his other leg into his jeans. He wriggled them over his hips and pulled up the zipper. "He didn't say it outright," he cautioned. "But it's what he meant. He said, *I was young, but I couldn't get her out of my head.* 'I heard it in his voice, like he trod water until he found you. It changed my perspective when I heard him say it and you guys made sense for the first time."

"Thanks!" Hana's sarcasm bit and Tama winced.

"I mean I understand your relationship. I need to stop having meaningless one-night stands and wait for my soul mate."

Hana shook her head and blinked. "I'm pleased for you, Tama. The meaningless sex only hurts you in the end." Her green eyes narrowed. "Who's the old man, Tama? Why was Logan talking about Caroline?"

"He wasn't talking about her!" Tama groaned and slapped his forehead. He pulled a pair of socks from his pocket and hopped on the spot to push his toes into them. "I'm in so much trouble. Forget everything. I'll drive to college and glue my lips together."

"You're making it worse," Hana insisted. "Just tell me."

Tama sat in the kitchen and weighed his options while Hana sipped a glass of water and stared at his bowed head. "Will you tell Logan I told you?" He sounded a mixture of scared and angry and Hana sighed.

"I don't know until you tell me," she replied. "Then I'll know."

"Logan should tell you himself," Tama grumbled and Hana's eyes lit with a sense of desperation.

"I'll ask him myself." She stood and folded her arms. "This is ridiculous."

"I'm sure he meant to tell you last night," Tama whined. "Then the cops came and you seemed upset."

Hana gulped. "So it's something bad?" She slumped forward. "You're talking in riddles and making it worse."

"You're tying me in knots!" Tama felt his loyalty stretch to breaking point, hammered to a fine line between Logan and Hana. "Uncle Logan won't trust me again and it's taken months to earn back his respect." Frustration flushed his cheeks and his fists balled by his sides.

"Just tell me," Hana pleaded. "Get it over with."

"I'm scared," he whispered. "You care about people's feelings. No woman ever showed me the loyalty you give Logan. You've changed my life and ruined me. I can't go back to what I had because I know there's more."

"Oh." Hana pushed an index finger between her lips. "I'm sorry."

"You make me want to tell you stuff," Tama whispered. "But I owe Logan everything."

Hana relinquished her hold on his secret and forced herself to let it go. "Forget it," she said, edging a smile onto her lips. "Logan will tell me if I'm meant to know." Insecurity bit at her soul and she struggled to push it away.

Tama felt a sudden rush of fealty mixed with gratitude and he reached for her fingers, crushing them in his hand. "I'll do it," he said. "I'll tell you who he spoke to, but Uncle Logan's gonna kill me."

Chapter 8

Logan stood on the grass outside St Bart's boarding house and watched as the little man in front of him waved his arms like a windmill. The horticulture teacher's eyes popped and bulged in threat of an imminent heart attack, infuriated further by Logan's apparent disinterest.

Logan heaved out a sigh as the yowling, nonsensical tirade ramped higher. The bell rang in the main building and he lifted his wrist and checked his watch. "I need to go," he stated in a neutral tone. "I can't trust my Year 9 English class to behave without supervision." He suspected the little idiots were already running around the classroom and would need detentions, which he didn't have time to supervise.

"I'm sick of this!" the horticulture teacher screeched and Logan winced. At six feet four inches, he dwarfed him, making the scene even more comical. But his shouting attracted unwanted attention from two nearby classrooms and Logan glanced up to see a rucksack plunge from an upstairs room in the main building. The squeak of its owner cut through the stillness, followed by the sound of a slap. His English class. Logan's patience snapped. He summed the annoying man up and assessed the threat, knowing with one well-aimed blow he could kill or maim him. He paused and cocked his head, wondering which one to choose.

"I'm leaving," he said instead. "Don't follow me this time."

"It's not good enough!" The horticulture teacher ran out in front of him and turned, blocking Logan's path. "Find out who did it."

Logan ground his teeth and forced out a measured reply. "How?" he demanded. "The cameras don't watch this area and I didn't arrive back until this morning. I don't know who sabotaged your compost heap, Graham."

"Look at it!" The horticulture teacher bounced up and down, both arms outstretched as he jabbed his fingers at the patch of churned mud. "It's ruined!"

Logan exhaled a long, calming breath and glanced at the sky. He spoke through gritted teeth. "I don't know who messed around in it and if I'm honest, I don't really care. It's a health hazard and I've told you countless times I don't want it here for this exact reason. It's mud. The boys can't leave it alone. It needs moving by the end of this week or I'll involve Angus."

"No, it's staying!" yelled the little man. He raised his fists and postured for a fight, thinking better of it as Logan raised one dark eyebrow. His right hand moved to grasp the handle of a shovel leaned up against the wall. He moderated his tone. "The horticulture boys need to learn about composting." He released a ragged sigh. "This is the best way to teach them. We dig a trench, we put the food scraps from the boarding house kitchens in and then we back-fill it and start again. It's in the curriculum."

"I don't care." Logan shrugged. "We back onto a gully and we have a rat problem. The pest control officer from the council says it's because you're feeding them." Logan tried to keep his voice level. "You need to find somewhere else to do your composting."

"We need to do it next to the vegetable plot," Graham snapped. "Are you telling me to move the veggies too?"

Logan paused and twisted his lips in thought. Then he nodded. "That's an even better idea. This area would make a great lawn with picnic tables. We could fix up a shade cloth and the boys could eat out here." He nodded. "Yeah, move everything. I don't want it here."

"No!" Graham shouted. A boy's face pressed against the window of the sick bay, retreating as Logan glared at him. The horticulture teacher hefted his shovel and dug it into the loamy soil, attempting to excavate the nearest trench which formed the centre of the argument. Someone had filled it in over the weekend. He pulled the dark earth back to where it came from and with it, potato peelings, carrot tops and other rotting items. "It's ruined!" he muttered to himself as food mixed with soil under his ministrations.

Logan watched, transfixed as the tiny man wielded the spade with expert precision. Squashy food crap spewed from the hole with every turn of the spade, filling the air with a rotting stench. His body tensed at the next turn of brown earth. "Is that ham?" he demanded, taking a step forward. "Bloody hell! You're only meant to put vegetable waste in there! No wonder the rats are coming for afternoon tea!" Exasperated, Logan shook his head and turned to leave. "Angus can sort this out," he bit. "It's way above my pay grade."

"Oh." Graham's body froze and Logan heard him gulp. The fire had gone from the horticulture teacher's voice and it caused Logan to grind to a halt. He watched as the spade hit something more solid than earth. "Oh, no." Graham shot him a look of sheer panic.

"What's that?" Logan pointed at the bottom of the spade to an object resembling a pink carrot.

Graham wiggled the spade and it caught against something beneath the surface. When it broke free, it brought the pink carrot with it. "It's a hand," he whispered. "Oh! Oh! It's a hand!" He dragged the spade across the soil and exposed an arm wearing a black school tracksuit.

"I don't believe this," Logan breathed. "I don't bloody believe it."

Graham dragged the spade further and with it came the hand, the arm, a torso and the side of a stiff, grey face. The compost heap had become a grave.

"Get out of there. Now!" Logan shouted, making the horticulture teacher jump as he stared down at the body. "Touch nothing else." Logan reached over and pulled him away by the collar, watching him leave deep footprints in the crime scene. He propped the sweating man against the wall of St Bart's and struggling with his other hand, pulled his cell phone from his jacket pocket.

"I don't feel so good," Graham spluttered as Logan stood with his large hand against the man's chest. He sagged, forcing Logan to press harder to keep him upright.

"Maybe send the cops and an ambulance," Logan told the operator. "We need the cops but the ambulance is academic. He's dead."

The horticulture teacher went a strange colour as reality hit him. He resembled one of the juicy green iceberg lettuces in the vegetable plot next door. As Logan jerked backwards with a curse, the little man vomited over the path and spread it into the soil. The absence of Logan's hand keeping him upright sent him flailing sideways and he sank to his knees.

"Nice one! You contaminated the evidence!" Logan snapped. "Keep it together, man!" Leaning over the trench as far as he dared, Logan peered at the partially covered body. He continued speaking to the operator. "It's a dude. He's wearing a school tracksuit top and what looks like black shorts." Logan heard the teacher groan behind him. The wind gusted and the soil shifted under its influence, cracking and pouring from the body as though attempting to escape. Logan squinted, trying to see without touching. "Ah, yep." He pointed at the shorts and then the pink hand, jabbing towards the half covered face near the end of the trench. "You should tell them to hurry. A colleague just decorated the body with his breakfast." He heard the teacher retch again and moved away, careful not to lean over the burial site. He needed to keep his own DNA away from the scene, not wanting to visit the inside of a police cell again any time soon. "I can see his knees and feet. Ah, yeah, that makes sense then."

The horticulture teacher spewed again, this time managing to swivel and spray the back wall of St Bart's. Logan heard continuous splashing on the concrete like a waterfall. He focussed on the bright, orange shoe laces peeking through the soil. "Stupid bugger," he mused. "Who did you piss off this time?"

Logan stood up straight and disconnected the call. The operator wanted to keep him talking, but he cut her off mid-sentence. He dialled the boarding house office and within minutes, two prefects appeared wearing their distinctive black-and-white striped blazers. "Right," Logan said. "The interval bell will go in fifteen minutes, so you stand there and you over there. Stop any boys from coming this way."

Logan stood on the path and blocked the boys' view of the body. Then he rang the headmaster's office. Amanda answered and her voice took on a simpering, nasal tone which he hated. "Oh, hi Logan," she gushed. "Are you coming over to see me today?"

"To see Angus," Logan corrected. "I need to speak to him."

"Oh, my gosh! Millie did the cutest thing this morning. You have to pop to my place on the way home and I'll get her to do it again."

"Angus. Please." Logan's voice remained calm, but he closed his eyes and counted to ten.

"Oh, okay." Amanda sounded disappointed. "I'll put you through." Logan sensed her holding her breath. "The light's gone in the hallway again. Would you mind dropping in later and looking at it?"

Logan pursed his lips. "Log it in the maintenance book," he suggested. He turned and winced at the orange laced shoes. "They'll get around to it."

"It's kinda urgent," Amanda argued. "You're so tall. It won't take you a minute."

"Put me through to Angus." The thinning veil of Logan's patience showed itself in the snippiness of his reply. The line clicked as Amanda pressed the relevant buttons and Angus' Scottish lilt droned from the handset on his antique desk.

"What is it, Du Rose? You know I've got this meeting with the board of trustees in a minute."

"I know." Logan formulated a sentence in his head, but Graham beat him to the punch. He vomited and threw the remains of his breakfast over his own shoes.

"What's happening?"

Logan imagined Angus straightening in his chair. "It's a bit complicated." He broke the bad news and Angus groaned. "Bloody hell! Who is it? Do we know?" he demanded.

Logan gave a sharp intake of breath, unsure whether to voice his suspicion. "I've a fair idea," he hedged.

The horticulture teacher barfed again, creating a small flood of second hand coffee between his feet. It dribbled over the edge of the pavement and created a rivulet in the brown earth. Logan lowered his voice to just above a whisper. "Remember the player who didn't show up on Saturday."

"Is someone listening?" Angus snapped.

"Yep," Logan replied. He winced as his colleague projectile filled the pot holes in the concrete.

"Okay." Angus drew out the word. "I know who you mean." He'd attended Saturday's game, standing under a school umbrella with the administrative assistant from the student centre. It sent the school rumor mill into overdrive. Angus chuckled. "Perhaps someone stepped on his crease."

Logan smirked and shook his head. He didn't reply and Angus covered his own error. "Sorry, that was disrespectful and crass. You know I wouldn't risk saying that to anyone else."

"Yup," Logan answered, cupping his hand over the phone speaker while the horticulture teacher retched some more. Nothing else came out and the man doubled over in pain.

The sound of sirens rent the air as Hamilton's finest piled through the front gate in squad cars. They wasted time looking for a vehicle route through the site to the boarding house without finding one. Having disturbed the whole school, they backed out onto Maui Street with their sirens still blaring and looked for the rear entrance.

As an ex student, Bodie knew the location of St Bart's entrance and arrived first. He walked around the corner and acknowledged his stepfather with an upward jerk of his head. "What's up?"

"A stiff." Logan pointed at the body at his feet. The gathering wind unwrapped it from its shallow grave with relentless determination. The horticulture teacher dredged up the last remnants of coffee from his gut, let out a moan and puked again. Bodie jumped back just in time and Logan laughed. "Nice dodge, goalie. See, that's where you're going wrong." He snorted again as Bodie gave him the middle finger. "Ooh officer!" Logan feigned shock. "That's no way to treat a member of the public."

Bodie mouthed something obscene and Logan smirked. "How come you always turn up to this crap? Don't they have any other cops in Hamilton?"

Bodie grimaced as the horticulture teacher glanced back over at the trench and then went in for the full projectile vomit, his stomach finding stores he didn't know he had. "Yeah, but I'd just tugged someone for speeding around the corner." He leaned over the trench. "Great!" he said without sympathy as vomit dribbled into it. "That will thrill the forensics team. Couldn't you take him further away?"

Logan kept his expression impassive. "The operator said I shouldn't touch anything, so I didn't. This guy dug him up which makes him part of the crime scene."

"Dug him up." The horticulture teacher gave a dramatic moan. "I dug him up." He sank to the ground looking as white as a sheet and the hand which mopped his brow shook.

Logan raised his eyebrow at Bodie. "You know what? This guy's a human vending machine that just keeps on giving."

"Screw you, Du Rose," his stepson grumbled. "You could have moved him away."

"Touching nothing this time." Logan held his hands out in front of him. "But you might want to let me go long enough to direct the traffic."

Bodie ignored him and took charge of the scene to the chagrin of the late arrivals who screamed up to the boarding house moments later. They cordoned off the area, keeping Logan and the horticulture teacher inside the tape. The clock ticked and the bell sounded, wreaking havoc behind them as boys stampeded towards the boarding house. The cops tried to contain the hungry throng but failed. Desperate for their usual sausage roll and morning pie, the testosterone filled masses used a back route and ended up at St Bart's dining room, anyway. They queued in front of the floor to ceiling ranch sliders, gawking and pointing.

Phones snapped covert photographs of the scene as the medical examiner arrived and Amanda kept busy answering calls from hysterical mothers who'd just received alarming texts. Within minutes the news spread across the Waikato. *Dead body found at the school*. Boys stood at the windows and munched pies while watching the dead groundsman recline in his makeshift grave.

A paramedic led the horticulture teacher to her waiting ambulance. Logan listened to him dry retch the length of the path. A uniformed officer followed with his notebook already out and a pen poised in his fingers. Logan eyed the mess on the pavement and found a clean patch of wall. He leaned back against it and closed his eyes. A stick of chewing gum from his pocket encased him in a haze of spearmint as he settled in for the wait.

"Mr Du Rose," Odering said with a sigh. "I thought we'd said our goodbyes." Logan gave an upward jerk of his chin in answer. Odering continued, "Your family seems to lurch from one disaster to another, doesn't it?"

Logan shrugged and fixed the blank look on his face. Odering's frustration oozed from him in waves. "I need to teach the next class." He folded the chewing gum wrapper into a neat square and placed it in his jacket pocket. "Let's just get this over with, Odering."

The medical examiner leaned over the trench. A rotting carrot and a half-eaten sandwich rested next to the dead man's foot. Odering waved his hand towards two female police officers carrying a pop up white tent. "Get that over the body!" he barked. "And someone pull those blinds down in there." He pointed towards the gawking boys. His glare settled on Logan. "You could have ordered them to do that, man! What were you thinking?"

Logan shrugged. "My assistance was rejected." He saw Bodie glance up and a pink hue crawled up his olive cheeks. He smirked and Hana's son gritted his teeth and looked away.

The police women battled the carcass of the white tent as the wind gusted. Logan tried not to stare at their antics. The breeze worked its way underneath the cloth and fought to send them both into orbit. Billowing like a parachute, it refused their efforts at taming it.

Odering took Logan's brief statement himself, not delegating it to one of the waiting uniforms. In his peripheral vision, Logan saw the tent achieve lift-off and one woman's feet leave the floor. He turned his laugh into a cough and Odering glared at him. "Finding this funny, Mr Du Rose?" he bit. "Want to come to the station and chat about it?"

"No, but thanks for the invitation." Logan took deep breaths and fought his laughter as the tent danced the women around the compost heap.

"Oh, there you are." Peter North trotted round the corner. He lifted one leg over the police tape and paused. "What are you doing?" He stood with one foot in the air as the tape fluttered between his legs. He forced his foot downwards and the plastic tape twanged. It snapped and the loose ends floated to the ground like ribbons. The wind seized them and spun them into the air around his head. Oblivious, Pete stepped into the crime scene. "Dodds wants you in his office now, Logan. Your Year 9 class pulled all the notices off the board and made them into airplanes." Pete's sneakers stopped in the middle of the vomit stain, his attention caught by the two flying police women. "That's funny," he remarked as his face split in a wide grin. "One more puff of wind and they'll be in Matamata."

Logan snorted and Odering fixed him with a steely eyed stare.

"Hey, love, watch what you're doing!" Pete yelled to the nearest tent wrestler as he noticed where her dancing feet took her. He tramped over the soil and almost flattened the medical examiner. "My Henrietta planted those potatoes! Don't stomp all over them like that!" Ignoring the shouts and yells of warning, Pete kept moving with his eye on the fluttering tent. "This isn't the best place for it," he said. "If you want to sunbathe, the soccer pitch is better. Or the tennis courts."

His fingers lay hold of a corner of the tent and he helped haul it back to earth. Logan forced himself to concentrate on his breathing and not release the bubble of raucous laughter building in his chest. Pete took a step backwards and lost his balance, pitching over and sitting on the partially exhumed body. "Bloody hell," he said, peering down before looking back at Logan. "Why has Collins planted himself?"

Chapter 9

Hamilton traffic proved uncooperative. A queue of cars stretched up Te Rapa Straight as far as the edge of town.

"What's taking so long?" Hana grumbled as Phoenix complained behind her.

"Dunno," Tama replied. "Maybe an accident. Climb in the back and sing a song or something."

"To move the traffic?" Hana turned to peer at him.

"No!" He shook his head and wound the window down to allow cool air into the car. "To settle your daughter."

Hana squeezed into the backseat with much complaining. She didn't apologise as she whacked the side of Tama's head with her hip. Phoenix winced and sucked her thumb. "She's got a stomach-ache," Hana murmured. "I overfed her."

"Yeah." Tama's half-hearted reply belied his nerves. He tapped his fingers on the steering wheel and wondered if Logan would let him pick his own method of transportation into the underworld. "He's gonna kill me," he sighed. "I've seen him fight." Tama admired the angular contours of his face in the rear-view mirror. "Such a waste." He sighed again.

"He wouldn't hurt you." Hana said the words and accompanied them with a wince. She'd forced Tama to split his loyalties and needed to take responsibility for the outcome.

They sat in the traffic for another ten minutes. Tama tapped, Hana fretted and Phoenix dropped off to sleep. Hana held her breath as the vehicles moved a few metres but then stopped again. Half the Hamilton police force rushed past, pushing through the intersection with their sirens roaring into the wintry sky.

"Must be time for morning tea," Tama said with a sneer. "They don't move so fast for much else!"

Hana ignored him and focused on thoughts of her father. "This is a big mistake," she breathed. "What am I doing? Turn the car round, please. Let's go home."

Tama slapped the steering wheel as an ambulance squeezed through the narrow gap between two cars. "We're not going anywhere right now, Ma! Just calm down. If we ever get to Victoria Street, you can decide what you want to do then."

Phoenix grunted in her sleep and filled her nappy. Hana groaned. "That's all I need!"

"I'll change her bum in the car," Tama offered. "You go in by yourself at first. That's if we ever get there."

The lights changed as the last police car sneaked across the intersection. The road cleared in seconds as the traffic moved away. Tama shook his head. "There's nothing to show for all that drama."

"Sounds like my life," Hana mused, and he shot her a look of rebuke in the mirror.

"No, it's something to do with all those cop cars and the ambulance."

In the motel car park, Hana closed her eyes and considered her options. "I need to know," she concluded. "I have questions that only he can answer."

"Then you should get going," Tama said. "Logan's gonna kill me, so at least make it worth it."

After a fortifying hug, Hana walked into the reception while Tama changed Phoenix's nappy on the passenger seat. Hana looked back and spotted chubby pink legs waving in the air. She hesitated, looking for excuses to delay, but the receptionist spoke to her. "Can I help you?"

"I'd like to see Robert McIntyre," Hana replied, whispering for reasons she couldn't fathom.

"Take a seat and I'll ring his room," the woman replied, a fake smile plastered on her lips. The receptionist had a short conversation with someone on the other end of the line and then called Hana over. "Room 42. Go into the car park and turn right. It's on that side of the building."

Outside, Hana walked through an archway into a courtyard. Cars were parked in front of units, but the numbering scheme evaded her with the faded signs. She looked around, feeling foolish.

"Hana!" A familiar voice called her name and she turned to see him stumbling towards her. He was almost three decades older, but still her father. "Hana! Bairn!" Robert McIntyre's voice caught and he held his arms out wide. His steps faltered on wavering legs. He seemed unashamed, drawing attention to himself without caring. The proud, reserved man was gone as he called a name which he'd uttered only in his prayers for too many years.

He almost bowled Hana over but she hid her shock at the feel of his frail body beneath her hands. The once burly Scotsman with a voice which boomed from the pulpit had receded into a fragile old man. Everything about him had declared power and authority but he'd become a shadow of that man, all clothes and winter jacket without flesh to hold them upright.

Hana buried her face against his collar bone and tried not to recount the wasted years as she breathed in the familiar scent of his favourite soap. She felt his great drops of grief tumble into her hair and clutched his raggedy body. When she pulled away, they spoke at the same time. "Sorry."

Their dual apology crossed the years, leaving healing in its wake. Robert led Hana to his motel room, his steps slow and unsteady. He closed the door behind them and pulled a chair from beneath a dressing table for her. "Sit, please," he begged. Hana watched him, sensing the differences in his behaviour. The years had stripped away arrogance and pride, leaving someone else underneath wearing a clean, new skin. He settled himself on the edge of the double bed and faced her.

"I didn't know if you'd come." Robert's face twitched with nervous energy. "Your husband promised to speak to you, but I wasn't sure he would." He left the rest of his thoughts about Logan unsaid and it caused a distracting lull in conversation. Hana's shoulders slumped with exhaustion; her emotions emptied out on the ground. Hating the silence, they both spoke at once and Hana's father held out his hands to prompt her to speak first.

"I owe you an apology, Dada," Hana said, ignoring his frantic head shake. "I never considered the shock factor for you when I turned up pregnant and trailing a boyfriend. It's ridiculous that I've spent the last twenty-six years thinking about it from my perspective and let it override the truth of my happy childhood. You deserved better from me. Will you forgive me, please?" A rawness struck her heart as though someone had peeled it.

Robert held up his hand. "Of course, I forgive you," he gushed. "I should apologise to you for my appalling behaviour that day. I've never since felt consumed by an anger so powerful, but it cost me everything. Oh, Hana. I'm so sorry."

"Thanks, Dada," she said. Her voice failed. "I don't know where to start. I never expected to see you again, so I haven't rehearsed what I wanted to say."

Her father smiled, his blue eyes the only thing which hadn't changed in the intervening years. "On the contrary, Hana," he said, "I've imagined this moment almost every day for the last twenty-six and a half years. And I decided long ago that I would take my only daughter for coffee."

Hana laughed. It seemed so unexpected that her frugal father would offer to spend money. She wanted to make a joke but daren't, sensing hysteria lurking beneath the thin veneer of her courage. "I'll tell Tama," she said, pulling her phone free and dialling his number.

Tama answered straight away. "Hey, I'm taking Phoe for a walk," he announced. Hana heard the icy wind blow around the phone and the shiver in his voice. "She's in her pram and the chicks are loving it." Hana tutted and he laughed. "Just kidding, Ma. I'm telling them she's my sister."

"Oh, Tama!" Hana sighed. "What about waiting for your soul mate?"

"I'm joking." His laughter tinkled through the phone. "Are you okay?"

"I'm fine. Dada wants to go for coffee, so we'll head along to the motel bar. You can meet us there when you've had enough of hawking my daughter far and wide." Hana swallowed. He'd asked if she felt okay and she didn't know how to answer.

Robert ordered two coffees and put it on his room tab. Then he sat next to his daughter. The embarrassing silence threatened to descend again and Hana tried to disperse it, not wanting to keep climbing out from beneath its weight. "Tama said you'd remarried," she said. "He couldn't remember her name."

"Elaine," Robert replied. His brow furrowed and his expression held concern.

Hana nodded. "Is there anything you want to ask me?"

For the next hour they chatted, catching up on each other's lives. Robert asked questions about Vik and their life together, how they ended up in New Zealand and about Bodie and Izzie. "I understand I'm a great-grandfather," he said.

Hana nodded. "Yes, Bodie has Jas and Izzie has Elizabeth, Vikram and Marcus Junior. The boys are twins, born last year." Hana swallowed and chewed her lower lip. She remembered her father's fear of defects and the way he reacted to anything which threatened his veneer of perfection. Hana took a deep breath and refused to deny her adorable granddaughter. "Elizabeth was born with Down Syndrome. She's an amazing little girl. The doctors didn't think she'd ever speak, but she's managing a few words now."

Hana looked away, fighting her tendency to babble. She missed Logan like a physical ache, understanding why he hadn't yet told her he'd found Robert. He'd wanted to accompany her to the meeting. He would have held her hand and plugged the awkward gaps. Hana bit her lip and worried about him finding out she'd jumped ahead. She'd cut him out, circumnavigating his wisdom and regretting it like she always did when she rebelled from beneath his well-intentioned protection.

"Did you know your brother lived here in Hamilton?" Robert asked, inclining his head to drink his coffee. Hana saw the hearing aid nestled in his left ear and realised again how much she'd missed. He used to hear the fridge opening in the kitchen from his study on the other side of the vicarage.

She gave a tight little nod. "Tama mentioned it," she answered. "Why is he here?"

Her father lifted an eyebrow, recognising the salient part of the story Tama left out. "He's working at the hospital," he said.

Hana nodded and steered the conversation away from Mark. "How are his nice wife and little boys?" she asked. She replaced the word *perfect*, which she automatically slotted into the sentence in her mind.

Robert shook his head. "We don't know, Hana. Claire left not long after that awful day. There were problems before that, but Mark chose not to see the problems under his nose until too late. I opened the door to him and Claire just hours before you arrived. Claire wanted a divorce and Mark didn't see it coming. He hoped we could convince her to stay married." Robert winced. "After our treatment of your baby's father, she made her mind up and moved out as soon as they got home."

"Oh." Hana covered her eyes with shaking fingers. The scene played out behind her eyelids on a loop. "I've always imagined him living a charmed life with two perfect sons and a perfect wife. Tea on the table and slippers by the fire. I assumed I was the family disgrace."

"No, bairn." Her father smiled. "It proved a day for shocks. Pregnancy and divorce in the space of two hours."

"Not a good day then?" Hana said, her voice soft.

Robert shook his head. "The worst. I lost a daughter, a daughter-in-law and three grandchildren that day." His complexion paled, turning grey in the dimly lit lounge. Hana touched his knee with feather light fingers.

"Let's not dwell, Dada."

Robert nodded. "Just one thing before we move on though. I knew nothing of the letter Mark wrote to you after Judith died." He drummed his fingers on the arm of his chair as though unable to contain a hidden beat. "I didn't know he told you not to come to the funeral." His eyes flashed as Hana nodded, fresh pain threatening to overwhelm them where they sat. "I didn't tell him to do that, Hana." Robert leaned closer. "I wrongly assumed you didn't want to come. Please forgive a foolish man for not following it up and checking with you? I apologise for that grave error of judgement."

"I look back now and it's like a catalogue of disasters," Hana whispered. "Little miscommunications which created a huge mess that seemed impossible to unravel. I should have written, but feared you'd ignore me and I couldn't bear that. I tried phoning. Once, I waited an hour for my turn to use the phone box on the corner of the promenade. I heard your voice and slammed the phone down. After three or four times of making a fool of myself, I gave up."

Robert reached for her hand and it felt unnatural to Hana. The undemonstrative father of her childhood kissed the back of her wrist. "Ah, sweetheart," he breathed. A tear dripped from the end of his chin and landed on the carpet. "I prayed you'd call back, but you never did."

Hana gulped. "Mark must be in his late fifties now," she said. Robert kept hold of her hand and nodded.

"He's an accomplished surgeon," he said with pride. "He arrived in New Zealand on a two-year contract last January. Mark's heading up the new surgical unit here and they've asked him to stay."

Hana nodded and caught the odd look in her father's eye. She withdrew her fingers from his grip and sat back against the seat. Her body became rigid as the puzzle pieces fitted together. The mysterious voice returned as an echo in her mind and she gasped. "He mended my wrist." She looked down at the welt rising from the soft, pale skin. "I heard his voice and blamed it on the medication."

Robert nodded. "He saved your life, Hana. After your little accident." He looked away with an awkward tilt of the head and Hana held her breath. "I made the mistake of asking your husband yesterday if you were mentally stable. He didn't appreciate it." Robert looked contrite, pursing his lips and wrinkling his nose.

Hana jerked. "I'm surprised he left your head on your shoulders," she bit.

Robert slumped in his seat and his head hung on a neck empty but for the sinews and tendons holding him together. "Mark phoned me in the middle of the night in great distress. He said he'd stopped the bleeding and promised he'd see you again. I waited by the telephone all the next day, but his call ruined my dreams of a reunion. You'd left the hospital and he couldn't find you. He thought you'd given a false address. The police detective wouldn't discuss your injuries with him or tell him what you were mixed up in. Mark wanted me to fly out straight away, but my oncologist refused. He made me see my radiotherapy through until the end. Mark promised he'd wait until I arrived, but I know he's visited the address you gave because he couldn't wait."

Hana blew out a breath. "It's better this way," she admitted. "I panicked after the surgery and left. Logan would have reacted in my defence if I'd woken up to find Mark standing by my bed." She shook her head. "It's all a blur. I think I've blocked out most of that week." She lied, desperate to move the conversation away from thoughts of Laval and the nightmare he represented. But she recalled clinging to the familiar voice of her surgeon. He'd told her she'd be okay. She remembered the feel of his breath on her cheek and the sensation of warm tears plopping onto her forehead. "I should have guessed," she whispered. "He sounded real because he was."

"You don't want to talk about it?" Robert asked. Hana saw the hunger in his eyes. He searched for reassurance. For his sake she allowed herself to venture back into the moment.

"It was an expensive crystal whisky tumbler," she said, banishing the mental image of her blood spraying an arc on the concrete driveway. She held her hand out, palm upwards for him to see.

Robert cringed and shook his head. "My poor wee girl," he whispered. "I'm so sorry."

"It looks this way because it got infected and reopened. Logan tried everything to get me back to the hospital. But nobody understood. I couldn't take the risk of being separated from Phoenix again. I believed if I took my eyes off her for a second time, she'd disappear and it would be my own fault."

Hana looked into her father's eyes and read her fears in the reflection of his blue irises. When he reached for her damaged wrist, she knew he understood, seeking contact to reassure himself she wouldn't evaporate into mist.

Hana closed her eyes and fought light-headedness. She sipped at her cooling coffee and tried to control the numbness that threatened to fog out her brain. When Robert leaned towards her, she jumped. "Hana, will you let me call your brother? He's desperate to see you."

Her brow knitted and she closed her eyes, not able to give him a straight answer. "I don't know, Dada," she admitted. "Can I think about it? I'm not quite ready to play the happy family yet."

Robert nodded and patted her hand. "I'm satisfied with that," he said. "I can't ask for more."

They chatted about Robert's life in England and he told her about his teaching career. Hana marvelled that he'd become the headmaster of the primary school she and Mark both attended. He entertained her with funny stories about the village. Hana shook her head. "So, you lived in the little cottage next to the school?" Her eyes widened. "We used to believe that place was haunted." She laughed. "Didn't some old lady live there and shout at us when tennis balls went over the wall?"

Robert chuckled and Hana delighted in the familiar sound of a Scotsman's mirth. "That's right," he said. "Mrs O'Rourke. Her husband worked as the school caretaker for twenty years. I don't remember her being an old lady though."

Hana snorted. "She was over a hundred!"

Her father threw his head back and laughed. Other customers turned to observe them as Robert mopped at his eyes with a patterned hanky from his breast pocket. "She was the age you are now!" he giggled. "Forty-six!"

Hana let the smile fall from her lips. She shook her head in disbelief. "She was definitely a hundred," she grumbled. "Over a hundred."

Tama wheeled the pram through the doorway into the resident's lounge. He paused for a moment until his gaze settled on Hana. Relief coasted across his worried expression. "Sorry, Ma," he said, pushing the pram towards her. "I had to come back. I didn't bring a coat." He put his cold hand against her cheek and she jumped. Robert observed their interaction with interest.

"Silly boy!" Hana breathed. Tama gave her a coy grin and sat next to her. He invaded the moment with the carelessness of a teenager, but his foot remained on the axle of the pram as he kept it moving. Phoenix snuggled beneath her blankets and sucked her thumb.

Robert looked longingly at her delicate olive face. "The child's stunning," he breathed. "She has the look of her father."

"What, scary?" Tama bit his lip and Robert frowned and refused the bait. Hana gave the slightest shake of her head and Tama obeyed, calling off the dogs at her bidding.

Phoenix twisted her head from side to side in her sleep as though her dreams demanded action. Hana reached forward and stroked her delicate forehead. Robert shifted his gaze to his daughter, forcing down the dreadful ache which bit at his fractured heart as he recognised his beloved Judith in every facet of her. The emerald green eyes and curly red hair caused him physical pain.

Tama jabbed his elbow into Hana's ribs as Robert's wife entered the lounge. She searched the room before finding her husband and her severe features relaxed into a smile. Robert gave a small, regal wave and Elaine started walking. She carried groceries but her footsteps slowed at the sight of Hana and Tama. Robert rose to his feet as she approached.

Hana gaped and then bounced upright like a marionette. Her fists curled and released against her thigh. "Aunty Elaine?" Her voice sounded tight and brittle.

Tama watched as the cracks showed in her feigned joviality. Hana reclaimed her seat after an attempt at air kissing Robert's wife. The pleasant meeting degenerated into long silences as she floundered. "I don't understand," she said at last. Her fingers shook as she pushed a loose red coil behind her ear. "I don't understand."

"What's bothering you?" Robert asked, his voice soothing and low. "Ask whatever you need to."

Hana shook her head. Her index finger jabbed at Elaine. "She made my mother's life miserable. You banned her from visiting. Now you've married your sister-in-law!" Tama's chin drew back into his neck and he winced. Hana's ire hiked far enough to make her stutter over her sentences. He reached out a gentle hand to stop her waving her arms and she shook him off. "Don't baby me!" she snapped at him. Her index finger continued its jabbing action in Elaine's direction. "You got what you wanted, didn't you? Mum let you visit once a year like clockwork. She tolerated your criticism and the way you sucked up to Dada, but she knew your game. You wanted what she had and now you've got it. Well done." Hana's slow applause attracted the attention of the room's other occupants. She rose and leaned forward, her eyes blazing. "You made her cry that last time. You broke her heart." Hana closed her eyes and remembered Judith's tear-streaked face and the fearful look in her eyes. She swallowed and fought for control. Elaine's green eyes remained unblinking as she stared at Hana. The less genteel of the McGillivray siblings, she wore her hair in a tight bun and her skin resembled alabaster.

Hana turned to her father and spread her arms wide. She stood, her expression conveying the overflow of her dismay. "Why, Dada?" she demanded. "Why her?"

Robert swallowed with an audible gulp and looked from Hana to his wife. He appeared lost for words as though confounded by his daughter's reaction. Hana backed away until her hip contacted a bar stool and she threw out a hand to save herself. Tama rose, seeing too late the situation spiralling out of control. He anticipated Logan's fury and heat rose into his chest, his actions indefensible.

"Hana, wait!" Robert pushed himself into a standing position, but Hana shook her head.

"I need to go," she breathed. "I should have stayed away." Her heart hammered in her chest and her fingers fumbled on the handle of the pram. Tama cupped her elbow in his palm and steadied her as she navigated chairs and tables. He looked back once to see Robert sink into his seat, his shoulders bowed and his expression crestfallen.

Outside, Tama panicked. "I'm sorry, Ma. I've stuffed up. We should have waited for Uncle Logan."

Hana shook her head. "I don't want to talk about it." She looked pitiful, her green eyes huge in her pale face and her teeth worrying at her bottom lip. Tama nodded, transferring the sleeping Phoenix into her car seat and dismantling the pram.

"I'm dead. Logan's gonna kill me." Tama's misery for Hana spread to himself.

"I won't tell him." Hana's voice held an uncharacteristic wobble. "Let's forget it happened."

A chill wind nipped at Tama's shirt sleeves and snatched at his jeans, reducing the temperature to a little above zero. Tama blew on his hands and jumped into the driver's seat. Hana climbed in next to him, her silence eerie. He started the engine and turned right out of the motel, crossing the four-lane road with care. Boundary Bridge seemed calm after the earlier traffic jam and within minutes, they crossed the river and headed towards the school site.

"Are you staying with us at the staff unit?" Hana asked. "Or do you want to go back to Culver's Cottage and fetch your ute?"

Tama shrugged. "Can I stay with you for now? I'll talk to Uncle Logan and then go back to the hotel. Jack lets me use his guest room and I can work for free while I sort out the fire brigade stuff."

"You know Alfred lives with Jack now, don't you?" Hana asked. "Will that be a problem for you?"

Tama shook his head and thought about his family tree. It resembled a case of bindweed. He gave a soulless laugh. "Do you mean Alfred who started out as my great uncle, before getting promoted to a grandfather because my uncle is really my father? That Alfred?"

Hana sighed and nodded. "Yeah."

"Na, it's okay." Tama reached across and captured Hana's writhing fingers in his left hand. "Alfred's cool with everything, even though his son's an idiot."

"I'm sorry Tama," Hana said, clasping her fingers through his. "You deserved better in a father."

Tama wrinkled his nose. "I don't like Michael. He's clever, good looking and knows it. His Du Rose genes got twisted somewhere along the way. He has no moral scruples either, from what I've heard." Tama snorted. "You know what I heard a few weeks ago? Michael and Aroha are dating again." He shook his head. "My parents are giving it another go after almost nineteen years. It makes me sick!"

Hana eyed him sideways in sympathy. "Parents, hey? Who'd have 'em?"

Tama shuddered and nodded. "Poppa Reuben was both father and mother to me in his own way. He discovered early on that Kane was vicious and sheltered me from the worst of it. Reuben wasn't the fool they've painted him. I wish Logan got to know him before he died." Tama wrinkled his nose and tapped a nervous beat on the steering wheel.

"Don't you have contact with your mother?" Hana asked.

Tama shook his head. "No. I don't want to. She abandoned me as a baby. Poppa Reuben wouldn't let her have me when she came back."

"At least she came back," Hana whispered. "It shows she cared."

"Maybe. Not enough."

"How do you know?" Hana's heart ached for a woman she'd never met, sympathising through Logan's very different side of the story.

"She didn't try that hard, did she?" Tama bit. "She could have seen me outside their control. Why didn't she come to sports days and school plays? Kane and Poppa couldn't have stopped her seeing me in public places. She didn't bother."

Hana stilled her tongue, recognising a desperate need to heal his life now she'd discovered her own beyond mending. Tama shook himself to clear his head and Hana reached forward and turned the heat up, thinking he suffered from the cold. But the chill biting Tama's heart originated in his history and not the spiteful wind blowing up from Antarctica.

"You might not want to hang around while I tell Uncle Logan about dropping out of college," Tama mused as they turned on to the back road to the boarding house. "I once saw him take out two guys without breaking a sweat. He used to tell me it's how you hit, not how hard."

Hana pulled a face and shook her head. "Don't be silly. Logan won't hit you. You have a plan and that will ease any misgivings over your decision. He just wants to see you settled and happy. It's all we ever want for our children, to know when we die, they're equipped to go on without us."

Hana thought about her mother, dying without knowing if her daughter could go on without her. "I wasn't," she muttered. "I wasn't equipped at all."

Tama turned to face her but left the question unspoken. He saw the anger in her expression. Her mother's death had robbed a teenager of valuable help and wisdom. Hana turned to stare at her baby's car seat. By the time her daughter was testing her wings, Hana would be in her sixties. The thought sobered her, not helped by the looming reality of the claustrophobic two-bedroom staff unit in her near future.

An unusual queue of traffic blocked the gate to St Bart's and cars moved one at a time. Tama strummed his fingers on the steering wheel. "I dunno what's going on." He tried to see ahead and noticed the flashing lights of an emergency vehicle blocking the entrance. He glanced at Hana, but she clambered into the back seat next to Phoenix and didn't see. "Nice bum," he commented, fluffing his fringe in the rear-view mirror.

"Shut up," Hana replied. "I can't wait until she can face forwards. I never know whether to sit with her or stay in the front."

"She was fine, Ma," Tama complained. "I can see her in the mirror. Don't fiddle with her. It took ages to get her to sleep."

"She's gorgeous." Hana smiled, a proud, maternal beam.

"Yep, just like I said." Tama eyed Hana in the mirror, knowing she'd panic when she saw the emergency lights. She'd assume it related to Logan. He held his breath as Hana leaned sideways and caught the flash of blue and red reflecting off the windscreen. Her eyes widened and her face paled. "No, Ma! Stop!" He flicked the switch and locked the rear doors to stop her bolting. Hana grappled with the lever.

"Let me out!" Her breathing sounded hoarse.

"No. Stay in the car!" he barked. He released his seatbelt and turned to snatch at her shirt. "Stop it!" He sounded angry, his command cutting through her fear like a knife. Hana heaved gulps of air as she froze, but her hand remained on the door handle. "They won't let you in, Ma. You need to sit here and let them deal with the cars. They're letting staff through look." He pointed at a vehicle moving through the blockade. "Here," he offered, digging around in the cup holder and handing over his cell phone. "Ring him."

Hana stared at the phone and then at Tama, her heart thudding blood through her brain. She glanced at her baby, hearing the little 'click, click' sound as Phoenix sucked her tiny thumb. Then she looked at the phone again, her eyes showing panic as Tama snatched it back. "I can see cop cars, Ma. If Uncle Logan hurt himself, there would only be an ambulance. This is massive. There are uniforms everywhere."

The traffic stilled again as an outgoing vehicle slipped through the barricade, its sleek black tinted windows masking its purpose. Tama watched it slide past and shook his head. "That's the undertaker, Ma. Someone's died." He reached behind and grasped both her shaking hands in his strong fingers. "Uncle Logan's fine, or Mr Blair would have rung one of us by now. It takes ages to process a body. You'd know if it was Logan."

"How do you know this stuff?" Hana demanded, her voice husky and fearful.

"I just do. It's not Logan." Tama withdrew his hand. "Put your seatbelt back on please, otherwise this cop at the gate will waste time giving you a ticket and it will take longer."

Hana obeyed, quickly inserting the plug and clicking it shut. The little red seatbelt light on the dashboard stopped blinking. A young woman at the gate wore her smart police uniform and Kevlar vest like a fashion statement. She looked stunning, her dark hair pulled back into a neat ponytail and striking blue eyes blinking beneath her hat Hana distracted herself by watching Tama preen himself in the mirror before the car in front moved forward. She smirked as he fumbled with the switch to lower his window.

"Hello." The girl leaned down and Hana caught the subtle strains of floral perfume. "Can I ask your business on the site today, please, sir?"

Tama tried to concentrate on her question and kept his eyes on her face. Her peachy skin looked flushed from the cold winter air and biting wind. "What?" he stammered.

The girl smiled and exhibited patience. "Why are you here, please, sir?" She leaned in the window and noticed Hana in the back seat. Hana released her seatbelt and leaned forward.

"My husband is a haemophiliac," she said. Her teeth gnawed her lower lip. "Is he hurt?"

Tama groaned. "No!" He sounded frustrated. "I told you it's not him."

"Driving licence please," the girl said. She kept her tone friendly but persuasive.

Tama dragged himself back from an alternate universe in which the female cop asked him for a date. He pushed his fingers into his back pocket, a look of dismay drifting across his olive face.

"Oh, no!" he exclaimed. His jeans were too tight for his fingers to search his front pocket. His face flushed. "Can I get out for a second?" he asked, his cheeks beetroot red. Hana watched through the window as the girl stood back and Tama unwound his tall body from the driver's seat. He towered over her and she stared at the buttons of his shirt as he dug around in one pocket and then the other. Her eyes flickered with amusement as he eventually produced the small plastic card from his wallet in the glove box. He handed it over, keeping his grey eyes fixed on her face as she examined it. Her eyes flicked up once as she checked the photo against the owner. Then she handed it back and smiled again, betraying nothing in her expression.

"Thank you, sir," she said. Her ponytail bounced as she turned. She walked to the vehicle behind them without a backward glance.

Tama watched for a second before climbing back into the car. It made a grating sound as he turned the key, forgetting he'd left it running. "Sorry, sorry," he hissed. The car pulled away and did kangaroo hops for a few metres before settling into a steady pace.

Hana leaned forward and peered through the gap between the seats. "I want to see Logan," she demanded. She frowned at the sight of Tama's pink ears. "Oh. What's wrong?" She bit her lower lip and stopped herself giggling at his discomfort. After the rotten meeting with her father she craved normality. Hugging Logan and taunting Tama went part of the way to healing the soreness.

Tama glanced away with a grumpy expression and muttered a swear word under his breath. He experienced a peculiar rush of emotions he didn't understand. "I think I like girls in uniform," he confessed. "Who knew?"

Hana smirked and turned in her seat. The girl's long chocolate hair danced in the wind and she hid a slender physique beneath her police uniform. Tama looked so vulnerable that Hana relented. "You've got enough problems right now without mixing in a hot police officer," she said. "You need to confess your woes to Logan and try not to tell him about my disastrous meeting with my father."

Tama groaned. "I can't lie to him, Ma. He'll know. Uncle Logan's got this sixth sense for trouble."

Hana nodded and their eyes met in the mirror's reflection. "I know. Please can we make sure he's okay before he kills you?"

Chapter 10

Tama unloaded the Honda and put their bags into the staff unit. Hana wrinkled her nose at the tiny space in which three adults and a baby would need to coexist.

"Try Logan's number again," Tama suggested.

Hana shrugged. "I got his voicemail." Her face became pinched with concern. "I left him a message asking him to call me."

"Don't read anything into it," Tama said with a sympathetic smile. "He's probably teaching."

Hana nodded and checked her watch. The police activity concentrated on the boarding house and she fought her fluttering heart. "You're right," she agreed. "If the emergency services came for Logan, the lady-cop at the gate would have recognised the name on your driving licence and pulled us aside. Du Rose isn't a common name, is it?"

Tama winced. "No, Ma. I'm sure Logan's fine. But my last name isn't Du Rose."

Hana missed the end of his sentence, distracted by the lunch bell sounding in the distance. Then she jumped at a knock on the door. Her eyes sparkled like emeralds as she ran across the lounge and wrenched it open. Amanda stood on the step, her eyes alight with scandal and gossip. "Let me in," she gushed. "I know what's happened."

"Hey," Hana greeted her, accepting her hug and standing back to let her into the narrow hallway. "We just arrived back from town. I'm worried about Logan." Hana's brow knitted and she chewed her bottom lip in a fit of nervousness. She fought the urge to rush to the boarding house and find her husband. Her fingers tapped an anxious beat against her thigh as her mind flicked back to Laval's threats against Logan months earlier. She'd gone to great lengths to keep him safe. Losing her first husband had devastated her. Losing Logan would kill her. She believed it with every fibre of her being.

Amanda kept Hana waiting in the spirit of all practiced gossips. She pulled a sachet of soup from her handbag. After flicking the switch on the kettle and loading two slices of bread into the toaster, she turned and leaned her backside against the counter. "I shouldn't be gossiping," she said with a naughty wink. Hana sensed she would anyway. For once, the notion didn't make her feel soiled. "Logan's fine. He called the cops. He and Compo from the horticulture department found a body in the compost trench behind the boarding house. I answered the phone to Logan when he rang Angus. He sounded snippy with me, understandable under the circumstances." She pouted as though Logan's perceived slight affected her more than it should.

"Whose body did they find?" Hana lowered her voice to a whisper. "Is it someone from the school?"

Amanda shrugged. "Dunno. The cops are all over the boarding house. Angus isn't giving anything away, but he called an emergency meeting with the Board of Trustees. Parents have been blowing up my phone since morning teatime."

"Poor Logan," Hana breathed. "What a shock for him."

"He sounded more annoyed than anything," Amanda said with a toss of her long hair. Something in the way she said it made Hana bristle. She'd noticed a low-key possessiveness in Amanda's attitude towards Logan of late.

"I'm sure it was shock," Hana said, biting her lip. The action stopped her teeth grinding.

"Perhaps. It seemed unusual because he's always so sweet to me." Amanda popped her bread from the toaster and smiled at Hana as she reached into a cupboard for a plate. "Oh, please, could you send him round later? I've spent all weekend with the loft hatch banging in the wind."

"I could stand on a kitchen chair and shut it," Hana offered.

Amanda shook her head. "Thanks, but Logan can do it. The bolt's rusted, or I'd have done it myself."

"They replaced them all when they renovated a few months ago," Hana said. A frown grooved a line into her forehead. "They did ours anyway."

Amanda flapped her hand in Hana's direction and turned to fill her mug with boiling water, bashing the soup mixture with a teaspoon. "It's fine. I've got other bits I need doing while he's over there."

Hana watched her friend's back with a sense of unease. She'd been here before with Caroline. Logan rolled his eyes every time Hana gave him one of Amanda's requests for help. "I'm not the bloody maintenance man!" he snapped last time. Hana defended her neighbour, advocating for a woman who'd lost so much. As she watched Amanda stir her soup, her heart gave a painful clench. Her last husband had picked a mistress from among his work colleagues. Hana closed her eyes and gave her head a small shake. Logan wouldn't. He'd promised a million times.

Amanda knew little about the body in the compost heap. She wasted half an hour speculating with nothing concrete to add beyond school gossip. Tama stayed clear of Amanda, playing with Phoenix in Hana's bedroom. The sound of raspberries on a fat little tummy followed excited baby giggles and drifted through the tiny unit to the lounge. "I didn't realise how good Māori men were with their children," Amanda mused. "Maybe that's what I need." She eyed the door to the hallway, but Tama didn't oblige with an appearance.

"Not all of them," Hana replied, thinking of Michael, Kane and a list of other Du Roses.

Amanda ignored her wisdom. "I need a tall, good looking Māori guy who's comfortable around children." Her eyelashes fluttered. "Do you know any?"

Hana pulled a face and avoided the undertone to Amanda's question. "You can't go looking for love with a racial shopping list," she muttered.

Amanda frowned and checked her watch. "I'll head to the day care centre and get Millie." She took her time gathering her scattered belongings and clearing up the soup powder she spilled on the kitchen counter. "Don't forget to send Logan over later."

Hana pursed her lips and contained the biting retort building in her head. She'd thought they might become friends when she arrived at the unit, but Amanda had her own agenda and she regretted allowing the woman to get close again after their last cataclysmic dispute.

As Amanda breezed through the front door with a wave, Hana shaded her eyes with her hand and looked across at the boarding house. "I'm just nipping across to St Bart's," she called to Tama. "Please watch Phoe for a little while." She heard his muted reply and pulled the front door closed behind her.

Hana took a shortcut, jogging across the cricket pitch. She listened for the sound of Larry Collins' quadbike and tensed, half expecting him to materialise from thin air and scream at her for stomping across the crease in her boots. Heaving a sigh of relief, she skipped up onto the access road behind the covered seating and punched the air with her fist. "Larry Collins, fifty-three. Hana Du Rose, one."

She made her way to Logan's office on the ground floor. Housed inside a cubicle with mirrored glass, the office enjoyed three unimpeded views of the corridor, lobby and stairs. It served as a cunning observatory for misbehaviour. Boys forgot they were under scrutiny and Logan solved many crimes without leaving his desk. Unfortunately, his deputy manager used it as a way of conducting his personal grooming habits while on duty, picking his nose, belly button and any other handy orifice. He thought because the mirrored glass hid his antics outside that nobody knew. Everybody knew. He left the evidence on his chair.

"Hey, Hana, how are you?" The sweet receptionist sat at her desk in the foyer. A retired grandmother, she loved her part-time job at the school. Her white curls moved in the breeze from the front door.

"Good thanks, Paula," Hana replied. "Looks like you've had a busy day."

Paula rolled her eyes beneath dark rimmed spectacles. "You could say that." She inhaled as the telephone trilled next to her hand and Hana winced in sympathy. She heard half of the conversation as she walked away. "No, none of our boys are in danger; your son is fine."

Hana knocked and entered the office, holding her breath in case Peter North was on duty. He had a horrible tendency to bounce from his chair and hug her, much to Logan's annoyance. Pete rarely washed his hands after a bout of nose digging, and it left Hana feeling as though she needed a shower.

Only Logan occupied the small office. He sat in his swivel chair with his right boot resting on the desk. A laptop balanced across his strong thighs and his right hand moved the mouse. The cursor scrolled through a spreadsheet of names. Hana resisted the desire to alternately kiss and slap him. "So, you are alive," she snapped. "Thanks for calling me back. I appreciate being at the top of your list."

Logan's smile revealed his tiredness. His hair stuck up on end where he'd run his hand through it. Black curls bounced against his dark lashes. The circles under his eyes betrayed a bone deep exhaustion. The phone rang on the desk next to him and he shook his head and ignored it. "Sorry, babe," he conceded. "I haven't got near my cell phone for hours. I should have flicked you a text."

His instant apology stripped the anger from Hana's temper, and she sighed. "Paula looked like she was struggling too." She jerked her head towards the trilling phone. "It might be her."

Logan shook his head. "It won't. She's stopped putting them through to me. I can't add anything extra to what she's saying, so what's the point?"

"Parents?" Hana asked, feeling the urge to defend the army of men and women concerned for their precious children.

Logan nodded. "And journalists."

The phone stopped and then began again, its irritating ring cutting the air with the sense of a relentless wasp. Hana leaned across her husband and grabbed the handset. "St Bart's office," she said with a professionalism born of practice. Logan raised an eyebrow and slipped his fingers beneath the hem of her shirt. Hana bit her lower lip as she tried to ignore him. "No, madam. The boys are fine and the police are dealing with all information releases." Hana listened to the tearful mother on the other end of the line. She shivered as Logan's hands worked forward until he cupped one of her full breasts in his palm. He smirked at her with a lazy expression. The phone cord wouldn't stretch enough for Hana to stand up, leaving her exposed to her husband's sensual exploration. "Yes, I understand your son might have texted you, but he knows nothing concrete. It's just teenage exaggeration. I'm sorry, I need to go." She bit back a groan as Logan found his way into the maternity bra, using one hand to unclasp it at the front. With a sigh of pleasure, he caressed the breasts which spilled into his hand.

Hana replaced the handset and shoved her husband's shoulder, grappling to contain herself in her gaping underwear. Her shirt hung open to the navel, leaving nothing to the imagination. "You're awful!" she exclaimed, squeaking in fright as a group of boys wandered past the office window.

Logan laughed and rubbed his eyes, disappointment wrinkling his nose as Hana stepped out of reach. He lifted the laptop and set it on the desk. "They can't see you," he said, running his hands over the back of his head. Hana pressed her shameless breasts back into the bra and fastened the clasp.

"You have a headache," she stated, recognising the telltale signs as Logan pressed scarred fingers against his temples.

"Yep," he replied with a nod. "Hardly surprising after this morning."

"Well, risky office sex isn't the best cure," Hana said, straightening her shirt.

"It might have helped." Logan smirked and gave her a coy look. "You won't know unless you let me try."

"You're a worry," she replied. "I'll give you a hug instead." She slapped his boot, so he removed his foot from the table before she settled in his lap. She laid her head on his shoulder and sighed as he wrapped his arms around her, jabbing him in the ribs when his hands wandered. The stress of the day seemed to melt away in the silence. Hana let the fear of losing Logan recede to the back of her mind, knowing it would creep back out at another opportune moment.

She jumped at a knock on the door, making Logan grunt as she elbowed him in the stomach. The newcomer didn't wait for an answer, turning the handle and entering without permission. He raised his eyebrows at Hana as she pushed herself upright and straightened her shirt. Guilt bloomed as a pink hue, covering her chest, neck and cheeks.

"Tama said you were over here." Bodie waved his arm in Hana's general direction. He assumed he'd caught his mother in indecency, misunderstanding the innocence of the moment he'd interrupted. He stared at the notice board on the back wall to avoid seeing her discomfort. His tone became snippy and defensive. "We've cleared up, so it's business as usual. I'm off now, but Odering wants to see both of you."

"Me?" Hana's voice squeaked. "Why does he want to see me? I wasn't here. I didn't find a body." Curiosity nudged at her. She'd been so desperate to find Logan unharmed; she hadn't given another thought to the actual dead person.

Logan sighed. "Don't worry, babe. He just wants to have another go at me." Hana's heart sank at the antagonism in his voice.

Bodie shrugged. "I'm not responsible for what he does. He's the boss, but he's mad at you. Who lets a witness puke all over the crime scene?"

Logan shook his head and glared at Hana's son. "You saw him, Bodie! The guy's a human vending machine. Thanks for standing up for me."

"Oh, did you stand up for him?" Hana addressed her son, the tension leaving her shoulders.

Logan snorted. "It was sarcasm, Hana."

She looked away from the men and closed her eyes, a familiar and destructive pattern of antagonism yawning in front of her. Bodie turned his attention to Hana, waiting until she opened her eyes and released the heavy sigh clogging her lungs. "Can Jas spend the day with you tomorrow, Mum? His school has a teacher only day, so we're stuck. I got put on an early shift and Amy already signed up for a late." Hana saw his jaw work through his cheek, his eyes flashing with a darkness she couldn't fathom.

"It's fine," she replied, forcing a smile onto her lips. "Will you drop him here?"

"Amy will," Bodie said. Relief softened the angles of his handsome face. "It's just for a couple of hours during the crossover. One o'clock until three at the latest." He turned to leave and then glanced back, his teeth gritting at the sight of Logan's hand reaching for Hana's. "By the way, Odering is the acting inspector on this case. He's enjoying his authority. Just so you're aware."

Logan's face lit up with a smirk and Hana nudged his shoulder, sensing his quick brain formulating a plan of maximum irritation. "Who's the policewoman at the back gate?" she asked. "She's pretty."

"Lucy?" Bodie's shoulders tensed and his expression radiated protectiveness. "She just broke up with her long-term boyfriend. She doesn't need another loser in her life. Tell your idiot nephew to stay away from her." He left without glancing back, slamming the door behind him.

Hana watched her son through the mirrored glass as he strode past the receptionist. Heaviness weighed her down, alongside the realisation she'd been duped. "It's all an act, isn't it? You've both been play acting friendly to please me, haven't you?" Her voice sounded sad. "And I fell for it."

Logan frowned and his expression turned nasty, his lip curling upwards in one corner. "Yep." His tone sounded biting. "Your son's a spoiled little jerk and I played along, despite his continuing poor attitude towards me. Now he can go to hell."

Hana jerked backwards at the curse, her lips parting in dismay. Logan kept his eyes averted, but she sensed his rage brewing under the surface. She'd seen it before, a steady rumble coming just before an earthquake. He didn't frighten her, though she pitied anyone else clashing swords with him in the next hour. "The issue is me, Logan. I keep praying he'll get over it. He misses his father and thinks you've replaced him. It's difficult. It's not personal."

Logan laughed outright, a spiteful sound with no trace of mirth. He rose and shoved the chair under the desk, his manner indicating an end to her visit.

"Logan?" she asked, perplexed as he froze her out.

He moved to another desk in the corner and began sifting through papers, making a pretence of looking for something. The tension made Hana suspicious and she pressed him for answers, not realising her foolishness until too late. "It's not personal. He'd be like this with any new husband I chose. It's not you."

Logan rounded on her and his hands balled at his sides. The misery in his face went deeper than she realised. "How can you be so blind?" He raised his voice and his words echoed off the glass walls. "We made a truce when you got hurt, Hana. But it was always one-sided. I honoured it, but he never intended to reciprocate. I'm '*the spare*' to him, not good enough to take over from the sainted Vikram Johal. Do you understand what it's like feeling barely tolerated by your wife's son? It's fine for me to look after his kid when he's desperate, but I get nothing in return. One minute, I believe it's all okay and then he sees us together and blows up again. I'm tired of it, Hana. Jas is exceptional, but his father's a dick. I'm not welcome in his precious family and I've given up kidding myself."

Hana faltered, the force of Logan's distress pinning her in place. He'd exposed a hidden pain and she had no answers for it. Her words wavered, hitting the wall of his defences and ricocheting. "What do you mean by, '*the spare*?" she asked. "I don't understand." She took a step forward and reached for his arm. He dodged her consolation and slammed a bunch of papers on the desk.

"I need to supervise supper in the dining room." He stormed from the office, the heels of his cowboy boots hitting the corridor tiles hard enough to cause damage. The door swung on its hinges and whacked the cabinet behind it.

Hana released her held breath. "Great," she murmured. "And God help any boy who pushes you too far tonight. He'll find himself on detention until he's thirty."

Hana left St Bart's with the weight of the world on her shoulders. With the sense of urgency removed, she used the path and didn't trespass over the cricket pitch. Tama looked up as she clicked the front door closed. He juggled Phoenix in one arm and a bowl of hot baby rice in the other. She grizzled, a pitiful, hopeless sound. "It's still too hot," Tama grumbled. "But she won't wait."

Hana took her daughter, breastfeeding her as a consolation prize while the rice cooled. She squirmed at the memory of Logan's soft touch against her sensitive breasts. Phoenix fed, waving her arms around her head as though conducting a silent orchestra. "I didn't intend to take so long," Hana said with a sigh. "I didn't find out who died, but Logan's fine. Ropeable, in fact."

Tama winced. "Oh. Which idiot riled him?"

"Bodie." Hana shook her head. "Logan said he feels like '*the spare*', but why would he say that?"

"Dunno." Tama bent and kissed Hana's forehead. "I'm nipping across to St Bart's and confessing everything to Uncle Logan. I just needed you to come home."

"Oh, no!" Hana's eyes widened. "That's a terrible idea right now. He's already angry and supervising tonight's food fight. Just give it a few days. For your own safety." Hana shook her head. "We don't need two dead bodies on site."

She sought to curb Tama's misplaced heroism, but found her efforts wasted. "I'll be fine, but maybe get the bandages ready just in case. If he's wound up anyway, I can't get the blame for making him angry." He straightened his tee shirt and gave himself a mental shake. "I'll see you later. Or not." Tama waggled his eyebrows and pushed his feet into his trainers. He appeared deaf to Hana's further protestations and left with a forced smile.

She groaned as the front door clicked behind him. Phoenix stopped feeding to reward her mother with a gummy smile. Hana laughed. "You know how to cheer me up, don't you baby?" she cooed. Her daughter beamed, unconcerned by the vibes of male aggro surrounding her tiny world.

Hana fed her the rice, giggling at the mess they made. Then she bathed her, breastfed her and put her into her cot. Phoenix sang to herself in her ethereal language before drifting off to sleep. Hana put the TV on but saw nothing of the images moving across the screen. Bored, she rang her daughter in Invercargill on her mobile, getting Marcus instead.

"Izzie's at church," he said. "What's wrong?"

"Nothing," Hana lied, hearing her son-in-law's snuff of disbelief stretch across the miles. She relented and confessed the day's events to the astute cleric. "Logan said something odd before, about Bodie. I think they've had a spat and I wanted to ask Izzie if she could tell me anything about it."

"Ah, tricky," Marcus replied with a hiss. "This is why a vicar should never marry his best friend's younger sister."

Hana sighed. "I'm wasting my time asking you, aren't I?"

"Pretty much," Marcus replied. "I'm sorry. I'm happy to listen, but I can't break a confidence. You wouldn't trust me again if I did."

Hana conceded, asking after Izzie and the children instead. Marcus let her speak to each of them and she soaked up the baby giggles and the sound of Elizabeth licking the phone. Marcus came back on the line to Hana's laughter. "I should get this lot to bed before my wife returns," he said, inferring a sufferance that didn't exist. His tone lowered. "Look, Hana, Izzie and I are standing with you in this. Bo might take a while, but until he accepts Logan, it's his loss. He's missing out, not you. You live your life, okay? He'll come around eventually."

"Thanks," Hana said, her chest knotting with anxiety as she ended the call. She rattled around the unit, hating Logan's night duties and putting off bedtime. After eight years of sleeping alone, it took no time at all to adjust to having someone warm next to her in bed. The enforced absence dictated by the boarding house rota felt like a trial.

Hana dug out an unfinished novel and took herself to bed. She fell asleep reading and didn't hear Tama's return after midnight.

Amy dropped Jas off at ten o'clock the next morning, three hours before Hana expected him. It took her by surprise and forced her to abandon a planned walk to the baby clinic to get Phoenix weighed.

"Oh, sorry," Amy said with a wince. She didn't look sorry. "Bodie said you wouldn't mind. I have a massage booked in Hamilton East and Jas is far too naughty to take with me."

"Right." Hana grimaced as Amy lifted Jas' bicycle from the back of her car. "He can't ride that out here by himself, not while school is open. There are cars and students. It's not safe." Hana gnawed on her lip as Amy ignored her observation and slammed the boot closed.

"Maybe you could go for a walk along the river with Hanny and Phoe," Amy suggested to Jas, bending to drop a kiss on top of his head.

"Yey!" His excitement notched higher and he wobbled his bicycle along the tiny lane towards the primary thoroughfare for the boarding house. "Let's go!"

"I'm not comfortable with that idea." Hana's eyes widened at the thought of the narrow path and the deep, unforgiving Waikato River. "I can't chase him if I'm pushing the pram. He might fall into the water."

"See ya!" Amy gave a wave of indifference and drove away, leaving Hana with the consequences of her empty promise.

Jas behaved with his father's characteristic belligerence, refusing to come indoors while Hana got Phoenix into the pram. The short walk around the school grounds didn't satisfy him, and he complained when she turned for home in response to Phoenix's hungry wails. "I want to go along the river!" he protested. "That was just a little walk. I want more than that rubbish one!"

The air seemed too thin around Hana, mirroring her reedy patience. The effort of keeping Jas pinned inside the unit robbed her of her energy and left her breathless. When she refused to let him ride his bike along the narrow hallway, he indulged in an impressive tantrum which included head banging and screaming.

She texted Logan and received nothing in reply. Her day had turned into a punishment for an unknown crime with Bodie at the root. She'd just got Phoenix off to sleep in her cot and walked into the kitchen to find something for lunch when she caught Jas escaping through the front door with his bicycle.

Hana's temper flared and she ran down the steps and seized the bike handles. "Oh, no you don't!" She raised her voice and Jas' lips parted in protest. A group of passing students stopped to watch, and Hana's colour flushed as she imagined the gossip headlines. '*Wife of boarding house master beats child on front doorstep.*'

"Get inside," she snarled, her voice oozing an uncharacteristic hardness. "I've had enough, Jas. Get inside."

"No!" he whined, yanking his bike from her grasp and screeching as it tumbled sideways off the steps. "Look what you did!"

Something in Hana snapped as Phoenix's wail cut through the air. She stamped down the steps to the lane and lifted the bike in one hand. Without caring where it landed, she marched it around the side of the unit and hurled it into the bushes. Jas dogged her steps, his voice rising to a wail loud enough to reach the main building. "Get inside," she snarled through gritted teeth. "I will not put up with this behaviour. No more bike until you learn to behave. Now, do as you're told."

She grabbed Jas' hand to stop him lurching into the bushes and frog marched him back to the unit. Phoenix had stopped crying and Hana's truck occupied the space at the bottom of the steps. Tama appeared from the hallway carrying the baby as Hana hauled Jas up the steps and slammed the front door behind her.

"What's going on?" Tama's grey eyes widened in concern and he frowned at the angry pixie growling and hissing at the end of Hana's wrist. "You left the door wide open and Phoe by herself!"

Hana gave a wooden nod and released Jas. He shocked them both by lurching at Tama. "You can't touch our baby!" he shouted, his voice loaded with indignation. "She's not yours. She's ours." He took a swipe at Tama and got enough lift to thump him in the ribs. Tama gave a grunt of pain and turned away.

"Sod off, shorty!" he spat. "Touch me again and I'll break your fingers." He shot Jas a look of disgust and left the room with Phoenix. Hana heard the bathroom door click shut.

"What is wrong with you?" she demanded, staring at Jas through eyes filled with disappointment. "I thought you were a nice boy, but your behaviour today is horrid."

"I am a nice boy," Jas protested. "But that Du Rose boy is not a nice boy. He's an assassite."

"A what?" Hana leaned forward, still not understanding the word when he repeated it. She tried to take his hand, but he dropped to his knees and folded onto the rug like a discarded towel. She didn't trust herself to engage with him further, stepping over his prone body and walking into the kitchen. Every breath seemed to catch in her chest and her energy trickled out through the soles of her feet. She placed both hands on the kitchen counter and bowed her head. "I can't do this," she whispered. "What's wrong with me?"

Tama reappeared. He ignored Jas as the child swiped at his feet when he stepped over him. Phoenix sucked her thumb in his arms and drifted back to sleep. "I changed her nappy. What's wrong with the kid?" He didn't hide his disdain. "Why's he behaving like that?"

Hana shook her head. "Because his mother made him a promise, I can't keep. Because he's been dumped on me three hours early and would rather be elsewhere. His consolation prize is riding his bike on the cricket pitch and I can't face another yelling at by Larry Bloody Collins. And I'm knackered." Hana pressed her forehead against the counter. "I need Logan and he's not talking to me."

"Logan?" Jas pushed his way past Tama, a note of hope creeping into his voice. "Take me to Poppa Logan, then. I love Poppa."

"He's at work," Hana replied. She sighed and stared at the fridge, looking for inspiration in its stainless-steel door. "It's lunchtime."

"You threw my bike, Hanny. That's naughty!"

"I'll get it back later," she promised. "Eat your lunch like a good boy and I'll consider another walk. But only if you behave." Exhaustion pressed at the edges of her psyche and Tama cocked his head to watch her. He frowned and padded along the hallway to put Phoenix back into her cot.

"We don't like that boy," Jas said, lowering his voice. "He's bad news."

Hana swallowed and recognised her son's words emerging from the child's rosebud lips. The exhaustion took an even tighter hold. "Well, I love him," she replied. "You should make your own decisions about people, Jas. It's not good to think badly of a person just because someone else does, even if it's someone you respect. Tama's a good, kind boy. If you look with your own eyes, you'll see that for yourself."

"Don't forget handsome." Tama grinned and nudged Hana aside to get to the fridge. "Good, kind and handsome. I'm making cheese on toast for lunch. Who wants to help?"

"I will." Jas narrowed his eyes. "But just so you know, I don't like bread, margarine, cheese or ham. Or plates." Tama rolled his eyes and hid his smirk behind the fridge door.

Hana left the boys to turn the kitchen into a sea of grated cheese and occupied herself sorting through a biscuit tin containing old photos. She divided them into two equal piles.

"I want pickles on mine," Jas demanded. Hana glanced up but couldn't see him over the counter.

She saw Tama shake his head. "Don't you mean, I want pickles on mine, please?" He waited for Jas to respond and then reached into the fridge to retrieve the jar. "And don't waste them. They're Logan's favourite."

Hana moved the photos off the table for the boys to eat, her stomach too knotted to join them. Tama made Jas help him clear up the kitchen and then found him pencils and paper for drawing.

"I'm bored," Jas declared after a few minutes, throwing the pencil across the room. It hit the TV screen and Hana's chest tensed.

"What a good job smacking is illegal in New Zealand," she muttered, maintaining a stony, impassive face. "Pick the pencil up," she told him. Jas slipped off his chair and dragged his feet across the rug. He displayed the flexibility of a geriatric as he bent for the pencil and made a great show of being unable to reach. "Just get it, Jas," Hana sighed.

"Mummy says, *or else*," he jibed as his fingers closed around the pencil.

Hana narrowed her eyes and gave a twisted smile. "I don't make empty promises, Jas," she said. "I'm so disgusted at your behaviour, I'm contemplating ringing your father."

"No! Don't ring him. Ring Poppa Logan and ask me to give him a telling off. I want him to tell me off!" The child's face dropped into an ugly frown and his dark eyes clouded as a tantrum brewed.

"I don't want my lovely husband to see you like this," Hana replied. "It would make him very sad and he's got enough to worry about at the moment."

"Are you gonna ring Daddy then?" Jas taunted and pushed against Hana's limit. She nodded and shifted the photos from her lap onto the floor.

Tama glanced up from the game on his phone. "Cool it, kid. What's wrong with you today?" He rose and ran a hand through his fringe. "He's doing my head in today."

"Where's my phone?" Hana stood and surveyed the kitchen counter as Jas increased his volume. "I think I left it charging in the bedroom."

"No, no!" Jas wailed. He bounced up and down next to Hana. "Please, don't do it. I wanted Poppa, not Daddy. I'll be good, I promise. Just get Poppa to tell me off."

Hana watched the devious child through narrowed eyes, seeing more of her son in him than she wanted to. She stared at him while he begged and cried until actual tears ran down his olive cheeks. Tama frowned and shook his head, returning to his game with an expression of scorn. "The kid's nuts," he said with a sigh. "Are you sure he's not a Du Rose? He's showing all the symptoms."

Hana leaned forward and lifted Jas' chin to capture his attention. "Last chance," she warned him. "I'm telling you; I've had enough! Start behaving or I'm calling Daddy out of work and sending you home with him."

Jas relented enough to sit on her knee and help her sort out the photos. As fast as Hana sifted them into piles, he mixed them up with an endless commentary. "Please look at them without touching, Jas," Hana urged. She heard the tiredness in her own voice. He'd ruined a snapshot of Vik holding a baby Izzie ,with a greasy thumb print and a blob of bogey.

Tama shuffled through to the lounge, his hair sticking up from an impromptu sleep on Hana's bed. He eyed Jas with nervousness and his brows furrowed. Oblivious, Jas pointed for the hundredth time to a photo of Vik. "Who's that?"

"Your granddad," Hana replied, struggling not to yell the name and managing a gravelled croak instead. "The same answer as the previous ninety-nine times. Why do you keep asking when I've already told you?"

Jas cocked his head, considering something before letting loose with another episode of whinging. "I want you to say something else. Not a granddad. I don't want that granddad. Poppa Logan's my granddad! This one is the spare one."

Hana's head whipped round so hard she heard her neck click. "What did you say?" His words resonated in her brain. Hana took a deep breath and calmed herself, knowing from experience Jas wouldn't tell her anything if she probed. "What on earth is a '*spare*'?" she asked, putting emphasis on the ultimate word. "What a funny expression." The photo of a teenage Bodie shook in her hand.

"Well," Jas began, settling himself in for a lengthy description like an old man telling a tale. "It's when you've already got a daddy and someone gives you another one you don't want. Like my Dad had one and then he got another one. But he doesn't want the new one. It's a spare one." He looked Hana square in the eye with a sad look shrouding his expression. "But I like Poppa Logan best. I don't like this other one and I don't want him." Jas picked up the spoiled photo and put it face down on the sofa arm. Then he chuckled and his lips spread into a grin. "See, he's gone now. Bye bye spare granddad."

Hana put both hands over her face, her son's cruelty revealed. He'd slated her husband in front of the child and then used Logan to babysit without conscience because it suited him. The pieces dropped into place with a date and time. A few weeks earlier while Hana still recovered from her wrist injury, Logan looked after Jas during an emergency. He'd taken the child to his Year 13 English class when the primary school closed for a water leak. Hana noticed Logan's dark silence later, but never understood it.

Peeping through her fingers at Tama, she saw his teeth gritted in the characteristic Du Rose-pissed-off-face and couldn't blame him. Shame prickled in her chest at Bodie's spite. She inhaled and smiled at Jas, keen not to blame him for repeating something he'd heard. She sought to change the mood considering the reason for Jas' awful behaviour. "Why don't we get away from here?" she suggested, seeing Tama's faint nod of acquiescence.

"Where?" Jas demanded.

"Let me think," Hana replied, forcing a smile onto her lips. "Let's put your bike in the truck and go to Hamilton Gardens?"

"Get your coat on," Tama said to Jas. He rose to his feet, his authoritative tone rewarded by immediate obedience. Jas ran to the hall cupboard to retrieve his jacket.

Tama fitted the bike and pram into the truck and they drove towards the rear gate next to St Bart's. He seemed quiet and Hana bit her lip to avoid prodding the hornet's nest. She regretted Tama's opinion on Bodie and there seemed nothing she could do to improve it.

A group of police officers stopped traffic on the gate again, speaking to each driver and recording their answers. The female police officer approached the vehicle and Hana grinned at the back of Tama's head as his fingers fumbled on the steering wheel. He blushed to a heated shade of red and she watched the tops of his ears start sweating.

Jas sat on a booster in the passenger seat, leaving Hana in the back by Phoenix. The bicycle wheel spun in the boot with the motion of Tama's jerky braking. The cop smiled and Hana watched satisfaction settle over her pointed features. "Hello again, sir," she said, tapping her pen on the pad in her hand. "We're making enquiries about an unexplained death. Please can you give me your movements over the weekend?"

"Hello!" Jas piped up and the officer gave him a momentary wave. He leaned sideways for the full effect. "Tama likes you," he said.

"Jas!" Hana exclaimed. Her eyes widened and she clamped her bottom lip between her teeth.

The cop blushed, but Jas hadn't finished disgracing himself yet. "I'm gonna be a pimp when I grow up."

"Right." The officer drew out the word, her eyes widening in shock. Tama groaned and tried to cover Jas' mouth with his hand.

The child dodged sideways to avoid the gag. "Yep, like on Miami Vice. I'm gonna have a big gold med-lion round my neck and lots of girls. You can call me Poof Daddy." Jas made his eyes bug wide and resembled a maniac.

Tama looked to Hana for help in the rear-view mirror and she intervened from the back seat. "We went to Huntly for the weekend," she said. "My husband works at the boarding house and we left the site for a break."

"Ah, Du Rose." The cop made the connection and looked at Tama with renewed interest.

"Do you want addresses and phone numbers?" Hana asked.

The woman nodded and jotted down their details. "So, you live here during the week?"

"Yeah, unfortunately," Hana breathed, covering her misgivings with a nod and a smile. "We get away as often as possible. We attended a soccer game here on Saturday morning, but most of the team arrived as a group. I guess we can all alibi each other."

"Do you think you need an alibi?" the cop demanded.

Tama's blush intensified on the backs of his ears and he shook his head. His frantic throat clearing indicated he felt very much out of his depth. "I don't think we need an alibi," he said, a falter in his speech. He spun around to glare at Hana, his widened eyes telling her to stop talking.

"Cool then, thanks." Lucy closed her notebook and stepped away from the car. Tama clumped on the gas, causing the wheels to screech in his haste. Hana rested her head back against her seat and wondered if the day could get any worse.

At the gardens, Jas belted around on his bike, getting underfoot with tourists and gardeners. "At least I'm burning calories," Hana puffed, trying to look on the bright side.

"You don't need to," Tama reassured her. "If you get any thinner, you'll drop down storm drains."

Hana paused, nodding and holding her chest. Tama took his eyes off the two-wheeled maniac and caught hold of the pram handle. "You okay?"

She nodded and glanced up at Jas as he wobbled around the side of Turtle Lake. "Just catching my breath," she gasped. "I'm unfit." She pointed her index finger as the child wavered too close to the edge. "Just grab that boy for me before he drowns, please."

"You nearly fell in, kid!" Tama said, retrieving Jas and hauling him back to Hana by the arm. The small bike dangled from his other hand, making the veins in his biceps stand out as ridges on the skin.

"I need a coffee," Hana conceded. "And a seat."

In the cafe, Jas whined for chips, pie and ice cream, which he didn't get. Tama dealt with him to Hana's relief. "Muffin or nothing," he told the boy, his voice emotionless and not caring either way. Hana gave Phoenix a covert feed under her fleece.

"Did you ever behave like that?" Hana asked as Tama sat Jas on a seat and told him not to move. The child eyed him sideways and capitulated, knowing he meant it.

"Not if I still wanted skin left on my backside," Tama admitted, sitting next to Jas and trapping the child between the adults. "I just made up for it when I got older because by then nobody cared."

The cops had left the school site by the time they arrived home, but Bodie waited outside the staff unit in his car. Jas kicked up a fuss when Tama transferred the bicycle from the Honda's boot to Bodie's.

"Tama," Hana whispered, "please can you take Jas to the swings with Phoenix for a few minutes?" She jerked her head towards Bodie and Tama shrugged.

"Don't waste your breath," he sighed. But he transferred the sleeping baby from the car seat into the pram and strode towards the playground, shooting a withering look in Bodie's direction.

"What's with the cuckoo?" Bodie asked as Hana unlocked the front door and gathered Jas' belongings together. She couldn't trust herself to speak until the brimming lahar of hot lava in her chest was under more control. "You trust that parasite with your kid?" he pressed and Hana bit hard on the inside of her mouth.

She handed her son the envelope of photographs and he peeked inside as though she'd handed him evidence of a crime. Hana watched him but his face remained closed. Rage bubbled in her chest and she wrestled the urge to shout at him, knowing it would end in an argument.

"Has he behaved?" Bodie dropped the envelope as though it held no value.

"No," Hana replied. Bodie shrugged with disinterest, stoking her temper even higher. "If you're interested," she said, a bite in her voice, "your son listens to everything you say, even when it's not for his ears. This afternoon, he entertained us with a complete repertoire of inappropriate action and horror movies which he apparently watches with you." Hana reeled off a list. "He informed a colleague of yours he intends to be a pimp when he grows up, like on Miami Vice. He also described how to heat meth on a spoon. In detail."

Bodie swore. "Little git! I swear I put him to bed, Mum. He must sneak back out. I watched a movie last night and a couple of scenes showed drug use."

Hana shook her head. "I don't care what you watch while Amy's at work, but you might rethink the porn." Bodie gasped and his olive cheeks heated. On the crest of an angry wave, Hana continued. "Apparently you refer to my husband as '*the spare,*' plus other derogatory terms which I have more dignity than to repeat. Your insults seem more cutting coming from the mouth of a child."

Bodie slumped onto a dining chair. He should have run away like he usually did; like she expected him to do. His continued presence took the wind from her sails. "What's your problem with my husband?" she asked, her tone softer. "And let's not forget Tama. Is he *the cuckoo* or *the parasite?*"

Bodie rubbed a hand over his eyes. He hung his head. "Logan's not Dad. He never will be."

"No," came Hana's swift retort. "Logan's faithful, for a start!"

"What?" Bodie's dark eyes flashed and the colour leaked from his cheeks. "What do you mean by that?" He half rose and Hana swallowed. The decade old secret hung like a weight in her chest, almost folding her double.

"Nothing." She ground her teeth, redirecting her rage at her son. Angry, black bile leaked from her psyche and she couldn't seem to stop it spilling free. "How dare you?" she half-shouted. "You're using us like unpaid childminders and slagging us off behind our backs. Logan took your son to his senior class to help you out and then you bad mouthed him, using horrid names which your son repeats to anyone who'll listen. Who the hell do you think you are? Logan's been nothing but kind to you and Izzie and you repay him like this?" Blood surged into Hana's chest and created a lightness in her head. Her body trembled from its velocity.

Bodie kept his head down but his jaw worked in his cheek. "He gave Izzie a fifty grand car." Devilment back lit his eyes as he looked up at her. "Or didn't you realise that?"

Hana licked her lips. She didn't but refused to admit it. "Logan booked your wedding reception and honeymoon at *his* hotel, free of charge! How mercenary and money grabbing can you get? I don't think I've ever been more ashamed of you than I am right now! You're nothing but a spoiled brat with an ungrateful streak which makes me feel physically sick!"

Hana picked up her cell phone and dialled the hotel reception. Bodie watched as without giving her name, she enquired about the cost of a wedding reception, listing the features of the package Logan had offered as a gift. With a shaking hand she wrote down an exorbitant figure and thanked the receptionist, hoping the woman hadn't recognised her voice.

She threw the paper onto the table in front of her son. "There you go," she said. "That was '*the spare's*' wedding gift to you."

Bodie gulped and his face lost its spiteful edge. He pushed the paper back across the table towards her. "Sorry," he said, biting his lip. "I didn't think about that."

"You will be sorry," Hana replied. The clang of steel rang in her voice. "You'll now be paying it. I won't allow you to abuse my husband's good nature anymore. Find the money or cancel the wedding reception. I'll leave you to explain to your fiancé."

Bodie rose, beads of sweat appearing on his forehead. "I don't have the money, Mum. Please don't do this."

Hana shook her head, her neck rubbery and unable to support it. "You should have thought of that before you taught your son a jaundiced nickname for my husband." She thumped the table between them with the flat of her hand, feeling the bones jar. "You might not like my life choices, Bodie Johal, but that's exactly what they are, *my life choices!*" She stood upright and pointed at the door. "Oh and find another idiot to child mind for free in future because I'm sick and tired of getting nothing in return from you but misery. And just so you're aware, Logan knows what you call him." Her green eyes blazed like emeralds. "I guess Jas informed him, probably out loud during his class, just to add to the humiliation. So, if you want to continue having a relationship with me, I suggest you grow up! I never asked you to like my husband. But I hoped you might show him some respect."

Hana swung on her heel and opened the front door. "Now if you don't mind, I'm exhausted. Your son was hard work for me and *the parasite*, which you'd understand if you paid him any quality attention. Goodbye."

Hana held the door open while her son walked past her. For the first time in his life, he appeared unable to string a sentence together.

"Oh, wait a moment," Hana added, running back to the table and seizing the envelope of photographs in shaking fingers. "Don't forget your wonderful memories will you. I wouldn't like you to miss out on reminiscing over the lovely life you think we had!"

As Bodie reached the bottom step, Hana slammed the door. She held her tears, damming them behind a failing wall as she leaned against the wall. She heard Jas demanding to see Logan and his wail of dismay as Bodie loaded him into the car. Then the engine started and her son drove away.

The tightness in her chest forced her to the bathroom where she vomited. Then she cried with great heaves, sitting on the cold tiles with her spine pressed against the side of the bath. Tama returned with her daughter, finding her sitting amid wads of wet toilet roll on the floor. "Oh, Ma," he whispered, kneeling and balancing the baby on his hip. Phoenix took swipes of Hana's hair, yanking a curl and trying to eat it. "How can I make it better?" he begged.

"You can't," Hana sniffed, the truth both simple and excruciating.

Hana fed her daughter on the sofa in the small lounge, grateful for the simple maternal pleasure of giving sustenance without rejection. Phoenix beamed and flapped Hana's shirt over her face, playing more than feeding. Tama plonked a cup of tea in Hana's hand and lifted the baby, winding her over his shoulder. "He's gonna screw that kid up," he declared, referring to Bodie and Jas. "It's the same pattern that Kane followed. I think it's called emotional neglect."

Hana sighed. "Where did you learn a term like that?"

"Bitter experience." Tama shrugged. He paced the floor as Phoenix released a disgusting burp over his left shoulder. Her vest rode up to reveal a slender back and the outline of her spine. "Jas started crying while we were at the swings. He adores Uncle Logan, but his dad won't let him even mention Logan's name. He's told him he's not his poppa. And I don't think things are as rosy as they seem with Amy. Jas said they had a massive argument this morning and she told him not to come back." He shook his head. "The stupid idiot doesn't recognise security and happiness when it's under his nose." Tama sounded wistful and Hana reached out to stroke his thigh, balancing her cup on the arm of the sofa.

"I don't know what to do," she breathed. "But yelling and throwing him out didn't help."

Tama smiled. "You're a taniwha, Hana Du Rose. Uncle Logan's lucky to have you."

Hana wrinkled her nose. "A water dragon? Thanks."

"A chief." Tama rolled his eyes. "Stop listening to pakeha Māori."

Hana's eyes misted as she ruminated over her words to Bodie. "A mother is supposed to back her children. I never understood women who took the stepparent's side over the child's. That's what I just did."

"He's not a child!" Tama sounded incredulous. "Hana, he's twenty-five years old!"

"Twenty-six," Hana acknowledged. "But I still feel in the wrong somehow."

"Well, don't." Tama patted the baby's back and listened to her suck her fist next to his ear.

Hana sipped her cooling tea and sighed. "I didn't hear you come in last night. How did it go with Logan? I don't think he's talking to me." She sounded sad and pursed her lips to stop the tears revisiting.

"He's more than a little distracted by the body in the veggie plot. He didn't mention his argument with you but I can see it's weighing on him. I told him about the fire service and he seemed philosophical about me leaving college, but I decided not to push my luck by telling him I took you to see your father." Tama winced and his eyes implored her with the impossible.

Hana sighed, wondering how the Du Roses attracted so many damaging secrets purely by default. "I must tell him eventually," she said. "I always think I'll be able to keep secrets from him, but I can't sustain it. He's like a human lie detector." She patted Tama's thigh as he paced past the sofa. "Don't worry though; I'll take the blame and say I made you."

"Good luck with that," Tama sighed.

Hana played with her daughter, before moving through their bedtime routine. She leaned over the side of the cot and watched Phoenix tumble into sleep. The delicate fronds of the child's dark eyelids brushed her soft cheeks as she sucked her thumb. Hana's heart grew heavy as the school site settled for the night and Logan's still didn't reappear. While Tama watched TV, Hana laid on the double bed and prayed over her dire circumstances. Exhaustion sucked her into a fractious sleep. She dreamed she rode in a shaky boat and despite her attempt to keep it still, it tipped. She grappled for the sides, but it tilted bow up. Dark water swirled below like an open maw. Her nails dug into the wood for purchase and the boat growled. Hana heard her name as she plunged into the freezing, murky waters. The tone sounded urgent and she recognised Logan's voice. Swimming hard to reach the surface, she found air and light, gasping as she thrashed against the surface.

Logan's powerful arms pinned her to the mattress and she clawed at his shirt. "I can't do it," she sobbed. "I can't save myself!"

"You don't need to," he replied. "I'm here."

Hana's chest heaved and her mind clouded. The back of her throat rasped with the nauseating sensation of rawness and acid. "I'm sorry," she blurted. "I didn't realise he called you that. This is terrible. I can't see a way out."

Logan stroked her hair and tucked her head beneath his chin. His warm arms surrounded Hana like a cage. "Don't worry about it," he breathed. "Things have a way of coming right all by themselves."

As the sensation of drowning faded, panic cleared from Hana's eyes. The light from the hallway cast a glow over the bedroom and the unit fell silent and still. "Where's Tama?" she asked, her voice hoarse.

"Sleeping," Logan replied. He released her head and lay back against the pillow. "I just got home and found you dreaming. I couldn't wake you."

Hana sat up and the dark stain on his shirt drew her gaze. "What happened?" she cried. Blood speckled his chin and left a streak across his cheek.

"It's fine," he soothed, "I sensed it coming."

"The headache?" Hana swallowed. She'd seen the warning signs.

Logan nodded. "Yeah. It started bleeding a couple of hours ago. I couldn't leave until it stopped. The doctor said I was overusing the medication, so I guess this is what happens. I'm fine. I've still got a headache, but the bleeding has slowed."

Hana stroked his cheek and pushed herself onto her knees. Sweat dotted her brow and a groggy sensation made her head spin. "The spray you put up your nose?" she asked, a yawn cutting through her sentence. Her fingers strayed into Logan's hair behind his ear.

"Yup." He nodded. "It's a quick fix, but not a permanent one. Haemophilia sucks."

"I love you," Hana whispered. "And Bo's an ass; I told him so."

Logan shook his head. "You shouldn't have done that," he replied, his voice level. He'd made a skill of not forming a wedge between Hana and her children. Bodie had forced him into that position, anyway. "I understand he resents me. But hearing Jas say it seemed more painful than I expected. I didn't expect to love that little guy, but he's grown on me. I didn't realise I felt like a spare until he said it."

Hana jerked backwards, the sharp prickle of guilt snaking up her spine. "I hope I haven't made you feel like a spare?"

"Not on purpose." Logan frowned and a drop of blood bounced off the button of his white shirt. He lifted a stained tissue and pressed it against his nostril.

"But I don't!" Hana's voice rose as she scrambled to defend herself against a veiled accusation.

Logan shrugged and his voice sounded muffled. "You wouldn't appreciate me talking about an old girlfriend. Yet I'm forced to face your marriage to Vikram Singh Johal every single day. All your memories of the last twenty odd years relate to him. I don't want to see his influence on your life any more than you want to see Caroline's on mine, but I get constant reminders. I see his face in your son's and when you talk about your kids, there he is again. If I talked about Caroline half as much as you talk about him, you'd have a fit. It makes me jealous and insecure. I'm still struggling to find my place in your life. Getting Bodie into trouble last year didn't help matters. He's suspicious of me, no matter what I do. It's why I love time at the hotel because Vik can't come with us there." Logan sat up and ran his hand across his top lip. A line of fresh blood transferred to the backs of his fingers. Stemming the blood kept him busy and he'd become candid by accident.

Hana couldn't think of a sensible retort. His words hurt, but she didn't want to stop him talking. The dilemma seemed like a knotted ball of knitting wool. She didn't recognise which strand to pull first to undo the mess. "I get it," she said to her husband and her heart clenched at seeing his raw agony. The window into Logan Du Rose's soul didn't open often. "I get it." She put her arms around his neck, feeling him relax beneath her. The blood from his nose responded to the sudden calm and stemmed. Logan pulled the tissue away and examined it in the dim light with a sigh.

Hana kissed him, transferring his blood onto her cheek. "I love you, Logan Du Rose," she whispered into his ear. "I didn't understand what genuine love was until I met you. You're the best thing that's happened to me in my lifetime and I won't stand by and listen to you being denigrated by anyone."

Logan smiled but his face held an uncharacteristic fear. "I never want you to choose between your children and me," he replied. "I'll lose."

Hana shook her head. "No," she replied. "It shouldn't be a case of winners and losers for my affection. I love you both, but he needs to grow up. I've withdrawn your kind gift of the wedding reception at the hotel."

"Oh. Wow." Logan's brows furrowed. "That's gonna hurt."

Hana snorted. "It already did. I rang the receptionist and quantified it in the thousands of dollars for him. He choked a little."

"I bet he did." Logan's eyes crinkled at the edges and he smiled. "You've got balls, Hana Du Rose."

"Yeah." She didn't sound sure. "I'd love to be a fly on the wall when he breaks the news to Amy that his mouth just cost him twenty-five grand."

"What if he apologises?" Logan sniffed and swiped the tissue under his nose.

"No idea." Hana sighed. "Let's deal with it if it happens. I think that should be your decision."

"At least Izzie likes me." Logan accepted the clean tissue Hana retrieved from her bedside table. But the comment steered the conversation along another difficult route.

"Yeah, about that," Hana said, her eyes widening. "Bodie mentioned something about a fifty-grand car."

Logan sank into the sheets and groaned, pushing his face into the pillows and leaving a trail of blood that would be impossible to remove.

Chapter 11

The next morning, Logan's nose still bled and his face looked swollen beneath his eyes. Hana drove him to the clinic in town with Phoenix in her car seat. Tama lounged around at the unit, hopping around in his sleeping bag. "He's up to something," Hana muttered as they sat in the doctor's waiting room with Logan holding a wad of tissue under his nose.

"I don't care right now," Logan grumbled. "I've got my own problems."

"We should have come here last night," Hana said, brushing her fringe from her eyes. Questing fingers reminded her she'd become distracted in the bathroom by Phoenix's cries and dealt with only one side of her hair. "I lost count of the number of times you choked on the blood in your throat; it terrified me." She yawned and covered her mouth. "I don't think I slept at all."

"Sorry." Logan glanced sideways, his eyes grey and laden with pain over the blood-spattered tissues.

"It's okay," Hana rubbed his thigh with her palm. "But I hope nobody sees our bedroom until I've been able to change the sheets. It looks like the scene of an axe murder."

Logan sighed. "My head's pounding," he complained, his voice muffled. "I wanted to see my own doctor."

Hana frowned. She remembered the private clinic and the man familiar with the Du Roses. She pursed her lips and Logan smiled from behind his tissues. "Tama's okay, Hana. He's doing fine. Don't worry about him; I know about the fire service stuff and told him I'd support him."

Hana nodded and rocked the car seat with her left foot. Phoenix stirred but remained sleeping. "I'm suspicious. He keeps borrowing the Honda and disappearing. He didn't want me to drive you here because he needed the car. Don't you think that's weird?" She lowered her voice to a whisper as a family sat next to them. She tried not to snigger at a four-year-old boy wearing a terracotta flowerpot on his head. Tufty hair stuck through the drainage hole at the top like a clump of blonde grass. The child swung his legs and chatted to his concerned father, his voice echoing in the pot. Hana's voice wavered with laughter as she tried to continue her conversation about Tama. "He's on track now and I don't want him detonating again."

Logan slipped his arm around Hana, but the tissue slipped in his other hand. Blood dribbled from his chin and hit the tiled floor with a splat. Several people in the waiting room looked alarmed and a few covered their curious children's eyes.

"You're starting to look really sick," Hana hissed, worry in her voice. Phoenix's eyes popped open and blinked. Hana held her breath. "She wakes up like you," she said, nudging Logan's elbow. "Look at her. She's ready for anything." Phoenix grinned and nodded her head.

"Do you have any more tissue?" Logan asked, his voice muffled. Bright red blood ran up his wrist and into his sleeve. The flowerpot wearer tilted his head back, so he could see where the growing drips on the floor originated from.

"I'll get some." Hana released a gurgling Phoenix from her car seat and sat her on her hip. As she was standing anyway, she approached the counter and lifted a box of communal tissues.

"Sorry for the wait. We're very busy," the receptionist said, a note of grudging apology in her tone. "Your husband is on the list."

Hana leaned forward, trying not to focus on the eighty bucks Logan paid an hour earlier as a starting fee. She glanced back at her husband and found him busy trying to find a clean piece of tissue. A red puddle increased between his cowboy boots. She lowered her voice. "Did my husband mention that he's a haemophiliac?"

The receptionist opened her mouth to utter the usual patter about not discussing patient details with third parties and Hana held her hand up to save her the bother. "Okay," she said. "But he's looking very pale and you might need a mop for the blood on the floor." She smiled, before returning to her seat. Mission accomplished. The receptionist half stood and peered over the counter. Her eyes widened at the sight of the puddle.

The woman disappeared into a back room and after a decent interval of whispering, a nurse appeared and called Logan's name. "Oh, dear!" she exclaimed at the mess. "Follow me and I'll just get that cleared up."

Hana trailed behind Logan carrying her daughter over her shoulder and balancing the car seat handle over her forearm. She sensed Logan's vibes of antagonism and knew he didn't want her in the treatment room. She shrugged them off and followed him in, taking a seat in the corner and bouncing Phoenix on her knee.

The nurse sent a colleague to mop the waiting room while she took Logan's blood pressure. She fitted the cuff over his upper arm and nodded at his tattoo. "That's beautiful," she said, admiring the stylish italics at the bottom of the swirling pattern. "Your whakapapa?"

Logan raised an eyebrow, ignoring the attempt at conversation. Hana shook her head in despair.

Used to men of few words, the nurse released the cuff and tutted at the results of her examination. "Your blood pressure and pulse are low; I'll fetch the doctor now."

The doctor arrived minutes later, already drawing fluid into a syringe. "You know what I'm going to say, don't you, Mr Du Rose?" he asked. He handed the syringe to the nurse and she popped the cap and pressed the needle into Logan's upper arm. The doctor put his hands on his hips and frowned. Hana's husband groaned.

"I'm not going," Logan snarled. "I don't have time for that today. It takes hours. I need some more nasal spray. It ran out."

"If this started from a headache, then I'm guessing you know the risks of continuing to use the spray?" A serious expression settled over the doctor's expression and Logan nodded.

"It's just a glitch," he replied, forcing confidence into his tone. "Just prescribe some more for me, please? I'll be fine."

"I'm not familiar with the risks." Hana sat in the corner and heard how small her voice sounded. "What risks?"

"Well," the doctor began, thrilled by a willing audience. He regaled Hana with a twenty-minute lecture on what might happen if Logan refused another Factor 8 infusion. Notes picked up from the patient database showed he'd been running on empty for quite some time. Hana's eyes narrowed as the man spoke and her glare shot daggers at her husband.

Despite his protests, Hana drove Logan to the state-run hospital in the south of the city. The doctor called ahead and directed them straight to the blood unit. Logan stomped through the tiled corridors with an edge of annoyance in his gait. The nurses knew him by sight and settled him into a side room. Within minutes he'd been settled and hooked up to a drip.

"You know the drill, Mr Du Rose," a dark-haired girl said as she inserted a needle into his raised vein. "Any tingling, headaches, nausea; you need to call someone. We're running a slow infusion, so we can withdraw if something goes wrong. Okay?"

Logan nodded and fixed his handsome features into an expression of boredom. He glared at the dripping bag as if hoping it would suddenly evacuate into his body. It hardly altered its volume over the next five minutes and Hana glanced up to find him leaning sideways to fiddle with a switch on the drip.

"Don't!" Hana growled. She stood and hoisted Phoenix onto her hip. The drip trolley moved with ease and she nudged it sideways, placing the visitor's chair between it and Logan. She effectively prevented him from hauling the drip closer. Reading the defiant tilt of his upper lip, she wagged her finger at him. "Don't even think about getting off that bed," she threatened. "I'll call the nurse." She snatched up the button the nurse left on the bed and her index finger hovered over the raised button. "I can't believe you've been putting this off when you need it!" she hissed. "We need you, Logan. In future, if a doctor tells you to get a Factor 8 infusion, you bloody get one!"

Logan wrinkled his nose and a raised vein ticked in the gap between his shirt collar and his neck. Hana shrugged. "Why don't I find a coffee vendor and get you something?" she suggested. She took Logan's slight nod as agreement and set off to follow the signage indicating a café lay between the emergency department and the maternity wing.

The signage failed her and left her lost and asking for directions. A tired doctor pointed towards the end of a sterile corridor. "Follow the people in green scrubs. They're on a break."

While Hana waited for an extra special coffee for her husband, she made some essential calls. Phoenix lurched at her phone and almost managed to snag it as Angus' voice boomed from the speaker. Phoenix stopped and her eyes widened in shock. Hana laughed. "Sorry, I'm just letting you know that Logan is in the hospital. He's having a Factor 8 infusion."

"Ah, yes," Angus replied. His tone told her he knew the drill and it irritated her that she was the last to know. "Make him stay away for a few days this time, will you? He always looks like crap after one of those."

"Great!" Hana replied. "At least now I know where he goes when he's unreachable."

Angus snorted. "He's a Du Rose, Hana dear. He'll be spilling secrets as he climbs into his coffin."

Hana shuddered at the thought and thanked Angus. "Can you get him cover for his classes at this late notice?"

He laughed. "I'll use it as an opportunity to audit the quality of Logan's classes. It's about time I got out from behind this desk and did some teaching."

Hana ended the call with a wince. "Awesome," she grumbled. "I'm sure Logan will love that." She pressed a kiss to the top of her daughter's head as Phoenix made another decent lurch for the phone. "Let's not tell Papa what the nice Mr Blair just said, shall we?"

Tama seemed slow answering his phone and Hana almost gave up. Her brow furrowed, wondering if he was ignoring her seeing as the device never left his vicinity. When he finally answered, Hana heard strange sounds in the background. "What's that funny noise?" she demanded. "Where are you?"

"I'm in town," Tama replied. His tone sounded snippy. "You guys didn't come back with the car, so I walked."

"Sorry. Logan's nosebleed turned into a sign of something more urgent," Hana said, hating the whining quality in her voice.

Tama brushed it off. "Well, watch your back. I've sat with him a few times during those drip-things and he's a horrible patient. He always leaves it too late because he hates them so much. By the time he gets forced into going, he's in one hell of a temper. It's like trapping a wasp in a matchbox and having to keep peeking inside."

It was such a good description of Logan it made Hana laugh out loud. "I'm getting him a coffee and a magazine," she said and Tama snorted.

"Okay, maybe drug the coffee with something to shut him up and get him a car magazine," he advised. "I need to go." Hana heard a strange drilling noise resume as the phone went dead.

"What's he up to?" she mused. Hana frowned at Phoenix. "He's nineteen, but I fear for your cousin's ability to make it to twenty." She smiled and accepted the coffees the barista handed across the counter. "Ah well, he's come this far alone. I guess I'll deal with him later."

Heading back to Logan with two coffees, a car magazine and a wriggling child proved no easy feat. Hana struggled with her load. It seemed little wonder that she missed a relevant sign and found herself lost in the bowels of the hospital. Corridors stretched ahead of her and the signs made little sense when she realised she didn't remember which ward she'd left Logan on. She searched for an information board as her chest tightened and a sense of panic gripped her reason. "Your father always says I can't find my way out of a paper bag. I'm proving him right."

Hana rounded a corner and saw a doctor peering through the glass of a vending machine. He tapped it with his fingers and swore. "Bloody thing! You did this yesterday! Just give me the chocolate bar," he groaned. His turban looked wonky and his white coat hung off tired shoulders.

"Hello, Dr Singh," Hana said. Relief flooded her chest at the sight of a familiar face. "I've got myself lost."

"Hello." Dr Singh gave Hana a cursory glance and shook his head at the vending machine. "This thing hates me."

Hana nodded. "I think this hospital hates me. The signs keep moving and I swear I'm walking in circles."

Dr Singh frowned. "Why are you in the general surgery unit?"

"Oh, am I?" Hana spun in a circle, looking for the elusive sign. "I didn't know."

"You're outside the surgical theatres." Dr Singh frowned. "I'm not sure how you got down here without being challenged by a staff member. Where should you be?"

Hana blinked. "I think that's the problem." Phoenix made a valiant lurch for the cardboard tray containing the coffee cups. The magazine fell to the floor with a papery slap. "Damn it!"

The tired doctor righted his tilting turban and retrieved the magazine. "Start at the beginning," he suggested.

Hana explained about Logan's condition and the Factor 8 infusion. Dr Singh clicked his fingers together and

Phoenix burst into raucous laughter. She looked at him with expectation, wanting him to do it again. "I remember!" he exclaimed. "Broken arm, punctured spleen? Tall, Māori guy with a bad attitude."

Hana swallowed. She pursed her lips to avoid agreeing. Dr Singh nodded and pointed back the way Hana had come. "You need to walk back to haematology. It's two right turns and a left. When you get back to the main corridor, follow the green line painted on the tiles."

"Thank you." Hana smiled with relief. Phoenix nodded her head and the coffee tray tilted at a horrible angle and brown liquid leaked through the hole at the top of hers. She puffed with exasperation. Dr Singh tapped the magazine with his index finger and waved it in front of her.

"You seem to have run out of hands," he chortled.

She nodded. "How about you have my coffee?" she suggested. "Then I just have the baby, one coffee and the magazine. I think I'll manage better without the cardboard tray."

"Are you sure?" The doctor eyed the coffee with furtive desperation.

"Yes." Hana nodded. "I didn't drink any." She handed over the tray and resettled her other burdens. Then she accepted Logan's coffee back and tucked the magazine under her arm. "That's better. Thank you."

Dr Singh took a sip of the drink and closed his eyes. "Perfect!" he exclaimed. He sighed. "I'm glad we met."

Hana smiled. "I'd better find my husband. Thanks for your help." She turned to leave and the doctor cleared his throat.

"Good luck with your husband. Du Rose? I remember him. He seems to think he can just 'get by' but this disease has a habit of getting its own back. He should take more care." Dr Singh jerked his head towards Phoenix. "He has a lot to lose."

Hana nodded and turned, but a shout made her halt. Phoenix held her breath.

"Dr Singh, Abdul?" The voice came from an opening theatre door facing Hana and the doctor turned. She moved aside as a surgeon emerged. He wore scrubs and a blue cloth hat hid his hair. A face mask dangled around his neck. His sideburns had run to varying shades of grey, but his physique looked tall and square.

Hana swallowed. Her blood seemed to stop flowing and a curious light-headedness gripped her.

"Can you scrub in for the next one?" the surgeon asked. He tilted his head, Dr Singh in his sights. "Motorcycle accident. Heading straight down from ED now. I'll come in once you assess him and get started. I just need to speak to the husband of my last emergency case and then I'll scrub in. Dr Smith is stuck next door with an emergency caesarean."

The English accent sounded clipped and his words precise. The surgeon's gaze lowered to Hana's face and his green eyes widened. She took a step backwards, her windpipe closing as her mind emptied. "Hana?" The surgeon's voice dropped to a whisper.

"Fine!" Dr Singh grumbled. "I just won't go home at all this week then!"

"Sorry." Mark McIntyre uttered the word without looking in the other man's direction. He took a step towards Hana, his earlier mission forgotten.

Hana watched Dr Singh's feet walk across the smooth lino, his comfy shoes squeaking as he strode through the theatre door. Phoenix lurched for the coffee cup and the magazine fell to the ground at the same time as hot liquid slopped over Hana's hand. She took another step backwards and urged her feet to turn.

"Don't!" Mark called. His voice lifted and Hana heard the begging edge to his tone. "Don't run, Hana," he whispered. "Please don't run from me?"

She closed her eyes as he halted her flight, leaving her with the options of either fighting or freezing. Unable to fight with Phoenix wiggling in her arms, Hana froze. Twenty-six years of anger and regret foreshortened to make their last awful communication feel like it happened yesterday. Phoenix sighed in her arms and Hana forced her eyes open. Her daughter studied Mark with a frightening intensity. Her brooding grey eyes mirrored Logan's studious nature but contained none of the closed emotion. The child issued one of her wonderful, accepting smiles and Mark McIntyre's face creased into a returning grin. He moved forward, captivated by the baby girl as he walked towards his sister and new niece.

Hana's feet refused to obey her orders to move and she remained paralysed like a rabbit in car headlights. Mark reached out and lifted the hand containing Logan's coffee. He removed the cup and turned her wrist over. Her body trembled at his touch, registering warm hands and a gentle grip. Glancing up, Hana saw her brother's pointed features narrow into a look of surprise. "What happened to this?" He sounded hurt, as though she'd somehow ruined his work. Then his face softened. "Did it get infected?" He winced. "Sorry."

Hana's lips pursed shut as her mind performed summersaults. Mark leaned closer and chucked Phoenix under her chin. The baby giggled and turned her face into Hana's shoulder as though embarrassed. Then she tilted her little face up as though wanting him to repeat the movement.

Hana's heavy silence drew Mark's attention back to her. He held out his hand. "I know you saw Dad," he said, his voice soft. "Please give me the chance to make it right with you. I'm sorrier than you can ever imagine for what happened between us. Can we meet? If I give you my phone number, will you ring me when you're free?"

Hana swallowed and stared at his open palm. Without being able to explain why she did it, she reached into her pocket and dragged out her mobile phone. Mark took it and tapped around on the screen for a moment. "I've added myself to your contacts' list for when you feel ready." He smirked. "I remember how much you hate trying to remember numbers." He patted the pants of his scrubs. "I'm due back in surgery now. Sorry, no phone to take yours on." His brow furrowed and Mark looked wrong footed and awkward, not like a man about to go into surgery and stick someone's broken body back together. He held out Hana's phone and she took it, trying not to touch his hand. Pain flared behind Mark's green irises. "Please call me, Hana?" he begged.

Noise sounded and the lift doors swished opened to signal Mark's next emergency. A porter pushed a bed through the open theatre door. A white face lay on the crisp pillow, the body swathed in wires and monitors. A nurse hurried next to the bed; her face filled with concern. Mark looked back, regret playing across his lips. "I'm needed," he said, his smile wistful. He leaned across and placed a kiss on his niece's forehead, as though loving his sister by proxy. He raised a grey eyebrow. "Anytime, Hana. Name the place. I'll be there." Then he turned and walked away, looking back only once at the carbon copy of the beautiful woman who raised him. Hana stood in the middle of the corridor, a porter negotiating her with a trolley as though she was a statue.

Hana returned to Logan in a fog, getting lost twice more and having no words to ask for directions. The coffee was luke-warm and a nurse let her heat it in the staff microwave. "Are you all right, love?" she asked as Hana slopped coffee on the counter. Hana gulped and nodded, clutching a wriggling Phoenix to her chest. "Are you sure?" the nurse persisted. "You look very pale."

"I'm fine," Hana lied. "Thanks for letting me use the microwave."

Logan looked like a man who'd rather be elsewhere, but whose body trapped him in place by dint of its faulty nature. Hana paused outside his door, seeing him slumped on the mattress with his arms folded. He never removed his gaze from the drip as though counting every plunging drop of liquid as it headed for his bloodstream. The nurse smiled at Phoenix. "She looks just like her daddy," she said, her voice lapsing into baby talk. Phoenix blinked and pushed her thumb into place between her lips.

Hana nodded. "How often should he do this?" she asked, not looking at the nurse.

"More than he does," the woman scoffed. "The girls call him Mr Broody. I'm sure there will be a few broken hearts now they've seen you and his gorgeous daughter." The woman smiled and withdrew, leaving Hana to take the coffee to her smouldering husband.

"You took ages," Logan grumbled.

"I got lost," Hana admitted. Her voice sounded small and Logan's eyes narrowed.

"What's wrong?" His tone sharpened as he switched from self-pity to concern. "Did something happen?"

Not wanting to lie to him, Hana avoided the question. She settled Phoenix on her knee and lifted her shirt to feed her daughter in the wide armchair in the corner of the room.

Logan flicked through the magazine and sipped his coffee. His grey eyes switched periodically to watching Hana and she sensed him biding his time. When her phone bleeped in her pocket, she reached for it with shaking fingers. Phoenix stopped sucking and peeked from beneath Hana's shirt. "It's Angus," Hana said. "He's covered your classes for the next few days. He wants to know about some test you've organised for tomorrow."

Logan grunted. "I don't need tomorrow off. I'll go back this afternoon."

Hana sighed and her fingers kept scrolling through her list of contacts. Searching under 'M' she found nothing and acknowledged the pang of disappointment.

"What's wrong, Hana?" Logan demanded.

"Nothing, just checking something." She heard herself lie and hated the sound of it. But the feeling of sorrow took hold of her emotions and she fought tears. Glancing at the corridor, she contemplated running back to the theatres and trying to find her brother. She had questions. Acknowledging her growing frustration, Hana's fingers scrolled backwards through the contacts, beginning with 'Z'. Had he only pretended to give her his number? He'd seemed sincere. Hana returned to the 'A' list, her heart sinking lower as her eyes flicked across the screen. Using the search feature, she looked for any recently added contacts.

At the very top of the list, she saw it. Mark had typed his phone number under a new contact called 'Aarsehole', using the Aa to make sure it stayed uppermost. Hana gave a reluctant smile. Always pedantic and teasing, he'd become funny in his old age. She turned her phone screen off, confused by the emotional assault besieging her soul.

Logan watched her through his eyelashes. Hana caught him looking and sighed. He'd inherited his mother's emotional radar which homed in on trouble like a heat seeking missile. "How are you feeling?" she asked, wanting to distract him as she sat Phoenix upright and patted her back.

Logan's eyes narrowed; his attention drawn to the flash of porcelain skin peeking from beneath her shirt. "Horny," he replied. A smirk lifted one side of his upper lip.

Hana laughed. "Want me to call a nurse for you?"

Logan faked indignation. "You'll do," he said. "Get over here wahine."

Hana rose and straightened her shirt to cover her breast. Phoenix wriggled over her shoulder, sucking her own hand with noisy gusto. Hana dipped to kiss Logan, pleased to see the blood-stained tissue looked no worse than it had a few minutes earlier. Her husband appeared less haggard. "You shouldn't be so secretive about your illness," she said, seeing Logan's eyes flash too late to stop herself. "It's a disease, not a judgement of weakness on your character."

"And you're qualified to say that because?" Logan challenged. "It's the Du Rose curse, Hana. Michael doesn't have it, but I do. How is that fair when he's a complete jerk?"

"It isn't fair!" Hana snapped. She saw a nurse appear in the doorway and turn away again at the sound of her raised voice. Her encounter with Mark drove a heady mix of emotions up to steal oxygen. "Life's not fair, you know that! It's not a curse, Logan, it's the culmination of a haemophiliac father and a carrier mother. You never stood a chance."

"And what about my daughter?" Logan's eyes blazed and he seized the tube leading into his vein.

"Don't you dare pull that out!" Hana spat as Phoenix's lips puckered in distress. "Your behaviour determines your strength or weakness. Logan Du Rose, you're behaving like a spoilt brat!"

His fingers twitched over the tube; his grey eyed gaze locked on Hana's face. She soothed her baby and glared at him. "Don't make me spank you," she said with a straight face, the unfortunate connotation enhanced by a secondary, accidental flash of breast as she hoisted her grizzling daughter higher.

Logan pursed his lips to suppress the smirk which teased at his eyes. He looked away to hide his amusement, feigning temper.

"I saw Dr Singh when I went for coffee," Hana said, changing the subject. She squeezed her bottom onto the edge of the bed so Phoenix could eyeball her father. The move was strategic, forcing him to face the one person he didn't want to disappoint.

Unable to resist his olive-skinned daughter, Logan lifted his hand and stroked the baby's wrist. She cooed and sang squelchy noises without removing her hand from her dribbling mouth. Logan laughed but the sound faded as he noticed gravity fighting against the drip of liquid in the pipe. He laid his hand flat on the bed and the liquid moved in the right direction again. "Who's Dr Singh?" he asked, his voice flat.

Hana sighed. "The surgeon who stuck you together again last year." She didn't want to remember how Tama caused his injuries. It seemed like too much of a paradox from the teenager in her home.

"Right." Logan sounded disinterested. "Why did you come back so upset? What did he say to you?"

Hana's heart sank into her boots. Would he always prove to be one step ahead of her? It was as though he moved the battle lines with his mind, leaving her exposed and vulnerable. She wasn't sure if she could face telling him about her father or brother yet. It still felt too raw and fragile.

Hana knew her face betrayed her as her husband relented. "Want me to leave it?" he asked. Hana fought tears of gratitude as she nodded. He'd shown more compassion than she would if the roles were reversed.

She stared at a poster on the wall, seeking her inner equilibrium and chastising herself for always forcing her way into his sensibilities in an awful need to know everything. He'd seen her distress and left her alone and for the millionth time since they married, Hana felt inadequate. "Thank you," she muttered. "We will talk, just not now." She leaned in and kissed his soft lips, her eyes glittering with unshed tears.

Phoenix grabbed a handful of Hana's hair and tried to eat it. Hana used up valuable moments of her life trying to separate tiny fingers from hair and strings of baby spit. Then the child fell asleep across the slope of her father's legs, her head lolling to the side. Logan rubbed her toes with his capable fingers and watched the amount in the drip bag deplete by slow degrees.

"Do you know how Barry died?" he asked, without looking up. Hana jumped and almost slid off the bed, his voice an unexpected intrusion into the silence.

She shook her head. "Your older brother? No."

"He fell off Jack's horse and landed on a fence post. A shard of wood went through his stomach." Logan looked up and their eyes met, Hana remaining rigid in an effort to preserve the rare moment of confidence. Her husband worried at his full lower lip. "It's ironic, isn't it? He and Kane split me open in the same place with a machete, but on purpose. Barry went to hospital and the surgeons stitched him up. I thought it served him right, but they'd given him an infected blood transfusion and he caught something nasty. He should have been on that train in London, not me." Logan sighed and shook his head. "I've always felt guilty for thinking he deserved everything he got. His scar looked neater than mine, but his more skilled doctors pumped blood into his veins that gave him hepatitis. Ma wouldn't let Alfred take him back to hospital because of the prejudice she felt for a brown woman with a moko tattoo on her chin. So, the doctors didn't find the infection until after he'd died. My ma really thought she could fix him with herbs from the bush and old wives' tales."

Logan's eyes narrowed as he shook the tube in his left hand, causing the bag of fluid to jangle against the metal rack. "If this isn't a curse, Hana, then what the hell is it?"

"I don't know," she whispered. "I don't know, darling, but I do know it's not a weakness."

They stayed silent after that. Hana shifted to the armchair and closed her eyes, praying for Logan and agonising over Mark and her father. She looked for the place in her heart where forgiveness should live. She saw Logan's guilt and bitterness and recognised it in herself. It felt frustrating to reach this same place again. She believed she'd let her negative feelings go, only to find herself at the same impasse years later. It marked a bridge she would spend her life crossing, finding herself back on the wrong side with no clue how she arrived there. Her mind wandered to her argument with Bodie and his attitude towards Logan and she mentally explored her son's emotions.

She'd replaced his father with a larger-than-life male and saw disappointment in her son's eyes every time he looked at her. An awful realisation dawned on her like a mist crawling off the mountains. It took over and reduced visibility to within its mind-altering perspective. Her father had replaced her beautiful mother with Elaine. As she named the feeling, the sting intensified and then evaporated. "I'm disappointed," she said out loud.

"Why?" Logan's voice sounded gruff and sulky. He glared at the drip as though his anger might speed up its progress.

"It makes sense." Hana sat up straighter. "I've been so cruel. Bodie has no right to dictate my life choices or stand judgement over me, so I can't do the same to him."

"What?" Logan's eyes flashed with suspicion and Hana bit her lip.

"No-one, sorry. I'm just rambling." She settled in the chair and fixed unseeing eyes on the poster again. The thought rumbled around in her head, justifying and then denying.

Logan Du Rose made her life worth living and whichever way Hana cut the cloth, it made the same garment. Her children could talk to her about their grief and concerns, but as adults, she wouldn't allow them to destroy her marriage. She needed to see Robert again and apologise for her behaviour to Aunty Elaine - his wife.

Logan made it to the end of the treatment, climbing off the bed with a similar level of enthusiasm as a released prisoner. The nurse smiled as she stuck a plaster over the infusion site in the crook of his arm but as soon as she left the room, Logan ripped it off and flicked it into the bin. Hana shook her head, knowing why she never saw evidence of his covert hospital visits. Logan gave her a beautiful smile and she shook her head. "You're a worry, Logan Du Rose," she said with a sigh.

They walked towards the multi-storey car park, paying an exorbitant fee to a machine near the stairs. "Well, that was expensive and boring," Logan grumbled. He clutched his magazine in one hand and ushered her towards the Honda.

"Not to mention a little lifesaving," Hana replied under her breath. She drove to a cafe on Victoria Street and fought for parking, beating out a larger SUV which couldn't squeeze into the space. She fed coins to the meter and followed the scent of fresh coffee. They settled in a corner, Phoenix snoring over her father's shoulder.

Hana took a deep breath and gave herself a mental shake. "I met my father," she said, fiddling with the sugar bowl. "But I'm sure you guessed that anyway."

Logan smirked. "You're not exactly subtle, Hana. Lying isn't a particularly strong skill in your toolbox. Thank goodness," he added. "Actually, your dad rang my cell phone last night. You didn't leave a number, so he rang the only one he had. He wanted to talk to you."

"Oh." Hana put her head down. Shame filled her chest. "I behaved so badly, Logan. I don't think he'll ever forgive me."

Logan said nothing, not confirming or denying. He kept his opinion to himself until asked. Their coffee arrived and Logan smiled at the blonde waitress. Her cheeks flushed pink and she scuttled away. Hana shook her head in exasperation he stirred his coffee with a look of confusion on his face. "What?" he demanded, catching her look of irritation.

Hana sighed, bored with explaining the source of the jealous streak which flashed in her green eyes. She knew it made her look sour and undeserving of the handsome man at her table. Fixing a serene look on her face, she tried not to scowl at the woman staring at her from behind the coffee machine. "You're hot property, Logan Du Rose," she sighed. "Again."

Logan shifted Phoenix onto his other shoulder, administering a soft kiss to her head. Through the corner of her eye, Hana saw the woman's face soften and her lips pucker into an 'o'. Hana gritted her teeth and kept the smile fixed in place. "Dunno what you mean," he replied.

Hana doubted that statement more than she wished to argue. She focussed on the blood staining his jacket. "What do you normally do after one of those transfusion thingies?" she asked, sipping her coffee.

"Go back to work," Logan replied with a shrug. "Pretend it didn't happen."

"Angus has given you sick leave for the next couple of days." She acknowledged the disappointment lodged in her chest that he might not want extra time with her. "I thought you might need it."

Logan shook his head. "I'll go back tomorrow. I used up enough sick leave last year with everything that happened. We can do whatever you want this afternoon. You have my undivided attention." His eyelashes shuttered without managing to hide his inner thoughts. She knew how he imagined spending a free afternoon. In bed.

Hana considered driving up to Culver's Cottage for peace and privacy. Her dreams floated away into the winter sky as Logan's phone rang and he answered it with his usual curt reply. "Yeah?" Her heart sank further when he handed the phone to her. "You should take this," he said.

Hana held the phone to her ear and her breath caught. She knew who it was without asking. Logan shifted Phoenix, laying her over his thighs and patting her back as she grumbled with colic. Robert McIntyre's lilting Scots accent wavered from the speaker. "Hello hen," he began, using the familiar expression. "I'm sorry to keep pestering your husband but we've come so far, hen. We need to talk to you, Elaine and I. To explain."

Hana imagined the pressure of not seeing one of her daughters for twenty-six years and then having less than a month to catch up. She took a deep breath. "Is now okay? We're already in town."

Hamilton Gardens café provided a ready venue and with Logan as her rear guard, Hana ventured there for the second time in a week. The gardens looked beautiful even in winter and offered a sense of peace and stability.

Logan pushed Phoenix in the pram, shortening his stride to cope with the axle of the back wheels. Robert and Elaine joined them at the entrance to the English garden and they wandered among pruned rose bushes and seasonal flowers. Hana's father appeared sprightlier than before, but Elaine struggled with the walking. An electric heater warmed the cafe and the group settled at a corner table where they could stash the pram without causing a bottleneck. Logan engaged in a heated discussion with Robert at the cash register over the bill while Hana wedged herself into a seat in the corner. She prepared to feed her waking daughter, covering her modesty with Logan's jacket. As though sensing the seriousness of the meeting, Phoenix took great pleasure in yanking it down.

Hana groaned. "Please don't, baby." She hauled the jacket back over her shoulder.

Elaine gave her a wooden smile and appeared to search for a response. The men arrived back at the table and she pressed her lips closed as though the moment had expired. Logan pulled out the chair next to Hana and indicated Robert should sit in it. He raised an eyebrow at Hana's look of alarm and sat opposite her. She saw the reason as her father settled in his seat and needed to turn to look at her. Without fuss, Logan had protected her dignity in his usual quiet way.

Phoenix's tummy started to fill and she quieted and stopped yanking at the jacket. The conversation about the weather ran out and an awkward silence filled the space. Even the appearance of the drinks and muffins failed to lighten the atmosphere. Hana sipped her coffee one-handed and felt the confession burn on her tongue. "I saw Mark today," she said. "At the hospital." Her father shifted in his seat to look at her and Logan smirked. Hana knew then he'd guessed.

"How was he?" Elaine asked, an eagerness in her voice which caught Hana unawares.

"Fine," she replied. "He gave me his phone number. We're going to meet sometime soon."

There seemed something disquieting about Elaine's eagerness for news of Mark. A stolen glance at Logan returned a raised eyebrow.

Elaine got to her feet; her legs unsteady as she looked around her. "I'll find the bathroom," she said, before giving Robert a pointed look. The moment seemed jarring and awkward.

"She's still jet lagged," Robert said as Elaine retreated to the other side of the cafe and disappeared through the bathroom door. He wiped muffin crumbs from his mouth with a handkerchief. "While she's away though, I need to explain something important. It's a factor which might help you make sense of everything." He turned in his seat to look at Hana, studying her from beneath his bushy, white eyebrows.

"Okay," she said, glancing sideways at Logan. Her husband's face showed polite interest but Hana saw beneath the veneer and knew he wasn't really interested. Neither expected the bombshell which Robert delivered, leaving Hana feeling betrayed but wiser.

"I suffered from mumps as a teenager and knew I couldn't father a child. Judith never minded. We loved each other and planned to enjoy a good life together. When Elaine was twenty, she fell pregnant back in Ireland to a Catholic boy. She came to us for help, not wanting the wrath of your Protestant grandparents. Life was very different back then."

Logan's gaze shot to Hana and he reached across the table for her hand. She gripped his fingers, sensing the coming storm might somehow unseat her. Robert cleared his throat and continued. "Judith and I adopted Mark and raised him as our own. We wanted to tell him the truth when he was eighteen, but Elaine grew impatient as the years progressed. With marriage, her circumstances changed and she wanted her son. In the middle of our disagreement, Judith fell pregnant with you, dear Hana."

Robert wiped his mouth with the handkerchief, dabbing with British propriety. "We permitted Elaine to visit us in England, but only as an aunt. Her marriage broke down and she stopped pressing us to tell the truth. We settled into a steady routine where she visited once a year and spent time with Mark." He inhaled and pursed his lips. Hana knew what was coming.

"She told him, didn't she? Just before my eighth birthday."

Robert nodded and his eyes misted with the film of the past. "Yes, she did. It broke Jude's heart and fractured the family. I sent Elaine away and told her not to return. It's one of my deepest regrets that we weren't honest with you at the time. It would have saved you much agony."

Hana gripped Logan's hand, squeezing the lifeline in white knuckled fingers. Robert released a pained sigh. "Many of Mark's subsequent issues stemmed from our dishonesty. A lack of trust crept into his marriage and led to disaster. His visit coinciding with yours seems like the cruellest twist of fate."

"Let's not go over it again," Hana begged. Logan frowned at the strain in her voice.

Robert shook his head. "That day has replayed in my mind a million different ways with a million different results. Please understand how sorry I am?" Tears shone against his bright blue irises and Hana nodded. Phoenix sighed from beneath the jacket as though adding her forgiveness. Robert smiled.

"In his worst moment, Mark reached out to Elaine and she contacted me. We shared his problems in common. In working together, we developed an affinity and became companions; two lonely, disillusioned people serving out our time in God's waiting room. We have affection for each other, Hana, but we're not soulmates. We've both loved and lost and are satisfied with our lot. I realise it came as a shock for you and I'm sorry. Please don't be too hard on Elaine. She's cared for me throughout my illness and the last fifteen years has been easier with someone to share life with as it draws to a close."

Hana shook her head and tried not to think of her father's mortality. It seemed such a cruel threat after all the wasted years. She considered her sentence for once before releasing it into the ether. "I'm happy you've had Aunty Elaine, Dada. I owe her an apology." She closed her eyes and pictured Bodie's angry face. "My children need to accept Logan for my sake. I can do the same for you."

Robert smiled, visibly grateful. Logan stared at Hana's hand firmly entwined with his and she read the doubt in his eyes.

Chapter 12

Hana found her positive resolve wilting as she met with Mark for the first time at a bar in Te Awa. The meeting sapped her energy in unexpected ways as she struggled to fit her brother into the role of cousin. She sympathised with Tama, rearranging his family to fit with his altered parentage.

Mark seemed tamer, as though life had knocked the sharp corners off him. Hana arrived to a drink already ordered for her and the first thing Mark said regarded the dreadful note he wrote after her mother died. "I sent it out of pure spite and jealousy, Hana. There's no excuse; I was a grown man and should have known better. It followed a lifetime of jealousy over you, wishing I could make Robert and Judith's 'real' baby go away." Mark lowered his eyes and avoided Hana's gaze. "It coloured my view and you didn't deserve the burden. It's ironic but I look back on the angst of my youth and wish profoundly I hadn't wasted my efforts on it. I'm the wrong side of fifty and I could use that time more wisely now."

Hana smiled and admitted, "You and me both. I've got twenty-six years to make up for."

They parted friends, cousins, brother and sister. It was awkward, like a badly fitting jigsaw puzzle, but at least they were both committed to sorting it out.

Pulling up outside the staff units, Hana wanted to settle in front of the TV with Logan. Exhaustion tugged at the fringes of her psyche and her heart knotted at the realisation they could be disturbed by a drama over at the boarding house. She let herself in the front door and put her keys on the small dining table, turning to find Amanda sitting on the two seater sofa with her husband.

Hana's face registered shock and Amanda had the decency to look guilty. The air in the lounge crackled with electricity and Amanda's cheeks looked flushed. Logan's face was expressionless and Hana froze in the centre of the open plan space. "What's going on?" she demanded, looking from one to another.

"I couldn't open my pickle jar," Amanda said, a smirk lifting the corners of her lips. Her eyes glittered with mischief and dilated pupils revealed her intoxication.

"Another one?" Hana said, a bite to her voice. Her gaze strayed to her husband and he focussed his attention on the TV. "I'm surprised you haven't turned into a pickle."

Amanda shrieked with laughter and slapped Logan's thigh with her palm. "Do I look like a pickle, darling?" she said to Logan and Hana saw him visibly wince. Grinding her teeth, Hana stomped to the hall cupboard, dumping her coat on a hanger and throwing it on the floor, knowing it would wind Logan up. Her heart pounded, filling her ears with the sound of blood and she felt jealousy course through her veins, green, nasty and vitriolic. She kicked herself for not stopping Amanda's crush months ago, sensing the other woman's loneliness and veiled lust when she eyed Tama and Logan. Hana pressed her forehead against the door frame and closed her eyes. Logan asked her for help last time Amanda requested his presence. There had been so many times lately.

"Stupid idiot," Hana chastised herself. "You're too nice for your own good."

Hana's brain screamed that there was nothing going on, but her heart recognised the possibility and it made her sick to her stomach. Inside her head an inner voice screamed, '*You can't live like this again.*'

Hana wondered fleetingly where Millie was as she checked on her baby. Phoenix was fast asleep in her cot, sucking her little thumb without a care in the world. Hana wished life could be as simple as having a full tummy and a soft bed. Hearing the rumble of voices down the hall, Hana stopped in the process of storming into the lounge and expelling Amanda. The other woman's voice sounded seductive and drunk. "I love seeing your muscles through your tee shirt," Amanda crooned. "Chris loved himself so there wasn't room for anyone else to love him, but you're different."

"God help me," Hana begged. She'd missed the danger looming, ignoring the lighthouse as it warned that the rocks were sharp and could wreck everything.

Hana slipped into the tiny laundry at the end of the unit, fingering the handle of Phoenix's pram and considering leaving with her. "I can't go in there," she whispered to her eerie reflection in the window. "I feel too mixed up." She thought about her sleeping baby and chastised her selfishness at thinking of dragging the child from her bed and taking her out into the cold night. "What can I do?" Hana panicked, hearing another volley of high pitched laughter from Amanda.

Darkness enveloped the school site and Hana watched the flickering lights in the main building, wondering what was going on. On an impulse and regretting the absence of her coat, she slipped out of the laundry door, closing it quietly behind her. The sickness deepened as Amanda's laugh cut through the silence of the night and Hana turned it on Logan. "Bloody men!" she hissed. "Bloody disloyal men!" She set off into the darkness, not knowing or caring where she would go.

The main buildings were busy with night classes and the car parks full. Hana sauntered around, looking in ground floor windows at adults learning French, Spanish, cooking and other interesting activities. She wondered if her brain would turn to mush if she kept living her current existence and she watched for a long while at the window of a pottery class, yearning to feel the clay beneath her fingers.

She wandered around until she arrived at the swimming pool. It was locked for the night and she stroked the wire fence, remembering her first kiss with Logan in the doorway of the changing rooms. Amanda's devious smile filtered into her memory and Hana banished all good thoughts of her husband. "He could've asked her to leave," she grumbled. "Unless he really does like her." Hana gulped as the thought took hold and she stared at the freezing water, her heart clenching at the threat of another failed marriage. "I can't do this again," she panicked. "I can't."

The deserted hockey turf was eerie, but the floodlights shone over the tennis courts. Hana walked towards the fenced courts, blinking in the bright lights after the darkness and isolation of everywhere else. One man played by himself, served tennis balls by a complicated machine which fired them at intervals. Hana counted seven seconds between balls. The man dealt with them competently, betraying his skill as an accomplished player. Hana stood and watched, fascinated by the pattern of movements he used in a steady rhythm, backhand, forehand and overhead, repeated over and over. The familiarity of the man's tennis game filled her with a sense of comfort, her fingers itching to hold the racquet and feel its weight and balance.

The player sensed someone watching and reaching in the pocket of his shorts, he felt for a remote control, ceasing the delivery machine's relentless ball firing. "Hey," he said, striding towards Hana with a smile on his face. Mid-thirties with white-blonde hair, the man possessed a sculpted physique and a kind, gentle face. He wasn't devastatingly good looking in a Du Rose way, but a pleasant nature shone through the easy grin.

"Hi," Hana replied, biting her lip with awkwardness. "Your game is fluid; you play well."

"Thanks," he said, his kiwi accent drawing out the syllable.

The man linked his fingers through the chain fence and studied Hana's face. She took a step back, feeling stupid.

"Partner me?" he asked, drawing the bolt back on the gate. He opened it wide and indicated with his arm that Hana should come inside. Without knowing why, Hana obeyed and found herself inside the courts. It brought back happy memories. "Do you play?" he asked, pointing to another racquet over by his bag.

"Not for a while," Hana said sadly, shaking her head.

"How come?" he asked and it was a strange question with myriad possible answers.

Hana shook her head. "I don't know," she replied. "Lots of reasons."

He pressed her, desperate to know. "What was it? Injury, busyness, work commitments, family; the list is endless."

"My tennis partner died," Hana said and it hit her as yet another thing Vik's death robbed her of.

"Oh, sorry," the man said. "I didn't mean to pry; you look familiar. Did you play competition doubles a few years back?"

Hana smiled and nodded slowly. "Ten years back actually. Mainly local, but a few area matches. We got rather good."

"You're not Hana Johal are you?" the man asked, his smile deepening. "You and your husband were awesome."

Hana laughed. "No, we just enjoyed ourselves. It was fun and something we could do together. Vik was the serious one. I played to spend time with him."

The man laughed and trotted over to the spare racquet nesting in its protective cover, unzipping it and placing it ceremoniously into her hands. "Come on," he said. "I'm bored with the machine. Play with me for a while."

Hana took the racquet and turned it over in her hands. It felt like an old friend, familiar and safe, welcoming her back in her time of need. Her companion urged her with a jerk of his head and Hana moved behind the back line. He served a fast ball without mercy and Hana returned it with a powerful backhand that made him run. He cheered and she smiled, enjoying doing something she loved. A far better player than her, he served and returned with consideration, not deliberately flooring her as he could have. Hana felt rusty, but they smashed away at the balls for another half an hour before her companion looked at his watch.

"I told Mr Blair I'd lock up by nine. Otherwise we get complaints from the residents at the back of the school about the lights," he called. He looked regretful as he walked over to the net to speak to Hana. "I've enjoyed myself. Don't suppose you'd fancy a 'come back'? I could use a good mixed doubles partner."

Hana shook her head, embarrassed by his compelling hero-worship-act. Making an excuse, she helped him retrieve the balls which had zinged around the court and returned them to the bucket on the machine. He released its stand and wheeled it over to the gate. Hana carried the racquets and his bag, trying to be helpful as he locked up the gate and shot the sprig from the padlock home. He smiled at her kindly and laid a hand on her shoulder. "I'm here most evenings," he said. "If you won't come out of retirement for me, I'd still love a decent sparring partner."

Hana offered a non-committal smile and a shrug. The exercise made her feel hot and bothered and an ache developed in her soul. It was always that way when she came across some part of her former married life she had enjoyed and lost. It was as though handling the tennis racquet made her vulnerable, offering her heart up for yet more hurt. Yet it felt so good to whack the ball with abandon and exorcise her negative emotion. "I have a young baby," she said, hearing her own breathlessness. "It's hard to get time to myself."

Disappointment made his young face crease, but he nodded once in understanding. "Fair enough," he conceded.

"Where do you want this?" Hana asked, indicating the heavy bag.

"Over here," he replied. His car was parked by the shed which the grounds staff used to store equipment and the man unlocked the boot and hefted the ball machine inside.

Hana opened the rear door and placed the two expensive racquets on the back seat. "They're expensive racquets," she said, closing the door. "That brand is awesome; I always hankered over one of those." Her voice sounded wistful and embarrassed she focussed her attention on the car. It was of nondescript colour in the darkness and could have been black, red or blue under the flickering light of the stars.

The man went over to the old shed and Hana heard him fighting with a rusty lock. He flicked a switch inside and the floodlights went off with a pop. Hana waited by the vehicle, wanting to leave but keen not to seem rude. It took a long while for the glow to disappear completely from the surface of the huge floodlights. "Thank you," she said as he reappeared. "I had fun."

He nodded and touched her shoulder again, his fingers making a gentle stroking movement. Without warning, he kissed her, his lips soft as they pressed over Hana's. She gasped and took a step backwards, stumbling over the curb. "Sorry, sorry," he said, catching her under her elbows. "I forgot how beautiful you were. You were my first major crush."

Hana peered into his face, desperate to remember this intriguing male. Something familiar screamed out at her and she opened her mouth to ask him where they'd met. When he dipped his head to kiss her again, Hana obeyed her pounding heart and escaped, ducking under his arm and breaking into a run. She felt his eyes raking her outline in the darkness and sped back to the unit. Hana didn't feel like going home but with nowhere else to go and Phoenix there, she had no choice.

Outside the semi-detached units which were hers and Amanda's, Hana saw lights on in her friend's. At least it meant that she'd left Logan alone. The thought of walking in on them kissing or worse made her feel ill. "He wouldn't!" she told herself but the nagging thought pestered her psyche and convinced her otherwise.

Hana sighed and tried the laundry door, tripping over the step and landing on her knees. The door's locked status meant her husband had been looking for her. *Fantastic!* She walked round to the front on leaden feet, finding that door also locked. Hana stamped her foot crossly. "He's deliberately making me knock to get in," she fumed, remembering her keys in the pocket of her coat in the hall cupboard. Feeling stubborn, she sat on the steps of the unit, not wanting to concede anything by knocking on the door and giving Logan more power than he already had over her. She sat for twenty minutes and decided that she might sleep there too. The stars were pretty overhead and reminded her of her baby's birth underneath the Milky Way six months ago.

God had different ideas though, turning the thermostat down to below zero. Hana's light pullover offered no help as she shivered on the door step, her foolish tantrum becoming more ridiculous as the minutes went by. She sneezed loudly, clapping her hand over her mouth but it was too late. She heard footsteps inside and Logan yanked the door open. Hana tumbled backwards into the hallway, catching herself at the last moment and banging her sore wrist on the door jamb. For a second the pain was excruciating, dulling to a faint throb as she got control. "Bloody hell!" she breathed, gripping either side of the scar to numb the ache.

Logan helped her up and led her inside, looking at her strangely. Hana recognised his scrutiny from the look he gave his mother when searching for signs of insanity. "Can you not?" she bit at him. It drove her mad, the way he examined her as he had his poor Bi-Polar mother, for signs she wasn't medicating.

Hana pushed him rudely out of her way and clomped along the hallway with her trainers on, deliberately ignoring her own, *shoes-off-at-the-door-of-this-tiny-shoebox* rule. She stripped off her clothes in the bedroom, uncomfortable as the sweat from the tennis practice dried in the cold night air and made her skin tight and sticky. Her hair was mussed and fluffy and she stomped into the bathroom for a shower and hair wash.

Logan followed, looking both worried and confused. The bathroom was tiny and it irritated her, his proximity when she needed room to breathe and think. Logan sat on the edge of the bath, getting wet as his wife washed her hair behind the shower curtain.

"Amanda was waiting to see you," Logan risked saying, hearing the snort of derision from behind the curtain.

"Whatever!" came Hana's curt reply.

"But she was. She's your friend, not mine."

Hana gave a nasty laugh, prompting Logan to whip the curtain back and get a face full of water. "What's that supposed to mean?" he spluttered.

Hana felt torn between wanting him to leave so she could calm down and wanting him to stay so she could argue. The latter desire won. "I don't have *friends*, Logan. I can't have friends around the Du Roses. Every time I get someone I can relate to, one of you screw it up for me. So, no she isn't my friend. *Not anymore!*"

Logan wiped his face on the hand towel, looking bemused. His confusion lit the blue touch paper on Hana's bomb. "Remember, my good friend of fifteen years, Anka? Tama's affair with her ended that for me. And now, Amanda, friend of four months seems to have a thing for you. How would you feel, arriving home and discovering me cuddling up to a man on the sofa? You'd go loco and don't bother denying it; you attacked a man for *talking* to me a few months ago. Double standards, Logan! So clearly, it's not safe for me to have friends but that's okay. I don't need other people. I love being lonely and miserable and not having a soul in the world to share my hopes and fears with, in case they make a play for one of you boys. It's wonderful. *My life is awesome!*"

"Hana!" Logan's face looked ashen as he reached out for her, her words cutting into him like a blade. She stepped over the side of the bath and slapped his hands away, nearly breaking her neck on the slippery floor. Managing to retain some dignity, she shrouded herself in one towel and balled her hair into another. The thought of sleeping with wet hair made Hana even grumpier. It was the worst feeling in the world; apart from childbirth, a broken arm, a shard of glass sticking out of her vein, or being told her husband just died under a truck. Maybe wet hair wasn't so bad.

Logan eyed Hana warily as she dried, her flesh pink and mottled by the heat. He ducked as she swung the towel to cover herself. He studied her through his stunning grey eyes, the long dark lashes swishing against his cheeks when he looked down.

"Please, stop staring at me," Hana hissed with exasperation, "you make me feel like a zoo animal."

"Well, you're behaving like one," he retorted, a veiled attempt at humour.

Hana spun round on the slippery floor and faced him. "Just stop it!" she shouted, raising her voice in the screechy pitch she hated. "Stop looking at me like you expect to see some kind of mental disorder! What will you do? Get me pills, send my children away....oh yeah sorry, you already did that!"

"Hey!" Logan got to his feet. The floor was soaked and his socks wet. As he reached out, he slipped and in trying to save himself, grabbed the metal towel rail on the wall. He swore as he pulled his hand away and blood dripped from a sliced index finger. He put it up to his mouth, trying to contain the flow.

"I'm sorry," Hana said, her rage instantly abated. She looked shamefaced as he ran it under the cold tap but when she tried to help, he pulled his finger away and turned his back on her.

"Just leave me alone!" he said, his eyes as grey as an angry sea. He left Hana to tidy the bathroom, her heavy heart weighing her down every time she leaned forward.

She wiped up the blood and mopped the water off the floor, putting off her return to the bedroom and the argument. Finally readying herself to placate her husband, she opened the door but found no sign of Logan. He wasn't in the unit.

Hana sat on the bed and cried, pressing her face into her palms and groaning from the pain of the heaviness in her chest. The cut to Logan's finger and subsequent blood loss rendered the factor eight infusion futile, as it leaked from his body so soon.

Phoenix woke for a feed and Hana welcomed the distraction of the smiling little girl, who beamed as her mother lifted her from the cot despite the late hour. Hana tried not to torture herself with thoughts of Logan, imagining him seeking comfort next door with the voluptuous and eager Amanda. "I hate how he makes me feel insane," she sobbed over her suckling child. "Maybe I am. Maybe I've caught it just by being married to a Du Rose." She thought of Miriam, upsetting herself with her last memory of her mother-in-law, screaming and dodging her sons to get to the fire and what? Save Reuben, or be with him in death? Her face resembled a ghoulish mask of insanity and mania as she fled into the flames and died with her lover in his inferno.

Hana felt the heat and heard the rushing whoosh of the fire as she sat on the bed, alone in her sadness and feeding the child born a day later. She stroked the little girl's delicate fingers and let her tears plop onto the baby suit. Phoenix only needed a top up and to say hello and Hana returned her to her cot with a full tummy and clean nappy.

Hana Du Rose didn't like the woman who stared back from the bathroom mirror as she washed her hands. Logan wasn't having an affair, even if Amanda wished he was. It was the *threat* of it which ate away at Hana's security and probably always would, thanks to Vik and his secret mistress. She'd been oblivious to his late nights and early mornings and the jobs which took him away from home in their final year together. Sometimes she hated Vik for dying because it denied her justice, not finding out until the day after his funeral when his tearful girlfriend turned up at her home. Hana felt livid at Amanda and furious at Logan and even more aggrieved with herself. "You sent him round to hers," she chastised the woman in the mirror. Red-rimmed eyes peered back at her, dark circles under the vibrant green eyes. "He didn't want to go, but you were so damn lonely and pleased to have friendship, you made him! Opening pickle jars, fixing light bulbs, bolting loft hatches." Hana sneered at her reflected self. "You're too bloody trusting, Hana Du Rose. When will you learn?"

Hana slapped moisturiser on her face and went to bed, grovelling around in her drawer for another novel. She fought the manic desire to rip it in two like a strong man ripping a telephone directory. Slender fingers stroked the cover and knew she wouldn't do it. Hana willed Logan to come home so she could look at his finger and finish the argument. The issues floated in the air, still unaddressed. She wanted a chance to say the clever things she'd thought of.

She fell asleep, lying diagonally across the double bed so Logan's return would wake her. But when she struggled from sleep the next morning, he wasn't there and she'd given herself backache.

Chapter 13

"I'm spending a few nights with friends," Tama informed her, biting his lip and furrowing his brow.

"Why?" Hana's face looked troubled at the thought of her only ally disappearing.

Tama rolled his eyes. "Because living with you and Uncle Logan is like being in a mine field, Ma. He's not talking to you and you're not talking to him. It's stupid."

"But I told you what he did!" Hana said. "I came back to find him sprawled on the sofa with my friend; what would you do?"

"No, Ma." Tama shook his head. "The story gets worse every time you tell it. If I didn't know better I'd think you were sabotaging your own happiness. Logan kept telling you he didn't want to help her out with her stupid problems but you wouldn't listen."

"I thought she was my friend," Hana sulked.

"No-one's your friend, Ma," Tama said, sadness in his eyes and his shoulders slumped. He hefted his bag over his shoulder and reached out a hand to stroke her red curls. "All we've got is family, babe. Don't you know that yet?"

A car honked in the lane and Tama left with a wave. "I don't even have family," Hana muttered to herself. She imagined herself crawling back to Bodie. "Hey, son. You were right; my husband's a jerk." Hana shook her head, choosing loneliness instead.

Bodie stayed away from his mother and Izzie never returned her call. Logan remained distinctly absent; always busy over at St Bart's, leaving Hana isolated and lonely. She rang the rest home and asked if she could visit Father Sinbad, yearning for the sound of his voice. Matron answered. "Hello, Hana," she said, sounding jovial. "He's not back from his holiday yet."

"But it's been two weeks," Hana said with surprise. "He only goes for a week."

"Usually," Matron replied. "The Catholic charity paid for ten days this year at another rest home in Russell just for a change of scenery for him."

"That was kind of them; he always loves going somewhere new and meeting other priests."

"Yes, he does." Matron's tone became serious. "He took a funny turn so they've kept him there for a bit longer. It's caused a problem for me because the lovely chap we've got in exchange really wants to go home now."

"Oh, dear. If you're talking to Father Sinbad, please give him my love, won't you?" Hana said. "Tell him I'll visit as soon as he's home and I hope it's nothing serious."

"It won't be," Matron promised. "He'll go on forever."

Hana avoided contact with her next door neighbour, hoping Amanda got the message without them needing to have a messy confrontational showdown.

Seeing her loneliness, Pastor Allen persuaded Hana to attend a Thursday mother and toddler group at church, but she found it compounded her isolation. Most of the women were in their twenties and Hana found no common ground, apart from the chubby babies each had on their hip. The women were related to one another or part of such a tight little friendship group, they didn't need Hana. The first meeting was a lonely, soul destroying experience, driving Hana deeper into herself and wrecking her confidence.

Escaping to the car while the other yummy mummies sang nursery rhymes, more for their own benefit than their drooling offspring, Hana started the engine and suffered a small crisis. "I don't know where to go," she told her smiling daughter. "Everywhere sucks!" Hana brushed away a tear from her cheek and bit her lip to distract her.

She listed her options on her fingers, finding none satisfactory. There was the empty Culver's Cottage, requiring work to open up and light a fire whilst juggling her baby. Or there was her scintillating life at the school site where the excitement was damn near killing her. Robert and Elaine, happy now they'd found Hana and mended their relationship, had headed off to see more of New Zealand than just Hamilton. Hana resented the days spent away from her, realising time was precious and she wanted more than they could give. She selfishly wanted twenty-six years of quality time squashed into the short few weeks before they left for England.

Hana pulled up to the intersection with the main road, sitting on the white line without indicating. "Where should I go, Phoe?" she asked her daughter. "Where do you fancy?"

Phoenix yawned and closed her eyes, leaving Hana to make the decision. "Fine," she said turning the car north. "But don't blame me." She cut across country until she met the junction with State Highway 1 and then headed towards Auckland. "I might not like my husband much at the moment, but I dislike myself more," she said to the sleeping child. Hana recognised she needed time to think and not worry, to get away from a former life which pulled and snagged at her like barbed wire. She was wise enough to see temptation in the sweet man with the tennis racquets, knowing she felt companionship with him in a dangerous way. The sensation of the strings pounding the tennis ball was exhilarating and Hana knew her reaction to Logan afterwards had channelled the pent up emotions released by the game. Hana saw how easy it was for Anka to bed the willing Tama, bored and stagnant in her own life and attracted by the excitement of his. The blonde man was sweet and kind and Hana sensed he had a vacancy for good company.

"What am I doing?" Hana groaned, making the turn towards Rangiriri. "I've just left my husband at the mercy of Amanda and her desperate DIY requirements. Tama's not even there to protect him." She tossed her red hair in defiance and decided if her marriage was in that much danger, it wasn't worth hanging around to watch it unravel. Her cheeks flushed at the memory of the gentle touch of the tennis player on her shoulder and guilt pricked at her. Logan would kill him. Yet somehow her husband believed it was okay to cuddle up on the sofa with the next door neighbour.

Hana arrived at the hotel at afternoon teatime, the bell sounding as she pitched in the front door carrying the car seat and change bag.

"Hey, Mrs Du Rose," the receptionist called. "Would you like help with your bags?"

Hana gave the woman a watery smile and looked at her belongings. It was then she realised she had nothing else with her and her face crumpled. The receptionist buzzed the kitchen for Leslie, dismayed by the level of Hana's upset and the Māori housekeeper waddled along the corridor at warp speed, seizing Hana in such a genuine embrace it left her bones rattling and her tears falling freely. "It's all gone wrong," Hana wailed and Leslie patted her back and waved away the other staff who came to watch.

The renewed contact with Robert reminded Hana of what she'd lost and she missed her mother with an unremitting ache. Leslie's maternal embrace was a painful proxy for Judith's absence and seemed to make Hana's hysteria worse. "Let's get you upstairs and out of the way of pryin' eyes," Leslie whispered, sensing the atmosphere of gossip descending. She took the car seat and change bag, letting Hana regain her dignity and leading the way up the spiral staircase to Logan's childhood room. Leslie pressed the numbers for access and pushed the door open.

As the door clicked behind them, Hana realised she didn't want to be there either; in the centre of more Du Rose territory. "I can't stay," she sobbed, while Leslie sat the car seat on the rug and returned for the child's distraught mother.

"Whatever's wrong, child?" the old woman asked softly, stroking Hana's arm with gentle brown fingers.

Hana began wailing like a five-year-old. "I've got no friends; I'm so lonely. Logan hates me."

Leslie sat on the bed with Hana enfolded in her comely arms and let her sob. It felt to Hana like mere minutes but it was actually forty-five of them. Three-quarters of an hour of sobbing, sniffing, nose blowing and then sitting with tears coursing silently down her face. If it gained credit as an Olympic sport, Hana Du Rose was a silver medal winner at crying. Leslie's uniform blouse was saturated with salt water and Hana felt cowed by exhaustion. As soon as she thought she might be okay to let go of the housekeeper, some other sad thought assailed her brain; her poor mother, her poor father or her even poorer brother and she started crying again. "I'm sorry," Hana managed to say eventually. "You have other places to be. It's okay if you need to go."

Leslie shook her head. "Na, Miss. Youse more important. You doesn't have to tell me if youse don't wanna though. Leslie's happy just to be with you." She stroked Hana's hair and let her sniff into her damp shoulder.

"I'm so sick of myself," Hana declared. "What must you think of me?"

Leslie smiled and pushed Hana's fringe back from her face with a crinkled olive palm. "I think youse heartsick, honey," she whispered.

Hana nodded and fetched a toilet roll from the ensuite, blowing into wads of it as the tears converted themselves into rivers of snot instead. "That's a good word for it," she admitted. "Heartsick. Yeah, that's how I feel."

Leslie fetched clean sheets and pillowcases from the laundry downstairs and helped Hana make the bed. "Will Mr Logan be arriving?" she dared to ask and Hana put her hand over her face and degenerated once again into waterworks, aiming for a gold medal in something of a sprint finish.

"It's early days," Leslie whispered, holding her tightly. "I left my poor Kiwi so many times that first year he looked surprised when I finally turned up for good. I think he'd forgot who I was." Leslie smiled. "There's been a lot to deal with, *kōtiro*. Give yourself a break."

Phoenix woke up and added to the din, discovering her stomach empty and feeling shocked and astounded at Hana's audacity for leaving it so. Despite having guests in the hotel and dinner to organise, Leslie disappeared with the baby, delighting in playing nursemaid and stuffing her full of pureed mashed potato, beef and vegetables. The housekeeper sat at the dining table through the archway like the queen, squawking orders to her workforce and enjoying the legitimate sit-down.

Hana raided the drawers and wardrobe in the bedroom, discovering enough clothing to last her and the baby a short while. She unearthed a packet of nappies she left there last time. They were too small, but she found a roll of tape to seal the child into them temporarily. The sleep suits were on the short side and Hana pulled a face, tears threatening at the scent of defeat. "No," she decided. "It's not the end of the world. I'll cut the feet out and Phoenix can look like a beatnik baby for a few days." She sat on the bed to fold the suits into a manageable pile but got no further.

The dreadful hitch in her chest from crying had exhausted her and Hana fell asleep sitting up, eventually face planting onto the mattress. Downstairs, her daughter thoroughly enjoyed the taste of Logan's beef herd, stuffed to brimming with the mash. Leslie sent a kitchen girl upstairs to let Hana know her baby needed milk, not surprised when the girl returned alone. "I peeped through the door and saw Mrs Du Rose flat on her face and snoring." The girl smirked and looked to the other housemaids for solidarity.

Leslie grimaced. "There's nothing funny about it and if I find you spreading gossip, there'll be trouble." She eyeballed the young woman who wiped the smirk from her lips. "She's family," Leslie reminded the women collectively, jabbing an index finger towards each of their faces. "And don't you forget it."

Leslie broke out a brand new feeder cup, ran it through the kitchen steriliser and warmed up cow's milk, spending the next half an hour laughing at the baby's ingenious way of drinking. "She's a bright little cookie," she said to the women as Phoenix waved the cup in the air for the hundredth time, showering everyone nearby with warm milk. The little girl laughed and sucked at the lip, gasping as too much shot into her mouth, surprising her. Then with a giggle, she repeated the whole process again.

"I don't think you're meant to give them cow's milk until they're two, Aunty," one of the kitchen girls warned.

The old lady shrugged. "It didn't do my *tamariki* any harm. Besides which, Mrs Du Rose isn't well so it'll have to do."

The girls raised their eyebrows at each other. Leslie was an amazing housekeeper even when Miriam Du Rose was alive, running the hotel in her absence when the missus took to her bed with depression. But they all gossiped behind Leslie's back when she was out of earshot.

"She's making free with that family now. She wouldn't have dared when Miriam Du Rose was alive."

"Mr Alfred moved into the bunkhouse extension with Jack so Leslie could have his apartment upstairs, but I heard he was seen leaving it early in the morning by a house maid."

"Jack?"

"No! Alfred Du Rose!"

"No way! You don't think that 'im and 'er are..."

"Eugh! That's disgusting. His wife's not six months dead."

"Yeah, but then he had a miserable existence with her loving his brother and all."

"And didn't Leslie and 'im have a bit of a fling many years ago? Wasn't there doubt about her youngest daughter being a Du Rose?"

"With Rueben Du Rose?"

"Alfred! Are you deaf?"

"No, shush! Mentioning that'll get you into big trouble. Miriam heard about it and threw a candlestick at Alfred's head; do you remember that?"

"It might be why Leslie's bossier now; because 'im and 'er are..."

"Well, she's certainly got a spring in her step."

"Maybe someone should tell Mrs Hana about her."

"Na, she looked real sick. I think she's got other things to worry about."

"Yeah, like keeping Logan Du Rose happy. Reckon I should offer to help her out? I could keep him busy for half an hour."

"Better than the old man, aye?"

"Hell yeah! Logan could keep going all night. We could take turns!"

"I don't think Alfred's got it in him. Mind you, if he's seeing to Leslie, maybe he has."

There was a peel of laughter as the kitchen girls waggled their eyebrows at each other. They pulled faces to show they were trying not to think about the old couple going at it above their heads in the attic flat.

The chirping of Hana's phone woke her. She groaned and rolled onto her back. "Shut up," she grumbled, putting her fingers in her ears to ignore it long enough to go back to sleep. Realisation made her sit up with a start, remembering her phone's inbuilt GPS tracker. Hana staggered around the room in her dozy state, hunting for the source of the noise. When she found it lurking in the side pocket of the change bag she resisted the urge to throw it across the room. Her fingers struggled with the power button and she turned it off and hurled herself backwards onto the bed. "I've got Phoe and nobody else matters," she decided in her self-pitying state. "The rest of you can get stuffed."

Hana snuggled under the sheets and reached for slumber again, knowing inwardly it was too late. Worries about Izzie and her father pervaded her peace and she sat up and rubbed her eyes. Turning the phone on, Hana saw two missed calls from Logan and a text from 'Aarsehole'. Wondering what Mark wanted and thinking she ought to rename him, she looked at his message. It was short and sweet. *Just got out of surgery and on my way back in. Loved talking the other night. I've missed my sister. X'*

Hana sighed with gratitude. At least someone cared about her for herself and not what she could provide. It was a strange irony that her tumultuous relationship with Mark was the one adding value to her life. Hana held the phone in her hand, tempted to ring her husband and reassure him Phoenix was okay.

Self-preservation stopped her. He might follow her in a desire to get the upper hand and Hana knew she needed a break from everyone in Hamilton, including Logan. She sent a nice text back to her brother and then stared at her contacts list, wondering whether to rename them all. Hana giggled like a child, entertaining herself deciding on alternative names. Anka could be 'Tart,' Tama could be 'Stud,' Mark could be himself and then change Logan to 'Aarsehole.' "I could have so much fun," Hana mused. "But what if I forget who's who? I can't ring someone and say, *'Oh sorry, I thought you were 'Git' but actually you're just 'Stupid,'* not with my memory."

Relenting, she sent a short text to her husband, hoping he'd noticed she was missing but figuring the two calls were because he needed something. *'Hope your finger's okay now. Phoenix is fine. Need space.'* Then she turned the phone off and stuffed it into the pocket of the bag, promising herself she wouldn't look at it again until she was ready to go home. *Whenever that was.*

Hana was starving and went in search of her baby and some dinner. She stumbled downstairs, staggering through the kitchen door and forgetting the room had changed.

"Through there, miss," a waitress said, pointing to the archway where the wall had been knocked through. Hana went into the new dining room, finding Leslie cuddling a very bloated Phoenix and reading a magazine. The baby's belly looked like it could explode and she was fast asleep. "I'm so sorry," Hana whispered. "I don't know what happened." She sank into a chair next to the housekeeper and ran her hands over her face, feeling her eyes bulging under her fingers. "I've got a frog-face haven't I?" she grumbled and Leslie chuckled.

"Better out than in."

"Dad used to say that about farts." Hana winced. She gazed around the room. "This looks good," she said, waving her arm.

"All your idea, miss," Leslie said, nodding her approval. The old doorway from the corridor had been reopened and a fire door added. As Hana watched, it opened gently.

Bobby stepped in quietly. He looked different from the man who hounded Hana the previous year. He'd grown a bushy beard and his blonde hair was long. If the cops came looking for 'Flick', they wouldn't find him. Hana smiled at him, trying to forget her puffy, unattractive eyes. "Hey, Bobby," she said.

He smiled back and nodded to Leslie, eyeing the old woman sideways. "Hello, miss, I heard you were back."

Hana's face fell. "Oh." She wondered if he'd heard her crying or if someone informed him she'd run away from her husband. The stock man's loyalty to Logan would trump any friendship she'd forged with him. Hana put her head down and turned her face away, thinking of an excuse to leave the room.

The sound of a loud band struck up in the ballroom, making the sleeping baby jump and shoot her arms out wide like a parachutist. "That's so cute," Leslie cackled. "I love how they do that."

Hana made a sound somewhere between a sigh and a sad chuckle.

"Can I talk to you, miss?" Bobby asked, hovering by the door and waiting for her to answer.

Hana took a fortifying breath and turned towards him, giving him a look of encouragement. "Of course, you can, Bobby. How can I help you?"

"I wondered if you wanted to go up to the new place, miss?" he asked, referring to the house Logan was building for his family at the top of the mountain. Hana sent a dart of fear towards Leslie, wondering if she'd live long enough to move in or if Logan would kill her out of frustration before the builders finished. She didn't want to be rude and nodded without commitment. Bobby's face lit up in a beam. "Awesome, miss," he declared with a grin of pleasure. "We'll set off after breakfast tomorrow. I'll come around the front for you at nine. Then you can see how far we've got and let me know if you want to make any changes. Will Mr Logan be coming?"

Hana shook her head and Bobby looked momentarily disappointed. He shrugged. "Never mind. You'll be living there so your opinion's just as good." He headed out the door smiling happily back at her. As soon as the door clicked shut behind him, Hana groaned and laid her forehead on the dining table, seeing at close range the wear and tear from years and years of use.

"I'll keep this little girl tomorrow," Leslie offered. "I'm off all day, so you take some time for yourself."

"But what about feeds and stuff?" Hana asked, looking for an excuse to get out of the trip.

Leslie snorted. "This little piggy scoffed a whole bowl of solids and a feeder cup of warm cow's milk. She's gonna be fine with Aunty Leslie looking after her."

"Traitor," Hana groaned. "There's no point me looking when I won't be living in it."

"It's not that bad, is it?" Leslie furrowed her brow and peered at Hana over her spectacles. "You haven't actually left Mr Logan, have you?"

"I don't know," Hana breathed, confusion in her eyes. "I couldn't go on like that, living in a shoe box with him not talking to me."

"Doesn't sound like Mr Logan," Leslie commented. "He's the shout and yell type normally."

"Yeah, he's done a bit of that too," Hana said, feeling tears smart the backs of her eyes again. "Then he just went quiet. I think I'm a big disappointment to him so I know I won't be living in that house. There's no point me even going up there."

Leslie squeezed her shoulder. "Things will work out for youse both," she predicted with a smile. "It's never as bad as it seems, miss. You have a ride up the mountain with Flick tomorrow and let the sunshine kiss you."

Hana smiled and relented. "At least I can go up on the quad bike if Bobby's taking me," she said, sounding relieved as she recalled the breakneck horse rides Logan had taken her on up there.

"There're tracks now," Leslie informed her, "where they sent the trucks up with wood and stuff. But I'd wear riding gear in case. The boys taught Bobby to ride and he loves every opportunity to get his handsome butt in the saddle."

Hana groaned again. She skipped food, deafened by the band bursting a gasket for the wedding guests in the ballroom and took her baby upstairs. Leslie took pity on her and arrived upstairs with hot soup and bread. She found Hana wandering around the bedroom looking lost, balancing the comatose child on one arm. "I haven't got the travel cot," Hana said, looking defeated. "And she's too big for the drawer now. I don't know what to do with her. She can't sleep in the bed because she can roll."

Leslie put the tray on the dressing table and returned five minutes later with a folded travel cot belonging to the hotel. Hana balanced the baby in one arm and ate standing up. Leslie set the cot up with sheets and blankets and Hana surrendered her child. "She feels heavier. What did you feed her?"

Leslie laughed and tapped her nose. Then she smiled and gave Hana a hug. "Settle down for the night and get a good rest." She took the tray and opened the room next door to allow Hana to raid her sister-in-law's closet for riding clothes. "I use Liza's clothes more than she does," Hana joked and Leslie laughed.

She fell asleep watching re-runs of English comedy programmes she hadn't seen for years and woke up, still fully dressed to the sound of Phoenix blowing straight through her nappy, vest and baby suit. It took an hour to sort the child out, resorting to bathing her in the bathroom sink. Hana silently cursed Aunty Leslie's beef and vegetables and not once either. "Far out child! You smell like a sewer pipe!"

The baby had extremely bad gas after the pebble-dashing of her undies, but suffered no other ill-effects.

Hana dressed her daughter in a footless sleep suit which she doctored with nail scissors by the light of the bedside lamp. "You look like the spawn of Barney Rubble," Hana yawned as she tried to give her a breastfeed. Phoenix managed a little but pulled a face after a while and fell asleep. Hana laid her in the cot, hoping and praying she didn't get another wake up call like that again. Without pyjamas, she found a tee shirt of Logan's in a drawer and slipped it over her naked body. Sorely tempted to check her phone again, Hana resisted, knowing whatever messages it showed possessed the potential to deny her a peaceful night's sleep. She conceded if the baby woke her up with another cement truck delivery, she'd permit herself to check, figuring she'd be up a good long while in that case anyway.

Chapter 14

Hana's breasts woke her at seven o'clock, unused to being ignored for so long by her infant. She woke the baby and coaxed her to feed which was unusual. The little girl seemed fine, sucking greedily and beaming at Hana. Her morning nappy was a little reminiscent of the night before, but not to the same extent. "You're a grown up girl," Hana crooned as she washed and dressed her baby and Phoenix squealed with delight. "I wonder what culinary delights Aunty Leslie has for you today? Whatever it is, I'll have to clean it up tonight!"

Phoenix laid on the bathroom floor while Hana showered, giggling with glee as her mother peeked out at her. The mountain spring water smelled and tasted so different from the town stuff and Hana felt clean and fresh. When she emerged from the shower cubicle, the baby had rolled over onto her stomach and was kissing the bathmat.

Hana wrapped herself in a towel and retrieved her daughter. "You're getting way too good at that," she said, praising the child. Hana laid her on the rug, calling to her from around the room and finding her in a different spot each time she spied on her. "How are you doing that?" Hana asked, moving her back to the bedside rug. She frantically snipped up another sleep suit and squeezed the child into it but while she applied mascara and lipstick in the mirror, the little girl removed both socks.

"Oh, Phoe, don't do that. You'll get cold feet," Hana said, kissing the twinkling olive toes. She stuffed them on again and packed more nappies and suits into the change bag, shoving the sellotape in too. She fitted the socks on again three more times before carrying infant and bag downstairs for Leslie.

"What's she doing?" Leslie asked in the kitchen, watching Phoenix bend double to rip off the socks, grunting and dribbling a trail behind her.

"Pulling her socks off," Hana said, wincing in apology. "I've run out of clothes."

Leslie took the baby and put the bag over her arm. "Come on, little *mokopuna*," she said, beaming. "Let's get you fed and that'll keep you too busy to strip naked."

"Do you think she'll be all right? I'm hoping I won't be long." Hana looked worried, twisting her fingers through each other.

"She'll be fine!" The older woman shooed her away, taking the little girl around the dining room to say hello to the hung over, sexed up wedding party from the night before.

"Ok, if you're sure." Hana dashed to the mud room at the back of the house, finding Liza's jodhpur boots and a pair of chaps to protect her calves. She sorted out the old hat of Miriam's Logan once gave to her and clamped it down over her hair. Then she doubted herself.

"What's wrong with you, *kōtiro?*" Leslie asked with a chuckle as Hana arrived back in the kitchen. "Youse got fleas girl?"

The other women rolled their eyes at Leslie's familiarity with her employer's wife, but Hana didn't notice. "I'll feel a total wally dressed as '*Penelope of Pony Club*' if Bobby turns up out front with a quad bike, or the Jeep," she whined.

"Shush woman and get youse arse out the front," Leslie snorted.

Hana hovered inside the hotel lobby, tidying up the magazines and straightening the flowers on coffee tables in the lobby. The clattering of hooves on the gravel made her heart quail. She wasn't confident on horseback and found it a trial with Logan. He always said he wouldn't go fast and then did as though his understanding of 'fast' was different to hers.

"I'm not riding that!" Hana pointed at the stomping white mare on the driveway, blinking in the brightness outside. Logan's horse eyed her haughtily and snaked her neck towards Bobby's hand.

"Enough!" he snapped at her, pulling his hand free and dropping the rope.

Hana shook her head and backed away. "Nope, I'm not coming," she said with determination.

Jack, the stable manager limped around the corner, waving his arms and causing both horses to act spooky. Hana wished he'd keep his body parts still and signed to him in his language to keep still. The deaf man read her hands and emphatically called her over, making his strange guttural noises and signing her to hurry. Hana shook her head and signed 'scared,' but he dismissed it, telling her Sacha would keep her safe.

Hana felt forty years fall from her life, leaving just six as she stamped her foot and pouted. Jack cackled loudly as Bobby struggled with Sacha and the gelding. "I don't want to," she whined, seeing Jack's eyes narrow as he locked his will against hers.

"Bloody get on!" Bobby shouted as Sacha aimed a kick at the gelding and Hana clumped reluctantly towards the mare. She tried not to look her in the eye, facing Logan's expensive tan saddle, her nose an inch away.

Jack intended to throw her onto Sacha's back, making Hana bend her left leg at the knee and using the spring in the joint to chuck her into the saddle. "No," she complained, flapping her hand behind her back. Jack grunted and slapped Hana's bum, taking her by surprise as he flung her skywards.

She almost stabbed herself on the horn of the pommel as she went up, saving herself from being flung clean over by the enthusiastic old man. Jack shortened the stirrups but refused to do the dangling girth up tighter, shaking his head and telling her with his hands to 'ride like a Du Rose.'

"I'll end up riding like a freakin' dead person," Hana wailed as Jack threw Bobby onto his mount the same way. To Hana's disgust, she noticed he rode Digger, the horse she often used. She pulled a face at him. "As soon as we get away from here," she whispered, "we're swapping!"

Bobby looked doubtful and set off in a clatter of hooves, going in a different direction from the one Logan favoured. A deep sandy track left the driveway fifty metres beyond the hotel gate, veering off left and making a steep climb up the mountain side. There were deep track marks from lorry wheels but the going was easy, despite the winter's abuse of the freshly dug earth. "Does this go all the way to the top?" Hana asked in surprise and Bobby turned and nodded.

"What a pity Logan's divorcing me," she muttered, "especially now I don't have to half kill myself visiting his favourite place on earth."

The dappled white mare snorted beneath her as though understanding Hana spoke disrespectful thoughts about her master. Sacha hated following, undoubtedly used to Logan leading any string of horsemen and Hana let her pull alongside Bobby, noticing the wild look in Digger's eyes at her appearance. "When can we swap?" Hana asked, her tone demanding.

"I can't ride her, miss," Bobby replied, giving her a look of complete sincerity. "She only carries Du Roses; nobody else. She'll buck me off quick as a flash. I've seen her do it." He patted Digger's neck with a tanned hand dusted in blonde hairs. "I'll stick with this old boy here, thanks."

Hana tutted like a small child, planning to ambush Digger when they stopped at the top. Sacha blew through her nostrils again, telling her off. "I'm not a Du Rose anyway," Hana complained under her breath. "I'm a..."

And there lay the root of the problem; Hana couldn't decide who she was. In the tennis courts under the stars she was momentarily Hana Johal, doubles tennis star. With her father and brother she was Hana McIntyre. But who was she really; Phoenix's mother, Logan's wife? Even her older children were Johals. Hana huffed and Sacha puffed and Bobby observed the females with alarm, wondering what he'd gotten himself into. He chatted to Hana, distracting her with facts about the build.

"Why are you managing the project?" Hana asked. "Is it something you enjoy?"

Bobby shrugged. "Kinda. I worked as a carpenter in a previous life, well, before things went wrong and I ended up as a fugitive." His brow furrowed and he fell silent.

"Are you happy here?" Hana asked.

Bobby nodded with enthusiasm, his cheeks colouring at the reason for his happiness, hoping Hana didn't guess. She didn't.

"But isn't it hard, being trapped up here, unable to go anywhere in case the cops spot you and arrest you? You must miss your family sometimes; my son said your stepbrother and his wife are lovely people."

Bobby shook his head long after Hana finished speaking. "The cops will find me one day, miss. When I need hospital treatment, or I have to leave for one of my boys; it's inevitable. I'm all right in the township. Mr Du Rose's word is law and if I'm okay by him, the townsfolk don't have a problem with me." He smiled sideways, his blue eyes glittering with passion. "I had my freedom and look what I did with it, miss. I burned myself and other people. Up here, I'm just me and I like who that is. I'm the man my step ma loved and had faith in. These people let me be him. *Bobby*." He grinned at Hana. "And I ain't riding that horse!"

Her face dropped and she looked grumpy. The horse snorted again as though laughing. "You horrid nag!" Hana exclaimed and Bobby threw his head back and laughed.

"Jack said it had to be this way - and he knows his horses," Bobby said sagely and Hana glared at him, determined to get her own way as soon as his backside left the gelding's saddle. "How's things with you nowadays, miss? Now Laval Senior's locked up and the other evil bastard's hanged himself."

Hana shook her head, surprising herself with her answer, "Coming apart at the seams."

Bobby held her gaze for a long moment and Hana felt conflicted. Despite her need for a confidante, gossip from the hotel went round the township like a bushfire. She looked at the hotel roof hundreds of metres below them and sighed. "Miss," Bobby said, his voice low, "I ain't no gossip. I don't speak about others in the hope they won't speak about me; I can stay here longer then. If nobody don't talk about me, the cops can't find me."

"I don't know where to start," Hana replied.

"Try the beginning."

Half an hour later, the riders had skirted native bush and mountains until finally they rode through a gap in the fence at the top of the mountain. The breeze was harder at altitude and the air colder. Hana had talked until she was hoarse and Bobby listened, giving her eye contact and the occasional nod of acknowledgement. She talked about her first marriage and the baggage she inadvertently dragged into her relationship with Logan. Hana told him about her father and brother and their recent meeting. She even confessed to her time on the tennis court with the man who knew she could play. Bobby's brow knitted at Hana's recount of arriving home to find Amanda draping herself over Logan on the sofa. He shook his head. "Man's an idiot if he's messing around behind your back," he said and Hana stared at the latent anger flashing in his blue eyes. His loyalty made her feel gratified. "I'd kill him myself!" he spat and Hana saw a flash of Flick, the other dangerous persona. Bobby shook his head seeing her fear and kept his eyes fixed on the horizon, making the effort to uncurl his fists.

At the top of the mountain, he dismounted, producing two halter ropes from the pockets of the saddle blanket and attaching them to the fence. He stripped off the tack and slipped rope halters over the beasts' faces, making sure they could graze but not roam. "It's no longer a paddock, miss," he said. "It's a building site."

Hana wandered around the site as Bobby checked items off a long handwritten list. "Where is everyone?" she asked. "Why's nobody working?"

"Waiting for supplies," Bobby replied. He waved his hand towards the structure. "The framing is metal. It's usually wood but the house will get a battering from the elements and needed tough, durable materials."

Hana nodded and clattered over the sturdy concrete base, using the doorways to give her an idea of the finished house. The tiled roof protected her from the cold breeze but subjected her to an unnerving whistle as the forceful air pressed around the structure. The back of the house had external plasterboard installed and the builders had begun fitting split brick over the top. It was a pretty material resembling Cotswold stone and Hana imagined the rooms enclosed by walls.

Port Waikato was a cluster of tiny dots in the distance far below, with the estuary and sea beyond it. "It will be a beautiful house," Hana said with sadness. "Logan's spared no expense."

Bobby smiled wistfully. "He's built it for you, miss."

Hana shook her head. "I don't think so, Bobby." She sighed. "You shouldn't tell him you brought me here; I think he'll be angry." She jerked her head towards the grazing white horse. "Maybe don't mention I rode his horse either. If he doesn't already hate me, he will then."

"You're wrong, miss. He adores you." Bobby looked up, checking dangling cables with interest. He nodded with approval at the veritable spaghetti covering the joists and running down walls. "All looks good," he said.

"Where will the power come from?" Hana asked, sure Logan had already told her a million times.

"Generator," Bobby replied. "That's what the tradies have been using. It works fine and there's a backup in case something goes wrong." He saw her swivel her head around and anticipated her next question. "There's a water tank and UV filter for rainwater. But there's also a natural spring a hundred metres north so you have a pump on that too." He smiled.

"Should be more than enough for when your girl's a teenager and using up all your hot water."

Bobby laughed, expecting her to join in but Hana didn't. She felt maudlin again. "I'll probably be dead by then or too old to get out of bed. She can use my share."

Hana turned away but found Bobby's strong hand on her upper arm. She saw his eyes flick to her wounded wrist, avoiding causing her pain. His face was close to hers. "Seems to me, miss, you spend too much time thinking." His breath caressed Hana's face, smelling of chewing gum. Bobby lowered his voice and stroked hair away from her cheeks with the back of his hand. "You've got to grab each day with both hands and wring out everything life has for you. Who cares if you feel too old to be a mother again or if some other woman's trying to seduce your husband? You have to put your head down and keep going because sometimes, answers are just around the next corner. Maybe you *should* play tennis again or take up Spanish or line dancing, but the important things are people, Hana. You just spent the last half hour telling me about the people who weren't in your life but now are. That's not a problem, miss, that's a blessing. Decide who you are and then align yourself with those people who let you be *her*. Stop trying to be a superwoman who's all things to all people. We get one go round and we're a long time dead!"

Bobby let go, his eyes flashing with fear as he saw his fingers clasped firmly around Hana's arm. Mutual trust passed between them and she nodded her acceptance. "Seen enough?" Bobby asked, his voice low and confidential and Hana nodded.

"I can't see myself living here," she replied, casting her eyes over the structure worth more money than she'd ever owned. Her green eyes met Bobby's concerned face and he cocked his head and looked sad for her.

"Come on, let's see if those bloody horses are still there," he whispered.

His laugh split the air as under her breath Hana replied, "I hope mine's not!"

Chapter 15

"But I don't want to." Hana complained like a child after they tacked the horses. "You ride her; you promised."

"I did not!" Bobby retorted.

"I bet you can mount her fine," Hana said. "You're lying because you don't want her either." Sacha turned her furry, dappled face towards Hana and her eyes looked sad. Hana ignored her. "Go on, try," she begged the stock man.

Bobby took the reins in his left hand and readied himself to mount the dappled-white mare. Sacha tossed her mane and stepped sideways as he lifted his foot towards the stirrup. He exhaled crossly and repeated the movement with the same result. Bobby tried again and again, looking like he was in a hopping competition and going nowhere fast. "See!" he spat crossly, giving up.

The mare's eyes developed a white rim around her dark brown iris, the blue wall eye on her left already threatening. Bobby leapt out of the way as Sacha turned her backside towards him, ripping the reins from his fingers and raising a back leg to kick him. He jumped out of the way and approached the mare's head, gingerly taking up the reins again as the veins in his neck stood out through his skin. "Get your backside on this mare or I'm leaving you here!" he snapped.

Bobby threw Hana into the saddle with gusto, getting bitten on the bum for trying to tighten the girth.

"You think you're the boss," Hana grumbled to the horse. "I don't understand why Logan loves you, you're a bitch."

Sacha tossed her magnificent mane and trotted towards the track home. Hana tried not to look at the kauri tree in the corner of the section where her husband's and baby's afterbirth were buried, tying them permanently to the *whenua*, the land. Her name would never deserve an inscription on the sacred, *tapu* tree, with a carved picture to denote her lineage. She was a marital interloper, a Du Rose by proxy.

The downward journey was quicker than the upward, the horses imagining Jack pouring feed into their buckets. They jogged steadily downward and Hana settled on Logan's horse, feeling safe enough.

They arrived in the stable yard around midday, making a spectacle for a group of Japanese tourists who captured Hana's ungainly descent on huge cameras around their tiny necks. Sacha showed off, stomping and whirling for her audience and Hana swore as she lifted the bridle off the large head and the horse winked at her. "Did you see that?" she asked Jack and he peered at her lips while Hana repeated it and then shrugged. Jack made Hana shower and groom the mare, enjoying watching her love-hate-relationship with the beast. "But you let Bobby go!" Hana complained and Jack rolled his eyes and ignored her, jabbing his head towards the hose pipe.

As she picked up the huge dinner plate hooves, Sacha rubbed her forehead up and down Hana's bottom, causing her to pitch forwards, grumbling. "Damn horse!" she complained. Jack watched her from the corner of his eye and enjoyed Hana's display of pique.

The Japanese tourists went on a short trek of their own, cameras bouncing around their necks and threatening to garrotte them if they got up any serious speed. Jack got Digger's feed ready in a yellow bucket, pointing out Sacha's diet on a blackboard in the feed room for Hana to mix. "A scoop of this and a pinch of that. *Far out!*" Hana whined, "It's like baking a chuffing cake! She's better fed than me."

Sacha ground her shod front feet noisily along the concrete until her rider appeared with a pink bucket. Hana had chaffage in her hair and over her fleece top. The huge wooden bin was nearly empty, making the tiny crumbs in the bottom hard to reach for someone small and slender. Hana balanced herself on the wooden edge using her stomach muscles, but overreached and fell in face first. She stood on her hands with her legs in the air considering adding vomit to the bin before managing to crawl her way out backwards. Miriam's hat remained at the bottom, unreachable.

Sacha gobbled her grains with greedy enthusiasm and Jack handed Hana's hat over, tears visible in his rheumy eyes. "You stood and watched me struggle, didn't you?" she raged and he pretended he didn't know what she was saying, snorting as he walked away.

When he released her from her duties, Hana stomped back to the mud room, kicking off Liza's boots and leaving the hat on its peg. She brushed her clothes outside the back door, coughing at the chaff dust which blew around her face.

Phoenix slept in her pram in the family dining and Hana stared at it in surprise. "You found my car keys?" she said, relieved. "I realised you might need the pram when I was half way up the mountain."

Leslie pushed the pram with her foot and continued reading her women's magazine, despite the chaos next door. The Japanese visitors who opted not to ride expected a picnic lunch for their coach trip to Rangiriri Pa – an old fortified Māori redoubt on the way back to Hamilton. "I'd quite like to go there," Hana commented. "I've never been."

"Youse go and get cleaned up," Leslie said, eyeing the shroud of dust coating Hana. The old woman seemed nervous as though forcing herself to relax. An odd atmosphere occupied the kitchen and dining room and Hana stared at Leslie without understanding.

"Have I done something wrong?" she asked.

Leslie shook her head. "No, miss. Get clean for lunch; everything's good here." Hana's baby looked porked, breathing heavily like her stomach might pop.

"What do you do to her?" Hana asked, staring at her child. "You realise she'll break the scales at the next baby weigh-in."

Leslie nodded and waved her away and Hana left the room, still feeling as though something was amiss.

She crashed into her room with a huge sigh, falling through the door with exhaustion after a disturbed night and an uncustomary ride. The reason for the nervous women downstairs lay on the king sized bed in his jeans with the telly playing. His motorbike jacket and helmet were on the floor in the corner. He already had the remote in his hand as though about to change channels but flicked the whole thing off instead.

Logan's black hair was glossy from the shower, the damp fringe flicking into his eyes. His torso and feet were bare, the muscles in his biceps ticking as he flexed his hands and turned to fix grey eyes on his wife.

The confidence and resolve Hana found on the mountain top trickled into her stomach, giving her a pain as it passed her belly button. She stood in the doorway as Logan unwound himself from the bed and planted his feet on the floor, saying nothing. A moment of pure panic drove Hana into stupidity and she turned and ran. Her feet skidded on the rimu floorboards in her socks but Logan's bare feet and longer legs caught her before she got very far. He wordlessly snatched her up in his strong arms and carried her wriggling body back to the bedroom, opening the door with his hip. "I'll scream," Hana threatened through gritted teeth as he laid her on the bed, chaff falling from every crinkle and crease in her clothing.

"Go on then," he said smiling, his sparkling grey eyes daring her to. "They know I'm good and that will just confirm it!"

Hana pushed at Logan's muscular chest, not sure why she fought anymore. His eyes flicked over her borrowed riding clothes and deft fingers separated her checked blouse from the cream coloured jodhpurs with ease. "I missed you, *wahine-*," he whispered, growing frustrated with the buttons of the blouse and pinging them off with a single rip. Logan spread the blouse open, his touch producing electric sensations across Hana's skin. She stopped fighting and swallowed all protest, her green eyes studying her husband with the same apprehension as the women downstairs. On home turf he was invigorated and formidable, a commander of a Māori army and Hana felt her belly flutter at his mastery of her.

His lips felt soft over hers, trembling as Logan pressed into Hana's mouth and ran his tongue over hers. Unable to stop the heat of excitement she gave in, just like she always did.

Logan smelled good, his cheeks and chin smooth from a recent shave and his kisses were tender and insistent. Hana tasted aftershave and inwardly cursed her complete lack of willpower, as her husband stripped her naked and set to work, reminding her why they were so good together.

"Did my horse get any chaff?" Logan asked later as he brushed dust and grains from the bed with a dustpan and brush from under the sink. "Or did you just roll in it and tease her?"

"How do you know I rode *your* horse?" Hana asked, pulling a face which showed her open disdain for the stroppy mare.

Logan snorted and pursed his lips. "I went to see her and Jack said she'd gone out with you and Flick. He can't ride her; she only carries Du Roses. That's the way I trained her and that's the way she'll stay." He walked to the bin in the corner to empty the dustpan but Hana plunged into another volley of sneezing.

"Don't put it in there." She grabbed it from him and carried it onto the balcony, watching with satisfaction as chaff flew away on the breeze. Logan smirked as he heard her shout apologies to the knot of Japanese tourists just getting onto their bus, being showered in natural grain.

"How does she know?" Hana asked as she closed the sliding door. Logan looked at her in confusion, his brain already onto the next thing. "The horse," Hana repeated. "How does she know whether you're a Du Rose or not?"

Logan bit his lip and looked sexy, masking a smile as he pulled his tee shirt over his head. "I don't know," he replied. "She just does. I broke her in after I came back from England to stay and she's bucked everyone else off her whole life."

Hana gulped and shook her head. "So she thinks I'm a Du Rose? Is it because I wore Liza's clothes?"

"No, Hana!" Logan's eyes bore into her face, reading her sense of inadequacy; the small fish in a massive pond, drowning. "You are a Du Rose and she knows it."

Hana shook her head and her expression was sceptical. "Whatever," she muttered. She'd insulted the mare from one end of the property to the other and the horse couldn't even tell a real Du Rose from a...whatever Hana was.

Logan's brow furrowed. "I'm not letting you go, Hana, so get used to it. You've belonged to me since I was fourteen so you were a Du Rose even before you knew it. Stop doubting yourself, *wahine*. You're mine."

Hana felt her heart pounding in her breast and a sense of violation eking across her flesh. Somehow Logan understood the root of her problem as though he possessed a secret route into her psyche. Her fear emerged as anger. "I could have been killed!" she exploded.

Logan's smile made her feel foolish instead. "Na, babe. I'm never that rough with you. I know just how you like it." He enfolded her in his arms and planted a sensuous kiss on her neck and Hana heard the moan escape her lips, feeling like the biggest pushover in the North Island.

They went downstairs to reclaim Phoenix and release Leslie, but the old woman was reluctant to hand her back. "Youse two have more time," she insisted. "I love having this little *moko*." Logan looked at the housekeeper oddly as she used the word for 'grandchild' and Leslie relinquished the baby and disappeared up to her apartment with more speed than Hana credited her with.

"Don't you like Leslie?" Hana asked, as she fed her daughter at the dining room table.

Logan shrugged. "We've never liked each other," he replied.

"Why?" Hana asked, watching Logan's eyes darken. Her heart sank. "Don't bother, Logan," she said spitefully. "It seems I'm only a Du Rose when it suits you." She ignored his awkward protests and fell silent. Phoenix produced another horrendous nappy half way through her feed and Hana made Logan deal with her. He was gone a long time.

Hana sat at the table enjoying a cup of tea and listening to the steady clatter of metal food trays and crockery in the industrial kitchen next door. It felt nice to be still for a little while. The women called to one another as they set up for afternoon tea and loaded trays for the restaurant dining room.

Logan returned with a happier baby and handed Phoenix over. "Leslie's been introducing her to boil-ups!" he exclaimed, disappearing to the outside bins with the reeking nappy.

"What's a boil-up?" Hana asked when he returned and Logan shrugged.

"It's everything boiled up."

It sounded logical but without details left the Englishwoman no wiser. Hana fed her baby for a while longer, silent as her brain worked. Logan paced the room, examining the builders' work in opening up the dining room and forming the archway to the kitchen. Logan scrutinised the cornice and skirting boards, nodding with approval. Hana shook her head, wondering how she ever passed muster in his perfectionist world or if he examined and picked at her faults when she was sleeping. She sighed and Phoenix popped out from her tee shirt and grinned. Hana smiled back and tickled the soles of her baby's feet. Phoenix laughed. "Use it or lose it, baby," Hana whispered and her daughter raised an eyebrow in an uncoordinated movement.

"S'up?" Logan asked, pulling out the chair next to Hana and plonking himself on it as though it was a horse. He needed a haircut and his fringe was permanently in his eyes, shuddering with the motion of his eyelashes. His striking looks melted Hana's resolve and she forced herself to look away.

"Nothing."

Logan waited with infinite patience, his grey eyes calm and peaceful like a smooth sea, hiding the danger beneath which could suck Hana in and crush her without mercy. The scar under his right eye looked messy but added to his sex appeal.

"The thing with Amanda," Hana began, as the silence addled her nerves. Her eyes flicked to Logan's face, seeking denial but getting none. "I don't know how to deal with stuff like that. I feel so threatened but you're gorgeous and other women like you." Hana swallowed, feeling an uncomfortable constriction in her chest as her pulse rate increased. "If I stay married to you, I have to relive the Caroline nightmare over and over again but with different women. Caroline's determination to get you back was traumatic and she made my life a living hell. I don't know how to cope because of Vik's affair. I freeze and do nothing because it doesn't matter what I do, I still lose. With Vik I believed I was the last one to know but was I? Did I see it happening like with Amanda and just ignore it?" Hana ran her free hand over her eyes. "I know I can't live like that; it messes with my head too much."

Logan waited for her to stop wrangling and then stroked his fingers down her cheek. "You said *if* you stay married. Are you thinking of not staying married to me, Hana?" His grey eyes bore into her soul, searching and leaving a trace of white light over the delicate surface. "Hana, don't you trust me?"

Hana thought about her answer, certain he would know if she lied. Logan seemed to understand her better than she did. She told him the truth, shaking her head with emphasis. "No, I don't know if I can live with women throwing themselves at you. And no, I don't trust you, Logan."

He nodded, understanding and compassion pouring through his eyes. He inhaled and smiled sadly at his wife. "Then there's nothing for it, is there?"

Hana's pupils dilated in fear at her husband's words. Was there no point continuing a marriage without trust? She wondered that herself often, not wanting to admit her worst fear. Worse than being widowed again was the nightmare of a partner's infidelity and living through the aftermath. Her brow furrowed and she tipped her head like a little bird sensing danger. "What do you mean?" she asked bravely, wishing she'd lied her damn head off.

"I'll have to earn your trust, won't I?" Logan said, taking her free hand in his, kissing the gold band on her ring finger and effortlessly making it seem highly erotic. "I'll show you how much I value our marriage, even if you never believe me. I personally prize honesty far above trust. Trust is earned, not given by right but honesty can be as hard to give and accept. I love your honesty, Hana. I'm satisfied with that for now."

Hana nodded and focussed on the baby, not wanting to fall into Logan's grey eyes without sealing over her vulnerability first. Logan took his index finger and pulled her head up, forcing her to allow him access to her soul. He smiled, mocking her bashfulness with a joke. "But I'm such a handsome devil there'll be more Amandas. I guess we need to work out a plan for you to cope."

Hana slapped Logan's leg, swearing at him and clapping her hand across her mouth looking mortified. "You're so bad for me!" she chastised. "But you're right. What *should* I have done about Amanda?"

Logan grew serious. "I needed you to react like I would if another man chased you. I don't leave you in any doubt I love you. I won't tolerate anyone muscling in on our marriage." Hana's mind drifted to the image of Logan picking Amanda's ex-husband up by the throat and splatting him against the window for standing too close to her. A guilty slice of her consciousness flicked to the tennis player's kiss and she kept her eyes away from Logan.

"I knew what she was up to," Logan continued. "I don't understand why she'd mess with our marriage when her husband wrecked theirs with his affairs, but lonely people do desperate things. It was harmless, flirty, needy crap and nothing physical. I should have spelled it out, but I thought you could see her game; it was so obvious. She refused to leave that night, insisting she needed to see you and short of throwing her out, I put up with her. I couldn't lay hands on her, Hana and I couldn't leave without taking Phoe. When I walked to the bedroom she followed me and that's all you saw; me trapped in the lounge with her because I daren't go anywhere else in the house. I wanted you to defend me - *us*. You needed to tell her to back off, not run away and leave me with the problem. When you finally got mad, you got mad at me and I did nothing wrong. I want you to stand up for yourself. You always jump onto the back foot and assume you can't compete, that you're not good enough. It's crap, Hana. I've told you I only ever wanted you but you don't hear me. You build this *I'm-not-good-enough-wall* and shut me out."

"Sorry," Hana whispered. "I did it again, didn't I? Just ran off without standing my ground."

She looked wretched and Logan pulled her in close, whispering into her curls, "At least this time it wasn't a plane ride, just a run up the highway home. But I wish you'd stop it. I never know whether to come after you or not."

"I never know whether I want you to either," she conceded and Logan laughed.

"Not much hope for me then is there?"

"Logan?"

"What?" his voice was soft and alluring.

"Am I meant to pick people up by the throat and splat them on windows?"

His laugh was low and melodious. "Na, babe. Your arms are way too spindly. I did that with good reason. I don't need you to be like me; one bull in our china shop is enough. Speaking to Amanda is fine; cat fights are ugly and a real turn off."

Logan jumped to his feet and held his hand out to Hana. "Come on, let's raid the chiller while the women are in the restaurant."

He emerged with the spoils of his mission and two spoons and carried the feast up to the bedroom. With Phoenix in the travel cot, they demolished the sherry trifle between them while the kitchen girls searched for it downstairs, blaming each other for misplacing it.

Chapter 16

Sunday arrived far too quickly. Hana woke feeling tetchy in anticipation of the drive back to Hamilton, resenting Logan's insistence she leave the relaxed environment of his hotel. Logan rode up to the new house on Sacha and returned in half the time it took his wife and stock man. Hana laid in bed feeding the baby as a veiled protest.

"That driveway's awesome isn't it?" Logan commented, laying a sleeping Phoenix in the cot. "I made it there and back in a fraction of the time it usually takes."

"Did you stop to pay homage to your name on the kauri tree?" Hana asked facetiously, snuggling into the sheets with her back towards him.

"Oh, you mean the symbol next to my name, the one with the big *ure*."

Hana turned and clapped her hand over his mouth as he mentioned the large phallic symbol on the *tiki* under his name. He laughed and scooted behind her, putting his hands underneath the tee shirt she wore to bed. "Actually," he said, his voice sultry. "I'm putting it on the trek for riding tours. The foreigners can photograph it."

"What it must be," Hana interrupted, "to have such a big...-*ego!*"

"Harsh," Logan replied, pushing his face through her hair and kissing her neck. "Now be a proper Māori wife and please your husband." He bit his lip, teasing her breasts out of her bra and dodging Hana's slaps.

"You arrogant man!" she shrieked, giggling as Logan eased her knickers down and smothered her lips with his.

Hana felt maudlin an hour later in the shower. "I don't want to go back," she complained, shouting over the sound of the water.

"Yeah, yeah," he replied. "I know, Hana."

"Well, don't make me then," she muttered and his handsome face appeared in the doorway.

"I am making you," he said. "You're my *wahine* and I want you with me. If you stay here you'll get bored and distract my housekeeper and leave me vulnerable to the lovely Amanda's charms."

Hana scowled and turned her back on him, bending to soap her thighs. "Last year you talked about coming back to run the hotel and farm yourself; why can't we do that?"

Logan snorted and pushed his hands into his front pockets, his naked torso sexy as he leaned against the doorframe. "You didn't want to, babe."

"What if I've changed my mind?" Hana ran her hands through her wet hair, pushing if off her face and lifting her chest, deliberately manipulating her husband. He smirked and studied her lithe body.

"Are you serious?" he asked, distracted.

"Why not?" Hana replied. "I live in a city and am as isolated as if I was here in the absolute middle of nowhere."

Logan's brow furrowed as he processed her statement, looking sceptical. "Ok," he answered. "But today you come back to town."

Hana rolled her eyes and turned her back, denying him any more pleasure when he wouldn't agree to her staying at the hotel. Logan smiled and returned to the bedroom, clumping around as he stripped the bed. Realising the battle was lost, Hana changed tack. "How come you missed the soccer match yesterday?" she called.

"Wasn't gonna happen," he shouted back. "The other team couldn't raise a full squad so forfeit. Just as well as I didn't want to play and with Collins gone, we don't have a good defender."

Emerging from the bathroom towelling her hair, Hana considered the stroppy groundsman who consistently berated anyone abusing his pristine sports ground. That included walking on it, running on it or even playing on it. Home games were a trial in the wet weather as Collins spent more time fitting clods of precious earth back into their slots than watching the ball. His skill as a defender came from a burning urge to keep the penalty boxes free of gouges or skids and at half time he always got into a temper, realising everyone would change ends. Sliding tackles were the source of instant outrage.

"It's been a week." Hana's brow creased as she squeezed water out of her long tresses into the towel. "Haven't the cops said anything about how he died or why he was in the trench?"

"Not to me." Logan stared at Hana's shapely body and bit his lip.

"No," she said, raising a finger in warning. He sighed and looked sulky.

"The last cop said they're having trouble reaching Collins' family, so can't release his name. It's a pity your son's giving me such a wide berth; he was usually a good source of information. Never mind. We know who died because I saw him and we've inexplicably been a groundsman short all week; people will have drawn their own conclusions. Somebody must know something." Logan continued stuffing his belongings into a backpack.

"I guess the police know what they're doing." Hana lobbed the damp towel on the floor by the door, ready to take to the laundry before they left.

Logan stared sadly at the unmade bed for a moment and Hana knew he didn't want to leave either. She put her arms around him, snuggling into his chest and breathing his aftershave deep into her lungs. "Let's stay here," she whispered. "Nobody would notice."

Logan squeezed her and kissed the top of her head. "Odering would love that. If we disappeared he'd assume I killed Collins. I bet he could find a way to prove it too. He'd probably send out Bodie to arrest me and they could have a double celebration."

"Oh, I didn't think of that," Hana said, chewing her lip. "How can he prove it if you didn't do it?"

Logan cocked his head and raised an eyebrow. "They can do anything, Hana." He dumped his backpack by the door. The room looked empty and unloved. As Hana pulled her sweater over her head and reached for her jeans, Logan grabbed her hand, forcing her to turn and look at him. "The other night," he said and her heart sank, hoping he wouldn't rake over her misery. "It wasn't the best idea for you to be wandering around site in the dark on your own. We don't know how Collins died or why. If there's something going on, we all need to be careful not to get caught up in it." He looked pointedly at the scar on Hana's wrist as it peeked out of her sleeve, gritty and sore after the horse ride. Hana nodded once to show she got the message and then bent to haul her jeans over her legs. She hid her face, not wanting Logan to see her guilt, unable to tell him *she hadn't been alone.*

Driving through Hamilton city, Hana tried to think positively about her return. Her father and Elaine would be back in town by the end of the week, she could see Mark often and her relationship with Izzie was fine; it was possible Marcus simply forgot to pass on her message. As for Bodie, he needed to sort out his own head and Hana decided to be patient.

Logan emptied the Honda while Hana fed the baby, arriving home before her on his motorbike. There wasn't much to unload as Hana arrived at the hotel empty handed.

Phoenix breast fed fine, but screwed up her little face and turned away from the baby rice, making a horrible whining sound. "She won't eat it," Hana said in frustration as Logan carried the change bag through the front door. She had a lump of rice in her hair and raised a finger to her daughter as Phoenix got ready to blow more at her. "No, Phoe! Naughty."

Logan ran his huge hand over the child's fluffy head and she beamed up at him. He leaned down and blew a raspberry on her neck. "You've had the good stuff now, haven't you girly? Daddy's prize moo cow."

Phoenix held her arms out to her side like she was flying and tipped forward and back in the high chair. She looked like a maniac and Hana laughed at her. Logan went to the small pantry and pulled out a cardboard box of rusks. Opening the foil wrapper inside, he broke off a shard and handed it to the baby. Phoenix made a few swipes at it, missing and then seizing it in an iron grip. It went straight into the hole at the front of her face, her eyes alight and excited. It wasn't shepherd's pie or boil-up-beef but it was sugary and different. She gummed it for a while until both she and the high chair were sufficiently smothered.

Logan's neat-freak tendencies were disturbed by the mess his daughter made and he dressed her in properly fitting clothes and changed her nappy. "That rusk's exhausted her," he whispered to Hana, putting her straight into her cot. Hana washed the high chair and the floor underneath it. "Fold it up and lean it against the wall," Logan said, hefting the high chair behind the table. "This place is too small to leave it out all the time." He sighed and looked around him. "Sometimes it feels more like a holiday caravan."

"It's a shoe box," Hana said wistfully.

A succession of sharp raps on the front door shook the whole house and made Hana jump. She opened it with a trembling hand, thinking her moment with Amanda might have arrived.

A uniformed police officer stood on the first step, a clipboard in his hand. He nodded to Hana. "We're making house to house enquiries relating to the suspicious death last week," he said, stopping as Hana's gaze drifted behind him. She wasn't listening, instead watching her son miss out her door and move on to another unit. She tuned back into the officer and stood back to let him in, not understanding why he was there. The officer wiped his feet and sat in the two-seater. Logan nodded to him and raised an eyebrow at Hana as though saying, *see, I told you so.*

Hana emptied the stagnant town water from the kettle and refilled it. "Tea, or coffee?" she asked the policeman and he looked surprised.

"Coffee, please." He looked young, very young, a-still-got-acne-kind-of-young. He slicked his blonde hair back with a trembling hand and Logan's eyes narrowed with interest. Hana looked out of the window and remembered a saying of her father's, '*When teachers and policemen look like children, you know you've gotten old.*'

Hana automatically made her husband coffee. He pulled out a dining chair and did his thing, turning it around and straddling it. It was an action he did it without thinking but the horrified look on the cop's face made Hana turn away to hide her smirk. Logan rested his chin on the back of the chair and studied the man as though he was a zoo exhibit. It was intimidating and Hana saw the cop bridle under Logan's obvious scrutiny.

'*Watch him!*' Acting Detective Inspector Odering told the young police officer. Even Senior Sergeant Johal refused to do this house and he was usually up for anything. The young officer tried to hide his nervousness and ignore Logan's intense stare.

Hana put the coffee next to her husband on the table and raised an eyebrow at him to tell him to stop. Logan smirked, knowing exactly what he was doing. Hana handed the young man his coffee and sat on the sofa with her back to the breakfast bar, sipping her tea and looking at him in expectation.

The officer cleared his throat and pulled the clipboard straight on his knee, beginning with routine questions. Hana answered looking to Logan for help, but he seemed happy for her to recount again where they were the previous weekend, what time they left and when they returned. Hana varied the pace of her speech, getting a bizarre kick from seeing the officer speed up and slow down his frantic scribbling.

"We've identified the deceased as a Mr Larry Collins, grounds keeper here," the officer said. Logan yawned but at least had the decency to cover his mouth. "When did you last see him?"

"Dead or alive?" Logan asked with a wicked glint in his eyes.

The officer became excited until his notes revealed Logan as the person who found the body. "Alive," he said, his attention focussing on him with renewed interest.

A heavy knock on the door prevented Hana answering the question. "It's like Piccadilly Circus!" she grumbled. "Just as we get the baby down, someone hammers on the door!"

With a glance of annoyance at the policeman, she moved quickly to open the door, preventing the visitor rapping again. A pink-cheeked Amanda stood on the front step. "Is Logan there?" she asked boldly, intent on brazening it out in the face of defeat. "I thought you left." Amanda sounded disappointed.

Hana took a deep breath and stepped outside, pulling the door closed behind her. "We've got a cop in there," she replied, hoping Amanda took the hint. She didn't. Still slightly on the chubby side, Amanda tossed her hair and replied, "Mine just left. I need Logan to help me with something."

"No!" Hana's retort was loud enough for the men inside to hear. "Logan won't be helping you now, not ever. Not to undo jars, taps or to warm your bed, if that's what you hoped. And seeing as you can't take a gentle hint, it's best you stay away from us altogether from now on, me included."

Amanda's face dropped as the full ramifications of Hana's words sank in. Extreme loneliness had caused her imagination to run wild, fantasising that the handsome man next door might be interested. She saw the reality of her error as she stood on the cold concrete with the pickle jar clutched in her hand. Having lost her only decent friend and willing babysitter Amanda felt foolish, but guilt made her angry. "What's he been saying?" she spat nastily.

Hana had no intention of arguing. She owed it to herself to guard her marriage with her life; it was God-given and she meant to keep hold of it. "I am sorry for you, Amanda," she said. "I know what it's like to raise children alone, those endless empty nights of worry and inadequacy. But I never tried to mask my own pain by reaching into someone else's marriage and smashing it to pieces." Hana shook her head, held up her hand palm outwards to signal the discussion was over and went inside, shutting the door assertively in Amanda's face.

Amanda's anger bubbled over into pure malice until she remembered Hana was meant to be looking after Millie the next day while she worked an extra half shift. Knowing Hana's kind and forgiving nature, she wondered if she should just turn up with the baby anyway. Otherwise, she was stuck. Amanda slouched back next door feeling a range of thwarted emotions, the strongest of all being self-pity.

Back inside the unit Hana found herself trembling. She hated confrontation and despite hoping to keep her distance from Amanda, had seen instantly it wouldn't work. The friendship was over and Hana's assertiveness shocked her. She clattered around in the small kitchen, aware the men waited for her. Boiling the kettle again, Hana made herself another drink to buy herself time. "Carry on without me," she told the cop, noticing the look of panic on his face. Logan smirked like an evil cartoon king and settled his gaze on the young man again.

Armed with another cup of tea, Hana felt calm enough to sit down again. Logan winked at her, his face positively beatific with happiness. Hana felt as though she'd passed an unwritten test, making *him* feel cherished. She craved a cuddle and felt the overwhelming urge to ground herself in Logan's physical strength.

"Is everything alright, Mrs Du Rose?" the policeman asked and Hana's eyes flicked to his face, wishing he'd leave.

"Everything's fine," she replied. "Are we done now?"

"I asked you when you last saw Mr Collins alive."

"Oh yes," Hana sighed, taking another sip of tea. "It was the Friday before he went missing, at lunchtime. The bell rang for lunch and I walked my daughter to the main field because I knew my husband would be training with the sports teachers there. We watched him for a while. That's when I saw Mr Collins."

The police officer wrote it down longhand on his clipboard. Logan's face took on a curiously dreamy look. He remembered Hana standing on the grass watching him sprint. Her long hair streamed out behind her in the breeze and she wore a pretty red dress and black tights and boots. She looked like an angel and he felt like a king. He remembered she disappeared and his brow furrowed. One minute she was there and the next she wasn't. Logan watched Hana's face, curious as the cop asked her the next question. "Where exactly was Mr Collins?"

"He was walking around the pitches checking the goal posts. I carried Phoenix, my baby, because he hates me pushing the pram over the grass. But he came up raging at me anyway because he said my boot heels dig in and ruin the turf. He told me to get off."

Logan exhaled loudly in exasperation, his fingers gripping the chair back as though he wanted to rip it off the base. "Bloody hell," he breathed.

"They were flat...are flat," Hana said conversationally and both men turned to look at her. "My boot heels," she said. "They're flat ones. They couldn't have dug in; he was being silly."

"What *exactly* did Mr Collins say to you?" the cop asked, frantically scribbling and sounding interested.

"I can't repeat it," Hana said confidently. "It was along the lines of, '*Get your bleep, bleep, bleeping, bleep off my bleep bleep bleeping grass, you bleep bleep stupid bleep!*'"

The policeman looked at her, frustrated. "I'm sorry ma'am, but for the purposes of your statement, it has to be verbatim."

Hana tutted and held out her hand for the clipboard. "I'll write it," she said. "But I might not spell some of it right."

When she finished, she prevented Logan from lurching at the clipboard, handing it directly to the police officer. He gave a low whistle, burying his smirk at some of the phonetic spelling.

"What did he say?" Logan asked, frustrated.

"That answers my next question," the policeman said, sounding disappointed. "Which was, did your husband know what he said. Obviously I can see he didn't."

"Absolutely not," said Hana, making the cop raise his eyebrows. "I told you, I couldn't repeat it; not foul language like that."

"So Mr Du Rose had no idea about this altercation?"

Hana realised the young man had gotten a whiff of a motive for murder and wasn't about to let it go easily. Logan sensed it too and wisely said nothing, keeping his opinions about Larry Collins for later.

"Look officer," Hana said with authority. "Mr Collins was always shouting at someone for something. If I told Logan every time he yelled at me for something since we moved onto the site, I'd be in danger of becoming boring. He yelled at me on Wednesday for putting my sheets on the communal washing line when he wanted to mow the grass, even though he mowed it the day before. He yelled at me on Thursday for double parking on the street outside when my neighbour had visitors and used up all the spaces and I needed to get my shopping and baby out of the car. On Friday, it was walking on the grass and if you want me to, I can go back further. He probably shouted at me every day since we moved in. I got used to it."

Logan shook his head in irritation. "Damn it, Hana! You should've said something and I'd have taken it up with Angus. It's not okay for a member of staff to abuse people like that. If you'd said something..." He shut up but obviously had more to say. Hana had no doubt she'd hear it later.

The policeman let the tempting thread of a lead fall harmlessly to the ground, pursuing a different track. "What about you, Mr Du Rose? When was the last time you saw Mr Collins?"

Logan settled down as he thought about his last conversation with the odious little man. He'd been his usual belligerent self. "It was before I went home on Friday afternoon around three-thirty, as the final bell had just gone. I walked across from St Bart's as we were leaving straight away and Larry almost ran me down on his quad bike. He was raging about the trenches at the back of the dining room. We have a rat problem and the horticulture teacher insists on collecting vegetable rubbish from the boarding house kitchens each day and putting it into a composting trench. It's an old fashioned way of composting and he's using it to demonstrate something to his students. But it's making a bad problem worse."

"What exactly did Mr Collins say to you?" the cop asked, scribbling away, needing to turn his sheet over and write on the back.

"Pretty much the same kind of things he said to my wife. Only probably modified somewhat. He knew he was wasting his time trying to intimidate me." Logan repeated his last conversation with the rude groundsman, adding, "I promised I'd talk to the horticulture teacher on Monday as soon as we were back in work. I agreed with him wholeheartedly that it's a health risk and if Compo still wouldn't listen to me, I'd escalate it to the principal. He grunted and left. I didn't see him again after that. Well, not until Compo dug him up anyway."

The policeman finally stopped scribbling and snapped the top back onto his pen, standing up to leave. He handed Hana his coffee mug and thanked them both, going out into the cold winter air.

"We've got a problem," Logan said thoughtfully to his wife after the front door closed behind the policeman. He wrapped his arms around her and pressed her cheek into his chest. "When Compo dug him up, I knew it was Larry Collins by the shoelaces, even though I couldn't see his face. He was proud of those soccer boots and said they were his 'lucky boots.' Then

I noticed his soccer shorts and shirt. That means he was on his way to the game when he was killed. Nobody can drive in sprigs, it's too dangerous. He must have intended to walk across the ground to the game. We were on the back fields, Hana, so none of us really has an alibi do we? It could have been any of the players or spectators couldn't it? One of us could be his killer."

Chapter 17

The morning sky was clear and blue, but the temperature struggled to get above zero. Phoenix woke early, forcing Hana to get up.

"Sorry," Logan said, walking into the kitchen with a towel wrapped around his waist. "The shower backs onto her wall; I didn't think about it." He winced and ran his hands through the glossy waves of hair at his temple, wiping his palms on the towel.

"I might forgive you," Hana said, watching the bowl of milk spin round in the microwave. "But only because you're naked."

Logan smirked. "I'm not naked."

Hana retrieved the bowl as the microwave pinged and pressed a rusk into the milk, watching it dissolve. Logan leaned across to flick the switch on the kettle and Hana yanked the towel, giggling as it pooled around his feet.

"Not funny!" he exclaimed as the first fifteen rugby team took a shortcut past the house.

"Hi, sir," they shouted, seeing only Logan's head and bare shoulders. He waved and waited until they passed before grappling for the towel.

Hana paused until he got it almost fixed around his waist and then yanked it again.

"Come back to bed," Logan said, grinning, clinging to the towel.

"Can't," Hana replied, losing the tug of war. Phoenix smelled the warm rusk and squealed.

"Yeah, yeah, excuses," he breathed, leaning in and kissing her neck.

"Hi, sir!" Another voice heralded the arrival of the second fifteen and Logan waved again.

"I hate this place!" he snapped, dropping to his knees and crawling to the bedroom. Phoenix spotted him as his head bobbed past the high chair and she squawked and giggled hysterically.

"Your daddy's a worry," Hana said, smiling at her daughter and sitting opposite. The child's eyes flashed with excitement at the sight of the steaming bowl and she waved her arms and opened her mouth like a baby bird. Phoenix loved the rusk mixture, woofing it quickly and topping up with a breastfeed. "That nice, baby?" Hana asked as the child burped easily and snoozed in her mother's arms.

Hana washed and changed her, finding her sleepy enough to pop into the pram while she showered and dressed.

"Caught ya," Logan said, sliding his arms around Hana's damp body as she towelled herself dry. He nipped the soft skin underneath her hair, his aftershave perfuming the surrounding air. "Now who's got the upper hand?"

"You have, Mr Du Rose," Hana breathed, turning to face him.

"Shame I'm due in the office early then, isn't it?" Logan smiled coyly at his wife and pulled her into him, smoothing her fringe away from her forehead. He sighed. "Odering wants to see me so I figure it's going to be a long day." He ran his palm over the small of her back. "See ya later, babe." He winked and left the room.

Hana wrinkled her nose and sulked. She dressed, a thought nagging at the back of her mind. "I'm sure I had to do something today," she mused. She tidied the tiny living area and then felt bored. Seizing the moment while Phoenix slept, she walked into town, arriving on the Boundary Bridge within half an hour. Mist drifted up from the river and Hana paused on the bridge to watch it wafting upwards as though alive. The Waikato River was the legendary source of the famous Hamilton fog, which dogged the city's reputation. "Oh no, Millie!" Hana clapped her hand over her mouth, remembering the forgotten obligation as the river surged beneath her. She quelled the instant flash of guilt. Amanda would be a fool to expect her to honour a babysitting session as though nothing had happened. "I wouldn't leave you with someone who was mad at *me*," she grumbled to the sleeping baby.

The baby opened as Hana arrived, the friendly shop assistant beckoning her in. "What can I help you with?" she asked, turning the sign in the doorway to 'open.'

"I'm just looking," Hana admitted, perusing the racks of baby clothes.

The assistant nodded and asked Hana to call her if she needed anything. "Where do I start?" Hana mused to herself, wandering through the shop. She eyed the baby food and bottle paraphernalia, contemplating buying ready meals for her hungry daughter. It was a risky business raising children, according to the experts. They lectured on the threat of bacteria, bugs and illnesses from pre-natal classes to warnings on virtually everything baby related. Hana successfully raised two healthy children without a mother's assistance and had the sense to know her child wouldn't necessarily be maimed if her feeding bowl and spoon went through the dishwasher instead of the steriliser.

"How's the steriliser working out?" the assistant called, remembering Hana from her last hurried visit. Hana smiled and nodded, not wanting to lie so saying nothing. "That was a good model you bought. We've sold heaps of them."

"Lovely," Hana said, moving guiltily to the other end of the shop. Before her disastrous kidnapping, Hana purchased a steriliser and bottles, expressing milk for her child while she went to reason with Michael Laval. Following Hana's absence and her time in hospital, even the sight of a rubber teat sent Phoenix into a panic and for a long time, plastic drink bottles produced an unhappy bottom lip and a whimper.

"How would you feel about writing a review?" the assistant called, hefting a mountain of baby vests onto the counter and beginning to stuff them onto tiny hangers.

"Oh, I'm not great at that kind of thing," Hana lied, remembering the shards of plastic still outside the laundry door. In a fit of anger after Hana's not so safe return, Logan took the expensive steriliser outside the back of the unit and smashed it into thousands of hazardous pieces, which he then swept up. With Bodie and Izzie, Hana went to great lengths to ensure their bottles and bowls were sterile before food or drink went into them. Then she caught them eating things off the carpet, licking the unhealthiest surfaces and putting everything into their mouths. Third time around she felt more philosophical about her child rearing expertise.

Balancing a metal basket on top of the pram, Hana examined the labels on the baby food, trying to make sure she didn't stuff her child full of chemicals. It all seemed a little too chemically enhanced and she settled on reasonably safe jars of cauliflower cheese and some apple puree.

Phoenix stayed asleep, swaddled up against the damp cold with blankets and clothing. Even the little hand near her face wore a cloth mitten, but Hana had cut the thumb out so she could still suck it. Hana examined the sleep suit range again, totting up the available cash in her purse. The rent from her Achilles Rise house covered the mortgage on Culver's Cottage and Logan gave her money each week for general housekeeping, although she wouldn't ask him for extra. He found her frugal attitude ironic after his previous fiance who ran through money like water and made him feel like a human cash point machine.

But that was the reason Hana felt she needed to be different. She had managed her money alone for nine years and her marriage to a multi-millionaire hadn't changed that.

Hana walked around the shop doing sums in her head, knowing after the supermarket shop and gas for the car, she wouldn't have enough left. The cash card for their joint account seemed to burn a hole in her wallet and she cringed. Fondling the pretty suits hanging on the rails, she texted Logan and waited, working out whether he'd be able to text back or not. He'd be in his tutor group, sorting out his boys for the day, reading out notices and dealing with problems.

She browsed, keeping her eye on three little suits for her baby which could replace the tight ones. The shop assistant hovered, desperate for a sale and Hana skirted the shop avoiding her, hoping she didn't suspect her of shop lifting. *Awkward*.

Her phone rang as her mind drifted, making her jump and ratch around in her pocket for its noisy shape. She hauled it out and answered in a whisper as though she was in church. Logan's voice echoed in the corridor outside his classroom. "Babe, get what you need. You don't have to ask me!" he said, for the hundredth time. "It's for our baby, you don't have to ask. Use the joint account; that's what it's for."

"I've forgotten the pin number," Hana stage whispered.

Logan smiled and reminded her, "It's your initials in binary, remember?"

"Oh, yeah. Thanks." Hana ended the call and put the phone back in her pocket.

Back at school, Logan stood in the corridor watching his class through the glass panel in the door. They sensed him looking and worked quietly, heads down. He shook his head and wondered if his wife would ever learn to trust her instincts where money was concerned. They were financially secure, yet she always asked him before using his money. Logan leaned against the wall, one knee bent and the sole of his boot against the plaster, thinking about Hana. Each time he told her she didn't need to ask, he retained a small hope she still would; not so it gave him power, but because it made him feel included. No one else in his life cared what Logan Du Rose thought unless they were schoolboys or an opponent he had dismembered physically or financially.

His mind strayed to Miriam. She'd cared in her own way and he missed her. The pain of her suicide had dulled to a familiar ache just under his breastbone. He wished she could rise from the dead like Hana's father and controlled a flash of jealousy.

Logan breathed out slowly, controlling the pain as a wad of paper flew through the air towards the front of the classroom. The boys nearest the door looked ashen, trying not to catch Logan's eye through the glass or warn the paper thrower. It wouldn't make any difference. The trajectory meant the teacher knew exactly who threw it. He waited with his hand on the door, bursting in as the next one whizzed across the room and catching the culprit with his arm still in the air. The stupid grin disappeared from the boy's face and he paled and chewed his lower lip. Logan closed the door quietly and beckoned to him with his finger, his stone grey eyes not looking amused as he pulled the wad of detention slips from his tight trouser pocket.

Hana bought four jars of baby food and two of the sleep suits. Then she headed along the street to a shop on the corner which would horrify Logan if he knew. She wandered into the second hand shop and browsed. Phoenix still needed clothes and it wasn't that Logan was a snob, but more that he grew up wearing seconds with no choice. It reminded him how life was for his family with Alfred Du Rose ruining a thriving family farm through lack of business acumen, watched by a brother who could have put it right, had he been allowed. The four Du Rose children were worked hard, fed the bare minimum and wore whatever came their way. Ironically the township folk didn't know how bad things were, or that the affluent farm was in a slow but certain decline. They might have shared had they known, but the Du Roses were too proud to admit their failings. Logan and his brothers wore each other's clothes, fighting over socks without holes in the winter and going to the cow shed with bare feet when they didn't win. Logan told Hana that once, when his feet were turning blue with cold and his toe nails were red rimmed with the pain of it, Michael told him to pee on his own feet to warm them. Logan couldn't, not even when his brother did and enjoyed the momentary warmth. "Harden up, man!" Michael exclaimed as Logan threw up behind the milking machine. It was the reason behind his compulsive neat freak trait as if living with nothing bred a mania for taking care of possessions. If it wasn't worn out, it stayed until he couldn't mend it any longer.

Hana found some lovely suits, cheap enough to pay for with the coins in her purse. She bought six, increasing in size to keep Phoenix dressed for a while. The bonus was a packet of pretty pink knitting wool in a bargain bin in the corner.

"That's beautiful," the elderly lady behind the counter remarked and Hana smiled.

"Yes, I've got a pattern for a matinee coat which would suit this colour."

"Wonderful," the woman remarked, peeking into the pram. "You got some needles, dear?"

Hana nodded, looking forward to Logan's next night duty when she could knit, instead of dreading it. "That was productive," she said happily to the sleeping baby, setting off for home. On the bridge her phone rang and she stopped and fished it out of her pocket, sticking a finger in one ear so she could hear against the traffic. She gathered it was Amy but couldn't understand what she was saying. "Sorry love," Hana shouted into the phone. "I can't hear you. Could you text me and I'll call you back when I'm off the bridge. It's too noisy here. I'll ring you back in a minute if that's okay." Then she hung up, hoping it wasn't an emergency.

Her phone beeped in her hand as she left the bridge and negotiated the traffic lights to cross the road. *Jas broke his arm yesterday and can't go to school until tomorrow. Bo was meant to come this morning so I could start work at 11 but got called in. I don't like to ask you again, but please could you come here for a few hours until he gets here?'*

Hana looked at the time on her phone, registering it was only nine-thirty and texted back she was around the corner. At the roundabout, she turned right instead of left and made her way to Amy's house on a side street in Claudelands. Amy flung the door open and greeted Hana with relief. "I don't know how I ever managed without you," she said. "I'm always in a mess when I see you lately."

Amy helped Hana bump the pram up the side steps and into the hallway, putting the brake on and peering in at Bodie's baby sister. "She's such a stunning little girl," she breathed.

The hallway was freezing so Hana left Phoenix in her blankets. She followed the young woman into the kitchen, nerves biting at her. "I'm not sure Bodie will be happy to see me here," she admitted. "He pointedly ignored me last night." Hana sat at the kitchen table, electing to keep her warm jacket on. "Sorry," she said abruptly, reaching under her chair, "I didn't take my shoes off."

"Don't," Amy said decisively as she filled the kettle. "You'll need the insulation!"

"Is Jas ok?" Hana asked concerned. Usually he appeared as soon as he heard her voice, enfolding her in one of his special cuddles which made her feel extraordinarily loved and wanted.

"Asleep on the sofa," Amy answered, bashing the tea bag in the mug hard enough to bust it open. She swore and started again. The kettle hadn't boiled yet, so she beat the bag for the sake of it. Already in uniform, Amy was wired and it made Hana nervous. "He had a dreadful night. I gave him the drugs they prescribed at the clinic and he threw up. I risked some at eight this morning and he's been asleep ever since."

"What happened?" Hana asked.

"Jas argued with his dad," Amy said, biting her lip and leaving the tea bag alone for a moment. "He kept saying he wanted Poppa Logan and not Bo and Bo stalked out and left us. He did a lot of swearing first, but went back to the police house. He was meant to come back an hour ago but texted to say he was at work. I don't even know if that's true or if he's just avoiding us, but I have this new boss at work who's making my life an absolute hell! Four of my colleagues have put in for a transfer. If I take today off after yesterday's fiasco at the hospital with Jas, he'll put me on report!"

Amy managed a mug of tea without bits floating on the surface and Hana took it gratefully. "I meant what happened with his arm," she said, sipping the hot liquid.

"Oh, Bodie took him to the swings and they were being silly on those overhanging bar things. Bo said another child pushed Jas when he was hanging and before he could grab him, Jas was on the ground with the bone sticking out of his arm. Bo said the kid's mother was apologetic, but he took him straight to the hospital. I got a call via the control room. This new guy won't let us have our cell phones on during shifts."

The young woman sounded at her wits end. Hana felt bad about pulling the plug on her free wedding but didn't see another solution under the circumstances. She reached out and took Amy's hand in hers and to her surprise, Amy dissolved into tears. "I'm sorry about your wedding," Hana said. "But I won't let Bo take Logan's generosity and then speak badly behind his back. What he said was spiteful and it hurt my husband, hearing Jas refer to him as *the spare*."

Amy cried even harder and Hana fetched a dish towel in the absence of tissues. She dried her tears but managed to stop herself before she blew her nose. "It's not just that," Amy sniffed. "My period's late as well now. We had a massive row after Bo came back from work. He said you'd told him he had to pay Logan back, so we'd have to delay getting married and I lost my temper. I told him it was all because of his big mouth, I was sick of him and we were finished." Amy ran her hand over the kitchen table and Hana pulled her elbows back in horror, guessing what came next. "I knew I was a week away from my period and it would be okay, but I don't think it is. It was all a bit spontaneous and frenzied and then Bo got up and left. He hasn't spoken to me properly since. We were trying to be good until we got married. Bodie felt strongly about it and I taunted him and accused him of trying to impress you and he got mad and we did it and now see where it's got us. *And* on the kitchen table. Jas could've come in or anything."

Hana patted Amy's hand and squeezed her fingers, trying to show love instead of condemnation. "Oh, no!" Amy groaned, putting her forehead on the table. "I shouldn't be telling you any of this."

"It's okay." Hana said softly, "stuff happens. He'll get back from it. He's probably just disappointed in himself."

"How come you're not mad?" Amy asked, sounding incredulous. "You weren't even mad when you found out about Jas. Does nothing shock you?"

Hana let go of Amy's hand and sat back in her chair, narrowing her eyes at the younger woman. "I was never mad. Believe me, I understand from bitter experience how these things happen. I guess I was disappointed at first but I got over it. The disappointment was more about my failure with Bodie than him having a son. It shouldn't have taken him a couple of months to tell me the truth and I feel cheated because I've missed four years of Jas' little life. He's a credit to you; you've done a good job, especially because you've done it alone and I know how hard that is. I never influenced Bodie not to sleep with you; that was his doing. I didn't sleep with Logan until after we married but I can't dictate to my grown up children."

"Bodie's angry," Amy said. "He thinks you've got double standards."

"What do you mean?" Hana looked confused.

Amy shook her head. "I shouldn't have said anything; ignore me."

"I can't now," Hana said, worry making furrows in her brow. "What did I do?"

"You said you didn't sleep with Logan and then had Phoenix eight months after you married."

Hana's jaw dropped and pain crossed her face. "Really? He thinks that?" She shook her head.

Amy waved her arms around. "See, I shouldn't have told you. It doesn't matter."

"It does to me." Hana clenched her jaw and seethed. "Phoenix was premature. She was underweight and tiny, born on top of a mountain after my mother-in-law bloody killed herself and I watched." Hana ran a shaking hand over her face.

"You're going to leave now, aren't you?" Amy's voice sounded pleading and her face crumpled. "Please don't go. I've nobody else to ask for help." She sat up, rubbing the remainder of her eye makeup all over her eyelids and cheeks, resembling a panda bear. "When Bodie turned up last year and worked out Jas was his son, it was like a dream come true. He visited all the time and I couldn't get enough of him. Then he got all religious on me and it ruined everything; I thought he'd gone off me. Then he proposed and explained we shouldn't sleep together and I didn't like it, but it was fine because there was an end in sight. He's really good…" Amy looked sideways at Hana again. Bodie's mother cringed.

"Yeah, maybe don't go there," Hana replied, wincing.

"Anyway, the other night was fantastic…" *Still too much-*, Hana thought, feeling embarrassed but Amy was oblivious. "Now I don't know where I stand. And when Jas started crying for Logan again last night, I thought Bo would blow a gasket. Sometimes he goes to this dark place and I can't follow him there. It's horrid. Maybe it'd be best if we stayed friends for Jas but left it at that."

The thought obviously caused her more misery than relief because Amy's tears flowed relentlessly. "What if I'm pregnant again? What will I do?"

Hana stood and put her arms around Amy, pulling her tightly into her. "It'll be okay," she whispered, "*it will be okay.*"

By the time Amy left for work at half past ten, she looked better. A fresh application of makeup and a good chat with Hana turned her back into the capable policewoman. She climbed into her beaten up old vehicle and went to work to face her new boss, along with all the other reluctant cops in her group. Her period was two days late and Hana convinced her it might be stress.

Jas snored on the sofa in the living room and Hana covered him with a throw she found on the back of a battered armchair. She wandered around tidying up, putting things away where she thought they might live, finding a heap of dirty washing on the floor of the laundry. Hana stuffed it into the machine and set it off, remembering the second hand sleep suits at the last minute and dragging them from the change bag. She shoved them into the whites wash reasoning at least if they were clean and ironed, Logan wouldn't know they were second hand.

Settling herself in the kitchen, Hana retrieved the wool and needles from the pram and cast on a line of knitting, beginning the little jacket. She knitted for an hour but neither of the children stirred so she raided the pantry and fridge, putting together a shepherd's pie for lunch for the boys, guessing she'd leave as soon as Bodie arrived. The sky outside remained a clear, beautiful blue after the mist although the cold breeze never lifted.

"Holidays at the end of next week," she whispered to herself, allowing the thought of escaping the staff unit to cheer her heart. She hoped they would go home to Culver's Cottage or back up to the hotel and looked forward to it as she mashed the potatoes. Hana put a tiny bowl of food aside for her baby, squishing it hard with a fork to make it extra mushy and hoping she wasn't half way through feeding her when Bodie arrived. Amy wasn't due home until six o'clock and Hana hoped she wasn't stuck there until then, not knowing if that was worse than being trapped in the kitchen with her son's obvious, glowering anger.

Phoenix woke up at midday and enjoyed her mother's cooking. "Try to keep it in your mouth, Phoe," Hana complained as the child poked it in and out with her tongue. She sat in Jas' booster chair, wedged against the table. There was an awkward moment as Phoenix sneezed with a mouthful of brown stuff. "Thanks," Hana groaned as she picked the bits out of her fringe. Phoenix ate the lot and Hana praised her. "You're so different to Izzie and Bo," she said. "They were picky and difficult, but you're just like your daddy. I think you'll be tall, like him."

The child's eyes widened with excitement as she searched the room for her father, disappointed when he didn't appear.

Hana relented and fed Phoenix a chocolate pudding. The baby ate half and then did a giant burp which shook the kitchen. Then she refused to eat anymore. Hana changed her nappy on the kitchen table and felt glad that the householders couldn't see her. "Let's not tell Aunty Amy," she told her daughter, feeling guilty at making such a small person complicit when she couldn't even speak. "I think this table's had enough action for a while."

Hana unloaded the washing machine one handed, balancing her baby on her hip. Phoenix seemed interested, watching intently, her grey eyes missing nothing. Hana kissed her on the side of her head and she smiled and made her own little kissing sounds. "Now, how do I hang it all on the line and hold you?" Hana pondered, seeing how overgrown and dank the back garden looked. Broken shards of pottery littered the concrete and the scrubby grass was mud and weeds.

In a feat of organisation and diplomacy which would have impressed the United Nations, Hana pushed the pram to the laundry and bumped it down the steps still holding the baby, then she put the heavy basket into the pram, tipping it by accident so half the contents needed putting back in. Leaving the back door open in case Jas called, Hana pushed the pram to the washing line and swapped the basket of clothes for the baby. "That was complicated," she told her daughter as she strapped her in. "I'm getting too old for this." The effort made her feel exhausted and Hana clutched at a momentary pain beneath her ribs. She pegged the washing on the line, hanging the fresh-smelling baby clothes nearest to the house to aid her getaway when Bodie returned.

When she turned around talking to Phoenix in a baby voice, she found her son watching her from the open doorway; his face unreadable. Hana snatched the little sleep suits down and turned, biting her lip. Bodie shook his head, taking them from her and hanging them back on the line. He put his arms around her and she didn't know whether to feel afraid or relieved. He said nothing as he bumped the pram up the back steps into the house, but he unclipped his sister and cuddled her to him for the very first time, letting her play with the buttons on his work shirt until she tried to pull them into her mouth.

"I thought you might be hungry." Hana dished up a plate of food and warming it in the microwave. Bodie picked at it for a while without enjoyment. Hana hovered, not daring to start a conversation which might escalate and leave her swiping the baby suits off the washing line in a hurry. Bodie kept Phoenix on his knee and she opened and shut her mouth like a little bird as he fed her his mashed potato. "She'll explode," Hana said, her voice sounding jarring and loud in the eerie silence.

"Sorry," Bodie replied, pushing the plate away.

With no further hope of more lunch and already topped up by a breastfeed, Phoenix popped her thumb in her mouth, leaned back against her brother's chest and dozed. Bodie cuddled her, looking pensive and exuding misery.

"I should check on Jas and then go," Hana said. She walked to the lounge and peered at the little boy asleep on the sofa. Soft snores meant he was fine, just suffering from lack of sleep and a drug induced peace. "He's still zonked out. Amy gave him some pills from the hospital so keep an eye on him…" She stopped herself telling her son how to look after his own child. "There's more pie if he's hungry when he wakes up," Hana said, trying to keep her voice light. She retrieved the suits off the line. They were damp but no longer wet. She folded them and shoved them under the pram inside the bag and rammed her knitting into the change bag, pushing the stitches up the needles and stabbing them into the ball of wool to stop them escaping. Then she wrestled a struggling baby into her coat and woolly hat and laid her in the pram. Bodie watched his mother preparing to leave, without comment. Hana got as far as the kitchen door.

"Mum," Bodie said, his voice barely a whisper.

Hana turned and faced him, her beautiful Indian son wrestling with conscience and rage. "Yes?"

"I don't know what to do about anything."

"I don't have any answers, Bodie." He pouted and looked disappointed as though having expected Hana to bail him out of his worries. Something in her snapped. "And just for the record, I wasn't pregnant when I married Logan; just in love." She bit her lip, knowing the next sentence would sound cruel but needed to be said. "Bo, I need to tell you something. I thought my father was dead, but he isn't; he's here in Hamilton but only for a few more weeks. I'm telling you so you can see him, if you want to."

"What?" Bodie looked confused and Hana put her hand up, asking him not to interrupt. "He's gone travelling and will be back on Friday. He'd like to see you. He married my aunt and...it's complicated." She shut up and considered her words without her own personal wrangling. "He's a good man, Bo. You'll like him. We had a misunderstanding many years ago and I haven't seen him since before you were born. Between us we've wasted a quarter of a century thinking badly of each other and yet missing each other. My brother, Mark's here too; he works at the hospital. I didn't know, but he repaired this." Hana pulled her sleeve up to reveal the mess of scarring on her wrist. "It's up to you anyway; let me know what you decide."

"Is this about you and me?" Bodie pursed his lips and stared at Hana. "Is this an allegory about kids who fall out with their parents? Are you warning me what will happen if I don't play nice and pretend everything's ok?"

Hana shook her head. "No, son; my father's genuinely in town. Your relationship with me is separate. I don't know what to do about us, sweetheart. You've pushed me beyond what's reasonable this time and I don't know how to be around you anymore. I accepted Amy but you can't seem to accept my husband. We've gone round in circles with this until I'm tired of it. You make your own decisions. Please tell Jas I was here and that I love him."

Hana bumped the pram down the front steps and went back to the unit, feeling sick about the whole conversation. A heaviness pervaded her movements and made her heart feel as though it was lodged in her stomach.

Bodie sat where Amy had hours earlier, his forehead in the same spot on the table. He felt like he'd been kicked in the stomach, not understanding how a dead man could suddenly reappear in New Zealand. "I can't cope with all this crap," he complained to the empty kitchen. He'd genuinely been called back to work that morning by an angry Odering. "What the hell were you thinking, man?" The detective yelled. "I asked you to collate the information from the house to house enquiries before you left yesterday."

"I didn't think it was that urgent and I needed to take care of my son," Bodie replied. "He broke his arm yesterday morning."

"So that's why you were late in?" Odering bawled and Bodie nodded, feeling like a schoolboy. "Job first, Johal!" Odering snapped.

"What, and end up like you?" Bodie replied, losing his temper. "Just let me go back to the job I signed on for and get yourself another sidekick!"

Odering shouted for a good ten minutes without drawing a breath. It was impressive as was the shade of purple his cheeks went. Bodie fixed his eyes on the wall and ignored him, hoping Odering lost his 'acting' inspector status and became his equal again. Then he'd give him a slap he wouldn't forget in a hurry.

To compound matters, Jas had kicked off on his return from hospital, wanting Logan. Bodie saw the red mist coming down over his eyeballs at his son's rejection of him for the tall Māori. He knew he was channelling his anger into a dangerous hatred of Logan and the problem was pure jealousy. He deliberately ignored Amy's frantic texts that morning, including the one which said in capital letters, 'YOU'RE AN ARSEHOLE, I MISSED MY PERIOD AND I HATE YOU.'

After finishing Odering's urgent paperwork, he headed straight for the rest home and the comforting old priest, Father Sinbad. Amy was already angry at him so Bodie chose avoidance as a reasonable tactic under stress. Father Sinbad was a steadying influence on him as usual, listening and not judging. Bodie told him everything, even the bit about the sex on the kitchen table. He fancied he saw a flicker of amusement in the priest's face, but couldn't be sure. The old Irishman prayed for him in Latin with his hand on the young man's head and it made Bodie want to cry. He stared at the chequered blanket lying on the useless legs, watching as unshed tears blurred the navy blues and reds into a colourless mess. Then the old man hauled himself forwards and kissed Bodie on the forehead with paternal tenderness. "I don't know what to do," Bodie whispered.

"Forgive yourself," Father Sinbad whispered back. "Abba Father heard you say sorry da first time. You don't have to keep saying it and punishing dat lovely girl of yourn. Hair shirts and birching are for fools who don't understand de power of forgiveness and grace. And dey are darn itchy, believe me! There's no need. Accept your wrongs and move on." The strong Irish accent was comforting and soft. "You know in yer heart dat it's not de Māori's fault. He's someone to blame for what you're feelin'. Let it go, young one, let it go."

A paroxysm of coughing sent Bodie to fetch a nurse. She fitted an oxygen mask over the old priest's face and asked him to leave. Bodie felt frightened then. "I didn't ask him about his holiday," Bodie said, his face ashen.

The matron soothed him. "Don't worry, his holiday wasn't great. He's had a few coughing fits lately; he'll be fine. Go home and I'll ring you if there's a problem." She patted Bodie's shoulder, remembering the small dark skinned boy who visited the priest for service points while still at school. The old man had no visitors and it was a match of unforeseeable success. The priest often talked to Bodie and Hana, although he never shared their secrets, which was a relief for the matron as it meant he didn't share hers either.

Bodie sat at the kitchen table and groaned with misery, ruing the terrible mess he'd made of his fresh start in Hamilton.

Hana wandered back to the unit as Phoenix shuffled around and then slept. She thought she might dry the sleep suits on the towel rail in the bathroom but wondered if she'd have the energy to do more than crawl in the front door. Tama's car was back at the unit and when Hana got in, she found Logan there too. "I'm glad you're home early," she said, feeling relief at the sight of his capable hands pulling the pram up the steps.

"Night duty, babe," he said apologetically. "Did you forget? I'm just doing some marking in my free period before I go over."

Hana nodded and tried not to look so upset, holding on to the thought of her knitting. "How's the marking going?" she asked and Logan shook his head.

"Hopeless, Tama keeps making me laugh."

Tama snorted and Hana looked from one to the other, feeling exasperated. Logan stroked his daughter's forehead and sat back at the table. "Oh, no, listen to this one," he said to an eager Tama, including Hana in his audience. "Question: Which way do Muslims face when praying?"

"Ooh, I know this one," Tama said. "East towards Mecca." He looked pleased with himself until Logan shook his head and read the boy's answer.

"Answer: F...f....f."

Hana looked at her husband, a quizzical look on her face. Logan only stuttered when he was nervous and he didn't seem unduly troubled.

"Frontwards!" he exclaimed. "Muslims face frontwards." The men dissolved into hysterics. "Question: Talk about a bible character and their achievements. This kid's written, '*Moses went up on Mount Cyanide to get the Ten Commandments. He died before he ever reached Canada.*' I shouldn't have taken this class," Logan wept, "I can't teach Year 9 Religious Studies; it's killing me!"

Hana pushed the pram into the baby's bedroom so Phoenix could continue sleeping without the men waking her. She went into her own bedroom and hung her jacket in the wardrobe, grateful for the warm air from the heat pump which made the unit more bearable than Amy's place. Hana swapped her boots for her slipper-socks and padded into the bathroom, turning the towel rail on and hanging the damp suits over it to dry.

Logan found her in the bedroom and laid on the bed, tapping his chest in invitation.

"I'll get mascara on your expensive shirt," Hana said, her brow knitting in frustration.

"Don't care," Logan replied and held his arms out to her. "What's the matter, babe? Where did you go? I thought you'd run away again." He nuzzled his face in her hair, breathing in the scent of shampoo and the strange aroma of Shepherd's Pie.

Hana shook her head and snuggled closer. "No, I'm still here."

"So why don't you sound happy about it?" Logan asked. "You didn't pick up your phone. I texted to tell you I was home but then the boy turned up."

Hana sighed, "Sorry, I turned it on silent so it didn't wake the children. Amy called me in a panic. Jas broke his arm yesterday and couldn't go to school and she had to go to work. So I babysat him until Bo got home."

"How was it?" Logan asked, determined to stay out of her relationship with her children but trying to show support and kindness.

"I honestly don't know," she replied. "He didn't want me to go at first, but then didn't talk. So I don't know; I guess it's just the same as it was last week."

"How's the little guy?" Logan asked, his soft spot for Jas obvious.

"He was asleep. Apparently he'd been up since yesterday so Amy gave him pills from the hospital. He seemed fine but slept on the sofa the whole time. She thought he could go back to school tomorrow, but he didn't look well enough. Who knows? Little boys are resilient. He could be crawling the walls by tomorrow, or I could get another call."

Hana sounded wistful and Logan bit his lip. "Sorry I'm doing so many lates," he sighed. "I hate the tiny single beds in the staff bedrooms. I get in my sleeping bag and sit in the restroom on the sofa. The beds aren't long enough and smell disgusting. I'd rather be here with you."

Logan kissed his wife with regret before leaving, taking his marking with him. Hana laid on the bed thinking and her husband's space was quickly filled by Tama, who slipped next to her and lay there, looking intense. Hana reached out and stroked his face. "I missed you," she said. "Where did you go?"

"On a date," he replied, his eyes shining and Hana groaned with dread. "No, it's fine this time, she's only a couple of years older than me and so hot. She's the same as you."

"Do you mean she's got orange hair or that she's knackered?" Hana asked, yawning and turning onto her back.

"No, Ma! Christian. She goes to church and everything."

Hana wondered fleetingly what *everything* was as she stared at the flickering spots on the ceiling. "Who is she?" She tried to sound interested, remembering Tama's infatuation with Anka and the utter misery it caused.

"She's that lady cop, her name's Lucy and she's twenty-two. We got on really well. We drove over to Tauranga for the day though because apparently I'm still a suspect in that guy's murder." Hana looked at him sideways and pulled a worried face. "No, it's okay," he reassured her, "you're a suspect too."

"Oh great," she said without enthusiasm. "I don't suppose Lucy told you anything about the case, did she?"

Tama smirked. "She might have," he said coyly, "but I don't want to risk her breaking up with me if I tell." He looked genuinely worried, gnawing at his full lower lip.

"It's ok; I don't need to know. I guess I'll find out soon enough," Hana replied. She stroked Tama's dark hair. "I think

Amy's in a bit of a mess financially," she said, changing the subject. "What do you think?"

Tama shrugged. "House is a dump. But don't cops get paid well?"

"It's not that," Hana replied. "When her husband let her have the house in the divorce settlement, he signed it over with mortgage still outstanding. They were in negative equity but she accepted it so he could move on after her affair. It's falling down and the upkeep's killing her. I'm guessing as a single mother she refused to name Bodie as the father, so for years she's been doing it tough. I feel sorry for her but I'm not sure how to help, especially as I just denied her a decent wedding reception."

"You're so sweet, Ma. Are you sure you got the right son at the hospital? Like, you didn't accidentally pick up the wrong brown baby?"

"Don't be mean."

Tama cuddled up to her, laying his head on her shoulder and Hana put her arm around him, reminding herself that despite his man's body, he was still an overgrown boy. She wondered if any other female in his world ever showed him physical affection not attached to a sexual encounter.

"Ma," he said quietly and she looked down at him. "Lucy said the dead guy was hit in the face with a blunt object. The medical examiner identified it as the shovel used to dig the trench. Lucy said the time of death was sometime on Saturday morning, which means it could have been anyone at the boarding house or soccer game. The cops still have no motive, apart from the fact the guy was a complete git."

Hana sighed. "I hope and pray Logan didn't touch that shovel."

"He didn't," Tama replied, "I asked her. Apparently it was one of the first things Odering checked."

"I bet," Hana breathed, feeling an overwhelming sense of relief. "I wonder why it took them so long to do the house to house stuff though. It was almost a week before they took my statement."

"Na, Lucy took mine last week, that night I babysat so you could meet your brother. She came round then and that's how I got the date with her. I went out when Logan got home and forgot to mention it. Sorry."

"Have you been with Lucy all week?" Hana asked. "You've been gone for days."

"Na, I went to stay with a mate from school. But I thought you might not like it."

Hana's radar went on red alert. "Why?" She tightened her grip around Tama's shoulder and moved her other hand around his neck in a head lock. "Do I have to beat you?"

"No," he laughed. "You've been married to my uncle too long!"

He jabbed her under the armpit with the hand he wasn't lying on and Hana squealed and let go. "I stayed with Gareth. He's at Waikato Uni and we met up by accident. He invited me to stay, so I did."

"Tama! Really? Was that a good idea?"

"I know. We were good mates before...you know."

"Before you bedded his mother?" Hana helped him out, realizing how much she was sounded like Logan.

"Yeah, actually. That stuffed things between us for a while. He said his parents are divorcing and his dad has met someone else. He hasn't seen much of Anka. Charlotte lives with Ivan. What I did was awful. Maybe they'd have stayed together and been fine, but Gareth didn't think so. He said his dad seems happier than he's been for years, so he forgave me. I'm grateful; he was my best mate through school." Tama stopped to draw breath. "I never understood how bad it was trying to take Anka away from them, not until that night you told me about your husband and his other woman. I saw how it affected you – how it still upsets you and I felt guilty for the first time. Now I'm just sorry and wish I hadn't gone there."

Hana squeezed his shoulder and kissed the top of his head. "I'm so proud of you, babe."

"Thanks, Ma." Tama shifted his head so he could fix his grey eyes on her face and said, "I wish you were my real mum."

Hana's heart melted and she almost fell for it. She gave him a disgusting sloppy wet kiss on his forehead and told him to get his hand off her bottom, or she'd definitely tell Logan.

Chapter 18

"Please can I borrow your car, Ma?" Tama dangled the Honda's keys in his brown fingers and chewed on his lower lip.

"What's wrong with yours?"

"I need an automatic, it's easier."

"Easier for what?" Hana narrowed her eyes and a flush passed over Tama's high cheekbones.

"Just stuff."

"Illegal stuff?"

"No!" Tama looked a mixture of offended and relieved, as though Hana's question inadvertently missed the issue and he was glad. "If I needed a getaway car, I wouldn't pick a *mummy mobile*, would I?"

"Fine, but you can fetch some shopping for me." Hana gave him a list and Logan's credit card, hoping it didn't turn out to be a huge mistake.

He left and she pottered around, sorting out her daughter and then looking through the baby's clothes, piling up those which no longer fitted. It felt strange touching the soft fabrics for a newborn, knowing it was the last time Hana would hold a tiny, fragile child belonging to her.

At the sound of the interval bell, she sought her husband, missing adult company. Hana found him taking a break in the staffroom surrounded by friends from the sports department. It took a while to cross the busy, congested room as her old colleagues wanted to look at the sleeping baby in her arms. "How are you doing?" twenty different teachers asked and Hana got bored with hearing herself reply with the same sentence. Hana beat down the sense of missing out on 'real' life and smiled woodenly with her answers, missing the camaraderie of colleagues and the wide and varied subjects they talked about with ease. The decision for her to give up work was a joint one.

"I'll support you with whatever you want, as long as between us, we make a stable upbringing for Phoe," Logan had said. "I'm happy to stay home if you find it too isolating; I don't mind."

Hana knew it wasn't the place or the work she missed but the constant human interaction which work fostered. Many of her friends had moved on or proved not to be real friends under pressure. Amanda sat at the table with the admin staff. A few waved and begged her to take the baby over. "Hasn't she grown!" they exclaimed, peeking at the dark eyelashes and bonny olive skin of Hana's snoozing daughter. "We haven't seen you for ages, Hana."

Hana smiled, biting back a ready retort that she lived on site, less than two hundred metres from their seats. Any of them could visit in a break or at lunchtime, but hadn't. Hana had learned the nature of people meant they would show interest in the things right in front of them, but give them no further thought once they were out of sight. She smiled and made her excuses, working her way towards the grey eyed man who appraised her from the moment she entered the room.

The males at Logan's table shifted their chairs politely backwards to admit Hana. She shook her head, scenting the heady aroma of alpha male and testosterone. "There's no spare chairs," she said, hefting Phoenix into her other arm. "I just came to say hello."

Logan pushed his chair back and slapped his thighs. "Sit here," he said with a twinkle in his eye. Hana's eyes widened and she cast her eyes around the room, sensing Amanda's stare boring holes in her back. Logan winked.

It felt awkward with an audience but Hana slid her bottom onto her husband's thighs and he slipped his arm around her waist. "How're you doing?" he whispered into her shoulder.

"Good thanks," Hana lied.

Pete North in a fit of showing off, took the sleeping child and sat with Phoenix over his shoulder. "I'm great with kids," he bragged as he patted her back in a steady rhythmic drum beat.

"Just not when they get to high school," one of the PE teachers commented under his breath.

Hana cringed as Phoenix breathed in dandruff and an alarming blue powder which could be anything. "What's the blue stuff on your jacket?" she asked Pete.

"Ah, that. Yeah, I drew a hopscotch outline for my Year 9s." He looked pleased with himself.

"Hopscotch?" The head of faculty leaned towards Pete as though he was intellectually disadvantaged. "That's not part of the curriculum."

"Doesn't matter," Pete replied with a shrug. "We had fun."

Logan stroked Hana's wedding ring and she watched him trying not to laugh as the head of faculty slammed his coffee on the table and stalked away, shaking his head.

A colleague pursed his lips and watched the man leave, tapping Pete on the shoulder. "North, it was hockey, man. Not hopscotch. They've got an assessment next week on muscle grouping and hockey's one of the studies. You've been teaching that as well, haven't you?"

Pete shook his head. "Na, bro. She'll be right."

His colleague swore and then covered his mouth, remembering the baby in their midst. He glanced at Logan, who rolled his eyes and shrugged.

"Tama's back," Hana said softly as the men turned to debating a dodgy refereeing decision at a rugby game the previous weekend. Half argued it was fine while the others disagreed.

"What do you think, Logan?" Pete demanded and Hana's husband shrugged.

"Didn't watch it; don't care."

Logan smiled at his wife and she saw the crow's feet at the corners of his beautiful eyes. It was a sign he smiled more nowadays and she wanted to stroke them. She resisted, knowing too much of a public display would upset the tolerant men at the table. The glint in Logan's eye, told her he'd read her mind. Hana felt instantly better in Logan's presence; he embodied for her everything which made her feel secure and loved as a woman. For almost a decade her faith sustained her, keeping her sane through the difficult, lonely years when she was tempted to trash everything about her marriage to Vik in the light of his indiscretion. "I feel really lucky," Hana breathed and felt Logan's arms tighten around her waist.

The bell rang all too quickly and the staffroom emptied, making Hana's heart weigh heavily in her chest. Logan stirred beneath her as Pete almost dropped Phoenix in his haste to get away. "Pete! Don't be a bloody idiot!" Logan growled, catching his daughter as Pete thrust her in their general direction and left.

Hana sighed and looked around the empty room filled with abandoned coffee cups and rubbish. The knot of loneliness grew.

"What's wrong, babe?" Logan asked, his voice a gentle rumble.

Hana shook her head, dipping her lips to meet his. She kissed him and he responded. "Won't you talk to me?" Logan asked, his grey eyes laden with concern.

"No, I can't," Hana admitted in a whisper. "Because I don't know myself." A little sound below made Hana look down, finding her baby's grey eyes staring up at her parents. When she got eye contact with Hana, Phoenix beamed and giggled. Something in her mouth made Hana start and bend closer to see, spotting two white dots on Phoenix's bottom gum. "Logan, she's got teeth!" Hana said in amazement, running her finger over the tiny ridges. "Phoe, show Daddy your little pearls."

Logan sat his daughter up and peered into her mouth as she sighed and looked around the staffroom. "Wow!" he said in wonderment. Everything was new; he'd never done fatherhood before, his child's first smile, her first roll over, first tooth and first steps. He rejoiced over each milestone with genuine enjoyment.

"I need a record of this," he said, handing Phoenix back to Hana. Logan grappled in his jacket pocket for his phone. "Turn her to face me, babe," he asked. "Smile, Phoe, baby, smile for Daddy." Logan stared at the photograph with pride. "That's gorgeous,"

Hana watched the wonder in his eyes and knew he'd look at it often, like he did all the cute photos he stored in a special folder on his phone called, '*Phoe*'.

Hana glanced at the clock. "You should go." She nudged his upper arm. "Don't you have a class?"

"No, I've got an hour at St Bart's now, so I can do the accounts. I'll walk back over with you." He reclaimed his daughter with a grin, besotted. "Wow, you're so gorgeous," he whispered. Phoenix squealed, trying to speak, so it came out as a series of little whispered noises. She swung her legs and flapped her hands and looked excited in her daddy's strong arms.

"Amy's broke," Hana said, keeping her voice low as they walked towards the boarding house. "I'm not sure how to help. I can't just give her money; I don't think she'd accept."

"How do you know she's not just careful with her money?" Logan peeled his gaze from his daughter for a moment.

"The house is a mess and it was freezing yesterday but the heaters were turned off. She was upset for a number of reasons and even though she didn't say it - I suspect that's one of them."

"Just let them have the wedding at the hotel," Logan suggested. "Bodie's never gonna like me but at least this way he might not hate me."

"No," Hana was adamant. "It's Bodie's mess and he can sort it out. I'm not backing down but if I can help Amy without being obvious, then I will."

Logan ran his free hand through his hair and holding onto Phoenix with one arm, clasped Hana's hand, interlacing their fingers. "I love my girls," he said happily. "I wish it could always be like this."

Hana smiled and nodded, feeling the same. The weight of the murder hung over the site like an albatross. "Where can we go for the holidays?" she asked, looking hopeful it would be far away from the school.

"Anywhere you like, my love," Logan replied, kissing her on the forehead and reluctantly handing his child back. "Have a think and let me know." He sauntered over to the boarding house, looking back occasionally and catching Hana's eye. She watched him walk away, admiring his tight backside and the swagger in his walk. It was tempting to wolf whistle but her natural English reserve prevented her following through.

Reaching the front door of the boarding house, Logan turned and waved. Hana picked up Phoenix's little hand and waved with it. She'd been trying to teach her, but it was the best they could muster at that moment. Logan waved again not wanting to go into the office.

Feeling the emotional tie stretching and hurting her chest, Hana turned away, going back to her current abode with heavy footsteps. She walked back to the unit experiencing a sense of power in her husband's trust. "Daddy said I can choose where we go for the holidays," she told her daughter. "Culver's Cottage or Daddy's hotel?"

Phoenix waggled her legs and rubbed her eyes, disinterested. Tama still wasn't back with the car or shopping so Hana raided the pantry and fridge and chopped things up to make baby food from scratch. Her first attempt wasn't bad. She managed a decent mix of vegetables, cooked in the saucepan until they were soft and then pushed through a sieve. It was fun, adding things

Phoenix might like to try. Except peas. Peas seemed reluctant to blend, staying as little green husks in Hana's glossy cement mix.

As lunchtime neared her daughter became fractious, bored with lying on her back with a bare bottom swiping at the dangly toys on Millie's old baby gym. Hana put a nappy on her child and sat her in the high chair to try out the food. "Right missy. Tell me what you think of this?" Hana asked, eyeing the baby gym with a guilty cringe. "I need to give that gym back to Amanda but I don't want to see her and I'm not sending Logan."

"Baba, baba," Phoenix said, opening her mouth so Hana could fill it with more vegetable gloop.

"Good idea," Hana agreed. "Tama can drop it round."

Phoenix gobbled her bowl of food, distressed when was gone. She grizzled and Hana wiped her face and offered her a breastfeed. "I can't overdo the solid food, baby," she told her. "Most of the mothers with babies your age aren't even feeding proper food yet. Izzie and Bodie survived but those women make me nervous; they're very critical of someone doing it differently to them and it makes me doubt myself."

Within twenty minutes, her child was comatose in her arms. Hana swaddled her up and lingered by the pram, tempted to lay her there instead of the cot. She nodded to herself and relented, covering Phoenix with blankets and fastening her reins to prevent accident. "Your brother managed to fall out of his pram when he wasn't much older than you. I still don't know how he sat himself up and ended up face first on the carpet." Hana remembered the awful scene of tears and recriminations. Vik, as always dealt passively with her hysterics and his son's screams.

Hana collected the washing from the laundry and ran to the communal washing line to hang it, leaving the front door open so she could see the pram, but worrying about Phoenix anyway. Running up the front steps with the empty basket she felt a hand on her arm and screamed.

"Sorry, miss, sorry, miss!" James had his hands up to his face in guilt at her fright. The Year 13 Korean student looked ill and wasn't wearing school uniform. Hana stared at him in surprise.

"James, why aren't you in class?" she said, still panting. "If Mr Du Rose sees you, he'll have a fit!"

"What is fit?" James asked, panicking.

Hana calmed herself, remembering his difficulty with aspects of English, especially phrases and jokes. "It's okay," she said, "he's at St Bart's. Why are you in mufti and not in class? Start at the beginning."

It wasn't appropriate to invite a student alone with her inside the unit, but tongues would wag harder if they sat on the steps. Hana hesitated, seeing beads of sweat break out on the teenager's forehead and noticing how he looked around him as if anxious. She opened the front door and indicated the lounge. "In you go, James. Take a seat."

"I don't need more seat," James said, kicking his shoes off and eyeing the sofas. "Big seats. No room in my small dorm."

"Would you like a drink though?" Hana offered. "Tea, coffee, water?"

James shook his head. "No, miss. Thank you." He bowed and sat down at Hana's invitation. She reached for her cell phone. "I need to tell Logan you're here with me," she said.

"No! No!" shrieked James, throwing Hana into a panic. She put her finger up to her lips.

"You'll wake the baby!" she hissed, flapping her arms. "I just put her in the pram."

"Sorry, miss, so sorry," he groaned, agony drifting over his silky complexion.

"James, what on earth is wrong?" she asked him, concerned.

"Yes, miss," he said, his face lighting up, "the earth is wrong. The man in the earth is wrong."

Hana struggled to control her exasperation at his misunderstanding of her phrase. Then his words struck her. "The man in the earth? James, do you mean the man buried at St Bart's?"

James nodded emphatically, his head moving rapidly up and down, up and down. His eyes looked full of hope and Hana's heart sank. Instinctively she understood he knew something, it was eating him up and he expected her to sort it out. "You help me, miss," he declared, confirming her worst fears. "You help me all my four years, seven months and twelve days like best good lady. You help me now."

"Tell me what you know," Hana said, resigned to becoming more embroiled than she wanted.

"Man in earth work here," James gushed. "Nasty man who shout all time at boy for no reason. He shout me for no reason. I very upset. Mother send model plane for me for celebration. I play out in paddock. Man in earth always shout." James employed hand actions to help his explanation, knocking the TV remote off the arm of the sofa during his demonstration of his model aeroplane flying. "I sorry," he said, retrieving it.

"You mean, Mr Collins?" Hana clarified and James' head nodded again like a toy doll.

"So, he shout and I take plane to back of St Bart's out of way. It go too far and I lose. I very very upset." James beat his breast dramatically to emphasise the extent of his upset. "Mother not afford plane. Very expensive. I go into bushes down...down...in back of St Bart's."

"Gully?" Hana tried to help him out. He nodded happily.

"Yes, I went gully. I look for plane but I walk far from St Bart's down to water where not allow to go." James looked at Hana, his eyes begging. "You not tell Mr Du Rose I disobey and go to water, no?"

Hana cringed. "I'll try not to, James," she promised. "I'll only tell him if I can't sort your problem out another way."

James nodded, satisfied and trusting. His face brightened. "There is plane, sitting in leaf. Yes, leaf. Plane stuck. Lot of leaf cover up. Wire hurt hand with electric charge, very sore." James clapped his hands, making Hana jump as he demonstrated something grabbing his fingers. "Trap on floor and plane stuck."

"Traps?" Hana interrupted. "In the gully? James, there can't be. Do you think someone's trapping possums?"

James shrugged and clapped again, causing Hana to glance at the pram. "I hear man come, man in earth. I hide and him step through leaf and find plane. He take plane. He water plant and take off leaf, many leaf. Then come out. He has plane in hand. I want plane back. Mother pay for plane. For me. I follow him. I go to shed and say, *'Give me plane, please? I lose.'* He say *'No, throw in trash!'* I very angry. Want plane back. I leave and find Mr North. I ask him to get plane and he say *'Yes,'* but still no plane. Mother ask in letter, do I enjoy plane? I need plane. You help me get back? Please, Miss, get me plane?"

Hana sat for a moment, digesting the student's strange tale. She looked at James's hopeful face and felt caught. "Which shed, James? The big one with the mowers and equipment in? Or the one by the swimming pool? When the baby wakes, I'll walk over with you and see..."

James shook his head vehemently. "No. Shed, shed."

"Is it open now?" Hana asked. "If you give me a couple of hours, I'll see if one of the other grounds staff will open it for me."

The boy's face dropped. "No, only man in earth have key. Other mens not get for me. No key."

Hana's eyes narrowed in confusion. Someone would have a master key to all the equipment sheds, otherwise none of the mowing or maintenance would have occurred in the last week. The realisation came with a flush to Hana's cheeks as she remembered the other shed and the tennis player's soft kiss outside it. "Do you mean the shed near the tennis courts?" she asked, feeling a sickness pervade her stomach as James nodded with eagerness.

"Yes, yes! You get me plane, miss?"

"Please James, can you give me a few days to sort this out for you? I'll see what I can do; I might have a plan. I don't have a key but I might know a man who has." The question was when could she sneak out and meet him?

James left and Hana cleaned up after her cooking frenzy, spooning the baby food into ice cube trays and freezing them. She picked up her knitting and watched pointless daytime television without seeing it as her brain replayed the conversation with James. She wondered if he'd exaggerated and the leaves he spoke of were innocent. Her gut told her they weren't. The cops must have searched the gully for clues so she figured she was reading too much into it.

Tama rocked up half way through the afternoon. He didn't look well.

"You forgot the shopping, didn't you?" Hana asked, staring at him. Tama grunted and kept his body slouched. "Did you wreck the car?" Hana stood as Tama shook his head, his grey eyes channelling anger and pain.

"No! Check if you want; it's fine." He dangled the keys in front of her.

Hana was suspicious, standing and putting her arms around Tama's stomach. "Haven't you got a cuddle for Aunty Hana?" she asked facetiously.

"No, ma!" He shied away and she knew then something was wrong.

"Tama!" she exclaimed. "You think I've learned nothing from months of watching Logan trying to hide injuries and ailments? Don't take me for a fool!"

"Leave me alone," Tama protested and backed away.

"Tell me!" Hana ordered, but he shook his head, high-tailing it to the bathroom and locking himself in. "Tama Du Rose, open this door right now!" Hana hissed through the wood, trying not to wake Phoenix. The teenager hid inside, refusing to come out or communicate and Hana was forced to admit defeat.

After school, Logan ducked a heads of department meeting. "I'm knackered, Angus," he complained to the principal. "You promised the night duties would ease but they haven't."

"I know," the Scotsman admitted. "The new guy doesn't arrive back in New Zealand until November."

Logan shook his head. "Hana hates it here, Angus. You knew this was only temporary at the start of the year. Pete and I spent the whole night dealing with two puking kids and now you expect me to sit in a bloody meeting with droning old men after a day's teaching?"

Angus bridled at Logan's description of his departmental meetings and then relented. "Fair enough, Mr Du Rose. You're excused for tonight."

"Just as well," Logan jibed. "Because I'm going anyway."

Angus' red hair moved in the breeze and he couldn't resist the urge to rein in his wilful employee. "Mr Du Rose!" he called, enjoying the satisfaction of Logan's pause and slow turn to face him. "Wives don't sit on their husband's knees in my staffroom. It's not appropriate."

An evil look crossed Logan's face. "No, you're right. It should have been the typist sitting on a student, shouldn't it? Or what about a Year 13 dean sitting on a sports teacher?"

"All right, Mr Du Rose." Exasperated and needing the final word, Angus turned and whisked away on quick footsteps.

Logan smirked and strode home. He walked into a disaster zone, finding his disgruntled wife hopping around in the lounge. "I'm desperate for the toilet and Tama's in there. He won't come out," Hana wailed. "I can't keep hammering on the door because the baby's asleep."

Logan peeked into the pram, meeting his daughter's grey eyed smile. "Not anymore," he said. He walked down the hallway with long strides, producing a ten cent coin from his trouser pocket. He used it to turn the bolt on the other side of the mechanism and gained entry to the bathroom in seconds. He shut the door behind him and Hana hopped around outside, keeping her legs crossed.

"Nope, you've had long enough," she grumbled after a few minutes, barging in to discover Logan inspecting something under Tama's shirt. She shoved them both out of the way and undid her jeans, jiggling on the spot in desperation. "I'm stripping off," she announced.

"Hana!" Logan exclaimed, shoving his hand over Tama's eyes and giving her an admonishing glance. He ushered his nephew from the room, closing the door behind him.

"Sorry, but I was desperate," Hana said, back in the lounge. "I kept saying I was. What's happening?"

Logan jerked his head towards Tama, a smirk on his face. "Go on, idiot. Tell her what you did."

Wincing in pain, the teenager gently removed his tee shirt, displaying a livid, angry mark on his side. The tattoo covered the area from under his left armpit ending somewhere inside his jeans. The wording was Māori and looked familiar. Hana moved closer for a better look and saw Tama wince. "Is this what you've been doing every day?" she asked and he nodded slowly. "Why didn't you say something?"

"That's what I asked him," Logan said crossly. "At least then it would have been spelled right!"

Hana put her hand up to her mouth, looking to Tama for confirmation and he closed his eyes and struggled to hold back his tears. "Darling," she said and touched his arm. "Can't you sort something out?" she asked her husband, so used to him fixing everything.

"I can give the tattoo artist a slap, but this idiot wrote it down for him so not really, no. It's not too bad; it's a grammatical error." He shook his head at Tama, his frown slipping into a smirk. "Pity you didn't research it *before* you let him write it indelibly on your skin, aye?"

Hana gave her husband a hard look. He knew the pain of wearing a faulty genealogy etched into his flesh. The *whakapapa* tattoo on his upper arm and shoulder took a wrong turn when it listed Alfred as his father, neglecting a fork it should have taken through Reuben Du Rose. Logan caught Hana's reprimand and felt its impact. "It's okay, mate. When it stops looking so angry it'll be cool. I never thought of doing anything like that. Well done, I approve. It's good to preserve our heritage."

Tama cheered up, allowing himself a tight smile.

"I love the font," Hana said with encouragement. "How can we help the pain go away?" She looked across at her husband, hope in her eyes.

Logan opened a kitchen drawer and pulled out a roll of plastic food wrap. "Get me the nappy rash cream from the change bag, please?" he asked Hana. When she returned with it, Logan made Tama coat the painful area with the cream. "You don't want it to dry out. Didn't they give you any instructions?" Tama shook his head. Logan tutted and rolled his eyes with annoyance. "If you'd asked, I'd have given you the address of my guy. He uses traditional methods and would've known straight away the wording wasn't right." He caught the look on Hana's face and dropped the urge to chastise the silly teenager. "It'll be okay. It looks bloody sore. Make sure you don't get an infection."

Logan waited for Tama to spread grease over the tattoo before wrapping him in plastic, going around his torso four times. He asked Hana for tape and sealed the unusual dressing. Pushing Tama's tee shirt over his head, Logan clipped him round the ear. "You're such a bloody dork!" he told him, then in a fit of un-Logan-like behaviour, grabbed and hugged the teenager, letting him go just as quickly. Tama's cheeks burned red with embarrassment and a deep sense of acceptance.

"Do you really like it?" he asked Logan.

"Don't push it, boy," Logan warned, his grey eyes flashing.

"Why don't we go out for dinner?" Hana suggested, keen to disband the dangerous vibes collecting around her. They wound up in a cafe on Victoria Street which was famous for its pancakes. After ordering from the menu the subject returned to Tama's unfortunate tattoo. "Why did you keep going back for more?" Hana asked. "You must have been about four times already."

"It's eight times and because it bloody hurt," Tama replied, ignoring Logan's snort of derision. "Today's was the worst though. I kept wanting to pass out!" Logan laughed and Tama glared at him. "It's hard on yer ribs. That's the most painful part of the body *apparently!*"

"Is that what he said to cheer you up after he picked your sorry ass off the floor?" Logan ran a hand over his face, avoiding Hana's raised eyebrow. "The tattooist must be glad it's over," he sniggered and Hana shook her head at him.

A loud group of English tourists raised their voices, causing a disturbance. They spoke in southern accents, behaving as though they owned the place and Hana cringed as Logan turned to watch them. "Don't stare," she hissed at him.

"Bloody English," he muttered, dodging her kick under the table.

"Stop," Hana begged. "It's embarrassing to be associated with people who can't behave properly through a common accent."

"Can you tell them to shut up?" Tama asked the waitress as she took their order and she shook her head.

"Chef already asked them. They're getting drunk and the blonde one threatened him. The owner says if they carry on, he'll call the cops but then they'll leave without paying."

A male child with the English party walked over to their table and stared at Hana.

"What you doing?" he said, pointing rudely at her. Hana turned her body so he couldn't see her breastfeeding the baby, pulling the blanket further round her daughter.

"Nothing," she said. "Please go back to your family."

The child had blonde curly hair and a superior air, even though he was around Jas' age. Luckily they were sitting in a booth with Hana furthest from his prying eyes, but Logan became increasingly frustrated as the child appeared again and stood there, watching them like they were zoo exhibits.

"Sod off, kid!" Tama hissed and the child poked his tongue out.

The inebriated tourists complained loudly about the service, the cleanliness of the perfectly acceptable cafe, the quality of the food and anything else they could think of whenever the waitress was within earshot. The errant child appeared again and Hana's hopes sank as his party found him cute. "Aw, in't he lovely sayin' 'ello to everyone?" his bleach blonde mother drooled.

"No, *actually*!" Tama exclaimed, but a roar of laughter broke out from the other end of the group's table and his comment was drowned out. The boys' food arrived, delivered by a waitress who seemed flustered and upset and apologised for the awkward clientele in the next booth.

"Excuse me, please," she said to the spectator at the end of the table, reaching over his head to lay the plates down.

"I don't think he's all there," Hana commented under her breath to Tama, jerking her head towards the weird child. "He might have a disability and they can't cope. Sometimes it's not the parent's fault." Her mind wandered to her beautiful granddaughter Elizabeth whom the world classed as *different*, with her Down syndrome and chromosomal anomaly.

"Can you see Marcus and Izzie putting up with this?" Logan asked, his patience waning.

Hana shook her head and admitted they wouldn't. Tama's pain affected his good humour as the child stole a chip from his plate "Just go!" he said, raising his voice to the little boy.

The child put his elbows on their table and grabbed another chip from Tama's plate. "No!" he said in a cocky voice. "Up yours!"

Tama's fragile tolerance snapped. He widened his eyes as though beginning a *haka*. Standing, he took a rigid stance with his arms folded and stuck out his tongue, flattening it against his lower lip and chin. His demeanour was terrifying, accompanied by a low growl which matched his warlike face. The child bolted.

Phoenix sat on Hana's knee and stared at her cousin in amazement. Hana expected her to wail with fright as her rosebud lips parted, but the little Māori girl let out a peal of laughter like tinkling bells at a Christmas fair. Her whole body rocked with pure delight. When she stopped giggling, her eyes pleaded with Tama to do it again. He widened his eyes and growled and the baby laughed so hard her grey eyes squeezed tight shut and tiny tears collected at their corners.

"You scared my son, you ignorant git!" the child's father bellowed, appearing at the end of Hana's table. He was a picture of arrogance, enjoying staring down the table at them and flexing arms which showed more flab than muscle. His shaven head and bulging blue eyes made up a picture of aggression and he reeked of alcohol.

Hana sensed trouble and her chest involuntarily tightened, hating confrontation. "Your son behaved rudely," she said. "We asked him nicely to leave."

"Do you know who I am?" the man spat, leaning over the table, his shoulder close to Tama's face.

Hana shook her head. "No. Should I?"

The man stood up like a spring, affronted by her ignorance. "I just won the English lottery," he said with a sneer. "So if my son wants to stand and stare at the natives, then he can."

Hana gritted her teeth, experiencing an overwhelming urge to slap the man for spoiling their meal out, not bothering to control his brat, and humiliating her by cultural association. From the corner of her eye Hana watched the frazzled waitress run into the kitchens to fetch someone, fearing there would be a fight with the tourist's clumsy playing of the race card.

Tama laid his knife and fork next to his pancake and stood, meeting Logan's eye as he did the same. The teenager had grown into a six feet, two inch male in the last year and still hadn't finished. Logan was six feet and four inches in his socks and they towered over the tourist. The Māori males looked muscular and fearsome compared to the overweight, five feet nothing Englishman. They fixed their unified grey eyes on him, taking in the '*I love London*' tee shirt, the hairy belly overhang peeking from underneath and the regulation lurid shorts. His European tourist uniform of white socks peeked through the toes of clumpy, unattractive sandals and Tama's sneer spoke volumes.

Hana watched the Englishman's Adam's apple bob as he realised he'd picked a fight he couldn't win. The booth behind Hana fell silent as none of the lottery winner's sycophantic friends rushed to his aid. Sweat poured down the side of his bulbous face as he struggled to work out how to extract his pompous self from the calamity.

As one, Hana's men made their eyes huge and round, bugging from their faces and showing their sclera like crazed maniacs. They flexed their huge arm muscles and stuck out their flattened tongues. *"Haaaaaaaah!"* they shouted in unison, filling the small cafe with their guttural, terrifying war cry.

Phoenix dissolved into a peal of hilarity and almost laughed herself off her mother's knee and underneath the table. Hana struggled to keep her upright and when she looked up, saw the tourists gathering their belongings and fleeing. Logan caught the obstreperous man's eye as he reached the door and the Māori jerked his head towards the till, wordlessly ordering him to settle his debt. He crept back, throwing a wad of New Zealand notes on the counter and glancing over his shoulder towards Hana's table.

As the last tourist left, slamming the door behind himself, Logan and Tama sat down and picked up their cutlery to a round of applause from the other diners. The chef appeared from the kitchen with the phone in his hand. "No," he said to the person on the other end. "They've gone now, but you might want to have a chat to them if they're walking round our city behaving like that." He disconnected and nodded to Logan. "Cops," he said, waving the handset.

Logan did an upward jerk of his head in acknowledgement while Tama whispered under his breath. "Like they'll come here for a few rowdy tourists?"

"I'll tell Lucy you said that," Hana commented, drawing a glare of dismay from her nephew.

"Don't?" he begged.

"Which *haka* would you have done?" she asked, curious.

"The one from our *marae*," Logan said, filling his mouth with pancake.

"Oh." Tama stopped with a forkful of food half way to his mouth. "I was gonna do the school one."

Hana snorted. "Oh, dear. You're both a worry," she laughed. "I'm so embarrassed by my kinsmen sometimes."

"They're not your kin," Logan said gruffly. "We are. You're a Kiwi now."

Hana's heart fluttered with the warmth of acceptance and she bit her lip and smiled at her formidable husband.

"Yeah," Tama agreed, flushed with his own sense of belonging. "We're family; just us."

Hana smiled and enjoyed being part of something, realising how much of an outsider she'd become.

Chapter 19

"Painkillers," Hana said, handing tablets to the teenager. "It might help."

"Thanks." Tama took the white pills and clasped the glass of water. "You're awesome, Ma." He laid down on the sofa and flicked through TV channels, alternating between loud pop music and cartoons.

Logan got underway with report writing, putting all his concentration into a neat, left handed slant. Phoenix went to sleep and Hana rattled around bored. Mindful of her promise to James, she muttered something about visiting a random wife in the staff accommodation and disappeared before either of the men could question her further.

Hana found her tennis partner already on the courts with his ball delivery machine. She let herself in through the gate and borrowed the spare racquet, conveniently lying next to the man's bag. Without speaking a word, the players whacked balls at each other with speed and abandon until they were both breathless and worn out. The tennis player welcomed Hana's presence with regular smiles as she made him duck and dive to return her volleys and she revelled in the familiar, physical exertion. Her muscles remembered the stance and demands on their flexibility, responding keenly, if a little rusty. The sparring finished before nine o'clock as before and Hana jogged around the court, fetching rogue balls and waiting while her partner locked up.

Hana stroked her finger across the name, '*Lachlan*' written on the racquet case as she zipped it up, fighting to remember anyone of that name. She remembered one Lachlan from school, but his hair was a sandy red and he wasn't as nice to look at as her partner. It seemed ridiculous to ask his name at this late stage, especially as he'd known hers from the start, so Hana tried to make conversation that might give her clues. "So, you remember me on the tennis circuit," she said matter-of-factly, caressing the expensive racquet cover. "Did you go to the Hamilton club?"

He nodded. "Yeah." His blonde hair whipped up in the icy breeze and he smiled. "I loved watching you play; you have a natural grace and your backhand is dynamite."

His compliment distracted Hana and she felt herself blush in the glow from the floodlights. "It *was* dynamite," she said sadly. "Now it's more like - rusty undischarged landmine."

He laughed, a deep, rumbling sound. Hana started in shock as his hand snaked gently around the back of her neck and he caressed her skin with strong fingers. She opened her mouth to protest but he covered her lips with an index finger smelling of tennis balls and rubber grips. "Sshh," he whispered. "You're a demon on the court, Hana Johal and a goddess off it. Leave me with my fantasies."

Hana swallowed and he let her go, pushing the moment no further as if knowing she'd refuse. Hana clutched the racquet case and he took it from her, laying it on the back seat of the car, his fingers brushing hers in the action. Tasting the air for danger and reaching into her surroundings, Hana felt only peace and confusion. "Come again?" the man asked, his jaw angular and handsome as his blue eyes bore into hers.

She nodded with slowness born of doubt and pointed back towards the floodlights, remembering the real reason she came. "The lights are still on."

"Oh, yeah. Thanks." The tennis player strode towards the darkened shed, jangling a set of keys in his hands. He sorted through them until he found the right one. Hana stuck close behind and watched as he drew the creaky door open, peering into the blackness inside. The model plane perched on an old desk in a dank corner. "That's where it is!" she said, pretending to sound surprised. "My nephew's plane came over here last week and he couldn't find it. He's been really upset."

"Where?" he asked, peering into the gloom.

Hana turned a devastating smile in his direction. "There," she replied, pointing a finger to direct his gaze. The tennis player ignored her raised hand, staring at her instead as though drinking in her beauty. Hana felt momentarily powerful and exploited the man's adoration, tossing her hair and testing her latent skill to reel him in. He seemed stunned, fixated on Hana's flushed complexion and windswept red locks and then he stepped back, allowing her into the shed.

"Help yourself," he said with a wobble in his voice.

Hana walked up the steps and into the metal container before her common sense kicked in. She chided herself for her own stupidity at having willingly trapped herself, wondering if she learned nothing from her experience with Laval and his stalking. She felt her heart rate hike and the familiar pounding in her ears. Her hand shook as she snatched up the plane in her right hand, finding it heavier than she expected.

Hana swallowed and walked towards the open door with purpose, expecting at any minute to find her exit barred. "Thanks," she said, her voice breathy and hollow.

"No problem," the tennis player said with a smile, standing back to let her pass and closing the door behind her after flicking off the switch for the floodlights.

The area plunged into an eerie darkness as Hana bid him a shaky goodnight and jogged home, hearing the huge floods audibly click until they were almost as black as the night, leaving a slight, discernible glimmer as they cooled. "*Idiot, idiot, idiot!-*" Hana admonished herself, finding her lungs protesting as she reached her front door. The plane in her hand seemed ridiculously insignificant compared to what it might have cost her, had the tennis player been a different kind of man. Hana heard his car start up and caught sight of it passing the end of her road, a nondescript colour and model in the darkness.

When her heart rate returned to almost normal, Hana knocked on the door. Logan opened it and studied his wife, concern in his eyes at her dishevelled appearance. He stood back to let her in, touching her lightly on the back. "Have you been running?" he asked, suspicion etched into his chiselled face.

"It's just a bit dark and scary out there," Hana replied truthfully. "It made me want to run home." Her hair was damp around her head and her cheeks pink and cold and she sensed Logan didn't believe her. "Look what I found," she said holding the plane aloft.

Tama looked up from his cramped position on the sofa, losing interest when he saw Hana didn't possess the remote control to make it fly.

"Where did you find that?" Logan's eyes narrowed and Hana gulped and shrugged.

"Just out there," she said, sticking as close to the truth as possible, knowing Logan would smell a lie at thirty paces. Logan took the plane from her hand and peered at it as Hana bent to remove her trainers.

"Did you know it was missing?" he asked, his grey eyes boring into the side of Hana's face. "Your mate, James has been bugging me about a plane he lost a while ago."

"I just found it by chance," Hana said, trying to sound innocent and engrossing herself with her knotted laces.

"So what's this all over it?" her husband replied, looking at her with a gaze which felt as though it left a physical wound.

"I've no idea." Hana peered at the greenery stuck in the plane's wings, relaxing with relief at being able to align with truth again. "I didn't see that in the dark." She reached out to poke at a fluttery leaf and Logan lifted it above her head, his eyes flashing.

"Don't touch it," he said, his voice hard. "You don't know what it is."

Hana shrugged and wrinkled her nose. "Well, it won't be poisonous, will it?" she scoffed. "Not in New Zealand."

"Did you know you can die from touching cow parsley?" Tama chimed, looking pleased with himself. "It's part of the hog weed family and contains a natural toxin that kills some people. It might be that."

Hana shook her head and smirked at Logan, seeking his unanimity in mocking the teenager. He didn't join in, eyeing her sideways as though she represented a risky filly who nobody else had managed to break. "Please can you give it back to James tomorrow?" she asked setting her expression to neutral.

Logan cocked his head and his eyes flashed. Guilt made Hana exasperated. "You said he's been bugging you for it, Logan, so please will you give it back?"

"Ok." He raised it above his head as Hana took another swipe for it. "I said I'd deal with it, Hana. Bloody hell, I'll put it down here so just leave it alone." He laid it underneath the table by his boots, out of the way in the cramped unit.

"Thanks." Hana feigned normality and yawned. "I think I'll go for a shower and then bed. Phoe keeps waking at four and it's playing havoc with me at the moment."

"Ok." Logan softened and leaned in for a kiss, stroking Hana's ruffled fringe away from her forehead. "I'll be down later."

As he heard the bathroom door click behind his wife, Logan turned to his nephew as the teenager sprawled on the sofa in his plastic wrap shroud. "I'm not going mad am I?" he asked. "That's hash on that plane, isn't it?"

Tama nodded with certainty and went back to watching the TV programme taking his mind off the pain in his ribs.

"What's my wife up to now?" Logan mused to himself and Tama shrugged, not caring.

Chapter 20

Logan strode across the field towards St Bart's, the morning frost heavy underfoot. The aeroplane dangled from his hand in a plastic bag, the bits of vivid green leaf absent from its fiberglass body. The Māori shook his head, narrowing his eyes at the time it took to separate the greenery from the plane and flush it down the toilet.

"What are you doing?" Tama had asked, staring over his shoulder as Logan sponged the plane's surface with a wet cloth after midnight.

"It was covered in marijuana, idiot!" Logan bit. "Do you think I should've just rolled it into a joint and offered Bodie some?"

"Ah, probably not," Tama replied. "Reckon Supercop's got it in for both of us lately."

"No kidding," Logan breathed. He climbed into bed in the early hours having cleared the house, including Hana's trainers and clothing of drugs.

"Want breakfast?" Hana asked as she wandered into the lounge and nudged her house guest with her toe.

"Na," Tama sighed. "Don't feel so good."

"Oh, that's worrying. Logan gone?" Hana yawned and stretched and the teenager nodded.

"Yeah."

"Did he take the plane for James?" she asked, casting her eyes around looking for it.

"Yeah."

Hana sighed. "Are you going to say anything other than *yeah* or *na* today?"

"Na."

Tama stayed in his sleeping bag and remained uncommunicative. He couldn't explain why the last inking session caused him more agony than all the others put together, but something to do with the wording disappearing into his boxer shorts and heading for his groin served as a clue. Hana did a load of washing, asking him to hang it on the line for her when it finished. Then she bundled up the baby and put her into the pram, walking into town with the clothes for the op shop and an idea she might visit the pharmacy and get something to help the suffering teenager.

The first pharmacist was unsympathetic when she told him about Tama's tattoo and she left empty handed. "If the tattoo artist isn't licenced, there's all sorts of risks; hepatitis, HIV and various other dangers associated with tattoos." The woman refused to sell Hana anything to help, insisting, "Get him to a doctor as quickly as possible."

After the op shop visit, Hana walked to Hamilton East and found a much nicer response. She came away with anti-bacterial cream and stronger painkillers. The Asian man spoke with kindness and understanding, agreeing with Logan's treatment of the area. "Yes, that's exactly what I'd suggest he does. Apply this cream four times a day and repeat the dressing twice a day. Your husband's right. It mustn't dry out or form a scab." He rolled up his sleeve and showed Hana a beautiful eagle which wrapped around his forearm.

"That's amazing!" she breathed, admiring the realism of the image. "Did it hurt?"

The pharmacist shrugged and laughed. "I wouldn't admit it. He'll be fine. Look out for symptoms such as fever or weeping from the tattoo and general unwellness. Otherwise, he'll just be sore for a few days and probably complain a lot."

Strolling along Grey Street, Hana enjoyed window shopping without being tempted to go inside. The sound of her name being called made her stop and look around her.

"Hana! Over here!" Hana's heart sank as she recognised Vik's old friend and Anka's ex-husband, calling to her from a parked car.

"Hi," Hana said, only half committed to the conversation. Their last talk hadn't been pleasant. "I'm just on my way somewhere," she lied. "And I'm sure you've got work to do."

Ivan gazed at her over the tops of his brown eyes, sensing Hana's reluctance. He opened the car door and unwound himself from the driver's seat, standing almost as tall as Logan. "I work for the council, Hana. You know how it works."

Hana bit her lip and smiled. Ivan worked for the council in a managerial role, working in some capacity with the elected city councillors. Anka had regaled her friend with hilarious stories over the years of the things the great and good of Hamilton got up to. "I'm was waiting for a colleague to turn up to visit a shop owner on the block, but he's just rung in sick. Would you like to go for coffee?"

"No, thanks. I have to go." Hana backed away, seeing the sadness cross Ivan's face.

"Please," he said, reaching for her arm. "I'd like you to stay and hear my apology."

And so Hana found herself sitting in the same cafe she met with Ivan's wife some months ago, deciding the place must be cursed with a spirit of awkward conversations. Hana wedged the pram between two tables and checked Phoenix was still asleep, contemplating waking her and using her as an excuse to escape. They chatted about general matters until Ivan asked if she'd seen Anka lately.

"Not since February," Hana answered, trying hard not to conjure up the vision of Tama's backside working its muscular way back into its boxer shorts, or Anka sitting on Hana's new sofa with her breasts spilling from her bra. Tama often referred to the lounge rug as the rectangle of passion, just to tease Hana.

Eventually, Ivan turned the conversation to his phone argument with Hana, over a year ago.

"I shouldn't have taken it out on you," he said. "You weren't to blame and I shouldn't have lashed out at you."

"It was an unbelievably difficult time for everyone," Hana muttered, desperate to change the conversation. "It wasn't a good time for me anyway but Anka's affair with Tama made it worse."

"Well," Ivan said, "with you knowing how it felt, you were the last person I should have fought with."

"What are you talking about?" Hana asked, something nasty seeping into her consciousness and wrapping itself around her heart.

Ivan swore and clamped his hand over his mouth. "Sorry, sorry, nothing. I meant nothing by it."

Hana stared him down, making him squirm using a tactic learned from watching Logan operate. She never removed her green eyes from his face and in the end, he cracked. "I meant with Vik having the affair before he died," Ivan said, feeling guilty as he watched the healthy pink colour drain from the pretty redhead's face. "Sorry, Hana; I forgot you didn't know. Please, forget I said anything."

"You knew?" Hana said, her voice a husky whisper. "How?"

Ivan stirred his coffee, having opened a can of worms he wasn't equipped to deal with. He waited a long moment before answering the crushed woman opposite him. "I met Vik the afternoon before he died. He was upset. We bumped into each other and he told me everything; that he'd met someone else and been seeing her for a long while, a year I think it was. He planned to tell you that day because he..." Ivan took a deep breath. "He was leaving with her, Hana. They had tickets booked for somewhere else, to go and sit it out for a while until you'd calmed down and then he planned to move in with her. I can't remember her name."

Hana's mind drifted back to that same day, over nine years previously. She was unwell, thinking it was a virus that wouldn't go away. Vik left for work and Hana called in sick after realising she wasn't well enough to go into school. She went back to bed feeling dreadful after sending Bodie and Izzie off on the bus. Waking up mid-morning she found her husband standing over her with an odd look on his face. Rushing to the toilet she was violently ill, shaking and shivering and knowing something was badly wrong. Vik drove her to the doctors and they diagnosed a kidney infection and tried to send her to hospital. She refused, accepting antibiotics and going home. She felt absolutely dreadful, coping with the shivers and sweats that went with the illness and the overwhelming back pain. Vik disappeared in the afternoon, promising Hana he'd return. He picked the children up from school and bought take-away for tea. Hana couldn't eat, going to bed early and having a fitful night.

The next day she felt slightly better but still not well enough to go to work, trying to sleep it off in the empty house. The frantic knocking mid-afternoon disturbed her and drove her to answer the front door to the two police officers, bearing the kind of news which had the power to destroy the hearer.

Ivan looked at her fearfully. "I said, he didn't leave you, Hana. So it was okay. He must have loved you and decided to stay."

Hana looked at him and he could see the shock in her face. Her coffee grew cold on the table and the baby snuffled in her pram. "I'm sorry," he said again, "I forgot you didn't know."

"I knew," Hana whispered.

Ivan looked relieved. "Thank goodness for that!" he gushed. "We all watched you for ages, wondering what to do. But it seemed you were oblivious, so we decided not to say anything."

"Who's *we?*" Hana asked with more courage than she felt.

Ivan realised instantly he'd gaffed again. Only the look on his face this time was unrepentant and cruel. Hana gritted her teeth and asked him again, "Who knew?"

"Me, Anka and the pastor. Pastor Ben, who left to go on mission in Vanuatu before Allen came."

Hana felt like someone who'd had a dreadful prank played on them, a prank that everyone else would find funny, except her. The fact Anka had known about her husband's infidelity hit her like a slap, rendering the safe years of their friendship – the pre Tama years – nothing but a big fat fake.

Hana stood up slowly, retrieving the pram and struggling as she forgot to take off the brake. She backed out of the space and left the shop, leaving Vik's old friend and ally to pay for the spilled coffee, gaily making its way across the table top and down onto the floor. She walked around in a daze, feeling stunned as her former life unravelled around her legs. Eventually, her wandering took her back to the unit, but she stood outside, not sure what to do next. A desire to see Logan drove her across the field to the boarding house, pushing the pram along the corridor to the office where her watch told her he might be at this time. She knocked on the door and opened it at his rough, "Come in," feeling relieved to see him leaned over the computer in a standing position.

"Hey love," he said, masking the inner wince he felt at her interruption. "It's not a good time, babe. Can we talk later?"

"I saw Ivan, and he said..."

"Who's Ivan?" Logan asked. Irritation crept into his voice.

"Anka's husband and..." Hana tried to begin again and distaste crossed Logan's face as he didn't bother to hide his dislike for Hana's former friend. He instinctively knew anything to do with her meant trouble.

"Hana, I've got something on right now. Could we talk about this later?" He gritted his teeth, under pressure but trying to be pleasant about it.

"They all knew, they all knew about Vik's affair, they knew!" she wailed.

Logan swore, using a word he rarely let escape his lips. It was enough to stop Hana in her tracks. The pen from his hand shattered as it hit the wall opposite. "Not *him* again!" he bit. "Can he not stay dead just for one day? Far out, Hana, it's over, long gone. Can't you move on? I thought you were married to me now! Please, I need to deal with something here and then we can talk later."

Hana backed away, feeling his temper oozing out across the room at her. Logan reached out for her, his eyes filled with regret. "I'm sorry, Hana, but you sure pick your moments. The cops are crawling all over the boarding house, driving me mad wanting to interview the boys!" The phone rang and he snatched it up. "What?" Someone's voice came out of the handset, sounding tinny and far away. "Look, I'm up to my eyeballs, Senior Sergeant Johal and I'm not your lackey. Pete's currently playing tag team with me because the principal wants an adult to sit in on all the interviews. That's in between teaching classes!" Bodie rang off and Logan sank into his chair, running his fingers through his hair. "Where the bloody hell are you, you stupid boy?" he muttered. He was tired, frustrated and fed up - currently trying to locate a student who wasn't where he was supposed to be. He ran a hand over his eyes and squeezed the painful bridge of his nose as another headache fought for traction in his senses. "Geez, who am I looking for again?" he asked himself, trying to remember the surname of the boy he was running through the timetable system. When he looked up, Hana was gone.

She ran along the corridor, pushing the pram ahead of her and almost smashing it into Acting Detective Inspector Odering as he came in the front doors. He held the left-hand door open for her, looking at her curiously as she failed to acknowledge him or return his greeting. He drew the obvious conclusion that something was rattling her and catching sight of her husband through the open door of the office, smirked to himself. Hoping Mr Du Rose was already wound up, the detective sauntered to his lair to upset him a bit more.

Outside in the wintry sunshine, Hana still didn't want to go back to the unit. She wanted to run far away but quelled the urge. Logan was fed up of flushing her out and she knew he would, even if it was only to say he was sorry. She stamped her foot angrily, recognising she wasn't cross with her husband, but herself. He was right. He'd already told her he felt bombarded by her first husband's influence on her life and she had disregarded his confession, dumping another lorry load onto his head. Hana felt like laying on the concrete and banging her own stupid head on the ground in the hope she might knock some sense into it. She bit back the surging, threatening feelings of betrayal and stamped over to the unit.

Inside, she gave Tama the cream and instructions from the nice pharmacist and grabbed her car keys. "Where are you going?" he demanded. "I'm bored now. Wait for me. I'll do this and come with you."

"I'm going to Culver's Cottage," Hana replied, feeling fractious and prickly. "And you're not even dressed. I want to go now." Hana refused to wait so the silly boy, clad only in his boxer shorts and sleeping bag, hopped out of the unit, down the steps and into the car, remaining ensconced in his bedding. He looked like a big blue caterpillar and it took him longer to get in the Honda than it did for Hana to transfer the sleeping baby into the vehicle. Despite his valiant efforts, Hana was uncommunicative for the journey up to Culver's Cottage.

Up at the house, Tama slithered across the living room floor and lit a fire, trying not to use the flammable sleeping bag and himself as kindling. Once it roared happily, he settled on the rug on his stomach to enjoy the Sky TV channels Logan got installed over the summer. Hana hauled the car seat into the living room. "Watch Phoe for me please?"

"What are you up to?" he asked.

"Mind your own beeswax," Hana replied. Tama turned back to watching a cartoon channel and she sighed. Then she got to work, rampaging around the house checking every room for evidence of her former husband in photographs or memorabilia. There weren't many and none of him by himself. They were pictures of her children but as their father, Vik appeared in some of them; holding a baby Izzie or resting his hand on Bodie's shoulder as he stood proudly wielding a soccer trophy. Hana had been trying to maintain continuity for her children, in her own way attempting not to trash the old as she brought in the new. But she acknowledged it as a massive fail. Bodie couldn't and wouldn't accept Logan and Izzie, who was entirely supportive, wasn't there to see them anyway.

Downstairs in the garage, Hana found two small crate boxes and lumbered them upstairs, laying them on the kitchen table. She divided the photographs, sharing them out between her two children, handing responsibility to the next generation. Hana had photo albums stashed away which amply recounted her children's growing up years with handwritten captions and those she kept for herself. There were only four and they sat safely on the bookshelf in the living room, at the bottom where they couldn't offend anyone. Hana saw Izzie sometimes in Phoenix and she reserved the right get the albums out and compare occasionally. There were more surplus pictures and Hana spent an hour dividing them. She left the framed photos in their current state. Her children could keep them like that or take them out.

Hana fired up her old laptop, putting it on to charge as she used it. She located all their recent downloaded photos, including a much older selfie Logan transferred from his old phone before Hana threw it into the gully to stop his ex fiance pestering him. It was taken on their wedding day, standing outside Hamilton registry office in the sunshine. Hana's green dress, which she borrowed from Anka, contrasted stunningly against her red hair and green eyes and Logan looked handsome. The excitement of their secret marriage shone through their eyes in the selfie, which contained part of Logan's arm. Hana remembered how precious their first day and night were as Mr and Mrs Du Rose; untouched by anyone else.

Hana created an album on the laptop and added a selection of photographs; her and Phoenix, Logan and Phoenix and some of herself with her older children. She discovered a lovely one of Logan with Izzie's three children balanced on top of him and added it to the file, reminded of his passion as he caught up with his pregnant, runaway wife. There was a picture of Logan and Jas sleeping on the sofa together, snuggled up with the tatty old Action Man peeking out from between them and looking fierce like a sentry. Hana downloaded them onto a USB stick.

"I'm nipping out; I won't be long. There's a packet of baby rice on the side in the kitchen if Phoe wakes and I've got my phone on me." Hana sighed as Tama snored and she checked her daughter who slept in the car seat with her thumb in her mouth. "Bye, Mum," she muttered to herself and left. Hana shot into Ngaruawahia to the pharmacy there, knowing they had photographic machines. Something which might have taken a child ten minutes, took Hana an hour. A complete techno-moron, she had several accidents and misprints before finally attracting the attention of an assistant who helped her print off the right size photographs and added attractive effects to the ones Hana pointed out. The girl was brilliant, softening the edges on the photo outside the registry office and making it look dreamy. "That was my secret wedding," Hana admitted, biting her lip and looking coy.

"Right then," the assistant exclaimed. "Sepia it is." She aged the photo digitally, making it look like a romantic 1950s picture.

"Your husband's gorgeous," the girl gushed and Hana smiled, feeling proud for once instead of threatened. She wondered if the girl would still think that if she told her that her last conversation with him included a '*b*' word, '*f*' word and something *that* Hana couldn't say, let alone spell, which may have been French. She paid for the photos and ventured next door to the $2 shop, spending another half an hour choosing from the cheap frames in the shop. Hana clanked through the frames, choosing ones that looked mock-antique and were the right size, struggling up to the till with her basket of wares, the bag of photos swinging from her right wrist.

Back at the house, she found Tama still on the floor, zoned out by the antics of Popeye and his Olives and to her surprise, Phoenix was wide awake next to him, swinging her legs in her car seat and watching the cartoon. Hana sighed, shaking her head in disbelief and laid her purchases on the kitchen table. She boiled the kettle and whipped up baby rice for Phoenix and a sandwich for her wounded soldier. Deciding to change her baby's nappy before she fed her, Hana took her to the bedroom and made sure she was clean and decent. Phoenix became tetchy half way through the process, grizzling and fearing lunch wasn't coming. She cheered up when Hana sat her on her knee and fed her, managing to keep the mess restricted to her face. Tama shuffled in and sat on a chair, his hair sticking up on end.

"You feeling better?" Hana asked and he nodded and tucked into his sandwich of just-about-defrosted-bread from the downstairs freezer and jam from the pantry. "Sorry," she said, "there's nothing fresh here."

She realised what a waste the house was, sitting on its mountain waiting for the occasional *runaway Hana* to turn up. Tama looked curiously at the bags on the table but didn't ask what they were. "Will you be okay to drive up to Auckland in a few days?" Hana said.

"About that, please can I borrow your car? I don't know if the ute will make it up there without making me scared it'll break down or cause me to be late."

"Course you can," Hana replied. "But don't be silly in it because I'll make sure the speeding tickets come back to you."

Tama nodded, finishing his sandwich and raiding the pantry for biscuits and other instant crap. Then, kissing Phoenix on top of her head and receiving a gummy smile for his efforts, he disappeared back to the TV and a feature-length edition of 'Rug Rats.'

After a breastfeed, Phoenix went into the living room with Tama, cuddling up with him on the sofa. When Hana checked on them later, they were both asleep with the child snuggled into his bare chest and her lower half stuffed down the sleeping bag. Hana took a photo of them on her phone, smiling at the sight of Tama sealed into plastic wrap like a food item.

Hana worked quickly, snipping up the photographs and slotting them into their new frames. Then she walked around the house, hanging them on the walls. It was good fun and felt releasing. She kept three back for the unit, stroking the glass of her favourite; a photo of Hana with Phoenix and Tama, taken by an obliging gardener at Hamilton Gardens recently. As Hana took down a picture over the fireplace and replaced it with the most expensive frame containing her and Logan's wedding selfie, she disturbed the pair on the sofa.

Phoenix pushed her little face into Tama's downy chest and sucked her thumb, trying to stay asleep, but he looked as though he'd been trapped in the same position for too long. "I'll take her," Hana whispered, swaddling her baby into her chest and giving her another breastfeed when she got stroppy. It gave Tama time to wake properly and stretch. "You need to get a shower so we can go back," she told him. "No, leave that." She pointed to the dressing as he dropped the sleeping bag and picked at the plastic. "It'll stop the soap getting onto it and I can redo it before we leave."

Tama nodded and padded to the shower, digging around in his bedroom drawers for clean clothes. He looked more human once he returned. The baby dozed back off in her car seat and Hana helped Tama rub the antibacterial, antiseptic cream into the bottom two lines of the *waiata* below his waistband. "Turn around and do your groin yourself," she said, not willing to shove her fingers anywhere near the randy boy's shorts. Hana held the cream and squeezed it out onto his finger while he used his other hand to keep his clothing away from it. He winced, but it didn't seem as painful as before.

"I think it's getting better, Ma. Thanks for getting all that stuff for me."

"It's soft skin down there, you idiot," Hana said. "But it's a beautiful piece of artwork. I love the font, how it's all squirly whirly and delicate. Is that the song Logan sings for Phoenix about guarding your inheritance?"

Tama nodded and his next words made her sad. "I don't have an inheritance. Kane doesn't want me and nor does Michael. I have no direct genealogical link to you guys other than uncle and aunty and I didn't feel I could get Logan's name on me without looking desperate. I don't own anything or anywhere so I thought I'd get the words of this old song tattooed on me. Our Māori heritage is descended from Hone Heke of the *Ngā Puhi* tribe, you know the chief who kept chopping the British flag pole down." He sighed. "I'm not even registered on the Māori roll for elections. So this is all I've got."

Hana reached up and put her arms around his neck, hugging him tightly and wishing she could do something to take his pain away. "I'd love to adopt you," she said quietly, "but I think you're too old. For what it's worth, we do think of you as ours."

Tama nodded and kissed the top of Hana's head. "I know, Ma," he replied, "I don't think I've ever felt so loved. It makes me feel safe. Kind of...invincible."

Hana shook her head, fearfully. "No, not invincible, love. *Invincible Tama* is a scary prospect and I don't want to rescue you from any more stupid situations."

He laughed and waved the roll of plastic wrap at her, accidentally poking her in the face. She slapped him on the arm and then rolled him into his unusual shroud. Hana couldn't find any masking tape at the last minute so used a length of duct tape, which she ripped into small pieces instead. "Good job it's not summer," she said, trying to look on the bright side, "you'd bake in there."

They tore themselves away and returned to Hamilton, arriving back on site an hour after the final bell sounded. Logan was at the unit but not in a better mood. He sat at the small table with a sheaf of reports in front of him and another heap on the floor. He kept muttering and scribbling through them with a red pen.

"I thought you did yours ages ago," Hana said, picking up one he'd completely defaced with corrections.

"I did!" he snapped. "But as head of department I have to check everyone under me. Angus has made me do the accounting and French departments as their heads seem incapable of writing English." He balled up a piece of A5 paper and threw it across the room, putting his head in his hands. "Phoenix could do better than these idiots! I don't know how some of them teach when they can't even write in full sentences." He got up and retrieved the wadded up paper, unscrewing it and trying to flatten it on the table under a bunch of others.

Hana and Tama retreated to the safety of the bedroom with the baby, lying on the bed and chatting. Logan appeared an hour later, his hair sticking up on end and dark circles forming under his eyes. He laid across the bottom of the bed, shoving Tama's feet out of his face.

Hana abandoned them after feeding Phoenix and went to the kitchen to rustle up dinner. She made a decently filling pasta dish and called them all to eat, shrugging at Logan's papers strewn across the table. Two men and a baby slept soundly on the bed, lying like an abandoned game of Jenga.

Hana dished herself up pasta and sat at the table. Taking the red pen, she dug into her memory banks for her English degree and set to work with the red pen on the report drafts. By the time Logan and Tama stumbled to the lounge with Phoenix, Hana had completed the corrections and stacked them alphabetically by student surname and pinned together by department. She felt uncannily pleased with herself.

Phoenix ate the thick soup Hana warmed up from her cooking exertions, sitting in her high chair and not spilling a drop. The men slumped on the sofa eating out of bowls and not communicating. Both brooded and Hana felt the loaded testosterone whipping around the room. They polished off the huge dish of pasta and Logan loaded the dirties into the dishwasher. Hana cleaned her daughter up and breast fed her, mindful of the little teeth in her bottom gums. Phoenix was smiley and happy, wanting to do more noise making than drinking and Hana gave up. "You're so gorgeous," she whispered to her daughter, receiving a gummy smile.

When her cell phone bleeped at her from the table, Hana found a text from Jas. *'Thanks Hanny and Poppa Logan for my new Action Man and outfit. I'm sending a photo.'* Clearly Amy was doing the texting. Another bleep heralded the photograph. A beaming Jas stood in Amy's kitchen sporting a full size army uniform and waving a matching Action Man doll. Hana spotted the old doll's feet hanging off the kitchen table in the background.

"Jas just sent a weird text," she said, sounding confused. "I didn't send him a gift."

"He did." Tama pointed his spoon at Logan and his uncle sighed.

"Thanks, big mouth."

"Oh, sorry. Was it a secret?" Tama smirked, not looking sorry.

"Aw, did you really send Jas a present?" Hana asked, pushing the memory of her angry husband from her mind and replacing it with the kind, bashful man at the kitchen sink.

"I ordered it online," Logan muttered.

Hana peered at the picture. Jas looked much better, his little blue cast sticking out of the camouflage jacket sleeve rigidly. She sent back a text to her grandson, telling him it was all Poppa's work and not hers. He sent back a kiss which Hana tried to show Logan, but he was still grumpy and she gave up.

"I did something for you today," Hana began, reaching for the bag containing the picture frames. Logan looked interested but the loud hammering on the front door heralded the arrival of her son in full uniform and Odering in civvies.

Logan let them in and Hana saw his patience hanging by a thread at the unexpected guests. Bodie was stiff and formal and Odering just plain aggravating. Tama shot off the sofa and went to Hana's room to watch the portable TV balanced on the cupboard. "You're working late," Hana said politely to the cops, laying Phoenix under the baby gym and thinking yet again she should return it to Amanda.

"Is it witching hour already?" Logan commented sarcastically. The men hung around, taking up valuable space until Hana invited them to sit. Logan crashed around in the kitchen, washing up the pasta dish and pointedly ignoring the police officers. The presence of the men seemed to fill the tiny space. It was like an uncomfortable game of Sardines. Hana felt claustrophobic.

"We're looking for a key, Mr Du Rose," Odering began. "It'll open a shed over by the tennis courts which we understand Mr Collins frequented."

Logan leaned on the breakfast bar, drying his hands on a towel. "Why would I know where the key is?" he snapped. "It's a school matter, not a St Bart's issue. Take it up with Angus."

"You were heard arguing with the deceased on the Thursday before his death. You wanted him to open the shed. What was that about?"

"Bloody hell!" Logan postured, his temper fraying by the second. "A student made a complaint about Collins to my deputy manager. He said Collins hid something of his in the shed and wouldn't give it back. I wanted to see if he had it."

"And did he?" Odering's voice was like syrup. Bodie's face was impassive as Hana watched.

"No idea," shrugged Logan. "He told me to 'bugger off,' said he wasn't opening the shed and I could do something to myself which I don't think is physically possible, even if I was tempted. I left it and intended to speak to Angus the following Monday. I saw Collins on Friday and we spoke about something else and then the next time I saw him, he was doing a convincing impression of a mole."

"Did you speak to Principal Blair?" Odering asked and Logan shook his head.

"Angus wasn't at school that week because he was at a conference in Dunedin. The next time I saw him was at a social soccer match and no, it didn't seem that important."

"So, it went out of your head, did it? Until when?" Odering's eyes widened like a wolf scenting blood.

"What?" Logan didn't understand the question.

"What reminded you about the student's property, Mr Du Rose? When did you think of it again?"

Logan paused, clearly trying to think on his feet. Hana sighed and closed her eyes, realising she'd put him in a difficult situation without meaning to. She decided to speak for herself and Logan widened his eyes the minute she opened her mouth, warning her with his expression to shut up. She ignored him, choosing truth as her only option, not understanding how very much she would be made to regret it.

"He was reminded about it when I showed him the object last night," Hana said from her corner. All eyes turned to her. Logan threw the towel onto the counter and folded his arms, leaning back against the sink. He looked angry and Hana wouldn't get eye contact with him. "I didn't know Logan was aware of it being missing because we didn't have a conversation about it before last night. The student came to me directly. I went to bed shortly after getting in and Logan returned it to James this morning."

"Are we talking about the model aeroplane? Belonging to..." Odering consulted his pocket book with exaggerated movements, even though he knew the boy's name from memory. "James Wong." He fixed an acid stare on Hana and so did Bodie. The only thing missing was the interrogation lighting and thumb screws and Hana would feel the scene was complete.

"That's right," she answered, injecting deadly calm into her voice. "James came to me upset about it. It was a gift from home. His mother works hard to keep him at the school and it was a generous present."

"We know all that," Odering said rudely, "where was it found?"

"In the shed," Hana said, hearing Logan's sharp intake of breath.

"By you?" the detective snapped.

Hana nodded and cringed at the look of anger on Odering's face. "And how did *you* get into the shed, when nobody else has been able to?" He spoke to her as though she was thick and it grated on Hana's nerves.

"Oh, I'm sure if you'd really wanted to, you could have crow-barred the door or something," she replied sweetly.

Odering stood up and strode over to Hana. He dwarfed her and she felt uncomfortable. She heard Logan's socks pad across the laminate floor and knew his instinct for protecting her might lead to him finally smacking the detective. She sensed he'd wanted to for a long time and knew she needed to stop him getting into trouble for her. Hana pushed herself to a standing position, putting her hand on top of the pile of papers to stop them shifting in the movement of bodies. Odering stood back and Logan visibly relaxed. Bodie stayed on the sofa like an obedient little dog. "*How* did you get into the shed?" the detective asked her again through gritted teeth.

"The tennis man let me in," she replied honestly. She had nothing to be worried about as long as she told the truth. Robert always promised her that. '*Tell the truth, hen. There's no fear in the truth.*'

"The what?" It was incredible. All three men said the same words at exactly the same moment. Hana giggled.

"The tennis man. He comes every night to play on the courts. He has a key to the shed because he turns the floodlights on and off from inside, instead of going back to the main building."

Odering whipped round and pointed an accusing finger at Bodie. "Who is this guy? If he comes every night why don't I know about him?"

Bodie was on his feet looking silly. "Nobody's ever mentioned him before!" he exclaimed, defending the investigation which had fallen on his shoulders. Hana looked at her son strangely.

"I thought you were a traffic cop," she said and Bodie glared at her.

"When does he come?" Odering snapped at Hana. "The tennis player; when does he come?"

"Just evenings. I wander out there and he's usually there. He said he comes most evenings. Angus knows about him because we have to turn the lights off around nine to avoid complaints from residents."

"What residents?" Logan asked.

"The ones round the back of..." Hana's face dropped. The courts were surrounded by gully, classrooms and sports pitches. She felt unnerved, wringing her hands and feeling the steady pulse beat increase in her chest.

"And why were you meeting this man at night?" Odering beaked at her, his nose pointy in his angry face. He didn't like being caught on the back foot and blamed Hana.

"I wasn't *meeting* him!" Hana sounded aghast, anger flaring in her eyes as she put her hands on her hips. "He was already there playing. I practiced against him, let him spar against me for variation. It's boring against a delivery machine all the time."

Odering swore and Hana grew frightened. Phoenix had stopped playing and lay on the rug, watching the tall men like a fragile ladybird in a dark forest.

"Why are you inferring things?" Hana cried, looking pointedly at Bodie, despite the fact he hadn't spoken. "I know you'd love it if Logan divorced me. Well, he probably will now. He's already sick of me! Now you're making it sound like I'm doing something wrong!"

Before anyone could react, Hana rushed across to her daughter, scooping her up and taking her to the bedroom while the men faced each other. She put the baby on the bed with Tama and then backed towards the door.

"S'up?" he asked without taking his eyes off the TV. She shook her head. *Nothing. Everything.*

Grabbing her trainers from the wardrobe, Hana slipped them onto her feet. She felt shaken and upset. The whole day had been blighted and ruined from the off. She was a one-woman-disaster-area. Logan would believe she was having an affair; her best friend had spent nine years studying her deceitfully for signs she knew about Vik's other woman and so had her pastor. *Her pastor!* Her son detested her and now she'd inadvertently walked into a whole heap of trouble without seeing it coming. No wonder Logan had wanted her to keep quiet.

Hana ran to the tennis courts, desperate to take her anger out on a round yellow ball, to hit it as though it was one of the men who seemed to think it was okay to dictate to and bully her into submission. Rounding the last corner, disappointment coursed through her veins like acid as she saw the darkness surrounding the courts. They looked cold and dead and Hana's heart sank like a stone. She pressed herself against the fence, feeling sharp wire cutting into her fingers as she gripped it and rested her forehead against the unforgiving diamond shapes it made. She heard a noise, but it sounded like it belonged to someone else, a dreadful gasping cry like a trapped animal. The sound returned to her, echoing off the concrete and bouncing back amidst the hiss of the trees along the gully side of the courts. Hana turned and sank to the ground, her fleece ripping on the broken, spiteful ends of metal and her fingers cutting and tearing the same way as she forgot to let go.

Hana cried fit to bust, gulping in great breaths between the sobs and causing her lungs to panic and constrict. She wondered inwardly why she was so affected by the men rounding on her and knew it was guilt for having a secret rendezvous with a stranger. She liked the tennis player and enjoyed his company, but craved the physical challenge of meeting his powerful serves and returning them with something like her old fire. All the while Hana held the racquet in her hand, she was over a decade younger, full of that zest for life which came with confidence and success. She was *good at something*, outside of being a wife and mother. It was a private pleasure, something she could indulge herself in, but the men had been horrified, twisting and turning it, putting a slant on it which it didn't deserve. They had ruined it and to make matters worse, the sanctuary of the tennis player wasn't even there.

Hana sniffed and wiped her nose on her sleeve. She felt unbelievably sad, grief stricken but not understanding why such an emotion would rear its head again. *I have so much to be grateful for!* She chided herself roughly, so that guilt added itself to the mix and made her even more miserable. The only thing missing she decided, was a mirror so she could watch herself cry and prolong the draining but cleansing feeling for longer. She sniffed and snotted on her sleeve again, reasoning it didn't matter. She felt and heard the rip down the back as she slid dramatically down the fence. Hana cried again, sad because it was one of her favourite fleeces.

The footsteps coming through the darkness were soft, discernible only by the grit under the sole of his boots. Logan folded himself in half and sat on the concrete next to Hana, leaning back against the fence and sighing. Hana wiped her sleeve across her face, putting more wet on than she took off. She changed sleeves and made a dreadful snorting noise trying to clean up her face. She felt Logan move next to her and suspected he was laughing.

"Go away!" Hana struggled to stand up, feeling stupid, but her husband seized her right wrist and pulled her back down, managing to get his arm around her. She fought against him pathetically, knowing it was futile but wanting to make a point. He kept a firm grip on her and kissed her once on the side of the head. Hana sighed, hating his power to make her feel better. "I wasn't doing anything wrong," she sniffed when the silence had eaten away at her nerves, "I was just playing tennis."

Logan said nothing and Hana resisted the urge to babble aimlessly, knowing it was at those moments she seemed to get herself into the most trouble. When he removed his arm and shifted his weight on the concrete, she felt cut loose and it wasn't a good sensation. Logan crossed his legs under him and leaned forward, sitting like a primary school child in assembly, incongruous with his six foot four inch height. "I never knew you were so good at tennis," he said quietly. "Bodie said you and his dad used to scoop up a lot of the local awards. Why didn't you tell me?"

Hana shrugged petulantly. "What's the point? It was another Hana in a whole other life."

Logan's heels dragged against the grit as he moved his feet. "We could have played. I'm not too bad, probably not as good as...Vik, but not completely uncoordinated."

He was reaching out to her, offering an olive branch but Hana didn't feel ready to take it yet. She exhaled and it came out more spitefully than she intended. "Don't mention his name, Logan. Remember how angry it makes you."

Logan sighed. "Yep, I deserved that. I'm sorry about before. What were you trying to tell me about Anka's husband?"

"Get lost, Logan." Hana heard him snuff and knew he was smiling. "I mean it!" she snapped. "Don't mention Vik when you don't want to hear it. He was a huge part of my life and I've spent all day trying to undo it. For you, Logan. *For you!* I wanted to show you the photos I made, but you weren't interested. So now I'm not interested in you. Just go away."

"Are you happy, Hana?" His question sounded sad.

"Yes!" she snapped, but it came out whiney and made her ashamed of herself.

"I realise it's not what you bargained for, staying in a shoebox and playing 'mummy' again, but if you wanted to go back to work, there's lots of options we can look at." Logan was trying hard to regain ground with his fuming wife.

"I don't know what I want," Hana sighed. "How can you help me if I can't help myself?"

"Well, I've been thinking," Logan said, turning towards her, "I could go part time if you want, so you can go back to work. Maihi would probably love the income for looking after Phoenix if there's any overlap. I'd give up working at the boarding house and we could live back up at Culver's Cottage. What do you think?"

Hana's brow furrowed as she thought about what he offered. It was a massive jump from where they were and she didn't know what to say. "I don't know *where* I would work anymore," she said sadly then. "I don't know if I could be bothered to get another job. I've lost all my confidence. Too much has happened."

"Actually, Angus asked if you'd be interested in a job on reception. Mrs-What's-Her-Name retires at the end of this year and he thought it might be ideal for you. I told him you might not want full time again and he suggested mornings. He could get someone else to job share the afternoons if you were interested. I said I'd ask."

Hana groaned. "I don't know, Logan. I don't know what to do!"

"It's okay," he said, reaching for her hand. "You don't have to tell him right now." He shifted next to her again, stretching out his long legs and leaning back against the fence. He put his arm around her and this time she didn't push him away.

"I always thought you wanted to go back up to the hotel and run it yourself," Hana said, surprised when he shrugged.

"Not yet. I'm not ready. I've run it at a distance for so many years I need a plan to ease myself back in if I'm staying for any length of time. I know I keep a tight rein on things, but you can't turn up and displace all the management you've had in place, especially when it's good management. The time will come, but not right now."

Hana nodded, understanding. "I'd have to work with Amanda if I took the reception job." She sounded regretful. Logan shook his head trying to catch up with her ability to flit about from subject to subject.

"Maybe not," he said, his tone mysterious. "She's actually not doing that well. Angus is frustrated with her. She's rubbish at passing on messages and is completely disorganised. Angus said she's worse than the last woman for gossiping. He can't tell her anything. He has to wait until the other lady comes in the afternoon and get her to do all the confidential stuff because he can't trust Amanda."

"Yeah, he's not the only one," Hana mused, chiding herself for feeling smug about Amanda's failure.

"Anyway," Logan said, "a lot can happen in a few months. We might not even be here."

"What...dead?" Hana said, horrified.

Logan laughed and it was a cheerful, welcome noise. "No, you egg! I was thinking about applying for a year's leave and taking you travelling. You could show me where you grew up and went to uni. Then we could look around Europe for a while. It'll be easier while Phoenix is still little because she won't complain about the things we want to see. What do you think?"

"Gosh," said Hana, surprised. "It sounds amazing!" They were both quiet for a moment as their thoughts ran unchecked. Then Hana said, "We could ride the Circle Line tube train and show Phoenix where we first met."

Logan kissed her tenderly and smiled in the darkness, thinking how strange it would feel, but also how perfect. "Hana," he whispered. "I need to sort something out with you."

Hana heard the weight in his tone and knew he intended to broach something major. She stiffened, wondering which of her many issues he would raise first. Logan cleared his throat. "Could you work on not bringing up the word 'divorce' every time you think I'm dirty at you? It'll make Phoenix feel insecure once she's old enough to understand what you mean. To be honest, it doesn't make me feel too great either."

"Sorry," Hana said instantly, feeling ashamed of herself at the obvious truth of her husband's words.

"More than not *saying* it, I need you to stop thinking it either. I've got no intention of letting you get off that lightly. I'll keep hold of you and make you suffer, not get rid of you, woman."

Hana said nothing, hearing his assurances but not believing them. Logan sensed it. "Look, I understand in your first marriage you felt insecure and unworthy of Vik. But I'm not him, Hana. I didn't marry you out of obligation or duty, I married you because you're the only person I've ever loved or wanted. We can't come back to this again; I don't know how to help you anymore. You need to *hear* what I'm saying and *believe* me this time."

Hana nodded against his shoulder and felt a curious feeling of relief, like sunshine on her skin. It was pleasant and edifying. "I worry..." she began and Logan interrupted her with a startling truth.

"Worrying's a sin. The chaplain told the boys at the last chapel service. He said it wasn't biblical – that if you're worrying, it's because you're relying on the wrong person. See, I do listen."

Hana felt slammed, closing her lips and knowing he was right. Without a suitable retort, for once she stayed silent.

"I suppose I shouldn't promise not to divorce you though, should I?" Logan said and his voice sounded full of doubt. "If you were unhappy and wanted me to let you go, I would...I think. I'd hate us to be like Mum and Dad...Alfred. I often wonder if things would have been better if my grandmother acted differently and made Alfred let Miriam go. It would've been awful, but perhaps better for Mum. She was so unhappy and I never knew my father. Hindsight's a funny thing isn't it?" He sounded unbelievably sad and Hana's heart ached for him.

"Ever since your mum and Reuben died," she said, "I've thought a lot about the same thing. I think instead of worrying that Vik married me for the wrong reasons and spending too many years trying to make it up to him, I should have just called it quits, thanked him for trying to do the right thing and parted friends. At least then, I'd have access to back up when Bodie went 'bush' for days, or stayed out drinking and smoking dope with his dodgy mates. Vik might be even be alive today."

Logan raised his eyebrows in the darkness, enjoying the thought of Supercop smoking dope but Hana hadn't finished. "Logan, maybe the secret is to carry on being brutally honest, even when it hurts. I can't imagine ever wanting to divorce you or be divorced by you, but if we get to that stage, instead of feeling trapped, maybe we can talk honestly and sort it out and change some stuff. Instead of receding into the pit of despair and then trying to crawl my way out, I should have been honest with Vik. He might have met me half way and I'll never know that now. It strikes me that the similarity between my marriage and your mother's is that we were both pretending we were happy and could make it right. But we couldn't; the odds were stacked against us both. I don't have to pretend with you, so maybe we got off to a better start but I *am* happy being married to you. My heart just needs to let my face know sometimes."

Logan smiled and hugged her tightly into him, whispering, "Thank goodness for that! I do love you, Hana."

He sat up, jiggling around underneath him with his hand. Hana wondered if he'd become invaded by one of the horrid night bugs that wandered around in the darkness. She watched the glow of his mobile phone as he retrieved it from his back pocket. "It's Tama. It says *'code red'*," he said, sounding bemused.

"That's Phoenix," Hana said knowledgeably. "It means she's squalling and he can't cope."

Hana worked her way up the fence backwards and heard her fleece give another rip. Logan helped her unhook herself and then wrapped his arms around her, kissing her and holding her tight. They held hands walking back to the unit and Hana dreaded having to face Tama and possibly Bodie and Odering.

Logan unlocked the front door and sent Hana up the steps ahead of him, noticing her hesitation. "You're all right. Supercop and Detective-Perfect left ages ago." As he turned back to the street, Logan glimpsed light bobbing around the gully end of the school site. It was a fraction of a second of torch flash, so slight he wondered if he'd imagined it but gut instinct told him he hadn't. "*What now? Like I need any more drama tonight!*"

"Pardon?" Hana asked, kicking her trainers off in the hallway.

"Nothing," Logan said, his brow furrowed with concern as he contemplated going to investigate. He hovered on the doorstep, feeling torn between his responsibilities.

"Come in, babe. It's freezing," Hana called.

"Yep, in a minute." Logan didn't want to leave Hana right then, sensing it would undo her confidence in him. But he feared the St Bart's boys might be on a night jaunt. They were ultimately his responsibility as manager and the adult in loco parentis. Logan shook his head and put his family first, not an easy thing to do when he felt something was wrong.

While Hana settled on the sofa with the not-too-impressed-Phoenix, Logan escaped to the bedroom and rang St Bart's office. "Pete," he whispered, "do a bed check and a head count. *Now*. Then ring me back."

Chapter 21

"I'm going for a run," Hana said, dragging her trainers from the hall cupboard and slipping them onto her feet. "I won't be long."

"Whoa, what?" Logan's face crinkled in surprise as he fastened the buttons of his work shirt. His belt hung unfastened from open trousers and Hana allowed her eyes to rove over the beautiful physicality of her relationship with Logan. "Hana!" he snapped. "Why are you going for a run?"

"I'm unfit," she stated, hearing the defensiveness in her tone. "Jogging home last night made me feel like a geriatric and I hate it. I was walking with Mrs Next Door but as that can't happen anymore, I'm taking responsibility for myself."

"But you walk everywhere with the pram," Logan said, wrapping his arms around Hana's trim waist. "You're perfect as you are." He kissed her neck, pushing her pony tail out of the way with his chin. "I can help you with cardio workouts," he whispered and Hana giggled and slapped his shoulder.

"Yeah, I bet you can," she joked. "I won't be long, I promise."

"Well, take your bloody phone this time," Logan chided her. "You left it last night."

Hana fell over Tama reaching for her phone as he roused himself from his nest on the lounge floor. "Can you tidy up in here before I come back?" she asked, keeping her tone light, so she didn't drive him away. "You can dump your sleeping stuff in Phoe's room."

"But I wanna lie on my sleeping bag and watch TV in the day," he grumbled and Hana sighed.

"Whatever," she said, resisting an argument and left.

As Logan pulled his boots on to leave, a knock at the door heralded Bodie. Logan opened the door and the policeman pushed his way inside without invitation. "Oh, hi Senior Sergeant Johal," Logan muttered. "Please come in. Oops, you already did." He ignored his step son, zipping up his cowboy boots and straightening his trousers. Tama smirked from his sleeping bag on the floor, tasting trouble.

"Will you be okay if I go to work?" Logan asked his nephew and Tama nodded. He leaned against the sofa with Phoenix dozing on his naked brown chest, half watching *Scooby Doo.* He sensed his uncle's antagonism for the cop and tuned into Logan's mood. Watching him keep a tight handle on his temper was always amusing, but only when someone else wound him up.

"Where's my mother?" Bodie demanded, tracking mud over the lounge floor and staring down at Tama.

Tama's eyes flicked towards Logan before answering, waiting for the blue touch paper to ignite and the fireworks to blaze. Logan stared at the back of Bodie's head, his eyes narrowed and his expression thunderous. "Hey, son," Logan said in a conversational tone, concentrating on Tama's smirk and bypassing Bodie with his question. "Do you think it's the same penalty for hitting a cop, as hitting an annoying cop you're indirectly related to when he walks into your house without invitation?"

"Na, reckon you'd get off with a caution," Tama answered, distracted by the antic of the cartoon characters. "Go for it." His lips brushed the downy head of the baby on his chest in a lazy kiss and Bodie swallowed and bit his lip in a wave of pure jealousy.

"Can I help you Officer?" Logan said, giving Bodie the full effect of his practiced sarcasm and the police officer straightened his back and headed towards the archway leading to the bedrooms.

"No, thanks. I'll find her myself," he spat. "I need to take a statement from *my* mother." Bodie emphasised possession with his stress on 'my' and Logan stepped in front of him, blocking the archway without making it look deliberate.

"She's gone out," he replied, his face expressionless. "See her later."

"Fantastic!" Bodie exclaimed spitefully. "Tell her I need to speak to her." As the young cop turned, he caught the smirk exchanged between the Māori men and felt a dreadful pang of nameless emotion which took his breath away and labelled itself. *Left out.* The men's close male bond looked so enviably strong, jealousy screamed inside Bodie's head like a charging rhino. "Stay out of my life!" he shouted at Logan, surprising himself with the vehemence in his voice.

Phoenix jumped on Tama's chest and gave a cry of alarm, compounding Bodie's guilt as the monster of the peace. Logan stood his ground, watching the young man's inner difficulty and wondering if the moment of truth had finally arrived. It had brewed under the surface like dirty water since their first meeting, when Bodie realised his mother and the tall, striking Māori were emotionally entangled.

Logan imagined Hana's misery if he allowed the detonation and stepped back, offering Bodie the chance to walk away. Bodie didn't move. "Just go mate," Logan said, his tone reasonable, but the young man's anger claimed too many of his brain cells for that to be possible.

"You think you can buy your way into my family?" Bodie hissed. "Sending stuff for *my* son and flashing your cash around like the Mafia Godfather you really are. You'll never replace my father, so don't even try! He was more than you'll ever be, Logan

Du bloody Rose. You're second best and even my mum knows it."

Logan fixed Bodie with a stare which made the young man feel as though his soul was stripped bare by the powerful grit coloured eyes drilling into it. Logan took a step into Bodie's personal space and stared at him from his great vantage point. Bodie felt intimidated as though he'd shrunk against the doubling of the other man's height. "Your father was amazing, was he?" Logan asked, his voice a hiss. Bodie blanched and balled his fists as Vikram Johal's sins tumbled through his mind.

Tama wiggled in his sleeping bag, trying to get free as he envisioned the situation getting out of control. He couldn't get involved with Phoenix in his arms and looked around for somewhere safe to put her. Wide awake, the child stared across the room at her powerful father as he dwarfed her foolish, cop-brother, her grey eyes studying Logan with too much wisdom for a tiny girl. Logan glanced across at Tama's frantic movements and connected spiritually with his daughter. Her eyes held his grandmother's reproach as surely as if the old woman stood across the room from him. The battle of wills ceased as instantly as it began and Logan stepped abruptly away from Bodie and drew a deep breath. "I don't know why you insist on maintaining this facade of 'poor me'," Logan said, trying hard to keep the bile from his voice. "You had a great upbringing with parents who both loved you. You know who you are and where you came from. You've had more love than Tama and I put together. You need to get over yourself, Bodie and get on with your own life, instead of trying to screw up Hana's. She doesn't deserve it. You might not like me, but I love her. Get used to it, man." He pointed again at the door, telling the uniformed officer, "Now get the hell out of my...house and don't come back until you've grown up."

Bodie didn't need a third invitation to leave. He yanked the door open and stormed down the steps, hatred oozing from every pore. He didn't close the door after him and strode away from the tiny unit feeling thwarted. Overtaken by a need for physical violence to cleanse his angry heart, Bodie had worked out exactly how to take Logan down and would have arrested him afterwards. Rage coursed through his veins at Logan's sudden change of heart which denied Bodie the taste of victory as he imagined clicking the handcuffs over his step father's olive wrists. "Another time, you bastard!" he spat into the empty street, hearing his words echo back to him from the brick walls of St Bart's. The young man stamped across the sports field, feeling foolish as the wet grass stained his trousers and covered his shoes. He remembered the last time a cop handcuffed Logan Du Rose and the cruel image bit at his anger; the metallic pressure on the Māori's fragile flesh causing wheals and bruises which bled into his arms like he'd been battered. Bodie balled his fists and felt the anger trickle away to dismay. He pressed his knuckles to his mouth as he stopped on the hallowed cricket crease and squeezed his eyes tightly shut, searching for the fury and finding only emptiness and fear.

Tama stood in the lounge in his boxer shorts, his sleeping bag slumped around his knees. Logan slammed the door behind his unwanted guest and hovered in the tiny entranceway, clenching and unclenching his fists. He avoided facing his perceptive daughter, dreading the sight of something else he couldn't cope with.

"Ha ha," Tama laughed, breaking the silence. "That's funny."

Logan stared at him, his equilibrium fighting to balance temper and pity. "What's funny?" he snapped. "I didn't see anything funny!"

"I know what you almost said to him," Tama snorted. "You nearly told him to *get the hell out of my shoebox*' didn't you?" Tama did an impression of Logan's deep voice and then ruined the effect with a high pitched giggle.

"Yeah." Logan nodded and gathered up the pile of reports on the table. He stalked across the room and kissed Phoenix on the forehead, avoiding her eyes and in his confusion, kissing Tama's as well. He couldn't take it back so he blagged it out, leaving for his tutor group and slamming the door behind him.

Tama touched the space on his head and smiled at the baby in his arms, who chewed the back of her hand. "Well, little sis," he said, happiness in his voice, "I think it's time we changed your bum, stinky pants!"

When Hana returned, she found Phoenix on her change mat on the double bed, kicking her legs in the air and singing. Tama knelt on the floor in his boxer shorts, digging around in the big cupboard drawers and pulling out baby-suits by the handful. "What are you doing?" Hana cried. "You're making a right mess!"

"They're all too small," Tama wailed, flinging another one on the floor. His fingers reached into the drawer above.

"Don't even think about it!" Hana snapped. "That's my knicker drawer!" She slapped his hand and Tama pouted. Hana bundled up the baby clothes and folded them on the bed. "I meant to take these to the op shop when I went yesterday," she said, touching the soft fabric and feeling maudlin. Phoenix burbled next to her and Hana blew a raspberry on her round, olive tummy. "You're such a big girl," she cooed, her kisses received with squeals of appreciation.

"That's not a compliment," Tama grumbled.

"I don't put your sexual intonation on everything though, do I?" Hana replied with sarcasm, rubbing her wrist across her forehead and seeming surprised by the line of sweat. "I'm so unfit, it's crazy. I did more walking than running."

"How far did you get?" Tama flopped onto the bed crossways, watching the baby suck her little toes in between singing. He put his face too near and she made a lurch for his head, grabbing a handful of hair and pulling surprisingly hard. Tama squealed and tickled her under the arms, making her let go.

"Not very far," Hana admitted. "I feel old."

"You are old," Tama replied unhelpfully and Hana slapped the back of his head. He ignored her, blowing raspberries on Phoenix's tummy until she giggled, occupying her while Hana retrieved the new sleep suits from the towel rail in the bathroom. "Get a nappy on her please, Tama," she said, pushing five suits into a drawer and holding up one with red cherries all over to admire. "I don't want her to pee with excitement and soak her vest and hair like last time."

"Ok," he agreed. Hana swapped the cherries for teddy bears and turned to find the baby wearing a clean nappy and Tama prancing around the bed wearing his warlike face. He stuck his tongue out and Phoenix giggled fit to bust. She sounded like an air raid siren, the noise increasing in volume, holding and then winding down until Tama did the funny thing again.

"Please love, you need to stop doing that," Hana whined, holding up the fluffy suit for his approval.

"But she loves it," he said. "That's cute." He pointed at the suit and cavorted around the bed again, the baby's eyes fixed on his antics.

"But next time Logan takes us to the *marae* and the *pōwhiri* begins, this child will be apoplectic in all the bits where you have to be quiet. Logan will be embarrassed. And if she wets herself like that during the *haka*, everyone will be offended."

Tama stopped to concentrate and then grinned. "Yeah, but it'll be so hilarious." He bugged his eyes and stuck out his tongue and the baby's face creased into hysterics. Hana slapped him on the backside and told him to get dressed. Phoenix tracked him out of the room with her eyes and then pulled a sad face. "Oh, stop it," Hana told her, "it's for your own good!"

Phoenix wasn't impressed with Hana's banishment of her entertainment and was uncooperative as her mother fitted tiny arms and legs into the cute little suit. Hana took her to the lounge for a feed, but already full of the breakfast rusk Logan fed her, she mucked around. "Tama, stop it!" Hana complained. "You're distracting her."

"I'm not," he lied, popping behind the kitchen counter. Phoenix laughed and sicked up milk, thankfully onto the bib.

Over at the boarding house, Logan finally sat down with his reports, not looking forward to wading through them. He noticed with surprise they were back in departmental order, better still - in class order. A quick shuffle through showed they were not only in alphabetical order by student surname, but had also been corrected with a red pen in a gentle, slanting hand. Gratitude washed over him, appreciating the beautiful redhead who just saved him an hour's work. He smiled and stroked the pages with tender fingers.

A knock on the door disturbed him and Logan ignored it, not bothering to examine the caller through the glass. The knock came again with more persistence and Logan stood and locked it, seeing Odering through the mirrored glass. "Piss off!" he shouted. "Go and mess with someone else; I don't have the energy."

"Open the bloody door, Du Rose!" Odering shouted, attracting attention from passing boys. Logan unlocked the office door and sat down, leaving the policeman to enter without invitation.

Logan shook his head. "I've had enough of you jokers for one day; I'm not in the mood, so go away."

"Are we talking about Senior Sergeant Johal?" Odering asked softly. "Or me?" He pulled out a chair from the desk next to Logan's and sat down. "I hope you got things sorted out with your wife last night."

"Like you actually care!" Logan scoffed.

Odering leaned forward in the creaky seat. "You *know* something, Mr Du Rose. And I'd like you to share it."

"Or else what?" Logan eyeballed him and the detective kept his cool, allowing himself to be observed by the piercing, grey eyes. Odering waited a few beats before answering. "Bodie Johal's been recommended to me as a kind of 'sidekick' as I climb the greasy pole at HQ. I can take that recommendation or I can squash it. It's up to you."

Logan looked at the detective aghast, a smile breaking over his face. "The kid hates my guts," he said in astonishment. "Why would you hand me his career on a plate? As my wife would say, 'you're barking' and I'd agree with her."

"Up to you, Mr Du Rose," the cop said airily as though he didn't care either way. "He saved your life last year jumping into that lake after you. If he hated you, he could have waited a few minutes so you drowned, but he didn't. You decide, Logan. I'm offering you the power and I know that's exactly how you like it; how you've always liked it." Odering stood and wandered around the office, looking at the wonky pictures on the wall which Logan spent his life straightening. Year group photos smiled back at him, generations of boarding house boys doing other things with their lives decades later. Odering turned on his polished shoes and clicked over to the door, putting his hand on the handle and waiting. Logan's hand brushed the pile of finished reports his wife had laboured over.

"Wait," he said as Odering depressed the handle. The man froze in position, without turning around. "Does Bodie want this?"

Odering nodded his head, smiling to himself. "More than you have any idea, mate." The detective's voice was soft and lyrical.

Logan hesitated and cleared his throat. "I strongly recommend you take the drug dogs into the gully fairly quickly. It might have been moved, but I suspect there's been significant activity down there recently. It'd be a great idea to bust that old shed open now too." Logan turned back to his reports as Odering nodded his head once.

"The one by the tennis courts?"

"Yep." Logan lowered his voice and told the Acting Detective Inspector in a clipped monotone, "If you double cross me on this, I'll make your life impossible. You have no idea what kind of friends I have in high places; just so you understand me." Logan picked up a pen, scribbling onto a blotter to make sure it worked.

The detective smiled broadly and his opponent heard it in his voice. "I think we understand each other perfectly, Logan. Haven't we always?"

Odering left the boarding house smiling from ear to ear. He summoned Bodie and ordered him to break into the shed, using whatever it took. Then he called the dog squad and sent them into the gully.

Logan shook his head and thought about the Old Boys' network. The old adage was true in New Zealand; it wasn't what you knew, but who. Odering was two years older than Logan in school. He was one of the good guys but still broke Logan's nose in a fight at the start of the younger boy's fifth form year, after Michael bedded Odering's younger sister. Michael possessed a terrible reputation, always staying out long after bedtime and getting other boys to cover for him. Karl Odering arranged a fight with Michael to defend his sister's honour but as usual, the cowardly charmer sent his haemophiliac kid brother.

"Where's your brother?" Odering demanded when faced with Logan. "Walk away, it's not your fight."

"He's not here." Logan's grey eyes observed the older boy with cool detachment. "So it's me or nothing."

"I can't fight you," Odering said again, glancing around at the gathered audience. "It's not a fair fight."

Logan shrugged. "It's me or nobody," he repeated.

Logan beat the taller, bigger boy to a pulp, taking an unlucky elbow to the face and shattering his nose in two places. He bled profusely over his opponent, terrifying the onlookers enough to break ranks and find an adult. Logan leaned over Odering, his blood running into the other boy's face and hissed, "Quits?"

Karl Odering nodded and they stood up, shook hands and walked away like it was nothing. Angus Blair appeared to clear up the mess and drove Logan to Auckland general hospital, yelling at him all the way there and all the way back. He would have continued his broad Scots diatribe during the procedure to set the boy's nose and give him a factor eight infusion, had the nursing staff allowed him into the room.

Logan recognised Karl Odering the previous year when he appeared by Hana's hospital bed after an attack. The ego dance began again, satisfying in a primitive, macho way. When angered, Odering revealed the scar above his left eyebrow which Logan caused with a well-timed head butt, and Odering enjoyed the slight kink in Logan's nose when he was trying to concentrate.

The teacher took his sheaf of reports and strode to the main building to deliver them, his cowboy boots clicking against the road. He slapped them on Amanda's desk and turned to walk away. "Logan," she called out. "What are these?"

"Reports," he said, his face blank. "Angus insists on seeing the quality of work his staff produce and he'll love those. *Not!*" He jerked his head towards the sheaf of paper and turned again

"Logan!" Amanda raised her voice, sounding desperate. He stopped and stood still without turning around. "What can I do to make it right again?" Amanda asked. "I miss Hana."

Logan's movements were effortless as he walked back into her office and leaned over the desk towards Amanda. Something nasty and latent brooded in his eyes and she swallowed. The receptionist waggled her ears and ignored the ringing phone, hoping to hear gossip. Logan's eyes made Amanda cringe with the intensity of his gaze. "I suggest," he said quietly. "I suggest you work out who the good guys are, as opposed to the bad guys. And then remember to shaft the right ones."

Amanda's hopes plummeted and anger lit her pink cheeks with embarrassment. Her pupils dilated at Logan's proximity and the musky scent of his aftershave. She wasn't over her fantasy and he saw it in her face. "Stay away from us, Amanda," he whispered and with a sad smile he left, taking the stairs up to the first floor three at a time on his long legs

Amanda sank into her office chair and put her head in her hands. She needed someone to look after Millie because there was an outbreak of diarrhoea at the nursery. Hana was her last hope. She shook her head at her own stupidity but the obsession refused to be banished and each sighting of Logan raced her heart and set her aquiver.

Logan's Year 11 class lined up outside his room and automatically straightened as they watched him stride towards them. A boy checking out a *'rateyourteacher'* app on his phone snorted. "Look at this," he whispered to his friend. "These are hilarious. *'Peter North runs like he's got a rod stuffed up his arse.'* It's signed, *Cowboy.*"

The boy next to him jabbed him in the ribs and he stopped and bit his lip as Logan looked at him in expectation. "Something you'd like to share, Mr Clarke?"

"Nothing, sir," the boy gulped, switching the phone off and shoving it in his pocket. Logan unlocked the classroom and the boys filed in.

"*Check his,*" his mate begged in a whisper, as they sat at their desks.

"*No point,*" the boy mouthed back. *"They're all so scared of him, they only put nice stuff!"*

Logan turned to the board and hid his smile. He loved that site. He checked it regularly and left the comment about Pete to see if he'd notice. Pete put a dodgy one back about Logan, but an administrator deleted it. Logan turned back to the class and rested his cowboy boot on the seat of the chair in front of him. He started teaching the finer points of the poetry of WB Yeats, with the faintest of crinkling around smiling eyes.

Chapter 22

"Have you got interview clothes for tomorrow?" Hana asked Tama as he stood in the lounge and pulled his tatty jeans up.

"Er...na...yeah...na." Tama muttered, using that dreadful Kiwi phrase which was more of a non-answer.

"Well, do you or don't you?" Hana asked, pouting.

"Na," he said and shook his head.

"So why didn't you say that!" Hana grumbled.

"I did!" he replied, his head shooting up and his face full of indignation.

Hana sighed and tutted as she fitted Phoenix into a coat, ready to go out. "Well, you'll need to look smart or they won't employ you," she said, seeing the dawning realisation in Tama's eyes.

"Oh, no!" he exclaimed, staring down at the holes in the knees of his jeans. "What will I do?"

An hour later and Hana dragged the young man along the mall, yanking his arm when he stopped to look in the windows of the gadget shops. "That's not why we're here," she grumbled, hauling him along.

"We won't find anything," Tama whined. "I've been in all the old-men's-shops and there's nothing."

"They're not old-men's-shops!" Hana bit, jabbing Tama in the ribs. "They're smart-men's-shops."

"Yeah, well they've never seen anyone my height," he grumbled, dragging his feet and sulking.

"I never knew he was so fussy!" Hana exclaimed to the shop assistant in the only remaining shop Tama hadn't yet rejected. "He's worse than a woman."

The male assistant bridled and looked offended, staring at Hana as though she'd slighted him personally. He muttered with sarcasm, "I don't think so, madam. He isn't complaining he 'aches all over'!"

Hana sniggered. "Fair enough." Hana looked into the pram to check her baby. Phoenix was awake and sitting up, reins keeping her secure. She cuddled a furry horse Tama bought her and Hana pushed it further into the pram to stop its legs dangling near the wheels. "Hold Fluffy tight," she told her daughter. "We can't lose him."

Phoenix squeezed the toy around its neck and her eyes widened with possession as Hana touched it. She'd developed an unhealthy dependence on the gift, looking for it in bed and wanting it with her when she went out. It filled Hana with dismay. Tama couldn't remember which shop he'd bought it in and memories of a crying Izzie came to mind as Hana eyed the toy warily. Poor Vik endured a three-hour round trip in the middle of the night during a snow storm to retrieve an ugly, squashed, fluffy green frog thing Izzie couldn't bear to be without. He'd arrived home exhausted after digging the car out of heavy snow drifts twice, only to find she'd cried herself to sleep.

The shop assistant's low whistle alerted Hana, as Tama stood in front of her wearing a smart white shirt and navy tie. Well fitted, dark trousers accentuated his trim figure and he appeared older. "Wow! You look amazing," Hana breathed.

"Scrubs up well, doesn't he?" the shop assistant stressed with pride, flapping at imaginary dust on Tama's shoulder. Tama's eyes bugged and Phoenix squealed with delight and flapped the furry horse at him.

"Does it look good?" he appealed to Hana, the coy version of the teenager seeming particularly endearing. He stuck his tongue out at the baby and she gurgled like a dirty drain.

"You look fantastic." Hana turned to the assistant. "We'll take them," she said.

Tama looked uncomfortable and shook his head. "No, Ma. It's too expensive and way out of my league. I don't want you to spend your money on me and I sure as hell can't afford it."

"Logan told me to use his credit card," Hana said. "So do as you're told." She sent him back to the changing room to remove the clothes, paying while he was in there. Tama returned in his tee shirt and holey jeans, swinging the shirt and trousers on the hanger with the tie trailing precariously over his shoulder.

"Too late," Hana said, seizing the clothes and handing them to the smiling shop assistant, who folded them neatly and placed them into a decent carrier bag.

"But, Ma, that's a lot of money." he protested. "People like me don't own clothes like that."

"It's a gift, sweetheart," Hana said, pushing Tama's arm. "And people like you are firemen, Tama, so they do."

"Thanks, Ma." Tama enfolded Hana in a hug, oblivious to the curious looks of passers-by.

"Shoes now," Hana said, enjoying her mission and pushing the pram towards a shoe shop. She didn't bother asking him what he wanted, realising he didn't really know. They trawled a few shoe shops until Hana found a pair of shiny shoes which would look smart and be easy to polish. Tama reminded her of a small boy as he sat on the bench seat and let her fit his big feet into the shoes and lace them up. Her mother's heart broke at the sight of his pleasure, knowing he'd experienced only the parenting attempts of Logan in his young life.

"You can put my shoes on every day," he said, loving the cossetting Hana provided. He fluttered long, dark eyelashes and resembled a child no older than Jas. Then he clumped around the shop, making Hana smirk as he admired his feet in every mirror he passed. "Phoe!" Tama popped like a jack-in-the-box around the side of a shelf as Hana stood with the pram nestled against her hip, holding his smelly trainers in one hand and lifting an elegant black stiletto with the other. Phoenix squealed with glee and Hana dropped the stiletto.

"Stop being naughty," Hana chided him and Tama and Phoenix giggled, sharing the same odd sense of humour.

Phoenix held her arms out to Tama, wanting to get out of the pram but Hana shook her head. "No, Tama, I don't want to start that game. Babies should stay in the pram when put there unless it's on fire. I'm getting too old to walk along pushing a pram and struggling to carry a heavy child who should be in it." Hana rubbed at her chest and frowned at the increasing breathlessness which plagued her.

"Ok, Ma. You're the boss."

The little girl whined and grumbled, but Tama popped up and down alongside the pram with her horse to distract her while Hana paid for his shoes.

"I'm desperate for coffee and a sit down." Hana said, wedging the box underneath the pram "Come on," she persuaded Tama, "I'm tired."

Tama ate hot chips, sharing them with the baby. She made a gummy mess whilst sitting on his knee. Phoenix became tetchy and Hana fed her for a while under a blanket until the wriggling stopped and the little girl fell asleep over her thighs. "Have you done any research for the interview tomorrow?" Hana asked, expecting Tama to produce his characteristic blank look.

"Yup," he replied. "I found blog sites where they talk about it. I've memorised the historical stuff they might ask me and I know what the requirements and training are, so I'm hoping that it will be okay. As long as nothing awful happens, I should be fine."

Hana smiled at him with approval, thinking how much he'd changed in the last six months. "You know we'll be proud of you no matter what happens, don't you?" she reassured.

Tama nodded. "That's why I'm doing this properly," he said, wiping the last chip through the remnants of ketchup and shoving it into his mouth. "I want you to be pleased with me."

Hana watched the teenager as she patted her child's back. His mind drifted and he degenerated back to checking out passing females with distracted grey eyes. Hana's love for the teen had grown from hatred and she questioned her own motives, wondering if she sought a replacement for her badly behaved son. Every time she went through the exercise it came back to the fact she genuinely loved Tama. He was a neat kid and Logan's almost continual backing verified it. Tama's lack of parental love meant he flourished under any sign of affection and Hana bit her lip, ashamed of her son's disdain of love when it wasn't attached to a dollar sign.

Hana ruffled Tama's hair. "Shall we go back to the unit? We should wash and iron that shirt before you wear it otherwise it might feel starchy and uncomfortable."

They arrived at the school site before the lunch bell sounded, greeted by pandemonium. Passing through the back gate, cop cars prevented further progress, parked on the grass verge and abandoned in the middle of the road.

"We can't get through," Tama commented, looking around him. He eyed the soccer pitch and Hana rolled her eyes.

"I know Collins can't shout at me anymore but I still wouldn't dare drive over his grass," she muttered. "Let's leave the car outside the gate and walk home. I'll put Phoe back in the pram. I wanted her to stay asleep but it can't be helped."

Hana backed the Honda through the gate, almost taking out a fast moving police car on its way in. "They're all maniacs," she gasped, catching the eye of Bodie as he slipped past her. Hana shook her head. "This is never going to get better," she sighed.

Tama unpacked the pram and they transferred the solid baby into it. A sleeping Phoenix was becoming a heavy Phoenix. She miraculously stayed asleep and Tama pushed the pram while Hana carried his clothing.

A shout as they stepped onto the healthy green grass made them both jump. Hana clutched her chest and Tama laughed. "Collins is in the mortuary, Hana. He's having a little sleep and waiting for a more conventional burial. Personally, I'd have left him in the compost heap; probably the most useful he'll ever be."

"Shut up!" Hana bit, spotting the uniformed male striding towards them. "Don't let them hear you say that."

"Can I ask where you're both going?" the cop said, his tone polite as he strode towards them, wearing a grey jumpsuit and black lace up boots. An enormous Alsatian with exceptionally pointy ears strutted along at his side on a very short lead.

"Home," Hana said, pointing over to the unit.

The police officer nodded. He was well-spoken, of Māori lineage with an air of confidence which was intimidating. "We have a warrant to search the site ma'am, so I'll accompany you to your home and let the dog have a run through."

Hana nodded as the dog wound its way around her pram, having a good sniff underneath and jumping up without putting his paws on it to stick his nose inside. Hana held her breath, hoping her child didn't open her eyes and find a terrifying beast with its face in hers. But the dog dismissed the pram and adults with a disinterested sniff. They didn't have whatever it was looking for.

They walked across the grass, dog and handler strolling along next to them as though out for a walk in the park together. Hana felt nervous and fought the urge to gabble about nothing in particular. The cop was tall and dwarfed Hana, making her feel vulnerable and inadequate. Tama winked at her and Hana's eyes widened, a sinking feeling occupying her stomach.

Hana unlocked the door to the unit and the cop entered first, looking around him and giving the dog a command. The Alsatian sat, its pointy ears twitching and its nose quivering as it saturated itself in the scents of Hana's tiny home. "Can you accompany me, ma'am?" the cop asked and Hana nodded. She followed as the Alsatian rushed around, checking each room with a series of snorts and sniffs. It circled the bed, sniffing in the bottom of cupboards and standing on its back legs to check the bath before moving on to the baby's room. Hana struggled to keep up and Tama had only just pushed the pram up the steps when they returned to the lounge with the dog leading.

"All done?" Hana asked and the cop narrowed his eyes and gave a pinched smile.

"Almost, ma'am." He let the dog sniff the small lounge and kitchen, moving quickly as its tail waved like a rudder. The animal pawed Tama's sleeping bag strewn across the sofa and then disregarded it, moving around the room and pushing its nose underneath the round dining table. Hana breathed a sigh of relief as the end came into sight and Phoenix snuffled in the pram.

The dog's tail began to wag in a frenzied anticipation of praise and it sat abruptly next to the dining table, staring at a point under the furthest chair. Its body became statuesque and Hana held her breath. "Good boy!" the cop exclaimed and pulled the dog away. The cop rewarded the dog with exaggerated enthusiasm and the Alsatian exhaled a series of excited snuffs, bouncing on his feathery feet and opening his mouth in a wide smile which made him look less terrifying.

The cop praised the dog and then turned to Hana. "My dog has indicated the scent of drugs. Is there anything you wish to tell me before I call it in?"

Hana and Tama looked at each other, her more bemused than him. "No," she breathed. "I can't explain it." In her panic, Hana noticed Tama fiddling with the pram hood with a guilty look on his face and she gaped at him. "Do you know anything about this?" she asked.

Tama bit his lip and smirked. "For once, Ma, no, I don't."

Hana looked to him for help, her face ashen. "I'm not accusing you of having anything," she whispered, tears in her eyes, desperate not to undo her faith building with the teen.

To her horror he chuckled. "I know you're not and I've never done drugs. There'll be a simple explanation, don't worry."

"Who else lives here?" the officer asked and Hana told him Logan's name. He nodded once and used his radio, not taking his eyes off the occupants of the room and leaving the dog on the laminated floor staring at the offending spot.

"What can it be?" Hana asked Tama, becoming frightened. "They arrested Logan for something he didn't do; they don't care if you're guilty."

The policeman gave Hana a disdainful glare and Tama put his arm around her, whispering, "It's fine, Ma. There's a million things it could be so don't go winding them up."

Within minutes, a crowd of people arrived and poured through the front door, tracking mud and grass without apology. Odering stepped in last, nodding to Hana with a serious face.

"He indicated there," the cop informed him, pointing underneath the table. "He's possibly picking up residue of marijuana or something harder. What do you want us to do? The guys can cordon the area off."

Odering chewed his bottom lip and thought for a long moment. He shook his head. "The idea of drug trafficking or pot smoking doesn't fit with my understanding of the Du Roses. Let me have a word with Mrs Du Rose," he said.

His colleague raised dark eyebrows and asked the dog to sit down, watching as Odering considered Hana. "What usually sits under that table?" he asked.

Hana pulled a face, wrinkling her nose and clutching Tama's sweatshirt in shaking fingers. "Sometimes Logan's boots, but we have to put things away. This place is too small to leave things out." She worried at her lip and flicked her eyes to Tama. "Help me out, love," she asked, begging with her eyes. "Nothing stays down there, does it?"

Tama lifted his head and eyeballed the detective, the smirk lighting his eyes with mischief. "Logan shoved that aeroplane under there so nobody stood on it."

Hana yanked his sleeve. "No, they're looking for drugs, Tama, not toys."

Odering raised his hand to silence her. "Is that the missing plane you retrieved from the shed the other night?" He fixed his eyes on her, his pupils dilating.

Relieved he seemed more interested in the plane than the alleged residue on her lounge floor, Hana swallowed. "Yes, the same plane. There were little maple leaves stuck in the joins and I brushed most of them off on the way back. The shed was covered in them and James told me the plane landed in foliage in the gully."

"What else did the boy say?" Odering asked, his voice soft. "I haven't received your statement yet."

"He didn't make much sense," Hana replied, feeling self-conscious as the tall, dark officer stared at her with increased interest. "He was rambling about electric wire and traps and confused me. His written English is impeccable but his speech can be a bit random. Logan took the plane back to him yesterday."

The cop's interest perked up and his dog stood, picking up the air of excitement. Odering jerked his head towards the door and his colleague left. Hana heard the dog barking outside and the man praising him. Odering touched Hana's upper arm lightly and she felt Tama stiffen next to her. "You just explained why the dog tracked from the shed right to your front door earlier," he said. "We took the dogs through the boarding house and one of them picked up the aeroplane straight away. Unfortunately, the young gentleman who owned it took exception to us seizing it and assaulted one of my officers."

Hana put her hand up to her mouth in dismay. "Oh no! Is James in trouble?"

Odering narrowed his brow as a reprimand and Hana swallowed, knowing she should enquire after his officer. "Yes, he is," he bit back.

"But he felt devastated about losing it. His family in Korea is dismally poor and he knew they went without food to send him a birthday present like that. It probably cost his mother a month's wages and he hasn't afforded to go home for four years. He came here when he was fourteen and it's been agony for him." Hana frowned. "You haven't arrested him have you? Oh gosh, he must be terrified!"

The detective shook his head and sighed. "Your husband acted for him admirably. He's keeping James in his office which is why he didn't rush here like he probably wanted to." Odering smirked. "Mr Du Rose is a little trapped." The thought gave him pleasure.

Hana paced the room, getting in the officer's way as she exorcised her anxiety. "Can I leave?" she asked, looking wildly at the door.

"No." Odering shook his head, deriving sadistic pleasure from keeping her prisoner.

Hana gulped and darted a look at Tama. He shook his head, reading her mind. Hana reached into the pram and lifted her daughter out, putting her over her shoulder. Phoenix sucked her hand and dribbled on her mother's blouse.

Odering looked away as Hana patted the baby's back, engaging in conversation with an officer examining the laminate floor under the table. Hana seized her moment and made a dash for the open unit door, avoiding the throng of cops in her way. Odering swore as she bolted, spinning around on his shiny shoes and watching her scurry away. Hana's ungainly run brought a smile to his lips, with the baby bouncing over her shoulder. He looked at Tama and shook his head. "What the hell does she think she's doing?" Odering marvelled and Tama shrugged, a giggle rising from his chest and shaking his torso.

"She's running from the po-po," Tama sniggered and Odering afforded a smirk at Hana's expense. "Can I go too?" Tama asked hopefully and Odering's smile disappeared.

"No."

Hana reached the boarding house with a heaving chest. The baby was heavy and her little body bumped around on Hana's shoulder so she feared she might brain damage her. She slowed down, feeling a fool and walking the rest of the way. Cops swarmed around the front of St. Bart's, blocking her way. "I want to see my husband," she insisted. "Logan Du Rose."

The officer standing in the doorway checked with a senior and allowed Hana to slip past him. "Check with me before you leave," he told her sternly. Hana grimaced, expecting to feel Odering's grip on her shoulder any second as he arrested her for running away. She glanced behind him but couldn't spot his lithe figure chasing after her.

Logan was in his office with James, the latter looking calmer than Hana expected. James leapt to his feet as Hana entered, recognising an ally and Logan looked relieved. "They take machine!" the student exclaimed, injustice screaming from his tone and stance.

"Only temporarily," Hana reassured him. "The detective will give it back soon. But you shouldn't have resisted them, James, it's made things worse for you."

"That's what I told him," Logan said, keeping his voice low and calm, "not that he'll listen to me."

Logan leaned against the wall in his familiar thinking position; knee bent and cowboy boot resting against the paint work. Tell-tale heel marks lined the wall, betraying the regularity of Logan's cruel use of it. "Hey, gorgeous." His gaze fixed on his smiling daughter and he took her from Hana, cradling her in his strong arms and kissing her forehead. She looked so peaceful and fragile it made him protective, yet he recognised a latent rage at the centre of his core, waiting to be directed at anyone who threatened her. He wondered if Alfred felt it when he held his brother's cuckoo and he missed the old man with an unexpected physical ache.

"Sit down, James," Hana told the agitated youth, who plonked into Logan's office chair with a thud.

"Police is bad," he ranted. "They make plane disappear and put me in prison. No happy. Want to go home to family. Have to leave!"

Hana stroked the boy's arm, pulling Pete's chair out to sit next to him. She noticed the pie stains and dandruff littered over its cushioned seat and squatted next to James instead. "Mr Du Rose will take care of everything," she promised, peering up at him through eyes full of belief in her husband's ability to fix the world's problems. Logan rolled his eyes at his daughter and she smiled. James doubled over and sobbed in a massive release of pent up terror.

Logan lowered his foot and turned to watch the corridors through the mirrored glass, observing the cops moving without haste. Dogs milled next to handlers, eager to be off. A signal was given and the cops disappeared in a rush like water down a drain, leaving a vacuum of emptiness behind.

"There they go," Logan muttered. He turned to face Hana. "I heard the cops say they'd found drug indications at our place," he said. She stood up, patting James on the back like an infant. "Was it that stupid...*thing*?" he asked, jerking his head towards the teenager and not wanting to upset him with mention of his toy.

Hana nodded. "How did you guess?" she asked her husband.

"It was covered in the stuff!" Logan replied scathingly. "And you'd have been wearing the residue like a flamin' second skin if I hadn't washed everything that night."

"You did that?" Hana asked. "You sound like a master criminal." She smirked. "You left a bit though."

Logan's storm grey eyes fixed on her face. "I was tired. I flushed the leaves down the toilet, disinfected the...*thing* and put it in a plastic bag. Then I washed my hands and didn't touch it again. I just didn't think about the floor. Guess I'd make a rubbish drug dealer."

"So how's the plane connected with all those cops?" Hana asked. "Has Collins' murder turned into a drugs bust?"

"I dunno." Logan sighed. "Last night when we got home I saw a light at the edge of the gully. Pete did a head count at St Bart's but accounted for everyone. At least the boys aren't involved."

"Last night? Why didn't you say something? We could've checked it out."

"That's *why* I didn't say anything!" Logan replied, rolling his eyes. "I'm not taking you into the gully at night and I've too much to lose nowadays to go blasting into situations anymore. I bided my time to see what else happened." Logan kissed his daughter, smiling at the reason for his reticence.

Hana smirked. "Liar. You planned to go tonight instead."

Logan laughed and didn't deny it. A dreadful thought occurred to Hana and she eyed the sniffing James with curiosity, hoping Odering's mind wasn't leaping in the same direction. She bit her lip and looked to her husband for reassurance and he shook his head. "At the doctor's for most of the morning with an infected toe," he whispered as James blew his nose and mopped tears from his olive cheeks. "Matron took him and they went for coffee afterwards. They left before eight o'clock and didn't come back until after lunch. She had four boys who needed appointments, so she sat and waited with them."

"That's good." Hana nodded with relief.

"Yeah, it is," Logan whispered, his words hidden in a sigh. "Because otherwise he'd be in custody right now. He totally lost it when they found the plane and that display of anger alone would set him up for a motive. Pete said he was out of control."

"Is this my fault?" Hana asked, hanging her head. "I should've warned you he was upset enough about it to ditch class and look for me."

Logan shook his head, distracted by the arrival of another group of police officers who collected in the foyer. "No, I knew he was anxious and should've done more to help." His eyes fixed on the uniformed men. "What're they doing now? Why can't they wait outside? This is a boarding house, not a bloody police social club!"

"You could ask them to leave," Hana suggested and Logan snorted.

"Yeah. Because they listen to me." The sarcasm in his voice made Hana wince and she turned back to James.

"I need to go home now, James," she said, her voice gentle. "But Mr Du Rose will look after you."

"Hang on," Logan hissed and Hana stood, watching as the knot of cops parted. Through the mirrored glass, Hana watched her son stride towards them and her breath caught in her chest. Almost the image of Vikram Johan, it seemed there was nothing of the young, frightened Hana McIntyre in him; he seemed like a stranger.

Bodie opened the door without knocking, unsurprised to find Hana standing next to James in Logan's office. He ignored his mother, grinding his teeth at the incongruous sight of his step father cradling the baby in his arms. There was a tenderness in the way the hard man held Bodie's half-sister and it came again, that feeling of being left out and excluded.

Hana got her brightest smile ready for her son, noticing the cut beneath his left eye. She held her arms out for Phoenix, standing on tip-toe to kiss her husband. "You want my statement now?" she asked Bodie, keeping her voice light.

He nodded, his face maintaining a professional blankness. Logan stepped away from the wall. "Can James go back to class, officer?" he asked. "I'll walk him over and you can use my office."

Bodie nodded once with a sharp, jerky movement and Logan squatted next to James. "Come on mate," he said gently, "let's get you to class. What do you have now? I'll walk you there and explain." Logan held his hand out towards James and touched him on the upper arm. "Come on, man, let's go."

The young man collapsed as though shot and crumpled to the floor. His eyes looked black with terror, his pupils massive. "No, no. Enough, enough. I go home, can't do this. It's too hard, too hard. I want my family. I am failure. They pay for me to be success and I am failure."

Hana closed her eyes and looked away in misery at the boy's anguish. He was the family protégé, the flagship sent away to gain an education which would repay his family's toil and faith in him for years to come. Logan shook his head and looked up at him. "You're nearly there, James. A few more months and it's all over; you can arrive home with qualifications and go to university, get a good job and help them." He balanced himself with one forearm across James's knees, ruffling the boy's poker straight dark hair with the other hand. "Mate," he whispered, "we've talked about this. You're *top* James, in every subject. You're in the running to be school Dux if you keep going – that's an honour. You'll go home a hero. You're not a failure so stop telling yourself that. Seeing your dreams just over the horizon's always the worst part. But it's not as bad as never seeing them at all. Come on James. Get a grip, man!"

James misunderstood the colloquial phrase and reached out for Logan's forearm, squeezing it in a firm grip. "Get grip," he repeated, nodding and drawing strength from the physical contact. He rallied, pushing the emotional strain from his face and trying to use Logan's arm to haul himself up.

Logan stood up and took a step back while James wrestled himself from the floor. "Come on," Logan said with authority, sounding like a teacher again. "Let's go."

At the doorway, Bodie stood back to let them pass and Logan ignored him as though he wasn't there. James bowed regally in front of him. "I very sorry for upset and smack round head. You keep plane; my gift to you for reparation."

With an encouraging jerk of Logan's head they left, striding along the corridor and stepping between the police bodies. Logan's head and shoulders rose above most of the police officers and Hana sighed. "The first time I met James he was lost in a downstairs hallway, frantically searching for his math's class. He's highly intelligent and will do something ground breaking in engineering or computers one day. The other boys make fun of him and he pretends he doesn't understand but sometimes I think he knows very well what they're saying." Hana's eyes flicked to her son, finding cold brown eyes and an impassive expression staring back. She gulped and swallowed. "Angus took him under his wing and tutored him for the whole of Year 9. He can write English better than me but struggles to speak it sometimes."

"Mum?" Bodie's voice held a spiteful edge and Hana's brow furrowed. "I don't care about some kid I don't know. Let's just get on with this."

"How can you be like that?" Hana asked. "He's a nice kid." She stared at the stranger in front of her.

"That's right," her son retorted, touching the cut beneath his eye and wincing. "You're always thinking of someone else."

Hana reacted as though stung by her son's accusation. Her face registered shock and sadness before receding to complacency. "What's happened to you?" she asked, her voice hushed. "I gave you everything I had and you've turned into a complete arse hole. I'm tired of this, Bodie Johal. I'm tired of a needy, selfish, grown man feeding off my emotions like a little boy. I'm so sorry that a terrified international student who's used to police making people disappear in the night, tried to defend himself against his perception of you." Hana clutched her daughter to her breast. "You've become a bitter, twisted little man," she snapped. "Vik would be disgusted because although he was an adulterer, he was still a man of courtesy and compassion. I'm disappointed in you, Bodie and the man you've become."

Phoenix began to grizzle and Hana shook her head. "You know what? I'd like someone else to take my statement, please. You can tell them where to find me."

Hana strode from St Bart's and arrived at the unit in distress. She asked Odering to take her statement and he obliged, not asking her reasons for rejecting his Sergeant. She told him everything she could remember about her tennis opponent, realising the nice young man had become a murder suspect.

"So, you played tennis with him twice at night?" Odering asked, his voice level.

Hana nodded. "I know it was stupid. He knew me from the tennis club years ago and seemed harmless. I'm certain he didn't kill Larry Collins. but I know you have an investigation to complete." She sighed and accepted the mug of tea Tama pressed into her cold fingers.

"What did he look like?" Odering asked. "Could you pick him out from a line up or a set of photos?"

Hana shook her head and wrinkled her nose. "He's tall, very blonde and good looking. But he looked like a lot of other tall, blonde, handsome men. I don't remember any distinguishing features apart from his very fair hair. I'm sorry." She sipped her tea. "Lachlan, I think his name was Lachlan; it was written on the case of the racquet I borrowed." Looking down, Hana saw Phoenix laying perfectly still across her thighs, studying her mother with an intense gaze. Her grey eyes were knowing and filled with unshared wisdom, uncanny for a baby.

The child volunteered a beautiful smile, her eyes crinkling like Logan's. "You're divine," Hana whispered.

"She looks like your husband's sister," Odering commented and Hana glanced at him in surprise.

"You know Liza?"

Odering sniffed. "She's tried some of my cases. The woman's got nerves of steel but she's stunning to look at."

Hana nodded. "None of my children look like me. Bo and Izzie look like their father, his Indian heritage screamed louder than mine. But sometimes I catch a face expression or a look that's mine and it's just enough to satisfy me."

"You're very beautiful," Odering whispered, his eyes sparkling in a way which affected the pit of Hana's stomach.

She shook her head. "No, my auburn hair and pale English skin can't compete with the Māori lineage of the Du Roses. They're beautiful."

Hana's heart cried out to the child of her middle age and received an answer. She smiled at her baby and the little mouth beamed wider, all innocent infant again. Hana sighed. "Are we done now? I feel quite tired."

Odering nodded and Hana hid in her bedroom for a while, enjoying a precious, quiet moment with her daughter. Phoenix rewarded her with little noises which were her attempt at speech, pursing up her delightful rosebud lips and blowing bubbles.

"They've found something," Tama said, bursting into the bedroom. "They all ran over to St Bart's. What do you think it is?"

"I don't know," Hana replied, rocking her daughter.

"Logan thinks there's a marijuana farm in the gully."

"There can't be. The cops would've found it weeks ago because they checked down there."

"They checked for clues in a murder case, not a drugs operation." Tama's eyes were wide with excitement.

Hana shook her head. "This is terrible. Larry Collins must have been involved with it and James saw him. What if someone saw James? Whoever killed Collins could intend to silence James. That means an innocent boy's in danger."

Chapter 23

Hana fed Phoenix mushed up casserole which she devoured before putting away a jar of apple crumble baby food. The effort of eating left the baby exhausted and after a short play with Tama and a change of nappy, she looked pleased to be in her cot.

"You eating, Ma?" Tama asked, making himself a sandwich.

Hana shook her head. "No, thanks. Everything gives me indigestion at the moment." She rubbed a hand over her chest and winced.

"See the doctor," Tama replied and Hana nodded.

"Yeah. I keep meaning to make an appointment."

"Do it now," he suggested and Hana frowned.

"I will," she said, making no effort to reach for her phone. "Have you ever seen a crop of marijuana?"

"Nope," Tama replied with his mouth filled with bread. "The growers set traps and stuff. Not safe places to be."

Hana paced the floor. "I wonder where it is; I know the gully reasonably well through helping with the gully restoration. It doesn't make sense; the boys go down there all the time. Whatever Collins hid must be outside the school site and closer to town. I thought it needed heat lamps and poly-tunnels."

"Don't even think about it." Tama eyed her nervously, reading the danger signs.

"I don't know what you're talking about," Hana lied. "I'm going for a lie down."

After five minutes, Tama crept along the hallway and discovered Hana searching in the shoe cupboard. She had a gum boot in one hand and a guilty look on her face. "I wondered where these were," she said, a picture of innocence. "They're my favourite ones."

"Yeah," Tama muttered, snatching it from her and shoving it on the top shelf. "And it's staying in here. Don't make me call Uncle Logan to sort you out!"

"Sort me out!" Hana scoffed. When Tama opened his mouth she put a finger to her lips. "Don't wake the baby." She flounced into her bedroom and closed the door and Tama hid the other boot in the pantry and phoned his uncle.

Logan appeared to find Hana in the laundry, fitting trainers on her feet. "Oh no, you don't!" he snapped from behind her. He sounded angry and Hana cringed, not hearing him creep up on her. "You go down there and the cops will arrest you. If they don't charge you for obstruction, you'll still make it look like you have a vested interest. They might start wondering if Collins had a female business partner."

"But I've never seen a patch of marijuana," Hana whined, "it sounds really technical and hard to grow. I thought I'd have a wander down and see."

"Do you think they're handing out tickets or something? *Gold coin donation for a look at the hash stash!*"

"Now you're being silly," Hana replied, pouting and folding her arms across her chest.

"No, you're the one being silly!" Logan retorted. He stalked into the bedroom and laid backwards on the bed. Dark circles ringed his eyes.

"How's James?" Hana asked climbing next to him and Logan shrugged.

"Weird. Not like James-weird but much, much weirder!"

Hana tutted. "You see that's the whole point," she said. "All this wanting to go home when he's so near finishing Year 13; it doesn't make sense. He's been homesick for almost five years so what's different now? I think he's scared of somebody. He knows something and feels unsafe staying here. Whoever frightened him must be more terrifying than turning up in Korea empty handed because every adult in his immediate family contributes to his education. James needs university entrance or he might as well not go home at all. Who could be more frightening to him than all those family members put together?"

Logan said nothing and his eyes remained shut, making Hana assume he'd fallen asleep. She smirked and lifted her bottom off the bed, taking her weight in her knees so as not to rock the mattress as she stood. The lure of the gully called and she smelled success. The mattress stayed level as she stood up straight, a smile of victory on her face. Almost there, she felt Logan's strong legs close around her thighs like a clamp. As hard as she wriggled, he wouldn't let go, laying on the bed with his arms above his head, smirking and watching her wrestle. As Hana grunted with exertion and temper, he sat up and lurched forwards, catching her and pulling her backwards on top of him. His arms wound around her middle, keeping hers firmly pinned by her sides so she couldn't get away. "Do you ever listen to anything I say?" he asked next to her ear, half amused, half cross.

"Yes!" she responded crossly. "I listen to you all the time! It doesn't mean I have to do what you say though." Logan tutted and didn't let her go.

"Hana Du Rose, you're a real pain sometimes."

"Don't you have somewhere to be?" Hana grumbled as her husband nuzzled at the back of her neck.

"Yep, and I'm here." Logan manoeuvred his wife off him by sliding her across his front and letting her fall to his right side. It was mean because he knew the skin on her left wrist was still tender and she wouldn't risk hurting it by resisting. It gave him the advantage as he tucked her under his arm and kept her pinned. "You're not going anywhere," he said firmly. "So nor am I!"

"I only wanted to look!" Hana bit. "I thought I might understand what happened when James went down there. seem It doesn't to add up."

"That's what Odering and your son are for. You know *them* don't you? *The cops!*"

Hana still argued. "You know what I'm talking about; I can see it in your face. James is scared and I want to know why."

Logan kept hold of his wife. "I know what you mean but there's nothing we can do about it. James wouldn't talk to Bodie, not before or after he thumped him in the face. I sat with James while he gave his statement the other day and all he wanted to talk about was the damn plane." Logan's eyes narrowed and the idea presented itself, a brainwave which wasn't of such epic proportions really. It was just logical.

Logan wouldn't let his wife go and found a way to keep her in the bed with him. "Stop!" she complained as he teased her blouse from her jeans. "Tama can hear."

"No, he's gone out," Logan breathed, pressing his lips to the soft skin above Hana's breasts.

"He texted you, didn't he?" Hana's voice sounded flat. "I'll kill him."

"Well, don't bury him in the compost heap." Logan's fingers worked their way into her jeans. His eyes had a sparkly quality and Hana knew it was useless resisting him, besides which, she didn't want to.

"You're a very bad boy," she sighed as he settled his lips over hers.

"Really?" Logan asked, his voice soft as he found the clasp at the back of her bra and popped it. Mischief lit his eyes and Hana laughed and shook her head.

Tama returned home absolutely filthy and thought he might have broken his finger. "They might look weedy but those Year 9s are pretty violent," he complained. He took one look at the lovebirds cuddled up on the sofa and felt glad he'd slunk out. Logan sat up, his legs clad in old tracksuit pants and his chest bare. Hana laid sideways with her legs over his and her husband massaged her feet through her socks.

Tama pulled a face. "Sometimes old people are really embarrassing," he grumbled.

"You'd know," Logan yawned. "You've bedded enough of them."

"Ha ha," Tama commented in a squeaky voice and Logan smirked. "At least you stopped your wife making a big mistake," he muttered, staring into the fridge.

Hana leaned backwards and glared at him. "Traitor!"

Tama shrugged. "I never appreciated how hard it was keeping a woman. They're more objectionable than stroppy heifers. Maybe I'm better off single."

"Hey buddy," Logan said to Tama over the top of Hana's head. "I've taken tomorrow off and wondered if you wanted company on the drive up to Auckland. If you're nervous, it might help to have someone else drive you."

"Naw, you big softie," Hana whispered to her husband, cuffing him round the back of the head and then ruffling his hair.

Tama's emotions moved through feeling thrilled to worried. Logan watched him with narrowed eyes. "Hey, it's fine," he soothed. "I don't mind if you'd rather go alone."

Tama put his head down and gazed at the floor. "It's not that. It's just you guys are both amazing. Tomorrow's interview is in a different place to the fitness stuff and I'd love you to come with me. I'm worrying about getting lost and being late."

Hana shook her head as Tama came to stand in front of her. "It'll be more stressful taking Phoe; I'll stay home with her and you can tell me all about it afterwards. You and Logan have some 'boy time.' I feel tired at the moment and think I'm coming down with something."

Tama smiled, thinking she was making an excuse. "I guess Phoe would make us work to her timetable," he agreed.

Logan looked at his wife sideways. "You are tired a lot but Phoe wakes up less at night. Why don't you book an appointment with the doctor?"

"I keep forgetting," Hana said, pursing her lips and avoiding Tama's narrowed gaze. "I'll do it tomorrow."

"Make sure you do," Logan said, asserting his authority. He rubbed her foot with renewed vigour. "I'll make sure you get a good rest during the holidays. They're only a week away."

Hana smiled and nodded. She fed the baby and went to bed early while Logan made a series of phone calls and nipped back to St Bart's. He was gone for hours.

In the morning, Hana helped Tama into his new clothes and Logan persuaded him to tie his necktie properly. "Come here, idiot," he said, pulling Tama towards him and tying it himself.

"You look amazing," Hana said, smiling with pride. She hugged and kissed the young man before walking him to the car. "Good luck, Tama. I'll be praying for you."

Logan stayed behind for a moment to kiss his wife goodbye and issue a strict warning. "Do *not* go near James today, Hana. He's got an assessment this afternoon so leave him for now. Please? Don't go asking him questions. He needs to concentrate and put his energies into this."

Hana smiled and faked her best obedient-wife-face. "The last thing I want to do is screw the boy's chances of getting the results he needs," she said, sounding convincing. "Make sure you drive carefully and text when you're on your way home. I need to clear my lovers out."

"I bet," Logan joked and slapped her bum.

"Stop, old people!" Tama complained through the passenger window. "I'm feeling delicate already."

Hana waved until they turned the corner and then tidied the unit for her brother's arrival. Mark instigated the visit and Hana looked forward to seeing him. Logan expected to be back after lunch and Hana thought that it a good opportunity for her brother to meet her boys. She felt self-conscious about the tiny shoebox doubling as a home for four people and she cleaned it, piling the detritus from Tama's haphazard living arrangements into the baby's room behind the door. "Time for a cup of tea," she sighed to herself, sitting on the sofa and feeling alarmed when she woke an hour later. Putting it down to a bad night with her teething baby, Hana ignored the tightness in her chest, blaming it on an unnatural sleeping position during the night. She slapped makeup on her tired, pale face and practiced smiling in the mirror.

Nervousness made her jittery with the anticipation of allowing Mark onto her turf and Hana kept busy, making a pasta dish for when the men got home. She pottered around, not daring to sit down again.

Mark's knock on the door was quiet and thoughtful, a man who knew what it was to have young children disturbed in the middle of the day. Hana opened the door with a smile, standing back to let him enter. She tried not to make excuses for the place, feeling claustrophobic in its confines under the pressure of the situation. Mark stepped inside and removed his shoes one-handed, placing them out of the doorway and then handed her a bunch of flowers wrapped in pink paper. "Thank you. They're beautiful." Hana took the carnations with care, overwhelmed by the tears which pricked behind her eyes. Under the guise of finding a vase and making tea, she collected herself, making small talk and asking Mark about work.

He gave scant details, but it sounded like a gruelling schedule. "I get ten days off in just over a week," he said, "to spend time with Mum and Dad."

Hana cringed hearing Mark call Aunty Elaine 'Mum' and she concentrated on putting his drink into his hand without getting eye contact. But Mark saw her grief. "Sorry, I forget I've had years to get used to it, but you've had only days. Do you realise our mother's been dead for twenty-six years soon?" His voice sounded soft and wistful and Hana nodded.

"I can tell you how many years, days, hours, minutes and seconds if you like. I to work it out daily at the moment," Hana sighed. "I missed her with my older children but it seems worse now. I'm not sure why."

Hana fetched a glass of water and sat on the sofa perpendicular to her brother's. Sitting on what Logan jokingly called 'Tama's throne' brought comfort, as well as an unhealthy dip in the cushions. She yawned, failing to cover it with her hand and apologised. "It was a bad night with the baby," she gushed, feeling ashamed of herself. "She's teething."

"It must be a big ask, going back to the beginning again with motherhood," Mark commented and Hana nodded.

"It's way harder. I was okay at the start but lately I'm struggling. It's just the time of year; I need some sunshine. I assumed when I remarried I was too old to get pregnant. I just got caught out."

Mark smirked good-naturedly. "Is that twice in one lifetime then?"

"Three times actually," Hana said, her cheeks pink and they both sniggered. "Bo and Izzie are close in age. I finished at university with an honours degree and two children. Vik always said we got value for money."

They both laughed and Hana remembered what a nice laugh Mark had. It was as though she had wiped out the good parts of him, allowing one awful memory to swallow them up.

"I wish I'd given Vik a chance to prove me wrong instead of reacting to a bad situation and making it worse," Mark said, wrinkling his nose in annoyance. "I've gone over it a million times and do it differently in my head each time. It's a pity we can't go back isn't it?"

Hana nodded. "Wouldn't it be amazing to take your wisdom back in time with you?"

"Absolutely." Mark smiled. "So where's your husband and the boy who sometimes lives with you?" Mark asked, trying to make polite conversation. "Dad said he's fiercely protective of you."

"Yes, he is," Hana replied, feeling grateful. "Logan's driven him to Auckland for an interview with the fire service."

"*Tama* is Māori isn't it?" Mark asked and Hana nodded.

"Ironically it means 'son' but he hasn't been anyone's son until now. Logan kept a fairly good handle on him as a distant uncle but since we married, we've taken responsibility for him. He's coming right and has heaps of potential. He just needs a help to steer occasionally."

The pair chatted and the ease of their last meeting returned as Mark talked about his life and what he'd done in the last twenty six years. "I've become a competent rock climber," he told her, "and I'm fascinated by the New Zealand bush." He expressed a keenness for exploring while he was there. "I've been offered a permanent contract but I don't know if I'll take it. I'd like to see as much of the country as possible in case I decide to return to England."

"What will you base your decision on?" Hana asked. He exhaled and looked pensive.

"Well, obviously you being here will make a difference. But Dad's been quite sick and I felt awful not being part of his treatment choices. It's not the same over the telephone. So that may prove to be the biggest factor. I also have two sons in the UK who I live in hope of seeing again one day."

Hana nodded, hearing the cry of his heart. "Kids hey," she said gently, thinking of her son. "Who'd have 'em?"

Mark laughed and agreed, wanting to know more about her children. Hana dragged out the envelope of photographs she'd set aside to post to Izzie and laid them out on the table to show to him. They offered a pictorial history of her life with Vik and filled in the gaps. Mark looked at each one, studying it with a surgeon's precision. It made Hana feel as though he was genuinely interested. She left him peering at a family photo taken in a portrait studio at Vik's parents' insistence. "That was taken before we emigrated," Hana said. "Vik's mother paid for it. She loved the children but hated me." The family laid on their fronts on a sea of grass, beaming. Vik had his arm around Izzie and Bodie had his arm around his mother. The lighting was fantastic and the grassy meadow awesome for a day out if it hadn't been fake.

Hana returned with Phoenix, who rubbed her eyes and peered at Mark from a tired, grumpy face. "This is Uncle Mark," Hana said, stroking her head.

"I'm not really, am I," Mark asked, his face sad. "If I was your brother, I would be."

Hana kissed her daughter's temple and sighed. "Look, Mark, I'll always think of you as my brother. I'm too old to cope with changes in status. Tama was a second cousin and now he's a nephew who calls me *Ma*. Logan always says family's what you make it. If it's alright with you, I'd prefer Uncle Mark."

Her handsome companion beamed and admired the baby, who peeked from Hana's shoulder. "She's beautiful," he agreed, looking lighter of heart. Phoenix rubbed her eyes and nose with one hand, giving herself a mussed up appearance, her downy curls sticking up on one side. Her grey eyes studied Mark until it became uncomfortable and then popped her thumb in her mouth and snuggled in, putting her other hand between her and Hana as though she was cold. Hana popped the kettle on to boil again. "Do you mind if I feed Phoenix?" she asked.

Mark shook his head. "It's fine, Hana; you don't need to ask."

She still felt embarrassed exposing her breast in front a man who'd become a stranger. Hana made coffee one-handed and laid it on the coffee table, sitting on the sofa with her daughter under her tee shirt. Luckily Phoenix drank instead of playing with everything in range; Hana's tee shirt, hair, her own hair, the sofa or Tama. Perhaps the absence of Tama was key.

Hana found herself sharing honestly with Mark about the situation with Bodie, telling him how her son resented Logan. "It's not like he's five and I've wheeled Logan in as the new 'daddy'," she vented, "he's twenty-six, for goodness sake. He has a fiance and a son. I accepted Jas straight away and I don't understand why Bodie can't return the favour."

Mark looked wistful. "I'm sure my sons went through the same thing when my ex-wife remarried. They won't speak to me, so I might never know."

"I'm sorry," Hana said. "You don't need to hear my problems."

"Is Jas Bodie's baby?" Mark asked, struggling to place the family members in order. Hana shook her head.

"No, he's a strapping five year old with attitude." She sighed. "That's not fair. He's gorgeous but the first time I met him was on my wedding day."

Mark's eyes widened as Hana described her first meeting with Jas. "Logan and I got married in secret. He threw this huge birthday party so my son-in-law could marry us in the sight of God and everyone came thinking it was my birthday. I arrived there to find my son sporting a hot blonde policewoman and a little boy with an uncanny likeness for my daughter and his late father. It was surreal." Hana shuddered. Perhaps it was how she told the dismal tale but Mark snorted with laughter.

"It wasn't funny!" Hana admonished him with a smirk on her face. "Oh and that was the night Izzie told me in tears she was expecting a baby which later turned out to be two babies! I'm really *off* the idea of family parties now, especially as I think I got pregnant that night!"

Mark serenaded her with his beautiful tinkling laugh. Phoenix sat on Hana's knee being winded and cracked a smile, displaying her little white pearly teeth for him. He smiled back at her. "You're going to be a little heart-breaker," he breathed. "She's stunning with her dark hair and skin and striking grey eyes," he commented and Hana felt pleased with her brother's approval.

"Don't say it," Hana said and Mark's brow knitted. Hana shook her head. "I saw you thinking it just then. You wondered if she carried the haemophiliac gene. I bet Dr Singh told you how he knew me. He probably told you why I was at the hospital too."

Mark nodded. "Your husband was having a Factor Eight infusion." He smiled. "Hana, it's a little too late to stroll into your life and start telling you what to do, don't you think?"

Hana laid the baby on the rug under the baby gym. In seconds, she had rolled over onto her tummy and tried to do the butterfly stroke on her belly.

"Just doing your lunch, Phoe," Hana called as Phoenix grizzled, popping more casserole cubes in a bowl. "It's pumpkin and kumara." Hana whacked the bowl into the microwave to heat up. "I'm coming, baby." Hana glanced at the rug, realising her child had gone quiet.

Mark had picked her up and held her on his hip. She reached up and touched dark hair going grey at the sides. The little girl didn't grab or pull, seeming to stroke his hair and face with the gentlest of hands. It made Hana want to cry again and she looked away.

By the time the casserole was ready, Phoenix recognised the sound of her bowl and spoon and peered avidly towards the kitchen. Mark put her into the high chair, struggling with the straps as she wriggled. "Can I feed her?" he asked shyly.

So Hana sat on a chair and watched her long-lost-brother, who was really her cousin, feed her baby daughter. Hana wasn't sure who enjoyed themselves the most. Mark did the old fashioned aeroplane moves, making Phoenix squeal as the spoon got close her mouth and then zoomed away again. Hana laughed. "I'm glad Tama's not here to see this. He has enough great ideas to get her going loco."

Hana nipped to the kitchen and mushed up blackberry crumble with a fork. The boys enjoyed it although they chewed theirs. Hana heated it up and sat it on the side for round two. "Dessert's on the side," she said, feeling proud of the illusion of capability. "We've got pasta cheese, but we'll have it when the boys get home."

The cheese crisped nicely on top of the pasta dish in the spotless oven and Hana closed it and put the oven glove back on its hook.

"Here they are now," she said, hearing the frantic knocking on the front door. Assuming it was an excited Tama, Hana flung the door wide and greeted the knocker with an expectant smile. On her doorstep she found the biology teacher who rented her Flagstaff house and her smile drooped in surprise. "Oh, hi er...hi," Hana said, replacing her smile and wishing she could remember his name. Logan called him, 'the biology teacher' and it was a bad habit they'd got into. "How can I help you?" she asked.

"There's a student asking for you. He won't come until you've seen him and I don't know what to do with him," the man gushed.

"Do you mean James?" Hana asked, wondering what other student would ask for her. "Are you sure he didn't ask for Logan? He'll be back soon."

"No, definitely you. He asked for you by name." The teacher nodded emphatically, beckoning with his hand and moving backwards off the step.

"I can't come," Hana said, looking conflicted. "I'm busy here." She looked back at Phoenix who eagerly filled her mouth with bright orange pumpkin casserole and Hana shook her head at the man. "I'm sorry. I have a guest as well; you'll have to find Pete or bring James here." She heard Logan's warning in her head, *Stay away from James. He has an assessment.*' "Doesn't James have an internal exam today?" she asked, showing her confusion.

The biology teacher looked pleased, nodding like a cartoon tortoise. "He won't do it until he's seen you," he said, looking relieved. "You have to come."

Hana shook her head again, severely conflicted. She couldn't abandon her child and brother, not even for someone as lovely as James. "Logan will sort it out when he gets home," Hana promised, even though he was technically on leave. She shook her head and turned away from the door, finding Mark standing behind her. Phoenix sat in her chair looking stuffed, holding her spoon with her hand and licking it. Hana noticed she held it in her left hand, like her daddy.

"You go if you need to," Mark said. "Phoenix and I will be fine for a few minutes. I can give her pudding and probably find her bedroom if she gets tired. If not, I'll play with her for a while, if I can remember how. I don't have to be in surgery for another two hours."

Hana swallowed, instinct telling her to wait for Logan. She looked at the biology teacher's flaccid face, seeing a line of sweat running into his collar. Not entirely sure why she didn't want to go, Hana just knew she didn't. She put her reluctance down to the overwhelming tiredness that seeped into her bones lately, but something else kept her dithering still. "We need to leave now," the biology teacher said, grabbing Hana's sore wrist and making her cry out.

"Hey, who are you?" Mark asked, sounding concerned. His brow knitted as he pushed his way past Hana.

"I work in the main building," the man blustered, his breath coming in quick pants. "Mrs Du Rose mentors a student who is having emotional difficulties and asking for her."

"It's fine, I'll come," Hana relented, hating the confrontation. Embarrassment forced her to stuff her feet into her trainers by the door and go with him. She looked back at Mark with an appeal for something in her eyes and he didn't understand. He watched her follow the teacher, stopping twice to fasten her laces. Mark quashed the feeling of unease, closing the front door as Phoenix dropped her spoon onto the floor with a clatter and peered over the side of her high chair at it. She beamed as he produced a blue one from the cutlery drawer and ran hot kettle water over it to make sure it was sterile. "Ever the doctor, my dear," he said with a smile as she whined in expectation. Then he began pushing the bright red mushy crumble between eager lips as though feeding a baby bird.

Mark's sense of disquiet remained though, especially when Hana hadn't returned after an hour.

Chapter 24

"It was so cool; I can't wait to tell Ma how it went," Tama gushed for the twelfth time between the outskirts of Auckland and the edge of Hamilton. "Never expected them to *want* me; I thought it was about them getting rid of applicants. My interviewer said I'm in the final five percent. There were over a hundred people at the first fitness test and they picked me!"

Logan looked sideways at the excited young man. He prayed to Hana's God to give the kid a break, just this once. "Hey, mate, it's gotta be your turn for something good to happen." He let the teenager prattle on and on about the other interviewees who sat nervously waiting for their interview and the camaraderie already budding. Logan smiled to himself, crinkling the ugly scar at the side of his right eye and looking forward to the upcoming holidays.

"Where do you want to be until you leave?" he asked and Tama furrowed his brow.

"Are you going back to the hotel or staying in Hamilton?" He clapped his hands in excitement. "Because I leave in just under two weeks to start my training." His eyes sparkled.

"I've told Hana she can choose," Logan said, "so Culver's Cottage or the hotel, but you're welcome at both."

"Hey, thanks Uncle," Tama said. "She was talking about the hotel yesterday, so I guess she's decided."

"That's awesome." Logan grinned, thrilled his favourite place was slowly becoming hers. "I'm considering asking her father and his wife to join us as guests and maybe her brother."

"I haven't met him," Tama commented.

"You will soon," Logan replied with a smirk.

"Will you ask Leslie to look after Phoe while you're at home?"

"Why?" Logan narrowed his eyes.

"To give Ma a break. She needs a proper rest; she looks permanently knackered."

"No, she doesn't!" Logan sounded offended and Tama changed the subject.

"Shall I pretend I didn't get in?" He giggled. "Yeah, that's what I'll do. I'll look really cut up and see how long I can trick her for."

Logan shook his head and sighed, wondering when the young man would stop behaving like a child.

Logan parked outside the unit and Tama couldn't contain himself. "That sad face is pathetic," Logan called as the teenager struggled to look miserable.

"Hurry up!" Tama hissed. "I don't wanna knock in case Phoe's sleeping. Please, be quick!" He bounded up the steps like a gazelle.

"Idiot!" Logan laughed and threw him the keys. Tama burst into the unit and Logan ran smack into the back of him as the teenager ground to a halt in the tiny hallway. Standing by the window was a stranger, a tall, dark haired man with green eyes and he clutched Hana's baby. Phoenix lay passively in his arms, a smudge of purple stuff around her tiny sleeping lips.

"What're you doing?" Tama snapped, his body stiffening.

Logan put a restraining hand on his upper arm, pushing past and offering his hand to the stranger cradling his child. "Logan Du Rose," he said politely. "I guess you must be Mark?"

Mark's face lit up. "Yes, Hana's...brother. Unfortunately, I need to leave in a short while. I'm operating at four. Hana put pasta in the oven for everyone, but I turned it down an hour ago to stop it burning."

"Is Hana in the bathroom or something?" Tama asked, still suspicious and fighting the urge to rip his adopted sister from the man's arms. Mark shook his head and looked concerned.

"No. I'm worried about her actually. A man came by and asked her to go with him. She didn't want to, but he persuaded her. I offered to look after Phoenix and she left after some deliberation. I've spent the last hour thinking it through and I'm certain she felt afraid. She gave me this odd stare as she left but I'm worried I read into it too much. We only just reconnected after almost three decades and I might be overreacting." Mark winced, looking apologetic. "I'm very glad you're here." The surgeon seemed uncharacteristically flustered.

Logan shook his head. "Start at the beginning. Who came for her?"

Mark scratched his head, mussing his neat hair but not for the first time that afternoon. "I don't think the man was called James because he intended to take her to see James. At least, she thought that's who he meant and he agreed with it. His actual words were 'a student' and Hana provided the name."

Logan ran his hands across his face, alarm bells sounding in peels in his head. Tama hadn't moved but fixed his grey eyes on Mark's face with terrifying intensity. "What did he look like?" He gnawed at his bottom lip and Logan shook his head.

"It's not Laval, Tama. Don't even go there. The old one's banged up and the young one's dead."

"My goodness!" Mark's tone contained horror. Tama repeated his question and Mark used his sharp surgeon's mind to recall the details of the caller, picking up on the men's panic. "I'm afraid short, balding and round will account for a lot of people," he said, his eyes channelling fear.

Tama took a step towards Logan. "She wouldn't leave Phoe, not after last time. No offence." He raised his hand to placate Hana's brother, who nodded.

"Yes, well clearly I have literally been left holding the baby and I really must go," Mark said and Tama rolled his eyes at the polite English reserve.

"This is really bad, Uncle Logan."

Logan stopped Tama's rambling with a look and turned to Mark. "You're right, the description's no help. But you're certain Hana knew the man."

"Yes." Mark chewed his lip. "Damn, I feel awful. She didn't say his name although she knew him and there was a queer moment when he grabbed at her wrist and she yelped in pain. Oh, my goodness, I'm so sorry. I should've realised."

Logan forced himself into action. "Son," he said to Tama, "please look after your sister. Mark, you come with me. Tama, call Bodie or Odering and if you can't get either of them, dial 111." He threw his phone at the young man who caught it one handed.

"Bloody hell!" he exclaimed, pointing to Hana's abandoned phone next to the kettle. "She didn't have a chance to take it."

Tama swallowed, panicking as Mark tried to hand him the baby.

"The police will find her," Mark said, shifting on his feet with anxiety. "I won't be much use, I'm afraid."

"You're coming anyway," Logan hissed and Mark's eyes widened.

Logan kissed his child on her sleeping forehead and stuffed Hana's phone in his pocket. Pushing Mark outside, he waved his arms in frustration. "Which way did they go?"

"That way," Mark pointed definitively towards the tennis courts and the gully. He seemed sure and Logan set off at a fast jog, Mark pacing alongside after tying his shoelaces. Larry's old shed door swung open and the men surprised a female cop who jumped, her striking blue eyes widening in alarm. A white suited man stood inside, fingerprinting the light switches.

"Did you see a woman go past here about an hour ago?" Logan asked, his breath coming quickly. "She's slender and pretty with auburn red hair. She was with a guy, short, fat and bald."

Mark winced at Logan's description and the forensic cop nodded. "Yep, they went down there towards the gully. My colleagues cordoned off the right fork, but they went left anyway. I shouted, but they ignored me so if you see them, they need to come back up. There's a police investigation."

Logan ran his hand over his face, trying to keep a cool head while his heart screamed at him to react. "Tell Odering Hana Du Rose is missing. Someone came for her and she's gone and we don't think it was willingly."

The forensic cop stopped brushing the doorframe and swore but the female reached for her radio. She looked familiar, but Logan had seen so many cops in the last week, he'd stopped noticing them. "I'm so sorry," she said, looking embarrassed. "I heard Jake shout but my sergeant briefed me to stay at the shed until it was examined but I should've investigated." She looked upset, turning away as the radio crackled on her stab vest.

"Go and see Tama," Logan interrupted, moving backwards at a quickening pace. "He's in the unit at the end with my daughter. He knows what the guy said before he took my wife." Logan called the rest of his sentence over his shoulder as he pursued Mark onto the slope into the gully.

"Sorry, I couldn't stand there talking when Hana might be hurt," Mark puffed, his breathing laboured.

The men crested the slope and Logan stopped, dropping to his knees and staring at the ground. An image of Hana in the same spot a year ago misted his vision as he searched the wet ground for footprints. A summer breeze blew her red hair as she stared up at him from the gully floor and Logan felt the same desire to kiss her. "Bastard!" he shouted and struck the floor with a closed fist.

"What? What?" Mark panicked, treading the ground as Logan blinked to clear the image. He trampled the area, destroying evidence of Hana and Logan shoved at his shin in frustration. Mark's shoe dislodged a stone and it skittered into the bush, thwacking off the bark of a native punga.

"What are you doing?" Mark asked with impatience, seeing only dead leaves and mud. *Lots of mud.* "The police will send dogs, won't they?"

Logan shook his head. "Hana's trainers were by the door this morning but not when we got home."

"No, she slipped them on," Mark confirmed.

Logan nodded, satisfied. "I bought them for her; they've got a distinctive mark underneath, a circle with an arrow through it. Look for that impression in the mud. Then we can track her without running around like idiots, wasting time." He glared at Mark. "And I'm not waiting for the cops this time."

Feeling chastised, Mark searched around for the pattern Logan described, seeing nothing but the muck of a wintery dirt track.

"Got it!" Logan called, moving off at speed. He ran along the track into the gully, the trees rising around the men and dimming the afternoon light. The noises changed from human-generated, distant cars, schoolboy shouts and laughter becoming feral; a mammal, a rustle, a bird call and the sense of being watched by myriad eyes. Mark shivered as the temperature dropped away from the face of the weak sun.

"I need to call the hospital and explain," Mark hissed, feeling the need to whisper. Logan ignored him and Mark jogged behind, texting an apologetic message to his colleague and pleading emergency. Twice he slithered in the mud and almost overbalanced in his effort to right himself. It was hard going as thick treacle spread underfoot the nearer they got to the water level. Small tributaries gathered pace, running towards the Mighty Waikato River and joining in a watery embrace all over Hamilton city, sacrificing themselves into its massive volume unnoticed. Logan ran on like a sure footed mountain goat. Even though his cowboy boots had smooth, worn soles, he didn't slip once and Mark huffed and puffed behind him, cursing his haphazard footing.

Stopping at a fork in the track Logan halted and dropped to his haunches, studying the churned mud with a bushman's eye. Mark watched in amazement as he separated hundreds of student footprints doing cross country from the single, partially obscured trainer tread. The circle and arrow took a left fork and disappeared as though Hana evaporated. "Don't follow me for a second." Logan jumped off the track and onto a steep bank a few metres above it. He disappeared over a ridge and then called to Mark. "This way!"

The older man treated the bank as though it was a rock face and navigated it with care, impressive despite his daily advance towards sixty.

"We really should wait for the cops," Mark whispered breathlessly as he caught up with him at the top of the ridge.

Logan shook his head dismissively. "No way. I'll find Hana myself and deal with whoever's with her." His eyes flashed with dark danger, twinkling in the dappled light beneath the trees.

Mark looked apprehensive. "I'm not a particularly good fighter. I swore off violence for life after the incident with Vik. It knocked me sick for weeks afterwards, not to mention finishing my dwindling marriage for good."

"Do I look like a man who cares?" Logan hissed, the whites of his eyes shining in the gloom. Mark shook his head and saw the latent fury in the Māori's face.

"Fine," he conceded. "At least I can offer you my medical services then." He followed like a faithful puppy as Logan half ran, half slid down the ridge, jumping off into a pile of leaves to cushion his landing. Mark copied, trusting finally that the other man knew what he was doing. The sides of the gully rose above them, higher than anyone passing through the city would guess. In places, the ridges were unassailable, sheer muddy faces worn by the passing of flood waters or slow nagging streams, depending on the season and weather. The mud was thicker at the bottom than Mark thought possible and clasped hold of his feet, threatening to pitch him over. Orange mud covered

Logan's expensive slacks to the backs of his knees and his cowboy boots vanished in a veneer of syrupy muck.

She came at them running, slipping and sliding in the mud, way off the beaten track. Her hair streamed red behind her like flames as she dipped and stumbled in the uneven landscape. Her breathing sounded ragged and laboured, her eyes like huge green emeralds in her white, frightened face. Mud streaked her face and hands from a tumble and ripped clothing streamed behind her, one layer indistinguishable from another. Hana rounded the bend and pitched straight into her husband, hitting and kicking, trying to scream but prevented by the constriction in her lungs.

Logan grabbed her forearms, even in panic avoiding the livid scar on her left wrist. "Hana, Hana, steady, babe. You're safe." He righted her as solidly as possible in the sliding earth and she clung to him, finding a lighthouse in the middle of a manic, stormy sea. Her breath caught in her chest and she gasped, pointing behind her and slipping as she pushed past Logan.

He worked it out, shoving Hana behind him and into Mark, just as the biology teacher rounded the bend and smashed straight into Logan's fist. He went down like a skittle, flailing a little before lying still, his glasses bent upwards from the bridge of his nose like transparent butterfly wings. Logan rubbed his knuckles and flexed his fingers, relieved they moved without obvious damage. Mark watched him deliberately hit with his right hand, a boxer's knockout punch. Logan kicked the man's legs, making sure he was unconscious, then embraced his trembling wife.

Mark stepped towards the man on the ground, his doctor's mind concerned. Logan shook his head, his eyes flashing. "Leave him."

"But he's injured!" Mark protested.

Logan's face became blank, the nothing in his eyes terrifying. "Make your choice," he hissed and Mark swallowed, recognising the ultimatum. Mark hesitated, watching the man's fingers twitch and fighting the urge to intervene.

Logan comforted Hana, keeping her tiny frame upright against his body, holding her up. Her breathing slowed but didn't lose its dreadful rasp. Mark reached out to take her pulse but pulled his hand back in fear, more lost than he'd ever felt. She left the unit in jeans and a floral top, both obliterated by brown and orange filth. Her blouse flapped at the shoulder showing a delicate, pale neck which was scratched and bleeding. The gully temperature dropped as daylight waned and Hana shivered with cold and shock. Logan stripped off his jacket revealing a neat, white shirt and cufflinks, an incongruous sight in the natural surroundings. "Here you go, babe." He slipped it around Hana's shaking shoulders and wrapped his arms around her again.

The man on the floor started to come round, shifting his legs and running his hand over his eyes, half submerged in water. Mark watched Logan's jaw tense as he turned slowly, still propping up his wife. A terrifying ruthlessness crossed his face, unleashing a blackness which was terrifying to see and Mark stepped forward, placing a hand on Logan's arm and shaking his head. "Don't," he said. "Please, don't."

Logan's brow furrowed and he glanced again at the flailing man before the hatred in his eyes faded and he nodded. Voices and the excited bark of a dog heralded the cavalry, sounding like a war party as the cops rounded the last bend and approached the mud stained group. "Mr Du Rose?" the dog handler shouted and Logan nodded, narrowing his grey eyes as the biology teacher pushed himself to a sitting position, disliking his partial lie down in the gully.

The burly police dog stretched its leash taut as it made for the adults, setting up a victorious bark. Logan watched over Hana's head as the handler patted the hound and rewarded its success. Other officers bypassed the giddy, slavering dog and stood over the man struggling in the water. Logan's hand itched to give him another slap, needing to feel the pain of his fingers breaking to release the angry pressure building in his head. He tried to breathe it out through his nose, willing it to go as Hana shivered under his jacket, her head pushed into his chest. Mark stood by feeling useless, his clothing wrecked by the unforgiving gully mud.

"What happened?" The most senior cop's voice sounded loud in the natural setting, jarringly bellicose against the trickling water and soft, rustling nikau palms.

Hana wailed, losing the last of her fragile nerve, "He wouldn't let me go..."

The police officer glanced at Logan, seeing his battle for control and nodded. "Get him up and cuff him," he told another officer. The dog, freshly rewarded, barked excitedly at its quarry as the biology teacher stumbled past, slipping and sliding without arms to balance him, a cop on either side. His nose bled in a steady trickle and Logan's jaw worked as the teacher got eye contact with him. Logan mouthed, '*You're dead*,' and the biology teacher paled.

"I didn't mean it," he squeaked, blood leaking into his mouth. "She saw me; I didn't have a choice."

Logan waited for the knot of cops to pass, listening to the senior cop cautioning the fat man that everything he said could be used in court action. Logan worked his jaw and chastised himself for listening to Mark.

"I'm sorry," Hana's brother said softly and Logan darted a glance towards him. "I wish I'd let you hit him," he admitted. "Sure feel like it myself now." Seeing the state of Hana compounded his guilt and Logan nodded, accepting the apology.

Logan turned his wife gently and pushed her in front of him, keeping a firm hold on her shoulders as she picked her way through the muck. It took half an hour to get up the track into school, a dreadful journey which Logan would relive in his mind a million times over the next few weeks, punishing himself for missing the cues to disaster. It felt endless, Mark trudging along silently behind. At the top of the track an ambulance waited, its back doors flung open. Tama paced in front of it, pushing a sleeping Phoenix in the pram, up and down, up and down. Wheel tracks in the gravel betrayed his expression of anxiety.

An ambulance woman made straight for Hana as she crested the brow of the hill, offering her a blanket and leading her by the arm to the back of her vehicle. "Come in here and let me check you over," she said, her tone light.

Reaching it, Hana saw the biology teacher sitting inside having a cut to his head dealt with by another paramedic. "No!" she cried. "You can't make me." She refused to go any nearer, reaching out a dirty hand for the hood of her pram and clinging to the fabric. "I want to go home," she said pitifully to Logan and he nodded, shaking his head at the ambulance woman.

"We'll be fine," he said. "Thanks." He led his wife around the back of the ambulance but the paramedic protested.

"She's got deep gashes on her arms and neck," she said, pointing at Hana's torn shirt. Embarrassed, Hana raised Logan's jacket and rearranged it over her cuts.

"Please, Logan," she begged. "I want to go."

Logan gritted his teeth. "You expect my wife to get in your van next to the guy who hurt her? Seriously?"

"Oh. I didn't know." The woman looked sorry and Logan relented.

"My brother-in-law's a surgeon. We'll be fine."

Mark's shoulders lifted and his posture altered at Logan's familial acknowledgement. It was acceptance of gigantic proportions for a man who felt he had no right to expect it. The three men and one pram flanked Hana protectively as they walked away from the milling cops and chatter of radios.

Odering stopped a male officer following them, shaking his head. "I know where to find them," he assured him. Then he raised an eyebrow. "Unless they take off elsewhere, which wouldn't be the first time the Du Roses gave me the slip." Odering crooked his finger at the female officer standing by the shed, her blonde hair flying free of her ponytail in the breeze. "Lucy, you go. Check her out as best you can, photograph anything important and bag her clothing. If she says *anything*, write it down."

"Yes, sir." The policewoman shadowed the family unnoticed, slipping into the unit behind Mark and ignoring the anger on Logan Du Rose's fearsome face when he noticed her. Tama's reaction was different.

"Luce! I'm glad you're here; it's been a bloody nightmare." He seized her in strong arms and buried his face in her blonde hair and the policewoman's cheeks pinked with embarrassment.

"No, Tama," she said, biting her lip. "I'm on duty."

Logan visibly relaxed. "So you're Lucy?" he said, smiling at her self-conscious nod. "Well, Lucy, I'm taking my wife to the bathroom to help her get this dirty clothing off."

"No! Please, Mr Du Rose. I have to be there!" Lucy followed them down the hallway, avoiding the blobs of mud littering the laminate floor.

"Leave her alone!" Logan snapped as Lucy pushed on the bathroom door, resisting his strength. He poked his face through the gap, his eyes centimetres away from Lucy's. "If you don't allow my wife her dignity, I'll throw you out. Do you get it?"

Lucy swallowed and nodded, holding out the clear plastic bag in her hand. "Please can you put everything in here?"

"Everything?" Logan's nose wrinkled and rage and fear blazed through his eyes.

"Yes, please. I'll wait here."

Logan accepted the plastic bag and shut the door in the policewoman's face. Lucy gazed at Tama who watched from the archway into the lounge and he rolled his eyes and drew a line across his throat.

Logan ran the shower, unable to look at Hana as she shivered in the corner. He readied his face, assuming a businesslike guise before turning towards her. A flutter of tears dripped from Hana's chin, bouncing off the linoleum like dropped pearls and Logan reacted instinctively, enfolding her. "Hey, baby, shh. Everything's gonna be okay now, I'm here."

"Why me?" Hana's voice sounded harsh, echoing off the tiles. "Why is it always me?" Her green eyes flashed with injustice and bitterness. "What's wrong with me, Logan?"

His arms tightened around her and he kissed the top of Hana's head. "Nothing, babe, nothing. This isn't your fault." His voice wobbled and he fought his demons by becoming busy. "Let's get this mud off you." He peeled his jacket away, dropping it onto the floor and seeing again the awful scratches and cuts on his wife's bare arms. Hana's nails were lined with orange mud, chipped and ragged. "Do you need help with your jeans?" Logan asked, chewing his lip.

Hana shook her head and fumbled with the zipper, hauling her pants down and struggling to step out of them. "This is ridiculous," she sighed with exasperation as they caught over her feet and turned inside out.

"Sit on the side of the bath," Logan told her. Hana sat and he pulled the material over her feet, taking her socks with them and throwing everything on top of his ruined jacket. Her jeans were shredded in places but had protected Hana's legs from the spiteful cutty grass and bush lawyer lurking in the gully. Faint red scratches marked her flesh and Logan watched her face for anxiety as he lifted her blouse over her head and undid her bra. As she stood naked in front of her husband, her body trembling from delayed shock, Logan noticed bruising round Hana's waist and upper arms. Hand marks on the underside of her jaw finished in deep scratches at the back of her neck and Logan balled his fists in fury.

"It hurts," Hana said, lifting her hair and pressing her fingers against the raw skin. She winced and Logan pulled her hands away.

"It's gonna sting but we need to wash it." He bit his lip. "Hana..."

Her green eyes turned towards him and Logan took a deep breath as she pressed her breastbone and closed her eyes.

Lucy knocked on the door, seeing the obvious agony in Logan's face as he opened it and handed the bag of clothes through a small slit. "We need a doctor to check her out," she whispered as sensitively as she could. "It's important; it might be the difference between her attacker going to prison and getting away with it."

Logan nodded. "Ok," he said. "We won't be long." Then he closed the door in Lucy's face and locked it.

"Won't I do?" Mark asked. "I'm her brother. It might be kinder."

Lucy shook her head. "Sorry, we have procedures. She has to be questioned properly and checked over by our doctor. I know it seems harsh, but it's about continuity of evidence. She shouldn't be showering here; my superior will kill me."

Mark nodded and sat on the sofa with a bump, rubbing his hands over his eyes. The baby slept in the pram and Tama inspected the contents of the oven, bringing out the cold pasta dish. "Was this our lunch?" he asked and Mark nodded. The cheese had become a wooden, impenetrable layer, brown and crusted. "Want some?" Tama asked and Mark shook his head. "I'm hungry," Tama mused, venting his anguish by exercising his best teenage skill. He filled a bowl and microwaved the pasta, pushing the leathery food between his lips with automaton movements.

"I feel bad for this," Mark whispered, changing his mind and copying him. They ate standing, leaning against the kitchen counter.

"It's only natural," Tama replied, his mouth full. "Once, Logan smacked me in the face and I ate five cheeseburgers. It really helped."

Mark stopped eating, the pasta tumbling from his halted fork. "Logan hit you in the face?"

"Ah yeah. But it was ages ago and I asked for it."

Mark swallowed and eyed the archway nervously. "That's awful. Your own uncle hit you?"

Tama raised an eyebrow and glared at Mark. "Yeah. But I did something wrong. Hana's first husband didn't ask you to beat the crap out of him for standing by her, did he?"

Mark's complexion paled and he placed his unfinished food on the counter with trembling hands. Oblivious, Tama folded wedges of rubbery cheese into parcels and popped them into his mouth one at a time, a sudden look of guilt crossing his face. "Oh. Sorry, Luce. Want some?"

"No, thanks." Lucy kept her vigil, leaning with her back against the archway, nervously fiddling with the curly wire of her radio earpiece.

"I might eat it all," he said, scraping the remnants into his bowl. "Logan never eats when he's had an upset." Tama wiped his mouth with the back of his hand and put the platter into the dishwasher, gobbling the last mouthfuls as he heard the sound of the bathroom door opening and voices.

Hana appeared in the lounge dressed in clean track pants and a hoodie of Logan's. "I'm not going!" she said miserably. "I need to feed my daughter."

As if on cue, Phoenix popped her head up, pulling a funny face as she strained to see over the side of the pram. Tama unhooked her straps, waiting for Hana to settle on the sofa before handing her the baby. Hana seemed oddly composed as she relaxed into the familiar routine with her child, but Logan paced the floor in his dirty clothes, unable to stand still.

"You and Mark need a shower, love," Hana remarked. "You're making a mess."

Logan looked down at the bottom of his pants and swore as if seeing the orange stained fabric for the first time. He turned on his heel and the others heard the linen cupboard door opening as he fetched a clean towel. Hana fed her baby, gently stroking Phoenix's downy head with fingers which shook less with every passing minute. Lucy waited by the front door and Tama sat on his usual seat, watching TV with the volume turned down. Mark felt too dirty to sit, hovering by the breakfast bar and feeling stunned by the calmness of his sister. In his memories, she was highly strung and volatile and he hardly recognised the girl she was in the woman regally feeding her baby on the sofa.

Hana felt his eyes on her and looked up, forcing a smile onto her face. "Sorry, Mark. It wasn't the afternoon I'd planned for us," she said. "You must be starving. I'll get you something to eat in a second."

Mark looked guilty and Tama half turned his head. "It's sweet, Ma, I've fed us both."

Mark bit his lip and pulled a face at his partner in crime as Logan emerged from the bathroom with a towel round his waist. "Bathroom's free," he said, running a slender hand through his dark waves. He turned and saw the look of horror on Lucy's face as his exposed scars came into view and bit his lip. "Can't you just go?" he asked nastily and Lucy blanched.

"No, I have to wait for your wife. My inspector wants us to leave now; he's already at the station." Lucy wished Odering would burst in, taking charge of a situation she had long since lost control of. She couldn't say he hadn't warned her. '-*Watch Du Rose*,' he'd said and she'd ignored him, thinking the handsome Māori was as puppy-dog-like as his nephew.

The hot water had angered Logan's scars, making them ridged and red, the operation wound from the removal of his spleen less awful than the ragged trail under his right arm. The latter snaked down his body, disappearing into the towel. Mark eyed it with a surgeon's interest, calculating the level of bacterial infection which might cause a mess like that, added to the complications of Logan's haemophilia.

Lucy couldn't take her eyes off it and Logan retreated to the bedroom to dress, feeling self-conscious and irritated by the strangers' presence in his safe place. Tama lent Mark clothes and the older man wandered into the lounge after his shower, clad in a pair of school track pants and a tee shirt which proclaimed the wearer to be 'too hot to handle' in neon print over a black background. "I look like a thug!" he complained and Tama sniggered.

Logan gave into his compulsion, sweeping and mopping the floors between the hallway and bathroom. He threw the hall rug out of the front door, unable to get the orange mud off. He eyed the lounge floor with eagerness, deciding he'd clean it later during the sleepless night he anticipated.

Mark's voice cut into the silence, clearing his throat and directing his question at Hana. "Have you any injuries you'd like me to look at?" he asked, keeping his tone light.

Logan stood transfixed as Hana smiled and shook her head. "Just bruising thanks, love and a few scratches. The biology teacher pulled me around and I fell a few times, but he didn't deliberately hurt me. He spent more time panicking about things I didn't understand. He was crazy..."

"Mrs Du Rose," Lucy interrupted. "I need you to come with me now and put your statement on tape. You remember the drill from last year, don't you?"

Hana nodded, winding her baby over her shoulder. Standing up, she handed Phoenix to Tama. "Please can you feed her something from the ice cube trays in the freezer?"

"Yup." He took the snuffling child and gave Hana a smile of encouragement.

Hana hunted in the hall cupboard for a pair of plimsolls, her finger too sore to tie laces. Logan walked up behind her. "What're you doing, babe? That cop looks like she's about to blow a gasket."

"Sorry." Hana sniffed and drew her sleeve across her eyes. "I usually grab my trainers but my fingers hurt too much to do laces and my boots have zips."

"I'll help you," he soothed, seeing the damp tear tracks on her cheeks. "Come out of the way and I'll fetch something."

Hana stood, resting her palm against the wall as she hauled herself up. Logan snatched a pair of ankle boots from the cupboard but Hana shook her head and backed away. "They'll look stupid with track pants," she said, her tone becoming hysterical. "I don't want to look stupid on top of everything else."

Logan gritted his teeth and reached towards the back of the cupboard. "Do these old tennis shoes still fit?" he asked, biting down on the growing irritation. At Hana's nod he helped to push her feet into them and fastened the laces.

"What about when they need to come off?" Her eyes were wide and frightened. "You won't be here when I have to take them off."

"I will," Logan promised. "Pete's covering my shift."

"I can't do this." Hana shook her head and backed away, tripping over the discarded ankle boots. "I can't live like this with you at work all the time and me alone. It's not safe for me here; I need to leave."

"Hey!" Logan pulled his flailing wife into his arms. "Let's deal with one thing at a time, babe."

Hana nodded and took fortifying breaths to calm herself, reassured by Logan's strength. "Ok," she whispered. "I'm ready."

In the lounge, Hana stood on tiptoe and hugged Mark, thanking him for coming to visit as though he'd popped in for tea and enjoyed a pleasant afternoon with his sister. She kissed him on the cheek and promised to call him. "Bye, Phoe, see you soon," Hana said, blowing a kiss to her daughter, who began to grizzle.

"She'll be fine," Tama said. "Get gone and then you might come back soon."

With a wide-eyed look of fear, Hana accepted the warm coat her husband handed her and climbed into the waiting police car. Logan accompanied her and Hana calmed, linking her sore fingers through his in the back of the car and staring blankly as the town whipped by through the windows.

At the police headquarters, Hana went to the suite she'd been in once before. "It's where they put women victims," she whispered to Logan and he frowned.

"How do you know?"

"I came here the night I was mugged by Flick's son. They took photographs and made a statement."

"You didn't know me then." Logan sat in the seat next to Hana, keeping hold of her hand.

She smiled, a pained, forced expression for his benefit. "But I had noticed you," she said wistfully. "I just didn't think you'd be interested in someone like me."

"Stop," Logan told her, his eyes narrowing. "You're beautiful, Hana. Don't go down that road; there's nothing wrong with you."

"So why does everyone attack me?" Her voice emerged as a whine and she closed her eyes, hating the sound of it.

Last time Hana sat alone in the prettily decorated room, but this time her husband accompanied her, his arm protectively around her shoulders. "I'm sorry I don't have answers, babe, I really am." The agony in his voice sounded painful and Hana selflessly suppressed her misery, hating the effect it had on Logan.

The police doctor took her behind a screen to assess her injuries, standing back for Lucy to photograph them. He asked searching and invasive questions which she answered truthfully. The fat little man was nothing like Laval. "He didn't touch me like that," she whispered, aware of Logan on the other side of the screen. "The biology teacher took me to the gully to frighten me into silence. He said if I saw what was there, it made me complicit." That he might have killed her seemed a distinct possibility. He'd done it before, after all.

The statement taking process happened in the suite. Gently, Lucy and another woman officer coaxed out Hana's tale. Logan kept physical contact with his wife throughout, giving her a sense of strength and protection with his thigh lightly touching hers.

"The biology teacher came to the house. He said a student wanted to see me and made it sound urgent. I assumed he meant James because he's been distressed the last few times I've seen him and the biology teacher agreed, although he didn't actually name James. I shouldn't have gone with him." Hana stopped and ran her hands over her face, wincing as her cuts oozed.

"What do you mean when you say, you shouldn't have gone, Hana?" Lucy's question made Hana's brow furrow.

"Why do you think?" Logan bit, gritting his teeth.

The other officer eyeballed him. "You need to stay quiet, Mr Du Rose, otherwise you must leave."

Hana fidgeted, Logan's anger communicating his stress. "I had an instinct about it," Hana admitted. "But I foolishly ignored it, not wanting to look stupid in front of Mark, my brother. The biology teacher took my arm and I cried out and it all seemed so ridiculous. I let the pressure get to me and should have stood my ground."

"What happened next?" the woman asked.

"We went towards the gully. It felt wrong and his grip on my arm was painful. At the old shed near the tennis courts, I saw another cop and you." Hana indicated Lucy with a jerk of her head. "I tried to make you understand I was in trouble but the biology teacher gripped my hand and twisted my sore wrist to stop me screaming. He had a knife and pushed it into my back." Hana rubbed at the skin on her left arm through her clothing as the memory disturbed her. "He said he'd go back for my baby and hurt her; he didn't even know her name." Hana turned towards Logan, her face a mask of horror. "He said he'd hurt her and I wasn't thinking straight. I didn't know if Mark could stop him if he went back to the house for Phoe. I should have thought it through. I can't believe I fell for his threats."

"It's natural," Lucy reassured her in a soft voice. "What mother wouldn't protect her child?"

"But it's not logical!" Hana snapped. "If he went back for Phoe, where would he put me? It's a bloody gully! He couldn't keep me and leave me, could he?"

Logan gritted his teeth and wished he'd given the man more than one slap to the head. Lucy widened her eyes in warning and he avoided stating the obvious. The man could've tied Hana to a tree and gone back, but the look of rage on her face made him bite his tongue. Instead, Logan took Hana's hand in his, grounding her in the present.

Lucy shook her head slowly at him. "Leave her to process it," she whispered. "Don't interfere."

Logan felt mercenary doing what was best for the cops in their quest to gather fresh, recollected evidence. He doubted it was best for his wife. She still woke in the night reliving her earlier kidnap, believing blood still spurted from her wrist and squeezing it so tightly she hurt herself again. Logan ignored the cop, stroking Hana's hand and concentrating on his wife's words as she focussed her blame on the unfortunate Lucy. "I wanted you to help me but you were busy. The whole thing felt unreal. He was hurting me; why couldn't you see that?"

Lucy gulped and Hana raged on. Her reaction seemed different to how she behaved after Laval kidnapped her. Then she had hidden from the memories, reluctantly given a police statement and cowered behind Logan's authority. He hoped her anger would see her through in a better state this time.

"I know it seems stupid that I went with him, but he's my tenant and I know him from work. I was scared of overreacting but now I feel so foolish." Hana snatched a tear from her cheek with careless fingers, rambling, going backwards and sideways without progressing. The female officers looked at each other in a well-used formula for dealing with hysterical victims of crime.

"Did Alec Petersen say anything to you as he pulled you along by your arm?" Lucy asked.

Hana and Logan stared in confusion. "Who?" Logan asked and the cops eyed each other warily.

"The man who took your wife into the gully." Lucy peered at her notes with a furrowed brow. "That's who we've got in custody anyway." She shot a nervous look at her colleague.

"The biology teacher," Hana sighed. "It's ridiculous. The school isn't huge but we could never remember his name. I should have learned it, not that it would have helped me." She pressed her hand over the top of her stomach and winced. "Do we have to do this now? I've got bad indigestion."

Logan put his arm around Hana, feeling her agitation as a vibration through his fingers. Pain made her breath catch in her chest. "She's had enough," Logan said, his voice a low, warning growl.

The other female cop left the room and returned seconds later, handing a pack of antacids to Hana. "I managed to catch the medic," she said with a smile. Hana took a tablet, thought for a moment and then took another, twisting the box around and around in her fingers. Logan confiscated it as she reached in for a third.

"I was asking you if the biology teacher said anything to you," Lucy continued.

Hana nodded. "Yes. He was furious about my rental property. I'm selling it and an agent looked around earlier in the week and let the tenants know I was listing it. He offered them first option, but they declined. The biology teacher was angry because they're happy there. He said they couldn't afford to buy the house and wanted to convince me not to sell. He said his wife was terribly upset and it was all my fault."

It didn't escape the notice of either cop that Logan Du Rose looked utterly stunned at his wife's revelation. He looked sideways at Hana with his mouth open and when she caught his eye, her face flooded with pain. "I wanted to surprise you, Logan. Everything you said outside the tennis courts was true. That house is part of the old Hana, Hana Johal. I'm not her anymore and I don't need her things. It marked part of my clearing out process." Hana smiled and her face lit up with an inner beauty. "It's been very releasing." She directed her words towards Lucy. "My husband's building the most beautiful house on top of a mountain. I wanted to sell some of my assets and contribute so it's mine too." Her face fell. "The biology teacher was furious. He insisted it wasn't about what I wanted, it was about what his wife wanted."

Logan looked away and rubbed his hand over his face. Hana sighed and her courage wavered. "He kept saying, '*I know you know about it.*' He kept saying that over and over again and I didn't know what he meant. He also said, '*You saw me.*' But I hadn't seen him for ages, not since I went to the staffroom to see Loge a week ago, or was it the start of this week?" Hana rubbed her hand across her stomach again asking, "I want to go now. Please could we do this tomorrow?"

Lucy shook her head, deliberately ignoring Logan who looked like he might take his wife and leave if she protested again. "Not much longer now, Hana," she said. "Tell us how you got that bruising round your waist and the scratches on your arms and neck?"

Hana let out a huge, impatient sigh. "He led me into the gully on the track, then he made me climb up a bank. I couldn't get up so he hauled me round the waist. It hurt and I cried out. I'd had enough and I knew I needed to get away. I pushed him and he shoved me backwards against a tree, holding me round my neck. It took my breath away and made me feel weak. After that, he shoved me in front of him so I couldn't turn. Parts of it were steep and I fell a lot. I kept grabbing roots and grass to stop me falling but the ferns were spiky and tore my hands and arms." Hana looked at her husband. "Did you know ferns were spiky? I didn't." She touched her stomach again in the same place and winced. "He produced this sharp knife thing near the shed when we saw the cops and after I pushed him, he dug that in my back a few times as he got angrier and angrier."

Logan shook his head and struggled to keep control. It explained the short nicks along Hana's lower back which he saw as he helped her shower. He knew if he reacted the cops would insist he left. It would leave his wife vulnerable and alone. *Again*. He worked at containing his fury, using old techniques to shield his emotions. He'd had years of practice and retreated as far behind the familiar mask as he dared, without detaching from the situation.

Hana continued, her head high as she exuded bravery. "We walked for ages along the gully, miles. I didn't know the gully was that long. Then we came to a really dense area. He made me go ahead into some bushes where there were loads of punga and other palms. I kept falling over the ground cover. Right in the middle was this electric fence on a battery thing and he turned it off with a key. Then he made me go in front and push through these tall leafy plants, like the ones on James' plane. He morphed into a biology teacher, telling me how much water the plants need and how often he has to go down there to make sure they're growing okay. He said he wanted to make enough to buy my house and had almost raised the deposit, but wanted me to wait before listing it and then he would pay full price. '*How did you find out about me?*' he asked and I kept quiet because I didn't know what he meant. He asked me again and I told him I didn't know anything about him, so he slapped me across the face. '*I saw you playing tennis and you saw me,*' he said. '*You waved and then you sent the agent round because you knew.*' I remembered seeing someone walking past, but it was dark and the floodlights from the courts blinded me to anything outside. If I waved, it would be out of politeness. I told him that and he called me a liar. He said Larry Collins and he alternated the runs to the furthest plantation and he was fed up of doing it by himself now. The cops found the other one, but they'd never find this one; it was too well hidden and he walked a different way every time."

"What else did Petersen say about Larry Collins?" Lucy asked.

Hana rubbed her stomach and ribs again. "He said Collins got greedy and harvested too early. They argued over it. He found out Collins sold privately to other buyers outside their agreement. Their regular buyer complained and threaten to cancel future orders if it didn't stop and said he wouldn't stop at ruining their business; he'd mess them up too."

Hana's breath caught in her chest and she filtered each exhale through pursed lips. "Please," she begged, "let me go now?"

As Lucy anticipated, Logan stood up to leave, his height intimidating and his body language full of challenge. He helped Hana from the sofa with tender, careful hands, despite his threatening stance.

"One more question," Lucy begged. Logan's grey eyes narrowed and his patience looked ready to snap. "You're sure you didn't know anything about the marijuana growing the teacher was doing?"

Logan looked incredulous and Lucy held up her hand. "I need her to verify that fact in case it comes up later."

Hana shook her head. "Of course I didn't!" Her eyes widened in shock. "I'm sorry; I've told you all I can." She turned to Logan. "Please, Logan, I want to go back to my daughter now."

Chapter 25

"Reception is through there," Lucy's colleague said, indicating a set of double doors. "Thanks for your help, Mrs Du Rose." She nodded and slipped through the access door disappearing from sight.

"Oh, crap!" Logan exhaled and added another swear word as Hana's body felt heavy against his, her legs moving mechanically.

"What?" she asked, too tired to panic.

"We came in the cop car. How do they expect us to get home? *Fantastic*. They've had what they wanted and we get dumped outside, surplus to requirements." Logan left Hana sitting on a grotty seat in the reception while he argued with the desk clerk.

"It's not my job to call you a taxi, sir. I'm a police officer, not a hotel concierge."

Logan opened his mouth to unleash a barrage of abuse, his fists balled on the counter.

"It's ok; I've got it," a familiar voice called to the clerk. Bodie appeared through the security door and Logan's heart sank. Hana caught Logan's eye and her look told him she didn't care how she got back to her baby, as long as she got back. He considered asking the desk clerk for a phone directory and calling his own taxi, realising it would only delay Hana and push her beyond what her fragile coping mechanisms could deal with. There was no room for egotistical pettiness and Logan shrugged at his wife, looking sorry for himself. Offering her his hand, he hauled her out of the seat, noticing plasters on some of the cuts to her hands while others were open to the air. There seemed no logic to the medic's choices as the open ones bled onto Logan's fingers and he gritted his teeth, wanting so much better for his wife.

"Take this," he whispered gently, reaching into his jeans pocket and pulling out the ever-present-clean-handkerchief. Hana looked at his hand in confusion. "You're bleeding," he said, jerking his head towards her hands.

"Thanks." Hana took the handkerchief with a smile of gratitude, using it to mop at her weeping cuts and pulling a face as they stung.

"Car's just here," Bodie's said, pointing to the front of the police station. Hana wondered fleetingly if the traffic wardens dared to ticket cops parked in the sixty-minute slots for too long.

Bodie started the engine and glanced in his rear view mirror. His passengers disconcerted him, having both opted to sit in the back of his smart BMW. He set off for the school site, pushing his way through the rush hour traffic. Nobody spoke. Hana stared through the window at the world passing by and Bodie saw in his rear view mirror how her husband watched her covertly When Hana turned and gave her husband a watery smile, his handsome face channelled a look of such utter love and affection it was as though Bodie saw him naked. Embarrassed, he turned his attention back to the traffic, doubting the comfortable dislike he'd shrouded himself in and wondering if he'd invented reasons to hate Logan Du Rose.

Bodie parked outside the unit and Logan opened Hana's door for her, ever the gentleman. "Thanks," he said politely as though in dismissal and Bodie felt a surge of anger that neither of them asked after his son's broken arm.

"Jas is fine thanks," he said with an edge of sarcasm and Hana looked back in surprise.

"Yes, I know. I spoke to him last night. Has something else happened?"

Bodie flushed red at his own foolishness, unaware of Hana's conversation with Jas. She gave her son an odd look and he got the feeling she knew something else too. Logan ushered Hana up the steps and Bodie saw her bend to remove her plimsolls before progressing into the hallway. Logan's dirty cowboy boots sat on the top step and he kicked another pair off his feet. Bodie watched as his step father turned and raised his eyebrow. "Are you coming or would you rather stand in the street pouting instead?"

Bodie hesitated, seeing himself as the problem in an eye watering moment of awful clarity. The conflict was self-made, deliberately misunderstanding everything so he could continue his one-man-pity-party. "Ok," he replied. Bodie gritted his teeth and followed Logan into the unit, kicking his shoes off as he closed the door behind him.

Phoenix sat on the rug, her legs splayed to balance herself as she clutched a plastic yellow duck in tiny hands. She swayed precariously as her parents entered the room, bringing with them a bitter winter draught. The child beamed, squeezing her grey eyes shut in pleasure at the sight of her family. Tama sat on the sofa behind her, his feet either side of her bottom to keep her stable. Bodie saw a stranger on the other two seater sofa, dark hair running to grey and a pair of silver-rimmed glasses balanced on his nose. "Hana, sweetheart, how are you?" He rose as Hana emerged from the hallway, greeting her with a warm embrace. Bodie watched Logan with interest, wondering why he didn't react to type.

"I'm making coffee," Logan said instead, "anyone else want some?"

Hana pointed to her son, hovering in the doorway and directed her sentence at the stranger. "Mark, this is my son, Bodie."

Mark stepped forward, letting go of his sister and offering his hand to the young man. Bodie recognised the clear green eyes and the puzzle fell into place. "You're my uncle," he said. "Mum's brother?"

Mark nodded and they shook hands. "Nice to meet you, Bodie."

Hana rubbed her sore neck and rolled her head around her shoulders as though it ached, an action not wasted on Logan. He went to her aid in seconds, making her sit next to Tama. "I'll get you some tea now," he said, showing all the hallmarks of devotion.

"Thanks, babe." Hana leaned forward and touched Phoenix, who twisted her head around on her shoulders with a smile. The little girl leaned back and played 'hidey boo' in Tama's trousers and the teenager ignored them as though it was usual.

Bodie felt jealousy rise in his chest and fought hard to push it away, battling his inner demons in a bid for peace. Logan poured steaming liquid into mugs on the breakfast bar, adding a jug of milk. "Coffee's here and tea's coming," he said, waving his hand towards Bodie and his uncle. Phoenix slumped down between Tama's feet and did a fake cry for attention when she saw her daddy bringing Hana a cup of tea.

Logan pulled a face at her and lifted her up. "Aren't you getting enough love?" he cooed and kissed her downy forehead. She clipped onto his hip and held on using his shirt in one clamped fist. He cuddled her and the baby rested her head on his shoulder. It was so touching and incongruous against the image Bodie had of Logan, it tested his battle lines.

Logan pottered in the kitchen with his daughter resting her head against his shoulder and watching his every movement. He poked around in the freezer and popped food into a bowl one handed. As the microwave door opened, Bodie and Mark made it to the spare sofa with their drinks and plonked themselves down. Silence reigned horribly.

"Isn't Dad back today?" Hana asked her brother, sounding exhausted.

"Meant to be," he replied, eyeing her with astute medical assessment. "But they got caught up at an army museum on the way up and decided to find a motel. They'll come back to Hamilton tomorrow instead. Mum finds the traveling tiring."

Hana nodded, relieved they'd missed the drama. "Please can we *not* tell them what happened? I don't think Dad needs the added worry at the moment."

Bodie stirred with curiosity. "What's wrong with your dad?" he asked Hana, but Mark answered.

"He's had lung cancer. He finished radiotherapy and came here on holiday. My mother has a congenital heart condition. Her sister, your grandmother also had it."

Bodie shook his head, confused. "I thought you were my mother's brother, but you somehow had a different mother?" He raised his hand in the air in an action which looked more dismissive than he intended. "Don't bother, it makes my head hurt. I need to get back to Amy and Jas." He finished his coffee and stood, putting his mug on the side. Logan stirred something in a bowl and Phoenix watched him. She had one tiny hand around his back and the other near her face so she could suck her thumb.

Logan looked up as he heard the mug scrape against the surface and smiled, nodding at his stepson. "Thanks for the ride home."

Bodie smiled back and waved at the room in general. "It's fine, see you all later."

"You off, Bo?" Hana asked and tried to get up.

"Far out, Ma!" Tama scoffed, putting both hands against her back to help her. He gave a shove and Hana giggled but there was little heart in it.

"Just wait," she asked her son, reaching into a drawer beneath the dining table. Hana pulled out an A4 sized envelope, handing it to him and biting her lip nervously. "I've sorted more photos out for you," she said. "And up at the house I've got pictures in frames and an album each for you and Izzie. I'll get yours to you soon."

Bodie took it and scrutinised Hana's face, searching for signs of rejection in favour of her shiny new life. He saw none. The only thing his mother's face contained was what Amy already told him – a woman trying to get on with the job of living and struggling to dovetail her old life into her new.

He thanked her and bent to kiss her on the cheek. "I hope you feel better tomorrow. I'll be on site for most of the day tidying up, so I'll pop in if that's okay."

Hana nodded. "You're always welcome, Bo," she said. "Logan's on duty Saturday night and Sunday and I'm not looking forward to dealing with the long hours alone." She smiled gratefully at her son and closed the door after him. As Mark got to his feet, Hana remembered his shift at work and clapped her hand over her mouth. "Mark, your job, I'm so sorry!"

"Don't be daft, Hana. A colleague covered and he owed me anyway. I did his shifts when his kids caught chickenpox. I'm not leaving straight away. I wanted to check you out if you'll let me. Something's bothering me and I want to assuage my fears. Would you mind?" he said, turning towards Logan.

"What?" Logan fought his daughter, trying to stuff her wriggly body into the high chair. "Phoe! Please, you're not getting your dinner until you stop squirming." She grizzled and held her arms out to Hana. "Ooh, nice pumpkin," Logan said, concentrating on the baby who sported a sad bottom lip. He wrinkled his nose at her. "You pout like your mother!" When he turned back, his wife and her brother had gone. He shrugged at Tama, a wasted action as the teenager ogled the television.

"Right, lie on the bed," Mark said, plumping the pillows.

"Ooh, doctor," Hana fawned. "My husband's in the next room."

"Idiot." Mark frowned. He took her left wrist, trying to slot his fingers into the space over her artery to take her pulse.

"Ouch!" Hana complained at the pressure over her scar, pulling her hand instinctively away.

Mark turned her hand over, palm upwards so he could look carefully at the old wound. "Hmmn," he said, sounding like an expensive plumber and making Hana smirk. "It shouldn't hurt that much still. I wonder if there's a shard of glass left in there. We felt sure we'd got it all, but it's not beyond the bounds of possibility there was a tiny particle we missed. It'll cause a sharp, gritty pain when pressed. Is that what it's like?"

Hana nodded. "Yes. It takes me by surprise because if I leave it alone, it doesn't hurt so I forget it's there."

"It may account for the infection afterwards as it's a foreign body." Mark turned her hand back over and laid it gently on the bed. "You were fortunate that night. An experienced paramedic got to you first, otherwise you could have bled out."

Seeing Hana's face drop and her mind stray back to that night, Mark distracted her, throwing his long body on the other side of the bed next to her. He took her right hand and repeated the exercise, getting no resistance this time. He pulled her arm across his stomach and pressed his fingers over the pulsing vein. "Your heart rate's very low, Hana. Didn't the doctor at the police station check you out?"

"Sort of. He didn't check that kind of stuff. He was more interested in the bruises and making sure the biology teacher hadn't...no, he didn't check my pulse. It wasn't a check-up like at the doctor's."

"Well, I want you to get one," Mark said with authority. "Judith...Mum wasn't much older than you when she died. This heart defect is hereditary so see your GP, please. I'll come with you if you like, but they must do a proper check and I don't have the right equipment here. It's important."

"Ok," Hana said passively, yawning with no intention of playing hypochondriac for her brother's benefit. "It's just because I'm tired after today."

"Don't be a hero; your children need you," Mark said, laying back against the pillows on Hana's usual side of the bed. "Crikey, I could go to sleep now."

"Know the feeling," Hana replied. "But my daughter will appear for a feed soon and I need to sleep when I'm sure I can get right through to the morning. Otherwise, I'll have nightmares after today."

"Well, I'm not prescribing pills until after you've seen that GP," Mark said stiffly and Hana wrinkled her nose.

"Spoilsport! Do you realise in the last eighteen months I've been chased, attacked, moved house, married, got pregnant and given birth in the middle of the bush. I've coped with a baby at my age, witnessed a house fire that killed two people, moved house again, been kidnapped, gained an extra adult child and been attacked again. It kind of takes its toll on the older body, you know."

Mark turned on his side and looked at Hana with a smile on his face. "Who'd have thought it, my kid sister a regular Nancy Drew? You were always such a wimpy child."

Hana laughed. "Gosh, show your age or what! *The Hardy Boys and Nancy Drew*, I used to get so scared watching that. Remember that time you sneaked into my room and terrified me witless after an episode of that? Dad came flying up the stairs and clipped you round the ear, big as you were!"

"I was mean to you, wasn't I? I was so jealous. Pathetic really." Mark laid on his back and looked at the freshly painted ceiling. "Something you couldn't have known was; the day you arrived home with your boyfriend, so obviously pregnant, you looked more beautiful than I'd ever seen you. You reminded me so much of Judith when she carried you, with your red hair and blushing cheeks, so fragile. It accentuated how much a part of *them* you were and *how much I wasn't*. I think it's what fuelled my anger. My marriage was imploding before my face and the little family unit I created – my very own family, was dissolving. And there you were, so pretty in your tight yellow dress, like a vision of beauty with hope and life in front of you. My temper ran so hot it was exhilarating. I actually felt in control for a change, even though I was far from it. I'm so sorry, Hana," he sighed.

Hana took his hand, threading her sore fingers through his, the plasters catching on his skin. "How about we start all over again," she whispered. "Hi, my name's Hana and I'm your little sister."

Mark giggled revealing a cute dimple in his cheek. He was so much like Elaine, Hana found it extraordinary she'd never noticed. Her brother sat up and put his feet on the floor, standing up and looking out of the window. "I should go," he said, stretching his arms high above his head and almost touching the ceiling. Hana sat up too and flexed her sore wrist. Her long hair flopped forward on her face looking mussed and untidy, adding to her wild prettiness.

"How can I get this sorted?" she asked, fed up of the continual discomfort but worried in case the cure was as traumatic as the injury. Mark stood over her, eyeing the long, red scar on Hana's wrist thoughtfully.

"You'd need an ultrasound or x-ray, although glass is notoriously difficult to see in certain sorts of scan. It's radiopaque, so a radiographer needs to decide how to find it. By the time I got to open the wound up properly, a larger chunk of glass had gone straight into the artery and partially blocked it, ironically fortunate. I suspect there's a tiny splinter inside the vein and I wouldn't want to muck around with it without doing some research. It was a terrible enough job trying to isolate and seal it in the first place. It could be a needle in a haystack. I'm not sure what to suggest because it won't break down over time. Hopefully, it won't move either."

"You're not making me feel any better," Hana said, pulling her sleeve over the scar. "You must be a rubbish doctor. First you make a right mess of my wrist and then you fill me with doom and gloom. You're a real shocker!" She laughed up at him and he shrugged.

"Sue me!"

When they emerged from the bedroom, Phoenix put her little head on one side and pulled a smiley, shy face with her mouth full of pudding. Tama was nowhere to be seen. "I sent him down the road for take-away food," Logan said. "Stay Mark, he'll get enough for everyone."

Hana watched her husband spooning food into Phoenix's face. She smiled as he opened and shut his own mouth in concentration and swallowed when she did. His tactic was business-like and calm and the child responded likewise. She didn't mess around like she did with Tama although his status as a big kid didn't help.

Mark accepted the extended hospitality and while Hana breast fed her daughter and picked at a plate of chips by her seat, the men sat at the dining table and scoffed a veritable feast. Logan watched his wife with an intensity almost painful to bear but ate little as Tama predicted. Mark wiped his mouth on a tissue and eyed the dark skinned man with respect. Logan left him in no doubt how much he adored Hana and their child with naked sincerity. It forced Mark to realise something; if he'd felt half as powerfully for his own wife all those years ago, things might have turned out differently.

As if reading his mind, Hana asked, "Do you see much of Carrie and the boys?"

Mark snorted with disdain and then regretted it as Logan shot him a dangerous look. "No. Sadly not. She remarried quickly enough to make me think she was already half way through the door before I noticed her dissatisfaction with me as a father and husband. I've no idea where she is and in the agony which followed our messy divorce, I also lost contact with my sons." Mark's brow furrowed and he pushed his plate away. "For years, money left my bank account and went into hers until the boys reached eighteen; then it ceased and with it, my last form of investment in their lives." He sighed. "The boys will both be in their thirties now. I've often wondered what they decided to do with their lives. Meeting you again and managing to put things right has given me the confidence to contemplate trying to find them. I'd like them to know dad before..." He trailed off, not wanting to upset Hana and engrossed himself in his cold coffee.

Logan excused himself and made a pot of tea, taking a cup to Hana on the sofa. "Hey," he said, sitting carefully next to her. His nosy daughter pushed up Hana's tee shirt to give him an upside down smile. He laughed and stroked her forehead and Phoenix giggled. Hana sat her up so she could see her daddy, patting her on the back to release the air bubbles. Phoenix put her fists up to her eyes and rubbed, betraying her tiredness.

"Come here, *kōtiro*." Logan held out his hands and she tipped forwards into them. Lying over his shoulder, Phoenix closed her eyes and began to fall asleep. "Hang on, baby," he whispered. "Nappy change and cot and then you can go to the land of Nod."

Hana watched her husband's strong frame bear the fragile child down the hallway, oozing adoration from every pore.

"He really loves you guys, doesn't he?" Mark commented, his voice low.

"Yup," Tama interrupted. "There's been a lot of people wished Logan Du Rose felt like that about them."

"Were you one of them?" Mark asked and Hana winced, dreading the teenager's reply.

"Hell yeah!" Tama wiped his mouth with the back of his hand. "I'd do anything for that man's approval but I never got it."

"You never got it?" Mark's eyes widened and he darted a glance towards Hana as she sipped her tea. She opened her mouth to defend her husband but Tama finished his point.

"No, I didn't get it because I was trying to earn it and when that didn't work, I did dumb stuff instead to get a reaction. Then Hana came along and just loved me for myself and when I realised what that felt like, I knew Logan always loved me, he just didn't say the words. Uncle doesn't give love easy, but when he does it's worth it. I had it all the time but was too dumb to see."

Mark's nod was slow and heavy with understanding. "Then that's what I need to do with my boys when I find them," he said. "I must love them, whether they feel like receiving it or not."

Mark left around nine o'clock and Hana crawled into bed shortly after, ignoring his good advice and taking a hefty sleeping tablet she found in the back of the bathroom cupboard. She peered at herself in the bathroom mirror, horrified by her white complexion and swallowed the tablet. "I don't think it's mine," she told her reflection. "I think it's a left-over from the previous occupant. Logan will have a fit." She crawled into bed and slept, the white tablet doing its work.

Her husband checked the little pot at the back of the bathroom cupboard as he got ready for bed, counting the contents and smirking. It *had* belonged to the previous resident, but he played the long game, replacing the real sleeping tablets with ordinary painkillers earlier that evening. It was underhand but Hana possessed a worrying affinity with out-of-date prescriptions and other people's medication, born of a complete lack of respect for drugs or chemicals. Logan hadn't yet worked out whether it was ignorance, or a blatant disregard for consequences. He still hadn't gotten over the time she'd taken ancient, dusty sleeping pills after a nasty scare before they were married. She greeted him bleary eyed the next day, getting half way to work before realising she still had her slippers on.

That night, Hana slept soundly under the influence of placebo painkillers and the firm belief she was successfully drugged.

Saturday dawned cold but bright and the soccer game between Waikato Presbyterian Old Boys and Staff and their counterparts in another local school, was not a fair fight. The opponents played dirty while the referee suffered a dreadful case of temporary blindness.

"This is ridiculous!" Bodie shouted as an opponent took his legs out from under him. "Are you bloody blind, ref?"

"It's social soccer!" the man yelled back. "I'm doing my best. I'm not a FIFA referee!" He threw the whistle on the ground and stomped off the pitch in a temper.

Peter North limped around the sideline feigning a calf injury, hobbling backwards as his team thundered towards him. "Pete," the goalkeeper cried, "referee the game, man. You don't have to do any running."

Logan shook his head and subbed himself off, standing next to Hana on the sidelines. "What kind of referee doesn't have to run?" he demanded. "Idiots!"

"The Pete sort of referee?" Hana asked, pointing as Pete donned the second hand whistle and wiped it on his filthy tracksuit pants.

Logan groaned and heaved out a huge sigh. Pete was an even worse judge of fouls, standing in the middle of the centre circle with a pained look on his face, instead of blowing the whistle. At one point, he turned to the spectators with an *oooh-that's-gonna-hurt* look on his face, while the players went crazy, screaming, *"Ref, ref!"* He blew the whistle with authority and made completely the wrong call.

When one of his own team yelled, "Why don't you put on one of the opposition's shirts, mate?" Pete threw his whistle down and followed the example of his predecessor.

"Oh what? Is he for real?" came the angry shouts behind him.

"I don't really wanna go back on," Logan grumbled as the coach performed frantic arm movements to get his attention.

"Well, why am I standing in the freezing cold like a fool then?" Hana protested. Her husband pulled a grouchy face and clomped over to the coach, running onto the pitch in a midfield position. He stuck his hand out at Hana and she wrinkled her nose.

Having stomped off the pitch, Pete headed home. By the time he reached his staff unit, the other team had reinstated the original referee, rendering Pete surplus to requirements. Hana was surprised to see him striding back towards the game with purpose and pushed the pram towards him. "Don't take it to heart," she said. "They step over that white line and become monsters."

"Oh, I don't care," he said, looking cross. "I dropped my house key somewhere on the pitch and need to look for it."

"Aren't you gonna wait until the end of the game?" Hana asked, watching as he ignored her and strode away. Every time there was a substitution or delay of any kind, he swooped onto the field and searched for the contents of his pocket.

"Aarrrrgggh!" he screamed, flattened by the technology teacher who powered down the left side of the pitch with a goal scoring opportunity. Bodie stood over the jumble of limbs waving his arms in fury. Pete sat up looking concussed and wobbly and was propped up against someone's rucksack on the sideline. Not satisfied with the damage he'd already done, he crawled back onto the pitch.

Tama played striker and when Pete blundered in front of him for the third time, peering at the ground like a hen searching for worms, Tama picked him up bodily and tipped him off the pitch. Hana laughed so hard she nearly wet herself.

The coach moved Logan into a defence position where he dwarfed the opposition players who shied away from his height. They scuffed the ball hopelessly wide as he ran at them without fear. Hence the ball stayed largely in the centre of the pitch, going back and forth and nowhere else, wearing a trench into Larry Collin's sacred earth.

Bodie switched into goalkeeper mode, clapping his huge gloves together in the cold and looking bored. He disappeared into the bushes for a pee and nobody noticed except Hana. Out of pity, she pushed the pram around to talk to him. "I don't think Manchester United will call anytime soon," she said, standing behind the goal.

Bodie looked round and sniggered. "Probably not." He eyed his mother from beneath his lashes. "You're looking very thin, Mum. And pale."

"It's just the stress of the last week," Hana bluffed, hiding her offence. "Something to do with living in a crime scene and having your long-lost father and brother turn up unexpectedly."

Bodie opened his mouth to speak but at that moment Pete, who was searching the back line for his key, took a hit straight to the face by a loose ball. He went down like a lead weight, landing with his arms and legs stretched out either side of him like road-kill. He looked unconscious.

"Get an ambulance," someone shouted. "But get him off the pitch first so we can carry on."

"Can't move him, don't be stupid!" someone else rebuked.

Angus knelt next to his sports teacher, slapping the florid face with enthusiasm. His girlfriend Heather, looked horrified. "Ooh, that's a bit hard, love," she reprimanded.

"Just a few more taps," Angus replied, clearly enjoying himself as he slapped Pete again.

The players tapped their feet impatiently on the grass as the referee went over to see if the body could be moved across the back line. "Is he unconscious?" he asked with concern.

"No!" Logan bellowed. "He isn't!" Upon reaching his friend, Logan grabbed Pete's nose in his fingers and gave it a sharp twist.

"Ow!" Pete squealed and the retraction of his knobbly legs freed up the white line for the game to continue as Logan used his foot to move the odious little man away. The whistle blew and the comedy sketch continued. Logan made some decent clearances from his half of the pitch, planting the ball at Tama's feet with perfect aim. Tama's opponent was not averse to repeated fouls involving the boy's legs more than the ball and as he went down for the fourth time, the teenager lost patience.

"You go up front!" Tama shouted at Logan, stomping over and taking his place during a restart of play. Logan shrugged and jogged up to the other end, playing a forward. He stood next to his new opponent, looking down on him and smiling viciously while raising one eyebrow in expectation. The defender looked around at his team members for someone else to swap with, but they mercilessly avoided his eye. As the ball came towards him,

Logan didn't need to jump to contact it with his head and his opponent bounced off him like a rubber ball.

"Goal!" the team screamed, celebrating and dancing at the equaliser as the ball shot into the net. They ran to Logan, pounding his back with elation. The whistle blew for a foul and all hell broke loose.

"You fouled the defender!" the referee shouted, posturing and pointing his whistle at Logan.

"He bounced off my chest," Logan replied, sounding hurt.

The referee shook his head. "Goal disallowed."

From then on the game degenerated into a violent mud bath and the ball was no longer the primary focus. Had poor Larry Collins not already been in another life, he would have beamed himself there. He wouldn't have stomached the complete desecration of his sacred turf as the players charged back and forth, chasing each other rather than the round, white object in the fray. Amidst it all, Logan put in a wonderful cross which found the science teacher's head and the back of the goal. When the referee put the whistle to his lips to challenge it, angry Presbyterian Boys' players surrounded him.

Logan jogged to see his wife and stepson in the goal mouth and Tama joined them. "This is a complete joke," the teen complained and Logan shrugged.

"It's just a good excuse for a run around for me," he replied nonchalantly, squatting down to smile at his daughter. Swaddled up in her pram, Phoenix giggled and burbled baby talk. Her mud covered daddy kissed her on the nose as she beamed up at him.

"You alright, babe?" Logan asked Hana, whose body quivered under her clothing.

She nodded and pulled her coat around her. "Yeah, it's just cold."

"No, you're just losing weight, Ma," Tama said, still sulking about the goal.

"Shut up!" Logan told him, warning the boy with fiery grey eyes. Rising to his full height, Logan looked towards the knot of bodies around the referee whose head was level with the players' shoulders. He inhaled as the whistle blew frantically from inside the circle. Logan shook his head. "I'm done here. It's a farce." He turned towards Bodie. "You played good, man. Wanna come back to ours for a shower? There'll be a queue, but you're welcome."

Bodie's face frowned with mistrust and he saw Hana roll her eyes in his peripheral vision. As she set off walking he nodded. "Thanks. It'll save me time as I'm due on duty at two o'clock. Odering told me to wear mufti as we're mainly clearing up here."

"Promotion?" Logan asked, an odd look in his eye.

"Maybe." Bodie looked at him with curiosity. "What've you heard?"

"Me?" Logan snorted and touched his chest. "From who?"

They caught up to Hana and she threw a comment over her shoulder. "You know the game's not over, don't you?"

"It is for us," Tama said like a sulky child and the three players walked casually around the edge of the pitch, unnoticed by the arguing throng surrounding the referee.

While Hana created a sandwich mountain, the men showered and changed into clean clothes. First out of the bathroom, Tama buttered bread and grated cheese while Hana quizzed him about his interview. "I'm so sorry, love. Last night should have been about celebrating you and instead..." Her brow knitted and Tama looked at her with curiosity in his face.

"Are you upset or in pain?" he asked. "Because it looks like pain to me." He placed the cheese grater on the counter and took Hana in his arms, pushing his face into her red hair and holding her tightly. "I love you, Ma," he whispered. "You'd tell me if there was something wrong, wouldn't you?"

"Of course I would, silly boy. I'm still shaken after yesterday is all." She patted his back like she did the baby's and Tama sniggered.

Bodie walked in and cleared his throat awkwardly, his face a badly veiled mask of jealousy. Tama ignored him, releasing Hana and resuming his grating. "I felt the interview went well at the time but I'm less confident after a night's sleep. I keep going over my answers in my head and wishing I'd said different things."

Hana smoothed a hand across his shoulders. "Sorry, I won't make you go over it again then. You can't change anything. But I bet you were amazing and they saw that. They wanted you anyway."

Bodie sat on a sofa and put his socks on, listening to the conversation without interjecting. He nodded to Hana's offer of coffee and she smiled and turned to pour some, whilst reassuring Tama and praying God would give the teenager a break. "Lucy was kind last night in the interview," she whispered, seeing how his cheeks pinked under the olive hue and he looked away embarrassed. Hana nudged him with her elbow and when he smiled back at her, they laughed. "Tama's got it bad," she joked.

Bodie sat at the table and ate sandwiches with Tama. Phoenix joined them in her high chair and sucked on a strip of cheese.

"Is Logan cleaning the bathroom?" Hana asked and the men shrugged. "He's been a long time," she mused, realising no sound came from behind the closed door.

"He might be taking a dump," Tama suggested and Hana tutted and shook her head.

"You coming for some lunch, Logan?" she asked, knocking on the bathroom door. When her husband opened it with a towel around his middle, he looked ashen and ruffled and Hana pushed her way through the gap and closed it behind her. "Logan, what's wrong?"

He faltered and Hana watched Logan's face as he floundered. She knew instinctively he was tempted to lie, to utter something that would placate her and soothe her worries whilst he internalised his own. "Truth, Logan," she said, her voice soothing. "Don't make something up."

Logan looked up at the ceiling and took a deep breath. "I keep thinking about yesterday and can't get it out of my head. I've spent years searching for you and now I've found you, feel powerless to hold on tight enough. Every time I look up, someone else is trying to hurt you and I feel a failure."

"You're certainly not that!" Hana exclaimed. "You were there when I needed you."

Logan shook his head. "I've operated in an emotionless world, controlled and cold for so long. My decisions were calculated and weighed against practical outcomes and there were very few surprises." He ran his hands through dark, tumbling curls. "Then along comes Hana Du Rose and unleashes these feelings of insecurity which hurt so much. I've realised how inadequate I am; I can't control anything or keep you safe. It's a physical ache, this fear that at any point it could all be over. My happiness hangs by a fragile thread, blowing in the winds of fate."

Logan's honesty stunned Hana as he laid his soul uncharacteristically bare. She saw that nothing in the world scared Logan Du Rose but that one tiny detail - the things which made his life worth living were the ones he had no human way of keeping.

She stood in front of Logan with her hands on his strong chest, looking up with genuine concern. "I know, babe, believe me I know. I'm not Nancy Drew; I can't laugh and shake it off while moving on to the next adventure in a week's time. These things take their toll and leave an aftertaste that doesn't disappear overnight." Hana saw her own fears reflected in her husband's eyes. "All I can do is keep giving you and my children into God's care because He can see what I can't. Life is fragile; Vik's tragic death taught me that." Hana ached for Logan, forced to agonise and worry without the ability to hand it over to a higher power and let it go. "It's okay," she said, resting her forehead against the downy, dark skin of his chest and feeling the dusting of hair move underneath her breath. She ran her hands up and around his shoulders and smiled as she felt her strong husband sigh. He started to kiss her, crushing her to him and Hana pushed him away giggling, knowing where it led. He smiled and the haunted look receded inside for the moment.

"You give me to God?" Logan asked, coiling a strand of red hair through his fingers.

Hana smiled. "Of course I do. Sometimes when I'm most vulnerable, I remember a memory verse my father taught me. *'The grass withers, the flower fades, but the word of our God stands forever.'* It's from the book of *Isaiah* and I was six when I learned it. The *Word* represents Jesus. Yesterday as I ran from the biology teacher, I realised if Jesus, *The Word* really can *stand forever*, the best thing I could do was get a good, firm grip on Him and hold on for dear life." Hana Du Rose looked at her husband through wise, green eyes. "Otherwise I'll torture myself and go insane because I can't do it in my own strength. *None of it.*"

She saw Logan bite the inside of his lower lip and knew she'd hit at the heart of his anxiety. He was like a superhero whose powers disappeared overnight and he'd leapt off a tall building, only to realise he could no longer fly. He'd reached the end of himself and had nowhere else to go. "Come and get some food," she said gently, "our daughter's sucking cheese and isn't sure if she likes it. It's hilarious, come and see."

Logan nodded, his face filled with agony. "This is too hard," he whispered, squeezing the bridge of his nose in scarred fingers. Hana pushed herself into his body and he crushed her in powerful arms. "I love you so much," he whispered and his body trembled. "I don't know what I'd do if..."

"Shh," Hana told him. "It'd be awful but you would cope. It's the most horrific experience but no less hideous because you imagined it a hundred times. I lived through it and so did my father and we survived, not always intact but we muddled through. Everything has a price, darling. The cost of me loving you and Phoe is opening myself up to the devastation which comes with loving and losing. But you know what? It's *worth* it and I wouldn't change anything just to spare myself misery." Hana reached up and stroked her husband's cheek. "It's the choice we make, Loge."

She released him, kissing the underside of his stubbly chin. Then she opened the door and walked away, knowing he needed to rationalise it for himself. Hana dug in the hall cupboard for her slippers, allowing the shoe rack the privilege of her words of wisdom. "Life is a private journey, walked out between a man and his maker."

Chapter 26

In the lounge, Tama fed Phoenix crusts of bread, banging her on the back as she coughed on rogue crumbs. Bodie looked uncomfortable and Hana sensed Tama had been asking him about the case. "Is the biology teacher still in custody?" she asked, reaching for a sandwich and sitting in the seat next to her daughter. Phoenix waved the crust and jabbered something unintelligible and Hana smiled and nodded, satisfying the tiny desire to be understood. The little girl did a huge nod and snapped the crust in two with her forehead, looking at the pieces with a mystified glare. Hana laughed and Phoenix giggled, squeezing up her grey eyes and producing a cheesy grin which showed little white teeth cutting through her gums. Hana stroked her hair and kissed her face, avoiding the mushed up cheese and crumbs around most of it.

Bodie finished his mouthful and sighed. "Yeah, he's still in the cells. They applied for an extension but Petersen's lawyer requested a medical assessment. He's a complete lunatic; raving on and making no sense. The drugs were definitely his - the first enclosure and the one he took you to. He and Larry Collins were in it together but it all went wrong a few weeks ago. Collins was a prolific user which explains his attitude and paranoia. The post-mortem showed he was as high as a kite on the morning he died. He was hit in the face with the spade from the trench and it broke his nose and caused a massive haemorrhage in his brain. Unfortunately, the forensics guys found so many fingerprints on the handle it's impossible to prove Peterson caused the fatal injury. I think you, Tama and Logan were the only people on site who *didn't* touch the murder weapon. It lived next to the trench so everyone passing picked it up, put it down or had a dig with it. Even Angus touched it. He fell over it the day before the murder and stood it up again although thirty teenage witnesses saw that happen. Where Petersen's concerned, we can prove motive and opportunity so hopefully the rest will fall into place."

"What about the tennis guy?" Tama asked. "Is he involved?"

Hana felt her appetite leave and the sandwich in her mouth turn to brick dust as Bodie replied. "That's the weird thing. Nobody else saw him on site, except Mum. Angus has no idea who he is and didn't give anyone permission to use the courts."

"Who told the biology teacher's poor wife?" Hana asked sadly, trying to change the subject. Her memories flicked to two police officers a decade ago, walking sombrely up the steps of the Achilles Rise house to impart bad news to her. In the back of her mind lingered the disquieting thought she had imagined the tennis player all along. Hana began to doubt herself.

"I did," Bodie spoke into the silence. "Poor bloody woman. She didn't have a clue. She thought he was either working late or having an affair because he kept disappearing and not showing up at home. When she challenged him he denied it and said he was working to buy the house and found some shift work making deliveries. He seemed sincere and showed her the bank balance so she believed him. He started the marijuana plants off in a propagator on the laundry window sill. The wife assumed it was curriculum stuff and didn't question it. She said their little girl knocked the tray off trying to open the window yesterday morning and he went absolutely mental. That was the last time they saw him. The wife put it all back together and stood the seedlings up. He told her they were maple saplings. She's devastated."

Hana covered her eyes with her hand, remembering the happy woman who bounced up two flights of stairs to the family room a year ago, heavily pregnant and begging Hana to let them rent the house.

"Mum?" Bodie was still speaking and Hana struggled to tune in. "Are you selling Achilles Rise?"

She sighed and nodded. "It's listed with the agent who rents it out for me. I just haven't managed to sign the paperwork yet."

Hana smiled at her husband as he entered the room and vacated the chair for him, grabbing a plate of sandwiches she'd rescued from the younger men's hungry hands. He thanked her and sat, not really hungry.

"I wondered if you'd let me buy it." Bodie bit his lip.

"No." Hana's answer came swiftly and the men stared at her. She flicked her hair behind her shoulder in defiance and Bodie looked disappointed. "This family should let that house go. We all need to stop hankering after the past. But I do have another proposition if you're interested. I've arranged to have Culver's Cottage valued so I can sell the land at the back to Maihi and Hemi. It will make the house less expensive and I'm willing to sell you that, if you want it."

Logan's mouth hung open, his sandwich suspended in mid-air. He shook his head in disbelief. Hana reached for his hand. "I love the house Logan's building and I want to put everything into it," she said. "I'm spread too thinly at the moment and need to cut down my responsibilities." She got eye contact with Bodie. "Talk to Amy and get back to me. Three agents can value it and Logan and I will take an average, but it's not a gift, Bodie. I'll be looking for a fair price. I'll give you first option but if we can't agree, it goes on the open market."

Bodie's face lit up. "It would be perfect; Jas and Amy love Culver's Cottage. Get the agents in and then we'll talk. That's awesome news."

"I'm not arguing with my children about money though," Hana reiterated. "Nothing's worth that and I *will* sell it if we can't agree."

"Ok." Bodie attacked another sandwich with gusto, a lightness in his heart not previously there.

Logan kept quiet, pleasure and hurt rivalling in his brain. Hana offered him security but hadn't discussed it with him and Logan wasn't used to being outmaneuvered. He narrowed his eyes at his daughter and pulled a face as she snatched a sandwich off his plate, dropping grated cheese onto the tray in front of her high chair and then flicking it around. She slapped her hands on it without coordination, flattening it into a yellow mess before rubbing her eyes and spreading it over her face. Hana dived in and pulled her arms up with one hand, deftly wiping the tiny face with a cloth in the other. "Mucky pup," she crooned, undoing Phoenix's straps and lifting her from the chair.

Hana sat on the sofa and got ready to feed the tired baby. Phoenix lay across her mother's thighs and kicked her legs with impatience. "I'm visiting Da this afternoon," Hana said conversationally, hoping Logan would offer to come.

"I'm on duty soon," he reminded her and Hana nodded and kept her eye roll to herself.

"A friend wants to see me." Tama looked sideways at Bodie and deliberately didn't name his colleague.

"And I've got work," Bodie said, looking at his watch. "Thanks for the shower and lunch." He smiled, a refreshing expression after the weeks of darkness. "I'll talk to Amy and let you know."

Everyone filtered away, but Logan drifted around the unit aimlessly while Hana got ready and put the baby in her car seat. "Are you cross I didn't discuss my plans with you?" she asked her husband but he shook his head. "So what's the matter?" she asked and Logan shrugged.

"Nothing, I'm fine." Agitation crept into his voice and Hana sighed. Admitting defeat she kissed him goodbye and headed out in the Honda.

Robert and Elaine's new motel was more upmarket after their long journey back from Wellington. When Hana knocked on their door with the car seat over her arm, she found them looking happy and rested. "Ah hen, how lovely to see ma wee girlie," Robert whispered, wrapping Hana in a firm hug.

"I'll make tea," Elaine offered, gripping the tiny kettle from the night stand.

"Don't worry, Lainey," Robert said. "Mark's meeting us at that little cafe we like, so why don't we head off there now and have a nice coffee altogether?"

They both looked at Hana for her approval and she gave it with good grace, hope nipping at her soul at the thought of being a family unit again, even a dysfunctional one. Hana fished the pram from the car and transferred her sleeping baby into it and the little group wandered along Victoria Street until they arrived at a cafe half way down. It wasn't too busy and they ordered, waiting in a booth for Mark and the drinks to arrive. "I ordered muffins and scones," Robert said, treating Hana like a child and waggling his bushy eyebrows. She laughed, a sharp pain in her chest at the memory of being a carefree little girl still in his eyes.

The sight of a slim, blonde woman waiting for a take-away coffee near the counter caught her eye and Hana took a slow intake of breath. The woman faced the shop window concentrating on the view of Victoria Street, her hair cut shorter than the last time Hana saw her. Excusing herself for a moment and clambering over her pram into the aisle, Hana tapped her on the arm, readying her smile.

"I saw you." Anka's smile seemed wistful as she turned. "I assumed you wouldn't want to talk."

"Sorry." Hana withdrew her hand. "Would you rather I didn't?"

Anka's emotions were confusing and impossible to read, but she shook her head. "No, please, I'm glad you did, I'm just surprised. I've done so much to hurt you; having sex with Tama in your lounge and..." Anka swallowed. "Ivan took great delight telling me about your conversation. He's such a bastard." Anka shook her head and examined the toes of her shiny red shoes.

Hana watched for deceit as she asked her question. "Did you know about Vik's affair before he died?" she asked bluntly.

Anka pulled a face and widened her eyes in horror. "No! Damn that man! *Ivan* did, he knew but didn't tell me until a few years ago when you started dating that relief teacher. He made a comment that maybe this one would be faithful and I made him tell me. I knew he'd told you the other day out of spite, but didn't realise he'd falsely implicated me." Anka shook her head, her customary composure gone.

"It's okay," Hana said. "It devastated me at the time because it made a mockery of friendships I relied on, but it doesn't matter anymore. I've got Logan and Phoenix and it's ancient history. Besides which, *I* knew and didn't tell."

"Why didn't you tell me?" Anka asked, looking hurt. Her lips turned down and she stared at her shoes again.

"Shame, I guess. Embarrassment. I wanted to preserve Vik's memory for his children, which turned out to be absolutely pointless. Bodie always knew and so did Marcus. Only Izzie is blissfully ignorant."

"What a mess," Anka sighed, shaking her head slowly. "For what it's worth, I'm sorry for any part I played in it." She touched Hana on the arm. "I'm also sorry for everything I've inflicted on you this last year. I've messed everything up."

Hana looked at her old friend, realising how much she'd missed her. Anka seemed more like her old self, thinner and less confident but certainly happier. "Anka," she said quietly, "I've missed you. We've both made mistakes but I forgive you everything."

There were tears in the other woman's eyes, desperate to take the proffered olive branch but knowing she didn't deserve it. Anka nodded. "Thank you," she whispered.

"Why don't you come and sit with us?" Hana invited, indicating the booth as her father and stepmother sipped their newly arrived coffee.

"Meet Robert, my da and Elaine, my stepmother." Hana fixed a wooden smile on her lips as she acknowledged Elaine, seeing her aunt's relief.

Anka shot her a look of mystification and cocked her head. Hana was thankful for her tact in not asking how Robert McIntyre had risen from the grave. "Nice to meet you," Anka said instead, nodding to the elderly couple. Robert dabbed his mouth with a handkerchief and rose to shake hands, overwriting the angry vision in Hana's head and replacing it with the gentleman she remembered.

Hana sat next to her friend and when nobody was looking, took her hand under the table and squeezed it, reminded of the words Pastor Allen spoke once. *'Unforgiveness is the cup of poison you pour for someone else and then drink yourself.'* Anka gulped and squeezed back, tears pricking the backs of her eyes. She started when a dark, handsome man approached the table and stood smiling at them with benevolence. "It became a party without me," Mark said, feigning disappointment. Robert laughed and shook his head.

"I should probably go," Anka said, rising.

"No, don't." Hana kept her hand over Anka's, forcing her to stay seated. "This is my brother, Mark," she said, shuffling into the corner so he could sit. He sat on her hand and Hana squeaked. "And he has a bony bottom!"

Mark leaned around Hana and gallantly shook hands with the pretty woman, a new spark of interest in his green eyes. Too late Hana realised her error and let out a slow exhale.

Phoenix whimpered in her pram and Hana shoved Mark out of the booth so she could go to her. He slotted himself back in, bailing Anka up in the corner and turning on his full charm for her benefit. An in-depth conversation ensued on health care, as Hana extracted her baby from the pram and removed her little jacket. Robert looked at Hana and smirked, nodding his head towards her brother and friend. Hana acknowledged a tiny sense of misgiving in her heart and the smile she returned was less than genuine. He winked as though he understood although he couldn't have guessed. Hana chided herself. She'd either forgiven, or she hadn't but to prove it, she'd have to let Anka's sins go.

Phoenix wasn't hungry but buoyant and happy once she properly woke. Hana asked the waitress for a soy fluffy; frothy milk in a tiny cup. When it came, she fed it to her daughter from a plastic spoon. In between each mouthful, Phoenix beamed at everyone around the table. "Big girl," Hana whispered in her ear and she smiled up at her mother and kicked her legs.

"How old is she now?" Anka asked, leaning forward so that she could see around Mark.

"Almost seven months," Hana said wistfully, thinking how quickly life disappeared.

"She's gorgeous," her friend complimented. "She's forward for her age isn't she?"

"I'm not sure. I don't see other mothers and babies at the moment and it's such a long time since Bo and Izzie, I can't remember what they were doing at this age," Hana admitted. "Logan and I spend a lot of time with her because she's the only one, so she might learn things early."

Phoenix chose that exact moment to beam up at her mother, her grey eyes round and knowing. She looked so much like Logan it made Hana smile. The group of accompanying adults let out a combined sigh to acknowledge her cuteness and Phoenix ruffled like a queen.

Anka stayed until her take away-cup was empty. She refused Mark's offer of a refill and excused herself. Hana handed Phoenix to her brother, standing up to let her friend out and walking onto the street with her. "Where are you living?" she asked.

"I've got an apartment over a restaurant close by. It's cool," she said. "I rent a parking space out back and they aren't noisy. It's nice sometimes to hear other people moving around and living their lives, less isolating. I'm working at the osteopath's offices again. They heard I was back and asked if I wanted my old job, so it worked out fine."

"Do you have a new cell phone number?" Hana asked. Her friend nodded and reaching in her bag, pulled her phone out.

"Remind me of yours, and I'll text so you can save it."

Hana read the number out and watched Anka's long, manicured fingers punch it deftly into her phone, frightened the other woman just took it out of politeness. Anka looked up and read the anxiety in Hana's face, pulling her into a warm hug. "Silly girl," she whispered, "I'll text you now. Then you can message me back and suggest another time to meet."

Hana nodded and saw Anka send a message to her new contact. She sighed with relief at the promise of a relationship restored, still terrified the tennis player was a lonely figment of her imagination. Hana felt lighter of spirit as she headed back inside the cafe to find her daughter singing a loud and interesting song for her captive audience.

"Anka seems lovely," Mark said, the twinkle in his green eyes giving him away. "What?" he laughed as Hana rolled her eyes at her father.

Elaine shook her head knowingly. "I'm sure I heard her tell you she was happy being single. Perhaps it was a hint she wished to stay that way?"

Mark shrugged nonchalantly and winked at his mother. "You always to assume the worst of me, mother dear. I'm fifty-six years old and very much past the *'love 'em and leave 'em'* stage. I thought she might be nice company for my upcoming works dinner, not a night of rampant debauchery in a hotel!"

Elaine looked suitably shocked, but Hana and Robert giggled, more at the elderly woman's discomfort than the thought of Anka and Mark. Hana resisted the urge to warn her brother to steer clear of Anka as she worked hard to put her life back together, deciding for once to keep her big mouth closed and let nature take its course.

"You seem uncomfortable," Mark whispered and Hana swallowed and shrugged.

"I'm fine," she lied, searching for the sense of unconditional forgiveness which evaded her.

Back at the unit, Tama and Lucy lounged together on the sofa behind the breakfast bar. Lucy looked different out of uniform, her blonde hair hanging long over her shoulders and makeup accentuating her beauty. Hana took it as a good sign that neither jumped as she blundered through the front door with a car seat and change bag. They talked in low voices, so Hana made a cup of tea one-handed and carried her still singing child to the bedroom for a feed. Phoenix wasn't interested, filled up by the soy milk fluffy and laid on the bed trying to eat her own toes. Hana played with her until she noticed the child was dozing off. "It's a lonely feeling, being ditched by your only companion," she breathed, ruffling Phoenix's soft curls and seeing her reach for her thumb. Hana changed her nappy without waking the infant and slipped her into the cot, feeling trapped with nowhere to go. She rattled around her bedroom until it was tidy but still boring.

In the hallway, Hana pulled long black boots over stockinged feet and marched into the lounge. Tama and Lucy had progressed beyond talking and sprang apart guiltily. Hana gave Tama a narrowed look. "Would you mind listening out for Phoe for a little while? You won't forget about her, will you?" Her face told him in an unspoken language what she expected.

Tama ran his hand through his hair and shook his head, non-verbally promising he'd behave "I won't forget her, Ma," he said.

Hana raised an eyebrow, reminding him of his eager tryst with Anka while Phoenix slept down the hall and Tama blanched. "I won't," he assured her.

"Thanks." Hana grabbed her phone from the baby change bag. She held it up in front of her face. "I've got this if you need me."

Hana walked across to St Bart's, nodding to Pete on reception as she passed. Dodging two rubber balls and the Year 9 body which followed them, Hana climbed the stairs to the top floor, finding the staff restroom and knocking on the middle of the bedroom doors.

"Hey, gorgeous. This is a nice surprise." Logan's sleeping bag lay on the single bed in a roll and Hana knew it wouldn't stay there. As soon as everyone else cleared out, he'd move into the rest room and keep vigil, detesting the confinement of the well-used room. A radiator blasted out heat, making the room stuffy and tropical and marking and work books littered the desk. Logan's tie dangled around his open shirt because even on Saturday Logan Du Rose dressed for work, donning a crisp, expensively tailored white shirt and bum-hugging black trousers. His wash bag sat on the shelf by the sink and the smell of his deodorant pervaded the air.

Hana shut the door behind her, keeping eye contact with her husband and slipping off her boots. He looked at her curiously as she climbed onto the bed and stood, pulling him towards her so she could kiss him at level height. Hana sought his eyes, unreadable pools of swirling greys turning blacker by the second.

"I've got dinner duty," Logan breathed, his lips twitching at the corners.

Hana shrugged. "Then you'll be late." She undid his shirt buttons one at a time, nipping at his bottom lip at the feel of each satisfying pop. Logan tried to put his arms around her but found his hands batted away as Hana teased and undressed him. Logan loved her so much it was like a physical pain in his ribs, made worse by his growing dependence on her. His heart stopped every time she walked into the same room still – after a year of marriage. It terrified the independent once lonely man that he might one day be forced to return to his former life without her. It left him emotionally stripped and vulnerable; to be so unutterably linked with another human being.

Hana enjoyed driving her husband mad. She touched her lips lightly to his muscular chest and shoulders, sensing she possessed him fully but knowing he'd only take so much teasing. It was fun while it lasted. She kissed, nibbled and breathed on his flesh until the gentle resistance of his wrists in her hands became like a tsunami and she couldn't stop his strong arms wrapping around her and pulling her down onto the bed. "I love you, Hana Du Rose," he whispered, slipping her dress over her head. His fingers shook as they brushed the red coils from her neck, letting them slither across her shoulders. "Don't leave me," he begged, his grey eyes flashing like a stormy sea.

"I won't," Hana promised, sighing as her breasts tumbled from her bra and Logan's lips covered hers.

Logan's temporary abode looked like a jumble sale with clothing mixed up on the floor and Hana's knickers hanging from the notice board. She snuggled into Logan's warm armpit and squinted, reading the words 'Fire Drill' which were partially obscured by her underwear. Hana covered one eye, so it read 'Fire' and then red lace, smirking to herself.

"Nice knickers," Logan sighed, smiling with his eyes closed. "Very irresistible."

"Mmnn," Hana sighed. "I noticed." She listened to her husband breathe in and out, glad she'd put more effort into the state of her underwear of late. A pair of elasticated, grey-washed-granny-knickers with holes in the sides wouldn't look so good, caught on a rogue drawing pin. "I might leave them there as a reminder," she threatened.

Logan turned on his side and wrapped his arms around her, muscles bulging under soft skin. "And leave me with the thought of you walking home across the paddock with no knickers on? You wouldn't."

Hana giggled and Logan kissed her, shrouding them in a haze of musky aftershave. She sighed. "Now I know what utter contentment feels like. I don't want to move ever again."

"Is Tama looking after Phoe?" Logan asked and Hana nodded into his chest.

"Yeah, I guess I should go back." Reality visited with its snake-like fingers of monotony, making food, tidying houses and going through the motions of life with its boring, necessary reminders. Hana sat up and pulled a face. The slippery sleeping bag shivered down her body revealing a breast and a delicious slice of porcelain stomach.

"Not yet." Logan kissed her again and shifted so he could pull her on top of him and Hana knew she'd be longer than promised. Logan moved so Hana straddled him, running his fingers down the soft skin of her back, his eyes roving over her body. "Tama can cope." His words brushed against Hana's hair and it shuddered in response, falling onto his chest and stroking the bulging pectorals. Logan bit his lip and reeled Hana in, smiling at her feigned resistance as she sank into his embrace. They pushed the mundanity of life aside for a few more minutes, looking for highs to sustain them in a temporary ecstasy.

"I feel like a naughty schoolgirl!" Hana exclaimed later in hushed tones as she sneaked out of Logan's room and into the restroom.

"Don't say that!" he chided, enfolding her from behind and kissing the back of her neck through her hair. "I'll take you back into my room."

Hana laughed and wriggled free. "Make me a cup of tea to take your mind off it."

Logan narrowed his eyes and slapped Hana's bottom but obeyed, his cowboy boots clicking on the lino floor. She contemplated asking him what was wrong earlier but guessed he wouldn't tell her. Hana wandered around the tired restroom and sank into a worn armchair, staring at a stain on the carpet by the collapsed sofa. "Is that your blood?" she asked, pulling a face and Logan nodded.

"Yeah. I think I need it back." He smirked, referring to his haemophilia in joking terms.

Hana shivered, remembering the incident and pushed the memory away in a rush. She grasped at the question which snaked its way into her mind, remembered from the previous day but not asked. "Where was James?" she said and a strange, unfathomable look crossed her husband's face.

"When?" Logan asked and looked away, alerting Hana's suspicious mind.

"When the biology teacher took me into the gully to see him. Where was he really?"

"Oh then," Logan answered, running his hand through his hair. "In his assessment, where I told you he'd be. So how's it going with Tama and his new squeeze? Do you trust them on their own?" Logan strived to change the subject far too eagerly, making Hana not want to at all.

"They're fine; he promised he'd behave. What other time did you think I was asking about James?" Hana asked, seeing guilt work its way across Logan's face. "Has he been somewhere?"

Logan shook his head and his eyes told her not to push but it turned her into a dog gnawing a bone; the opposite of his intention. Hana shifted onto the couch next to him. "I'll tickle it out of you then," she threatened, slipping her fingers between his knees and squeezing at the sensitive tendons. When Logan made a grab for her hands, Hana jabbed him in the ribs and made him squirm.

"Hana, don't!" Logan warned. There was something serious in the way he took her hands in his and stared into her eyes. "Don't."

"But you're ticklish," she said, her eyes heralding mischief.

His irises shone gritty and sparkled as though shot through with diamonds, emphasising his authority. "Hana, please leave this. For now. *Please?*" It was said as a question but implied instruction. Hana's enthusiastic lover took a backseat beneath the man of authority and Hana felt it like a violent slap to the face.

She snatched her hands away, knitting her brow and grinding her jaw. "More secrets!" she spat. "So much for agreements." She *hated* being told what to do, feeling a rebellious spirit force its way to the top. Sixteen years of marriage to a competent decision-maker who ran his relationship like a project, built up a core of resistance which threatened to explode. "Are you asking me, or telling me?" she demanded, voice low and green eyes flashing with defiance.

Logan ran his hand across his jaw and then through his hair, betraying his distress and Hana felt a flash of dread as he replied, "Hana, I'm *begging you.*"

Chapter 27

Hana's walk back to the staff units did little to assuage the unsettled feeling Logan's words created. She walked carefully around the edge of the sports field, acknowledging Larry Collins' continuing influence on the life of the school.

Knocking on the front door of her unit with a heavy heart, Hana was surprised to be greeted by Lucy, who stood back to reveal a scene of touching domestication. Tama set cutlery on the table and balanced Phoenix on his hip and it made Hana smile. "We cooked dinner," Lucy said with enthusiasm as a chocolate covered Jas appeared from the small kitchen with a grin on his face.

"And you've been breeding children," Hana said jokily, regretting it as Tama pouted.

"Definitely not!" he said prudishly. "They're all yours!"

Lucy's face gained a heated flush, mottling her delicate skin. "I'm a Christian; I don't agree with sex before marriage," she whispered.

Hana nodded. "Me too. Good on you." She disguised her smirk with a cough, knowing God had an interesting sense of humour. Tama was the male version of a whore and seemed serious enough about Lucy to curb his habits. She sneaked a sideways look at the teenager, seeing only contentment. Perhaps boundaries with women were all he ever needed.

Lucy peered at Hana as though expecting her to say more. "I didn't sleep with Logan until we were married," Hana said, trying to inject solidarity into the situation as she dropped her boots onto the floor of the hall cupboard. Tama clattered a fork onto the table, making Phoenix jump and grizzle.

"Really?" he said, his face mischievous. "He kept that bloody quiet!"

Hana lifted her finger and pointed it at him, narrowing her eyes and cocking her head. "Don't start!" she warned and Tama bit his lip.

"Sorry," he said, a grin straining at the corners of his mouth. "But I guess it explains how you're always..."

"Tama, thank you!" Hana said sharply and he smirked and went back to setting the table. In his confusion he handed the baby on his hip a metal spoon to play with.

"Yeah, I probably wouldn't do that," Hana suggested.

"She's fine," Tama argued, yelping as Phoenix whacked him on the chin and then banged herself on the forehead. Hana reached out to take her daughter and Phoenix did a fake cry and a smirk, launching forwards into her mother's arms like a miniature drunkard. Hana decided to play along.

"Did your nasty bro' hurt poor baby?" she said in a sickly, crooning voice and Tama looked momentarily annoyed until he realised she'd referred to him as Phoenix's bro' in front of Lucy. Then he felt included and soppy, looking so much like a big puppy it was endearing.

Hana decided not to help his cause any further, taking the baby to the bathroom for a quick wash in the sink. Jas came too and handed her things, watching as the baby splashed around in the water and Hana struggled to keep her sitting upright. Phoenix squealed and covered her small companion with soap bubbles, laughing when he patted them around his chin and tried to get her to say, *"Bush Santa."*

"So where's Mum and Dad?" Hana asked. Jas shrugged and didn't look bothered at being abandoned in her house.

"I've got my rucksack with things I might need," he said, "in case I stay the night."

"Oh, nice," Hana remarked with a smile, wondering where his parents thought she'd put him to bed.

"Let's get you changed into your pyjamas before dinner," she suggested. "I can fix a plastic bag over your cast and you can hop in the shower."

"You're not allowed to hop in the shower. Mummy says it's dangerous."

"Haha, funny guy," Hana scoffed and ruffled the boy's hair. "Come on, you get ready and I'll find the bag."

Jas' new Action Man sat on the edge of the bath and watched the splashy process. "Can he come in?" Jas begged. "He loves it."

"No!" Hana protested, brushing her daughter's wispy hair. "He'll get waterlogged like the last one."

In the kitchen, Tama had produced a half decent dinner of spaghetti bolognese with copious amounts of cheese. They gathered around the tiny table to eat and Hana eyed Lucy's plate with interest. Perhaps Tama thought his new girlfriend was too thin, dishing up Mount Kilimanjaro for her to summit. Hana remembered Miriam's need to feed everyone and how it was the older woman's way of showing love. She wondered if Lucy realised how much affection was on her plate.

"You gave me heaps," Lucy gasped, her face shining under an unhealthy sheen of sweat. The mouthfuls seemed to get harder to press between her lips.

Jas beamed across the table at his grandmother, twirling his fork competently in the pasta for a one-armed-bandit. His fight with the chocolate spread hadn't dented his appetite. "Why did the visitor drop the little parcel off?" Hana asked casually, careful not to make the little boy feel unwelcome.

"Huh?" Tama looked gormless and Hana shook her head in frustration.

"She means me," Jas said, pointing to his clean pyjama shirt with a sauce covered spoon. "I'm the little parcel" He winked at Hana with an exaggerated motion involving his whole face and she flushed with embarrassment.

"You're too clever for your own good," she muttered and Jas grinned.

"Thanks, Hanny. That's nice."

"Oh, his dad dropped him off. Amy's already at work but Bodie got called in. He's gone to the boarding house."

"Why?" Hana's fork remained poised in mid-air.

"There's a very naughty boy there." Jas waved his spoon and flicked sauce backwards onto the wall. "He told lies and Dad's gonna beat him up and lock him in the cells."

Hana pulled a face. "I think you've got something a bit wrong there."

"Nope." Jas shook his head. "Daddy said it on the phone. He said the boy got seen in the naughty place so he's gonna get him."

"What boy?" Hana asked, her breathing quickening in fear. "Do you know his name?"

Jas shook his head. "Nope. Where's Poppa?"

"He's at work, sweetheart. And no, you can't see him tonight."

"He knows the boy," Jas said, sticking his fork up his nose and wincing at the pain.

Hana's chest felt tight and she resisted the urge to run across the field to the boarding house. Her altercation with Logan rose inside her like a spikey thing. She hated it when he wasn't straight with her and it hit her in the guts like a body blow for being dumb enough to believe they were past that kind of closed behaviour.

In an attempt to distract herself, Hana made an unfortunate error of judgement. "I bumped into Anka today when I was with my dad," she said, picking over her food but not making much progress. It was more interesting watching Lucy deal with her food mountain and Phoenix play with a string of spaghetti in her high chair. The baby wore a plastic bib like a strait jacket and Hana wondered if she should have offered Lucy the spare one. She seemed to be dropping her dinner down

"Thanks for that." Tama visibly paled and Hana felt cruel, regretting mentioning her friend. When the silence grew embarrassing, Lucy interjected in a break from her one-woman-spaghetti-eating-competition.

"Sorry, who's Anka?"

Tama's cutlery hovered over his plate and even Phoenix stopped pushing the white worm around her tray in interest, fixing her grey eyes on her mother.

"She's an old friend of mine," Hana hedged, "I haven't seen her for a while."

"Why's that?" asked Lucy, ever the policewoman.

Tama looked at Hana intently, making her suffer and self-destructing at the same time. Hana felt herself wither with humiliation. "Yeah *Hana*," he said. "Why is that?"

She changed tack, trying to stop the moment getting out of hand and turning it back onto herself. "We had a fall out a year ago. Anka had an affair and it detonated her marriage. She hated on me because I tried to talk her out of it. Instead of sticking by her, I judged her. But I saw her today and I've missed her. I don't have enough friends just to let them go because of a bad choice. I can't say anything to punish her more than she has herself; Anka's lost everything."

Lucy stared at her spaghetti mountain and sighed. "My last boyfriend cheated on me," she said sadly. "We were engaged for four years and he'd been seeing this other girl for two of them. It's debilitating to be on the other end of it."

Hana nodded. "I know. But people make mistakes and they're all redeemable. I'm glad I'm friends with Anka again."

Lucy didn't look convinced. "It's hard. He still goes to my church and it's awkward. I don't have anyone to sit with because our joint friends supported him."

Hana patted Lucy's hand, her face filled with understanding. Vik hadn't been around after his affair but Hana knew it would have decimated their church.

"What's an affair?" Jas piped up, his mouth full of pasta. Phoenix laughed at his face expression and he squeezed pasta through a gap in his teeth, sending her into hysterics. Hana shook her head slowly at him and gave him the face.

"What church do you attend?" Hana asked Lucy, hoping to move the conversation away from Anka and allow Tama to breathe normally again. She grabbed his hand under the table by way of apology but he didn't respond, his fingers stiff and unyielding.

"Ships have anchors," Jas said helpfully, "massive big fat ones. So does Popeye. He has anchor tattoos on his big, giantnormous arms." He looked across at Phoenix, having a private conversation with her, "He goes *raaaah* like this when Bluto gets his Oliveoil and he eats the green stuff. It goes up his veins into his armpits to make a lump and he goes *raaaah!*" Jas bugged his eyes and flexed the spindly muscles on his good arm. Phoenix looked momentarily stunned and then realised he was doing the favourite face which Tama did. She screamed in delight and banged the tray of her high chair in glee, desperate for him to do it again. "Dad's got Popeye arms under his uniform," Jas said conversationally, "but his come popping up from Marmite, not green stuff." He scratched his ear with his spoon, spreading sauce up the side of his face, his brain working out some complicated scenario. "Do you still do that green stuff in your pants?" he asked Phoenix, who nodded happily without coordination.

Hana watched in horror as Jas put his fork down and Action Man's head appeared above the lip of the table. "That's not spinach, Jas," Hana warned. "Let's not go there."

"I go to the night services at The Zone," Lucy said, "I like it there and don't feel like changing when I didn't do anything wrong."

"If you're planning on going tomorrow, I'll come," Hana offered. "I've been before and liked it. That's if Logan or Tama will look after Phoenix."

Tama looked Hana square in the eye. "Ask Uncle Logan to babysit. I'll come to church."

Hana cocked her head and stared at Tama with curiosity, trying to work out his motive. She narrowed her eyes and smirked, guessing he didn't want her to be alone with Lucy in case she betrayed him again. "Right then," Hana said, getting up to fetch her baby's food bowl from the microwave, "that's settled. Church tomorrow night at The Zone."

"Right!" Tama replied, burying his fork back into his spaghetti, looking more sick than hungry.

An apologetic Amy collected Jas at ten o'clock that night, scraping him off Hana's bed and grateful he was already in his pyjamas. Logan worked all day on Sunday and Hana avoided him, sensing he was up to something. He borrowed the Honda at lunchtime and brought it back late in the afternoon. He appeared around five-thirty looking tired and overwrought, his tie loose and his top button undone.

"Dinner's in the microwave," Hana said, pointing to a plate of food. "It needs heating."

"Thanks, but I'm not hungry," he replied and Hana shrugged.

"Whatever."

Phoenix was fed, bathed and ready for bed, kicking her legs under the baby gym on the lounge rug. Tama appeared in his interview clothes and shiny shoes, ready to go to church and Logan gaped in surprise. "Who died?" he asked. "Have I missed a funeral?"

Hana smiled with approval and disappeared to the bedroom to shed her jeans, not wanting to make Tama look out of place. She reappeared in a pretty dress and her long black boots. "Where are you all going?" Logan asked, looking lost.

"Church," Hana replied curtly. "Wanna come and confess some sins?" She said it jokily but Logan looked stung. Hana wished she could lose her voice for a short time until she learned to think about the things that came out of her mouth.

Sensing the fraught atmosphere, Tama went out to the car to start it up and wipe the gathering ice from the windscreen while Hana bent down for one last kiss from her baby. Phoenix squealed and puckered her lips, making Hana laugh. The air bubbles on her cheek were the best the child could manage.

Hana stood up and wiped the goo off but when she turned, she found her husband standing close. He held onto her forearms with an iron grip, his face impassive and frightening because of the complete lack of emotion there. "Hana," he said seriously, "I don't expect you to like all the decisions I make, but at least respect them. I know I said it didn't matter but sometimes I just wish you'd trust me." He leaned down and touched his lips tantalisingly to hers, disregarding the glossy lipstick. He made her heart melt and slide into her boots and she hated him for it. "Do you have to go?" he asked, his breath soft on her face and Hana fought the urge to fall into bed with him, losing herself in his embrace. Logan's thumbs brushed sensuously along the delicate skin of her forearms. He knew exactly what he was doing to her.

Hana swallowed and nodded. "I promised."

Logan nodded once, his fringe brushing Hana's forehead and making her want to scream. He dropped her arms and stood back, allowing her room to pass. Hana felt conflicted and dithered on the spot in confusion, her heart vying for attention over her head.

"Go on, go," Logan said gently and kissed her again, making it worse. He turned her round and with his hands on her shoulders, guided her towards the door and down the front steps. He waved once and shut the door as his wife climbed into the passenger seat next to Tama.

Hana felt a horrid emptiness begin in the pit of her stomach and touched the spot under her ribs.

"You don't wanna go, do you?" Tama asked and Hana frowned.

"I try not to break my promises," she said, sounding sulky.

"So what do they do at this place?" Tama said, looking for guidance.

"It's like a school assembly, but bigger," Hana said, trying to be helpful. "But from what I remember, it's charismatic, so people move around more and put their arms up and stuff." A horrid thought occurred to her. "You do what you want. Don't feel like you have to copy other people. It's an act of worship, not a line dancing class." She had dreadful visions of Lucy going to the altar for prayer and finding Tama standing eagerly behind her. Church could be a traumatic experience for newcomers.

"So, it *is* like line dancing, or it *isn't?*" Tama asked facetiously and Hana glared at him.

"I'm sorry for mentioning Anka. It just popped out because I'd seen her."

"And because you'd had a bust-up with my uncle again," Tama smirked. "You always take it out on everyone else."

"No, I do not!" Hana replied, her voice hiking at the end of her sentence.

"Yes you do - like now. What did he say to set you off again?"

"Nothing!" Hana wailed, frustrated at what her reaction revealed. "He's up to something and I can't get it out of him."

"Then trust him," Tama replied, "it's simple."

Hana sulked all the way to church, fixing a plastic smile on her face as she went through the double doors. The well-intentioned person on the door was a 'hugger,' which was amusing from Hana's point of view and terrifying from poor Tama's. Not used to physical contact, the teenager looked unnerved by the woman who threw her arms around his neck and administered a meaty snog to the side of his cheek. Enthusiastic enough to suck him in, the woman's actions brought laughter from between Hana's lips. "You did well," she sniggered, patting Tama on the back as he progressed through the entranceway towards the next obstacle wiping sweat from his brow.

The 'shaker' was a man given the job of shaking hands and handing out leaflets. He pumped Tama's hand ardently and thanked him four times for coming. "Are you new here?" he said, his eyes glinting with the scent of fresh blood.

"We're just visiting," Hana said, giving Tama a hearty shove towards the seating area and snagging a leaflet as she dived past. "They mean well," she hissed as they passed a group of young people.

"They're scary!" Tama whined. "Are you sure they only want my soul?"

"Yeah, pretty much," Hana sighed, wishing she felt less jaded. "But you did great, sweetheart. Logan would have left after the hugger but you kept going. Well done."

"Logan would've left before the hugger!" Tama corrected her.

They found seats away from the gathered knots of people, greeted by well-meaning people along the way. Tama stared at Hana in surprise. "Do you know everyone in Hamilton?" he demanded.

"To be fair, I've been in Christian circles for a lot of years," Hana replied. "Churches are like big washing machines; we go round and round and potentially come out cleaner." Hana recognised signs that Tama felt overwhelmed and sheltered him as best as she could.

Their ineptitude at locating anyone in the dimly lit atmosphere meant Lucy had to find them. She sat alone in the back row looking sad and isolated until she spotted them further along. She waved to Hana as she and Tama screwed their heads round trying to find her. "There she is!" Hana said and nudged Tama. His expression became bashful.

"Thank you for coming," Lucy gushed, hugging Hana and Tama in turn. His eyes grew round as Lucy's enthusiasm mimicked that of the lady on the door and he glanced at her sideways. Hana shook her head at him and winked. "I didn't know if you meant it," Lucy said, raising her voice over the band's first chords.

"I try not to say things I don't mean," Hana reassured her, Lucy's enthusiasm making the journey out into the cold worthwhile.

Lucy sat between them as though seeking shelter and Hana noticed a group of young adults gathered in a row of seats in front. She watched as they whispered to each other, turning around and staring at Lucy and her guests. Hana felt anger prickle inside her chest at their rudeness, especially in a place designated as safe and when they turned again as one and stared in their direction, she lost her patience. "Hi!" she yelled at the top of her voice, just as the band paused between beautiful, melodic background songs. Hana eyeballed each one of the youths, communicating the reprimand through her wooden smile and flashing green eyes. She resembled a lunatic, waving frantically like a redheaded Barbie doll and the reaction was instant. The group faced the front like a choreographic move and resisted the urge to stare again. "Perhaps their consciences finally kicked in," Hana whispered to Lucy. One could always hope.

Tama put his arm protectively around his new girlfriend and Hana flanked her other side. Between them they offered Du Rose solidarity. Tama didn't seem freaked out by the worship which was loud and meaningful, but Hana felt chided by the message of the preacher. His style was different to Pastor Allen's as he moved around the front of the church, forcing his audience to follow with their eyes and not fall asleep. He was energetic and controversial with a clear brief not to sugar coat his message. "*We are all only one heartbeat away from eternity.*"

Hana shouldn't have needed reminding, but she did. Her first husband had gone to work one day and not returned and she knew everything existed by the grace of God. She prayed silently with honesty and self-awareness. If she was one heartbeat away from eternity, perhaps it was time to get her own life in order instead of meddling in everyone else's. The preach was about making it right with God but convicted Hana at another level as she contemplated her spat with Logan. Life was too short and she ached to seek Logan's forgiveness as well as her maker's.

As they stood to sing the final hymn, it hit her with such clarity she sat down with a bump. Tama looked across at her in concern. He squatted in front of Lucy and whispered in Hana's ear. "What's up, Ma?"

Hana shook her head. "I'm fine but I know what Logan's up to."

At the end of the service, Tama handed her the car keys. "I'm going to an all-night cafe with Lucy and some of her nicer friends," he said. "Will you be okay on your own?"

Hana nodded and kissed him on the cheek, hurrying home as fast as she dared without getting a speeding ticket. Taking a deep breath, she let herself into the unit, discovering Logan and her daughter laid on the lounge rug. Logan balanced on his side smiling at Phoenix, who kicked her legs beneath the baby gym. They both looked as Hana came in, kicked her boots off and sat on the sofa. "Hey." Logan smiled at his wife. He looked gorgeous; his grey eyes surrounded by long black lashes were happy and his hair flopped forwards over his eyebrows. He lay on his side, resting his body on one elbow with his hand against the left side of his face. He glanced at Hana and flicked a dangling bear so it jiggled and Phoenix giggled.

"Listen," he said with excitement. "Say it again, Phoe. Dada, dada."

The little girl cooed and waved her arms and legs, beaming at her father. She pursed her rosebud lips and repeated his words, "Dadadadada!"

Hana laughed and clapped, biting her bottom lip with pleasure. "You're so lucky!" she said to her husband and he beamed.

"I'll teach her to say Mama too," he promised.

Hana smiled. "She was always going to say Dada first," she said generously. "She adores you."

Phoenix grew tired of performing to order after a while and the novelty of her parents' elation wore thin. She became fractious and Hana fed her to sleep, sitting on the sofa while Logan made a drink. He brought the mug of tea and sat next to his wife, gently massaging the baby's tiny feet through the sleep suit as she drank and snoozed. "I've worked it out," Hana said quietly, taking the mug. "Call it divine intervention."

"I thought you might," Logan replied and his wife showed her surprise, emerald eyes widening as she turned to face him.

"Why?"

Logan sighed and put both arms behind his head, leaning back against the seat. His shirt came up and showed his stomach and Hana resisted the urge to stroke the smooth olive skin beneath. "Because we agreed we'd be honest with each other and I don't want to keep secrets. You're an intelligent woman and I wanted you to work it out. But I needed to give you time to understand my reasons for acting as I have."

Hana nodded once and felt a wave of sadness. *One heartbeat away from eternity.* "I'd have liked the chance to say goodbye," she said and a glossy tear rolled down her cheek.

Logan put his arm around her. "No time. I needed to move him as soon as he'd done that last Level 3 assessment. He achieved Level 3 with Excellence based on internal assessments, without having to set foot in any of his exams. It had to be that way. That was the internal assessment he sat last week when I asked you to leave him alone. I organised it and my offsider in the department sat with him while he did it. I wanted to know he'd leave here with everything he needed. He's got university entrance and can do whatever he needs to provide for his family."

"But he's a murderer," Hana said. "How on earth can he live with that?"

"Firstly, James only *thinks* he's a murderer, not that he'd listen to me and secondly it was self-defence. He was waiting for Matron to fetch the van to do the run to the doctors and saw Collins through the dining room window. He went to ask for that damn plane and they argued. Collins attacked him with the shovel and from what James says, the man was high and didn't make sense. He prodded the boy with it but kept falling over. James said the man went mad, telling him he was a dirty immigrant and should go home. The boy snapped, grabbed the spade and jabbed Collins in the chest with the handle. He reckons Collins fell backwards straight into the trench."

"So he covered the body and went off to the doctor's about an infected toe?" Hana was incredulous. "He should have stayed and faced what he did. This will haunt him for the rest of his life. We don't get to be judge and jury on stuff like this, Logan; it's wrong!"

Logan shook his head. "Collins was moving around when James left. He was thrashing around trying to get out of the mud and yelling at James. The biology teacher did it, Hana, not the kid. The post-mortem said he was hit in the face by the metal end of the shovel and James is adamant he poked him in the chest with the handle. It doesn't fit with a blunt force trauma to Collins' face. Peterson did it and buried him. Would you rather James stayed here and waited it out while his family starved in a village in Korea, all their dreams of solvency gone? He was their last hope, Hana. I needed to give him a chance to start over somewhere else."

"It's not right," Hana said. "I don't know if I can live with this."

"I know it doesn't help," Logan said gently, "but Collins sold dope to the older boys. He was pedalling it in school, not to the boarders thank goodness, but to the day boys. He ran a wholesale business from that shed by the tennis courts."

Hana shook her head to clear her brain. "Why did nobody notice? And how did you get James out of the country? Bodie got called into work to go and see a student at the boarding house so the cops are looking for him."

Logan frowned and Hana's body tensed in anticipation. "Che helped me. His guys shipped James out through a back door. I gave him cash from the sale of my Triumph so it's untraceable and away he went, to a new life and hopefully a good job."

"Not Che!" Hana cried, disturbing Phoenix who splayed her arms in her sleep. "I thought you cut ties with the Triads!"

"I have," Logan replied through gritted teeth. "But I needed him to do this. It'll be fine."

"No it won't! You'll owe Che now and what will he demand in return?"

"Nothing, Hana." Logan smoothed his hand over her red curls. "Trust me."

"But I'd have liked to see James first," Hana maintained.

Logan interjected, "No, Hana! You'd have tried to convince him to do the right thing. He was terrified. It started that day in the office when you came over and he kept saying he wanted to go home. He was so odd it began unravelling then. I asked him about it and that night, Pete caught him trying to take an overdose of stuff; just a cocktail of crap. He was a mess."

"Then he should have seen a doctor, a mental health worker and a pastor! Not a bunch of Triad henchmen," Hana bit, feeling upset and tainted by her guilty knowledge. "What will happen to the biology teacher? Have they charged him with murder?"

"Just about. It's a matter of hours according to Odering because a lot of the evidence is circumstantial."

"So why move James?" Hana stuck her chin out and looked defiant. "Why not leave him here?"

Logan shook his head. "One of the other boys saw him argue with Collins and gave a statement to Odering last night. He called his mother and she drove down and took him to the police station. James needed to leave. He couldn't cope with any more dealings with the cops. He was a wreck as it was. Cops are often corrupt where he comes from and he didn't handle their questions well, especially as he believed he'd killed Collins. He thumped Bodie, did you know that?"

Hana nodded. "So I gathered." She thought back to the cut on Bo's face and James' apology in Logan's office. He wasn't saying sorry for hitting, but for hitting *him*. "Did you drive him away this afternoon when you used the car?" she asked sadly.

Logan nodded and stretched again. "I met Che's guys at a service station in South Auckland and James went off with them. He seemed happy to be going. He gave me this regal bow and then ruined it by sobbing all over my shirt. Oh..." Logan reached down and grappled around in his front pocket, pulling out a crumpled envelope with Hana's name on. "He asked me to give you this."

Hana took the envelope in her hand, twisting it over and over, looking at the neat, spiky writing. She thought about the frightened Year 9, forgetting to answer to the western name he'd chosen for himself and constantly lost in the school building. He'd sat with Hana often in the days before he made friends. She helped him get a part-time job so he could buy his own textbooks without bothering his mother in Korea, writing a painstaking curriculum vitae over long hours of word switching and trying to make him sound like a good candidate. James loved Phoenix and was kind to Jas after the accident with Action Man, rebuilding him limb by limb and gluing on the mop of black hair. Hana sniffed. "The hair James glued onto Action Man is lost in a hand dryer." She rubbed a hand roughly across her eyes. "Unless McDonald's really did post it back to Jas."

While Logan winded Phoenix and took her to the cot, Hana unfolded the envelope and slipped her fingernail beneath the fold. It was a tatty white envelope and the letter inside comprised of A4 lined refill paper covered in scratchy writing. She read it four times before Logan returned and the ache in her heart was still painful. Hana pushed it towards Logan and he shook his head. "It's okay, babe. It's private so I don't need to read it but you know you can't keep it, don't you?"

'Dearest Miss,

You have been like mother and friend to me. I will not forget. You did give me your own food when I missed breakfast and you help me get job. But best, is that you listen to me, accept me and understand me. That one thing had more value than all others put together. Home has been calling me for a long while and all this killings has made me need family more than ever. Mr Du

Rose has given me chance to be somebody and I am grateful. I will make you proud of me. One day, my name will make you smile.

Your friend for evermore.

James.'

Hana read the precious letter one final time and folded it in half as Logan held his hand out. She placed it into his palm with obvious reluctance. Her husband gave a sad smile and pushed the refill back into the envelope before moving out of Hana's sight. She heard the click of the barbeque lighter and smelled the paper burning, as her husband destroyed a letter which could be misread by other eyes seeking a murderer in the face of a frightened, teenage boy, who'd already spent far too long away from home.

Chapter 28

Hana lifted her chin into the bracing fresh air as she wandered along the main road, trying to clear her head. Red coils streamed out behind her and she searched for peace, connecting with the sleeping baby in the pram. Phoenix stirred and Hana stopped and stroked the soft cheek with her hand before releasing the tiny thumb from the blankets and watching her baby push it between her lips.

Hana thought of James and felt the heaviness descend over her heart. Logan had burned her letter and then taken her to bed to console her. '*I'm sorry,*' he'd whispered in the darkness, resting his weight on one elbow to avoid crushing her. '*I don't know how else we could have done it.*' Hana shook her head and wondered if it would always be that way, their different moral codes colliding and inflicting damage and destruction wherever they touched.

Hana's sedentary life jarred against the taste of danger which rose without warning from her husband's past, flooring her with its outlandish violence and betraying the terrifying nature of the line he once walked. "Why involve Che again?" she raged under her breath, remembering how the Triad queen had stared at her with spiteful, gimlet eyes. The ruthlessness in the woman's face had stripped her bare and Logan's easy acceptance of their ways drove a wedge between them which rocked their young marriage to its core. But Hana Du Rose loved her husband and if he'd moved James out of New Zealand, she had to believe it was for the best. She just dreaded the awkward moment when the police demanded to know where their suspect was and Hana found her son standing before her with his eyebrow raised in disgust. *One heartbeat away from eternity.* The phrase caught at her imagination and wouldn't go away. "We're all headed for eternity," Hana grumbled, "but where we get to spend it is the real question."

Her feet took her up the road to the rest home where her old friend lived. Father Sinbad welcomed her as enthusiastically as always, but the sight of the oxygen mask over his face alarmed Hana. "What's wrong?" She parked the pram in the corner and perched on his bed, reaching for his wrinkled hand. His wheelchair looked empty by the window, bisected by a shaft of brilliant light as its owner fought for each breath.

"The wind is cold but the sun's shining," Hana said, glad Father Sinbad's blind eyes couldn't see the terror on her face. "It's nice in your wheelchair."

"Aye," he rasped. "Nice."

"Is this what holidays do for you?" Hana asked, lightening her voice to mask the fear. "Maybe I shouldn't bother."

"Oh ye know," Father Sinbad rasped, momentarily pulling the mask down so he could speak. "I was always in da waitin' room for de Lord. I be tinking dat he's left da throne room and is on his way down for me."

"No!" Hana shouted in her vehemence. "Don't say that! It's nothing, you'll make it through!"

The old priest left the mask dangling from his ears and patted her hand beneath giant, gnarled fingers bent from twisting rosary beads. "I'm tired me darlin', tired of bein' blinded, tired of bein' old and tired of bein' here on dis planet anymore. I want to run and jump and dance wit me maker. It's time for me to go, Hana Du Rose. Be pleased for me."

"I can't be pleased," Hana whispered. "Don't ask me to be." The tears came thick and fast, taking her by surprise. "I'll be lost without you. I need you to be here; please don't give up. Don't leave me." A breath caught in her chest, pausing her selfish tirade and Father Sinbad gave her a beatific smile and squeezed her hand.

"You and yer boy have been da joy of me life and don't you forget it. I've delighted in ye, truly I have. I'll see ye soon in da twinkling of an eye. Know dat I love you, Hana Du Rose. If I had a daughter, she'd have been just like you."

Hana cried and the old man comforted her with gentle pats on her bowed head. Her tears splashed on his bed sheets like summer rain and he replaced his mask with a shaking hand. "I'm being selfish," Hana hiccoughed, "but the thought of you not being here is too much to bear."

"Hush," the old priest soothed. "One day we'll all be together in heaven and you'll be amazed at what a dashin' wee fella I am. I'll get me legs back and me eyes. D'ya know I've never seen yer pretty face? I'll see if me imaginings are close to da real thing."

A pair of strong hands gripped Hana's shoulders and she turned, hurriedly wiping her hand over her eyes. Matron's eyes were blurred by tears and she nodded to Hana. "Thirty years of running this home and you'll be the hardest to let go of, Father," she whispered and the old man tried to chortle, choking on the sound. "You're the godliest man I've ever known, a walking confessional and a fount of extreme wisdom." Matron gulped as the old priest didn't answer. "You should go," she said to Hana, patting her shoulder.

Hana's eyes widened in dismay. "No, let me stay, please? I'll stop crying, I promise."

"Is that all right, Father?" Matron asked, sadness filling her eyes at the lack of response.

Hana texted Bodie, but he was on duty and didn't reply. Phoenix slept through the massive event unaware as a great and powerful man of God departed the earth. Hana cried soundlessly as the old man's breathing became shallow, each shuddering movement of his chest a valiant effort to cling to life. Matron turned up the oxygen and sent for the doctor but Father Sinbad had made up his mind. He was ready to go home.

As Hana sat with him stroking his hand beneath hers, his breathing became regular and normal and a beautiful smile played on his lips. Hope filled Hana's heart and she watched as Father Sinbad's eyes opened wide with wonder as though the blind man could suddenly see; his useless pupils dilated and his gaze fixed on something unseen near his wheelchair. Hana pressed the buzzer for Matron, believing the old man was reviving and hearing the woman's feet pound along the corridor.

With joy in his powerful voice, Father Sinbad stretched out his arm towards the empty wheelchair bathed in sunlight and said, "I knew ye'd come for me." The smile on his face looked ethereal, disappearing as his hand fell limply onto the bed and his soul shucked itself free. Free of the increasingly inadequate body, free of eyes blinded too soon and free from the extreme pain of living.

Hana felt sure she heard a whisper in the breeze, a gentle male voice saying, *"Well done, good and faithful servant."* The voice was there and then gone, drowned out by the sound of her own sobs.

The doctor arrived and shook his head, removing the mask from Father Sinbad's face and laying the old man's hands gently across his stomach as he failed to find a pulse. "Goodbye old friend," he said, his professional demeanour temporarily slipped.

Matron led an inconsolable Hana to her office and kept her there, plying her with tea and rocking the pram to keep the baby asleep. "Let me call your son," Matron said. "I can't let you leave like this."

Hana shook her head. "He's not answering. I'll be fine." She cut a pitiful figure pushing her pram like an automaton, not even sure in what direction she walked. Her mind went over and over everything and a quote from Shakespeare's

Anthony and Cleopatra rang in her ears. That the world should continue with such ignorance seemed incongruous. The words of Octavius, *"The breaking of so great a thing should make a greater crack,"* ran through her head like a mantra alongside the awful realisation that Father Sinbad was no longer a heartbeat away from eternity anymore. He was already there. *"Oh, God,"* she sobbed all the way home. *"Oh, God."*

Hana arrived home in a dreadful state. Phoenix was awake and hungry but unusually for her, not creating a scene. "What's happened?" Tama gushed, already reaching for his phone.

"No," Hana begged, "don't call Logan. I just need time."

Tama made Hana a drink and held the wriggly baby while she got ready to feed her. Hana's ashen, tear streaked face made him afraid. Her breaths came in agonising hitches and her halting sentences gave him no comfort. "Let me get Uncle?" he pleaded, handing the child over. "He'll know how to make you feel better."

"No," Hana insisted, certain her husband couldn't possibly understand her grief. What she'd lost couldn't be explained with words.

Father Sinbad's funeral took place in the catholic cathedral in Hamilton two days later. Hana attended in a pretty purple dress in his honour, distraught to find the beautiful church empty. Bodie met her at the door in full dress uniform and remarked on the absent congregation. "Bloody Christians," he said. "He gave them his whole life and they couldn't even show up to say goodbye."

"Father Sinbad loved purple," Hana whispered tearfully, smoothing her dress and denying herself a vent for her feelings. "He always said God was purple." She fingered the silky material which was far too thin for such a blustery day and shivered in the cool of the church interior. Bodie sat next to her, holding her hand and wishing he'd seen the text that would have allowed him a personal goodbye.

The church laid on a small wake for their old priest and a few people stood around eating and talking about his influence on their lives. Loved and revered by Hana, she wished she had known his true value before it was too late. It was her ridiculous fantasy that his funeral would be a huge affair, attended by the grateful masses of Hamilton humanity keen to reward his lifetime of service. It was a foolish dream and the blind priest had been left to rot. "Nobody cared," she whimpered to Bodie as silent tears ran off the end of her chin and stained the silk of her dress with darker lines of purple.

"I know," he whispered back. "I never realised we were the only people who went to see him. I always believed there were others."

Hana stood with Matron during the wake, chatting about nothing and desperately trying to contain the waterfall of tears which threatened to burst forth and wash everyone away. Bodie made his excuses and went to work, leaving Hana to walk home. She clip-clopped along the street in her high heels feeling bereft, as yet another of her tent pegs wrenched from the ground leaving her shaky and vulnerable.

Hana felt numb for the next few days as though her heart stopped at the same moment as the old man's and waited to begin again. She was on autopilot and couldn't seem to touch reality. It eluded her, like a knitter trying to make a sweater from fog.

Logan and Tama showed their concern but Hana shut down and refused to communicate, walking from day to day in a lost dream world. "I've invited Robert and Elaine to the hotel for the first week of the holidays," Logan said, taking the washing basket from Hana and laying it on the ground. "I thought you could have some quality time with them when they get back from Auckland."

"Thanks," Hana nodded, her tone dull. She pressed the top of her stomach again and winced.

"You should get that looked at," Logan said, noticing her movement. "Want me to come with you? It might be an ulcer."

"No, thanks." Hana shook her head and let her husband draw her into his chest, breathing in his masculine scent and aftershave and feeling nothing but emptiness. "We're all one heartbeat away from eternity," she whispered.

"What?" Logan pushed her shoulders so he could look at her, his eyes filled with sympathy.

"I'm not crazy!" Hana snapped. "Don't look at me like you examined your mother. I'm not mentally ill."

"I never said you were." Logan dropped his arms and took a step back, cut by Hana's biting remark. He strode from the laundry and she heaved a sigh of relief, receding into the peace and safety of her own misery.

"All good?" Tama asked as Logan strode into the lounge and hurled himself on the sofa.

"No," he replied. "Maybe it wasn't such a good idea to invite Hana's olds home."

Tama nodded. "Know what you mean. She seems really fragile at the moment although it's not surprising. She's lost pretty much everyone who ever showed her friendship. Does she look real skinny to you? She does to me."

"I don't know how to sort this," Logan told Tama, grateful the teenager seemed happy to hang around Hana like river mist. "Thanks for taking care of her. I just tried to get her to see the doctor and she bit my head off."

"Friday and the end of the term can't come soon enough, aye?" Tama said with a smile and patted Logan's shoulder.

"True dat," Hana's husband replied.

Hana sat on the bed an hour later, twisting her wedding ring and staring off into the distance. Logan sought her out to say goodbye as he went to his next class. "Hey," he said gently, knowing how futile his words of consolation would sound, clanging into the vacuum of pain. But he tried. "I love you, Hana Du Rose," he whispered into her hair. "Just hold onto that for now." He lowered himself onto the bed and put his arm around her, trying to absorb the negative misery through physical contact.

The bell clanged from the main building like a death knell, calling him back to work. Hana felt like a tiny bird under his strong arms and Logan felt a frisson of fear. Hana didn't react as he stood to leave, looking up at him as though noticing he was there.

A bus stocked to bursting with staff travelled from the school to Larry Collins' funeral the following day. The very same Catholic Church which echoed emptily with the sound of the priest's voice for a gentle, worthy man, was packed to the rafters with well-wishers for a man whom everyone hated. None of the Du Roses attended, despite Angus insisting Logan must go for the sake of appearances. "I'm telling you to go!" Angus shouted as the final car departed. He fiddled with his tartan tie and bristled with anger. "It looks bad if you don't! I want a show of solidarity from all my department heads."

"We'll be late, Mr Blair," Amanda interjected, straightening her skirt and jangling her car keys. Angus ignored her, raising his bushy red eyebrows to Logan.

"Sack me if you don't like it." Logan's voice sounded low and powerful, causing the older man's eyes to bug in surprise. Logan leaned in towards Angus' face stating calmly, "I'll be a hypocrite for no man!"

"I'll see you when I get back!" Angus spat and Logan gave him a sarcastic wave as the principal spilled from the front reception like bubbling lava.

Hana wandered aimlessly around the school grounds with her pram the following day, faking a smile for two female teachers supervising sports classes. "Hey, Hana," the blonde woman said. "Didn't see you at the funeral yesterday. The flowers were beautiful and the church was packed."

Her colleague nodded. "It was very moving."

Hana's jaw dropped in misery and she made no comment, pushing her pram through the middle of a dangerous game of moon-ball. Three Year 9s narrowly missed her as they hurtled by after the enormous ball, shrieking and giggling with a joviality Hana didn't even notice.

Tears coursed down her face as Hana strode home, incensed at the unfairness of life. Arriving home in a state of high agitation and misery, it was left to Tama to pick up the pieces. "It's not fair," she sobbed. "How can such a loving, godly man be celebrated by so few when a hated, spiteful, crooked drug pusher gets falsely lauded by so many? They're all liars!" she wailed.

"I know, Ma," he whispered, wrapping his arms around her and holding her trembling body. "It sucks; it's not fair."

By lunchtime on Friday, Logan was ready to leave and loaded the car with Tama. "Don't you have a class?" the young man asked as they lugged suitcases down the front steps.

"Angus said I could go during my free. School ends early today and the boarders have gone already."

"Did he ball you out for not going to Collins' funeral?" Tama asked, frowning.

"Yep," Logan replied. "Do I look like I care?"

Tama snorted and shook his head. "You sound like me, Uncle."

Logan stopped for a moment, fingering a ridge on the metalwork around the rear door. He narrowed his eyes and smiled at Tama. "No, son, I think you probably sound like me." He bit his lip and laughed as Tama's eyes twinkled.

Hana played with her baby on the lounge rug, finding the unquestioning nature of her daughter safer than the furtive looks and worried faces of her men. "Time to go, babe," Logan said, lifting Phoenix into his arms. "Let's go home."

Tama locked up as Logan stuffed Hana and his child into the back of the Honda and they arrived at the hotel before afternoon tea time, coasting down the long mountain road and crunching onto the welcoming gravel within record time.

Hana emerged from the back of the vehicle and inhaled fresh mountain air. She closed her eyes and tasted peace and cleanliness, breathing properly for the first time since the old priest left her behind. She touched her right palm to her lips, remembering how he passed onto the other side while holding her hand. It felt sore as though he'd left a scorch on her flesh. Surrounded by the green of the mountains and the azure blue sky, Hana drew in a huge, life-giving breath which went deep into her lungs and exhaled in a rush.

"You ok?" Logan watched her, his grey eyes bright as he struggled to mask his inner concern.

"Yeah. I am now." The shroud lifted and Hana felt the numbness tumble away as the Logan's ancestors rallied around her in the earth, bringing healing. "I feel the *tangata whenua*," Hana said, her voice sounding distant.

Logan nodded with instant understanding. "Good," he said. "You go in, I'll bring the gear up with the boy."

Hana sought Leslie in the laundry room and the Māori woman whooped with pleasure, embracing her in a bone crushing hug. "Now then my *kōtiro*, come and talk with old Leslie and tell her what you've been up to."

"I don't know where to start," Hana admitted as the reappearance of her father, the kidnapping and Father Sinbad's death played across her vision like a soap opera.

"At the beginning," Leslie said, patting the upturned bottom of a laundry basket. Hana sat and poured out her woes to the housekeeper while Leslie loaded huge washing machines with white towels and sheets. While the industrial machines clanked and rumbled they spoke with their heads close together like co-conspirators, drowned out by the noise. "I can't tell Logan how I feel," Hana sighed. "He still hasn't dealt with Miriam's death and what happened with Reuben. I can't load this on him too."

Leslie nodded. "Foolish men," she agreed. "Dealing with stuff isn't the Du Rose way. They bottle it up and then one day it hits the ground like a molotov cocktail and everythin' around 'em goes boom!" She clapped her hands to mimic an explosion and Hana smiled at the childishness of the old lady's imagery.

"It doesn't help he feels Alfred's abandoned him too. I think that's the ultimate cruelty. It's one thing to lose a father you never knew you had, but to lose the stand in too is dreadful."

"I hear ya," Leslie replied, "I'm workin' on it." She gave Hana one of her hundred watt smiles and the other woman felt reassured.

In Logan's childhood bedroom with its blue wallpaper and big double bed, Hana laid on her back feeling hopeful for the first time in days, her sanity partly restored.

Chapter 29

"I'll take you up to your room," Logan said, smiling at Robert. "You must be tired."

"I'll take them, Mr Du Rose," Leslie said, bustling forward. "Mr Michael's old room?"

"Yeah." Logan nodded. "Next to the lift."

"Thank you, Logan," Robert said appreciatively, taking Elaine's arm. Her face channelled an unhealthy grey and her breathing sounded hoarse.

Hana sat in the family dining room next to the kitchen, feeding Phoenix and staring through the long sash windows onto the driveway. Cars buzzed in and out of the car park as guests arrived and departed, keeping the hotel staff busy and in employment.

Logan left to talk to Jack and Tama was around somewhere. Hana browsed the tourist magazine on the table as Phoenix fed herself to sleep. Every time Hana thought she could safely stand, the baby disturbed and suckled again. Hana flicked the page over to a review of Logan's hotel and reread it. The photographs were stunning. *'Definitely a five-star destination,'* the journalist had written. *'Where natural beauty meets unequalled quality.'*

There was a picture of a bush walk Logan's men spent last summer putting in and the gravel path up to a stunning lookout over the valley. It was a good write up and had already drawn international visitors. The business was thriving and Hana felt a flicker of pleasure for her husband, coupled with jealousy at the journalist. Hana suspected she fancied Logan, reading between the lines and detecting the sense of awe and fascination with the imposing Māori. "Bad luck," she sighed. "He's taken."

Hana looked up at the sound of footsteps on the gravel driveway, surprised to find herself looking into the face of a pretty Māori woman, smartly dressed and on her way to the hotel entrance. She looked familiar, smiling and waving at Hana, who couldn't get her hand up in time to wave back. "I bet I looked a right idiot," she commented to the dozing child, "gormless, sitting at the table goggling out of the window."

She laid the baby over her thighs under cover of the table and fastened her bra, waiting for a minute. She dreaded nipping into the corridor and running into the pretty guest. It would be awkward, far too late to smile and wave. When the kitchen door opened, Hana assumed it was Leslie returning to prepare lunch and ignored it.

"It's all different!" exclaimed a confused male voice and Hana turned, seeing Michael and the guest standing in confusion inside the kitchen door. She stood and laid Phoenix over her shoulder, walking through the new archway to greet her brother-in-law.

"Hello," Hana said, leaning forward so Michael could kiss her on the cheek. His grey eyes smiled back at her and he waved his arm expansively.

"What's going on?"

"The Health people didn't like the family hanging around in the kitchen. It's fair enough; trying to feed a hundred guests food prepared in sterile conditions with Alfred sitting at the table in his socks, covered in cow poo."

Michael put his head back and laughed. It sounded so like Logan it was uncanny. "It looks good," he said, looking around. "We popped back for the weekend. I knew it'd be okay."

"It's fine," Hana said and then frowned. "Oh, dear. Logan put my father in your room because it was nearest the lift. We only arrived an hour ago."

The facade of goodwill melted and Michael looked petulant. "Yes," he said, not bothering to hide his annoyance. "They'll have to move. Where's Logan?"

"With Jack," Hana replied, resisting the urge to slap the arrogant doctor's face.

Without bothering to introduce Hana to his companion, Michael strode from the kitchen and Hana heard his heels click along the corridor. The atmosphere felt awkward and Hana's plan to put the baby in the travel cot and chill out for a while seemed under threat. "Can I get you a drink or something to eat?" she asked politely as the woman looked around her.

"Can I have warm milk, please? It helps with the morning sickness."

Hana started in surprise. "You're pregnant?" she asked and the woman nodded. "Congratulations," Hana said.

The woman seemed familiar but the look of distaste on her face betrayed her sickness. Hana led her through to the dining room table and offered her a seat. One-handed, she grabbed milk from the industrial chiller and heated it in the microwave. Phoenix disturbed in the chiller, wriggling against the cold as Hana replaced the milk but remained asleep.

"Here you go." Hana took the hot milk to the visitor and looked out of the window while she sipped it. "How far on are you?" she asked, interested.

"Almost three months," the woman replied, laying the mug on the table. "I was younger the first time around so this was a shock."

Hana smiled. "There's no reason it shouldn't be fine."

The woman smiled at Hana's encouragement. "You sound like you know what you're talking about. Do you have older children then?" she asked.

Hana nodded, but her face clouded at the thought of her antagonistic son. "Yes, I have a son who's twenty-six and a daughter of twenty-five. Girls are definitely easier, well, I hope so anyway." She kissed Phoenix on the side of her soft little face and prayed she turned out half as amenable as her gorgeous Isobel.

"I agree," the woman shared, looking apprehensive. "My son's been difficult. We haven't spoken for years." She looked sad and Hana felt sorry.

"Been there," she replied wistfully.

There came the clamour of raised voices and the dining room door opened, admitting a harried looking Logan. Seconds later Michael appeared through the kitchen door, looking embarrassed by his error. "I'm not moving Hana's parents," Logan said, his teeth gritted and Michael stood with his hands on the back of the woman's chair. Hana's jaw dropped with the realisation they were together and she looked at them both with renewed interest.

"It's *my* room," Michael said stubbornly.

Hana gnawed her lip feeling guilty. "It's okay," she began but the warning flash of anger in Logan's eyes silenced her. She looked away and patted her baby's back, hoping one of them backed down. As the argument progressed, she realised with increasing certainty; it wasn't going to happen.

Logan drew himself up to his full height and glared at his older brother. "Actually it's *my* room, *my* house and *my* land. Hana's family is *my* family. You're welcome to visit, but in future a phone call is necessary. If I can pick up the phone and let Leslie know *I'm* coming back, I don't think it's too difficult for you to do the same. Barry's old room is free and you're welcome to it."

"I don't want Barry's room! Geez mate, what's wrong with you? I'll have Liza's!" Michael capitulated.

Hana opened her mouth to speak but Logan shot her another warning look and she closed it again. The grey of his eyes looked stormy and dark, an eruption of Du Rose fury very near the surface. "Liza's room's in use," he growled, not mentioning Tama.

"Move someone!" Michael snapped. "I'm family!"

Hana gulped and widened her eyes at the stupidity of Michael's assertion, considering his demotion from brother to half-brother. The irony wasn't wasted on Logan. "Take Barry's room." Logan enunciated every word. "Or leave!"

Logan ignored the woman and Hana figured he was too busy with the argument to notice. But she intercepted an odd look cross her husband's face as Logan glanced across at the woman who sipped her milk looking uncomfortable.

Hana sensed a hidden issue and felt sorry for the guest caught in the middle. She smiled reassuringly as she caught the woman's eye and hoped the storm would pass; a futile hope as it turned out.

Michael glared at Logan. "When did you become such a..."

Logan interrupted him, holding up his hand. "Such a what, Michael? *Such a businessman?* That might be when I sunk my own money into saving this house and farm and you refused to buy in when I begged you. So don't whine about not having your room kept free all year round *half-brother!*"

Hana was finally glad she'd learned to keep her big mouth shut, saving her from a serious blunder. She stared at Logan and cocked her head, unaware he'd begged his brother for financial help to save his family from bankruptcy. Glancing sideways at Michael's companion, Hana recognised the heated blush of morning sickness and sympathised as the woman became paler by the second. She went into the kitchen and dragged the plastic dustbin through the archway into the dining room as the poor woman reeled and clapped a hand over her mouth.

Logan stared at Hana in bewilderment as she pulled it behind her one-handed, the black bin bag folded neatly over the top and her sleeping daughter lolling on her hip. His face was a mix of curiosity and confusion as Hana pulled the bin up next to the woman at the table just as she retched. "In here," Hana said softly and she turned sharply, spotted the remains of the dining room's scrambled egg breakfast at the bottom of the bin and threw up, adding a full cup of warm milk plus other splattered offerings.

The men stopped arguing and Logan wrinkled his face in distaste. Neither helped the women, scandalous as one of them was an emergency doctor. They both stared as Hana struggled to hold her baby in one hand and rub the woman's back with the other. "Logan!" Hana snapped as Phoenix lolled backwards and the woman pushed her face into the bin and vomited again.

Logan swore and started as though slapped. "She's pregnant?" he said in disgust as he hefted his daughter over his shoulder. "Bloody marvellous!"

Hana's mouth opened in surprise at her husband's cruelty and she shook her head in dismay, running into the kitchen to grab a glass and clattering at the sink.

"Drink this water," she told the poor woman. "Sip it slowly to take the taste away. It's miserable; I know."

The olive skinned woman cried over the dustbin, her stomach doing cartwheels beneath her ribs. Michael watched with a look of misery on his face but it was Logan who occupied his attention, Logan and the tiny girl in his arms.

"Come on," Hana said, realising the best place for her was bed. "You need to lie down."

The woman rose with deliberate movements, head bowed as she struggled to keep it together. Hana led her from the dining room and into the corridor, barking back at Michael with authority, "Get rid of that bin bag in the skip and disinfect the dustbin. Quickly, before Leslie notices!"

He nodded and tore his gaze from Logan as Hana let the door close behind her, still holding the woman's arm. She led her up the back, spiral staircase to the first floor, hoping she could remember which room once belonged to the late Du Rose Hana found the room but paused outside in dismay. "I don't know the keypad code," she said, her voice laced with disgust. "I'm an idiot!"

The woman leaned heavily against her and Hana felt her trembling through their joined fingers. "I'm sorry," Hana breathed, babbling in her confusion. "All the private rooms have keypads but the guest suites have cards..."

"I feel faint," the woman murmured and Hana panicked. She led her back along the corridor to the room she shared with Logan, opening the door and settling her in the comfy armchair by the ranch slider. Remembering the relief of fresh air after a bout of sickness, Hana pushed open the sliding doors which took up most of one wall, allowing the cool winter air to flood the room and put colour back into the woman's cheeks.

She looked up at Hana with gratitude, her face pale and her deep brown eyes dull and listless. "They said you were lovely," she mouthed, her voice a weak huff of air and words.

"Who did?" Hana asked, but the woman drew her legs underneath her and closed her eyes, concentrating on regaining control of her body.

"I'll get you a peppermint tea," Hana said. "That used to help me." She sorted through the sachets by the kettle and steeped the bag in hot water, setting the mug carefully next to the woman's chair. Then she closed the doors, feeling the room chill too much to be bearable. "Does that feel better?" she asked her guest.

A knock on the door was followed by numbers being punched into the keypad and Hana readied herself for Logan's angry entrance. "Ma, you'll never guess what..." Tama piled in beaming but the smile froze at the sight of the woman. He pointed towards Hana's guest with accusation in his eyes. "What's *she* doing here?" He baulked at Hana as though she'd stabbed him and his voice sounded pitiful. "Ma, why are you being *nice* to *her?*"

Hana took Tama's arm and ushered him from the bedroom, pulling the door closed behind her. "What have I done?" she asked, her voice laced with concern.

"That's *her!*" Tama hissed, balling his fists by his side. "That's my mother."

Hana clapped her hand over her mouth as devastation bit at her core, the betrayal reflected in Tama's eyes. "Oh no!" she moaned. She lurched at the young man, fixing her arms around his waist. "I'm *so* sorry. I had no idea."

"That's fine then." Relieved, he returned her embrace.

"Nobody tells me anything," Hana grumbled. "What can I do? She's been throwing up in the kitchen. Do you think I should ask her to leave the room or settle her somewhere else?" Hana balanced the nagging guilt against her loyalty to Tama. "I didn't realise, sweetheart. Logan and Michael were squaring off downstairs and..."

"Michael's here?" Tama's face hardened and he backed away from Hana.

She saw it then like a neon signal on the wall opposite, flashing and glowing and condemning her for missing the signs. Hana sighed. "I'm so stupid! Logan's rudeness makes sense if he was trying to get rid of Michael and his new girlfriend rather than upset you." She closed her eyes and resisted banging her head against the wall. "I despair of myself and my interfering nature. Now I've made a bad situation worse."

Tama stroked her hair and kissed her forehead. "It's okay. I get it."

"Logan offered them Barry's room," Hana said feebly and Tama smirked.

"That's good; Michael won't stay there. Nobody ever stays there," he said with relief in his voice.

Hana floundered. Logan hadn't come to help, maybe wanting her to stew in her own juice and she gnawed on her bottom lip, wondering how to extricate herself from the dreadful, self-made disaster. "I don't know what to do," she whispered.

Tama shrugged and walked away. Either he didn't know or just didn't care. It was still the same result – Hana was alone with her error. She let herself back into the bedroom, feeling unsure of herself. The woman stood on the balcony, leaning over the edge with her elbows on the balustrade. Even from behind, she looked sorry for herself. She spoke as Hana stood next to her, her voice laden with regret. "I told you. He hates me."

A tear dripped off the end of her nose, landing somewhere in the gravel below. Hana resisted filling the airwaves with empty platitudes. It resonated deep inside her own heart, drawing echoes of her relationship with Bodie. "It feels like crap, doesn't it?" she sympathised.

"Aroha," the woman said, offering Hana her hand. "My name's Aroha. You must be Logan's wife. I heard you were different from the rest of them. Thanks for being so kind. I feel better now. I should get out of your way."

Hana smiled, shaking hands and leaning against the balustrade. "I don't know what else I can do now," she said. "It's only right that I stick by Tama. I made him a promise and try hard not to break them. If you go back to the kitchen, Michael will have sorted something out with Logan by now."

"He didn't think you'd be here," Aroha said. "Otherwise, we wouldn't have come. Michael rarely gets a weekend off work and thought we'd be able to talk here." She sighed heavily and ran her hand over her abdomen. "Your baby's beautiful. You must think badly of me, leaving Tama. It always sounds awful in the telling, but at the time I didn't know what to do for the best."

Hana shook her head. "It's not my place to judge, love. I've done things I'm not that proud of, for what seemed the best reasons at the time. I understand sometimes we don't think we have a choice."

A vision crept into Hana's mind. She had expressed milk and sterilised bottles, walking out of the unit and leaving her eight week old baby with Tama. She attempted to bargain with a man who didn't understand reason and almost not returned. "Yes," she sighed. "I certainly understand bad choices first hand."

Aroha studied the redhead, recognising the inner pain of conviction and knowing Hana understood. She felt a kinship which made her heart ache as it would remain unfulfilled. Tama would see to that. "Tama called you, 'Ma' which means he's attached to you."

Hana nodded slowly, not wanting to compound Aroha's agony.

"I'm pleased," the other woman said. "I'm glad he has someone. I've spent eighteen years regretting my decision to run from Kane, leaving Tama asleep in his cot. I was seventeen when I left. Kane would have killed me if I hadn't. Michael was twenty-four and just finishing medical school. He should have known better, but he swept me off my feet. It was a childish mistake trying to pass Tama off as Kane's. He beat me until I confessed and when I went back for my baby, Reuben refused to let me take him. He said it was my punishment, the same as his." Aroha gulped and shook her head. "I should have guessed Kane would turn his wrath and spite on my beautiful little boy, twisting and tainting his lovely nature into something destructive and ugly." She looked at Hana with hope in her dark eyes. "Maybe you can make a difference to him and I'm glad. I wish it could be me but it can't." Aroha gave her blessing even though it was like a knife cutting deep into her heart. She turned, smiling at Hana before letting herself out of the room.

Hana sank into the armchair, weighed down by Aroha's regret and misery. She'd heard the woman's story from Logan, but his dismissive recount hadn't covered the awfulness of the situation. The Du Rose men were hard and unyielding. Few women survived for long in their world. Hana shut her eyes and prayed for Aroha and Tama. She trusted that God could see the bigger picture as she sighed and lay back in the chair, folding her legs beneath her. The energy to go back downstairs eluded her and Hana suspected she was in disgrace with Logan. She figured her baby would holler for her eventually, forcing him to find her. The cool breeze from the open ranch slider kissed her skin until it cooled and Hana hunkered down into the chair. "Just one minute more," she promised herself.

Wet baby kisses slobbered over her cheek, dragging Hana from sleep. "Ugh!" She rubbed at her skin, feeling the baby's dribble mingling with her own. She grimaced and rose from the chair, shoving her husband out of the way as she staggered towards the bathroom.

"I held her over your face to wake you up, but I didn't expect her to lick you!" Logan apologised from the doorway. "I don't think the kissing lessons are going as successfully as the waving lessons."

Hana grunted and splashed cold water on her face. "Just leave me alone for a minute. I need to wake up." She heard the snippiness in her voice and regretted it, clinging to the edge of the sink as the floor undulated beneath her.

"Are you ok?" Logan asked, his voice chastened and Hana nodded and curbed her irritation.

"Yeah. Afternoon sleeping makes me ratty. I only sat down for a minute." Hana sighed and patted her face dry, alarmed by the grey faced woman in the mirror. She returned to the armchair, rubbing her eyes and stifling a yawn as she stared in disgust at her grizzling daughter. "What did you feed her?" Hana peered at the yellow crust around Phoenix's rosebud lips and shook her head. "I don't want that all over my bra."

"It's only rusk," Logan argued as the baby cranked up her protest over the delay. "Sorry, I forgot to wipe her mouth. Shall I do it now?"

"Yes!" Hana sighed, sitting the baby up and grimacing as she thrashed around.

Logan fumbled with a baby wipe, putting it around the wriggling mouth and alarmed at how much came off. "Sorry," he muttered. "I've changed her nappy."

Hana knew he sought absolution for his behaviour towards Tama's sick mother and a mean part of her wanted to deny him. Knowing she was in the wrong for undermining him made her self-righteousness pointless.

Logan sighed as he attacked the baby's mouth with another wipe, his eyebrows raised and his face close to Hana's. "You're the only person on the planet who makes me afraid," he murmured. "I hate it when we fall out."

Hana snorted. "I don't scare you, idiot! I'm no match for your might."

"No, but you can break me with one look," he whispered.

Hana winced as the baby latched on to her breast and fed hungrily. Logan's masculine scent intoxicated her and she felt her resolve weaken. "I'm an outsider," she mused, surprising herself at the random sentence which conveyed her fractured status within the Du Roses. "I don't fit into your history."

Logan shook his head and squatted next to her, his forearms on her knees. "No, Hana. You don't know our history. That's different to not fitting in. There's generations of us twisted together like supplejack vine. How can you expect to unravel it in a year?"

Hana nodded, accepting his truth and picturing the brown vine which spread through the bush. Vigorous and hardy, it wound its way around the native plants, thwarted by nothing. "Sorry about before," she relented. "I made a right mess of everything as usual."

To her surprise, Logan wrinkled his nose and smiled. He sat on the arm of the chair, pulling Hana's head against his waist and stroking her hair. He sighed. "She'll be right," he said.

Hana tried not to roll her eyes in exasperation at the Kiwi man's mantra. They said it casually about burst pipes, missing children, not enough toilet roll in desperate circumstances and situations beyond their control. 'Kiwi ingenuity' they called it, but Hana wanted to rename it, 'Kiwi stupidity' because it made light of some enormous problems. "I hate that expression," she grumbled.

"Now you've admitted it, I'll say it more to annoy you," Logan replied and Hana heard the smile in his voice.

"I might have to kill you," she jested.

Logan snorted. "Then be careful where you bury my body. I know about the English fetish for burying spouses under patios so make sure it's a damn long one."

The spectre of death hushed the room with its black shroud and took Hana's breath away, unexpected and grim. She bit her lip to give herself something else to focus on. "Has Michael left?" she asked, patting the baby's delicate back.

"Na, they're both downstairs having afternoon tea with your father and Elaine."

Hana groaned. "Fancy falling asleep in the day," she complained. "What must they think of me? They drove all this way to see me and I've been up here all afternoon."

"Yeah, nana-naps aren't usually your thing." Logan's breath whooshed against Hana's hair. "That's why I left you. It might be the stress recently. We'll have a quiet couple of weeks and do whatever you feel like." Logan kissed the top of her head, enjoying her scent and stroked his baby's cheek with his free hand. Phoenix popped out of her mother's tee shirt and beamed.

"Use it or lose it, baby," Hana grumbled, not wanting to muck around. Phoenix took the hint and fed efficiently, collapsing afterwards and snoring in Hana's arms. "Did Michael tell you Aroha's pregnant?" Hana asked.

"No!" he said, his voice dull. He passed no comment and Hana didn't have the energy to press him for a verdict.

Logan carried the baby downstairs and put her in the pram, wheeling it along to the family dining room.

"Ah, my dear!" Robert stood as Hana walked in, kissing her on the cheek and patting the chair beside him. Elaine sat on his other side and smiled fondly at Hana. The elderly couple looked happy and rested after the journey to the hotel.

"I feel awful for falling asleep," Hana apologised and they waved it off indulgently. Michael nodded from across the table and Aroha looked sick again. Hana reached inside her jeans pocket and pulled out sachets of peppermint tea, pushing them across to the other woman. Aroha looked grateful, splashing hot water from the urn over one of them and sipping slowly.

"This is so generous of you, Logan," Robert said in his brogue accent, "are you sure we can't contribute?"

Michael looked up in surprise from his huge slab of fruit cake and had the decency to look guilty, Logan's earlier words ringing in his ears. It wasn't the Du Rose family home anymore; it was his business.

Logan shook his head at Robert, finishing his mouthful of apple. He sat with his other arm resting casually across the back of Hana's chair and his cowboy boot across the bar underneath. "Actually, I'd welcome your advice about something. Hana says you're a keen gardener and I'm trying to make a memorial garden. I'd be grateful for your help."

Michael stopped chewing and looked at Logan sideways. Hana couldn't read all the emotions in his face but he channelled a curious mix of jealousy and anger. Miriam's absence as both mother and hotel house manager had created a different dynamic. The hotel was Logan's domain and Michael struggled with the new era.

"I'd be delighted, my dear boy," Robert gushed. "And Elaine's something of an expert on different shrubs and bedding plants. We'd love to help you."

"That's great. I'll take you up to the site one day next week. We can use the Jeep now the new road's in." He laughed at Hana, who pulled a face. "I always make my wife ride up."

Elaine looked suitably relieved she wouldn't have to straddle a horse and Robert giggled like a schoolboy, covertly spotting the look which crossed her face. Hana felt grateful for his happiness, the pain of her mother's loss subdued by recent events. The elderly couple excused themselves and tottered upstairs to find walking shoes in their luggage.

"I gave your dad a map of the shorter bush walks," Logan said, brushing a curl from Hana's cheek as she pushed a scone around her plate. His brow knitted and he narrowed his eyes. "Do you want to go with them?" he asked.

"They didn't invite me," she said, sounding sad.

"Just tag along," Logan suggested and Hana shook her head.

"I'll get my feet up while Phoe's asleep." She punctuated her sentence with a yawn. "A foot massage might be nice."

Logan bit his lip and smirked. Hana widened her eyes in mock horror and he ran his finger lightly down the back of her neck, smiling at the shiver it induced. "Let's go then," he said, moderating his enthusiasm with a sideways glance at Michael.

As Logan stood up, red stuff erupted down his tee shirt. He put his hand up to his nose, squeezing with his fingers and putting his head down. "Oh, crap! Not again."

Hana dragged Phoenix's towelling square from under the pram, glad it was clean as she held it up to Logan's face. "try to contain it in this," she said, wincing at the blood spatters around his feet.

Michael watched with clinical interest but Aroha looked sick again. Hana turned her back on them to shield some of the gore. Logan's tee shirt soaked up the blood so quickly, it stuck to his chest and he pulled it away from his skin with his free hand.

"Hold on a sec," Hana said, shifting the scarlet square of towel beneath the flow. She smirked. "You look like an axe murderer." She saw only her husband's eyes over the towel and he rolled them in an exaggerated movement, tugging at his shirt.

"Noo ssherrt," he tried to tell her, his speech impeded by the blood and subsequent swelling. He tugged again and blood sprayed over Hana's arms.

"Okay ,okay," she soothed. "I've got the message, but there's not much point now; it's ruined."

Logan muttered something unintelligible and tugged again. Hana pulled at the hem and extracted his arms one by one as he swapped hands holding the towel. Blood marked the wooden floor making a dreadful, sticky sound as their feet moved over it. Aroha moved back in her chair to avoid the red spray, giving her a great view of Logan's impressively muscular torso and first-hand sighting of the dreadful scar which snaked its way up the side of his body. It was ugly and gnarled looking and Hana heard the other woman's reaction as Aroha's breath caught in her throat. Hana gritted her teeth, cursing the tactless reaction. A glance at Logan found him oblivious, his face pushed into the crimson towel.

Aroha put her hand up to her mouth and Hana moved to block her from view, knowing how self-conscious he was. Michael observed the scar with a surgeon's eye, but his interest strayed towards the tattoo on Logan's upper arm and shoulder. In blocking Aroha, Hana opened a clear line of sight for Michael. The tee shirt hung limply in Hana's hand and she stroked Logan's hair away from his eyes. "You ok?" she whispered and her husband nodded, squinting through one eye as the constant blood flow swelled his tortured blood vessels and induced a headache.

Hana eyed the pram and the route to the doorway which took her past Michael and she caught the smirk on his face as he read the lines of ruined genealogy on his half-brother's skin. Hana's eyes narrowed in dismay at the ugly grin of victory. He looked thrilled that Logan's *whakapapa* was wrong and she bristled with anger and loyalty. She glared into his grey eyes and saw his expression alter, moving from amusement to rage in an instant.

At first, Hana couldn't work out why and glanced at Logan in confusion. In beautiful, gothic font, the words, *Hana – Phoenix – Tama Du Rose* wrapped around Logan's bulging bicep with a flourish. Michael's eyes became gimlet hard and he stood, flexing his fists. Hana felt the danger descend over the room as rage filled Michael's face. His jawline grew granite hard and Hana saw his teeth grind beneath the skin of his cheek. Logan wasn't in any position to defend himself and Hana yanked on his arm with urgency. "Let's get to the bathroom," she hissed. "We need to move."

Logan saw nothing, his head bowed and his face shrouded in the towel. He trusted Hana and moved forwards at her direction. Sweat beaded on Michael's forehead as he stoked himself into a frenzy of jealousy and panic rose in Hana's chest. She yanked on Logan's wrist and the towel came away from his nose, pebbling the floor with droplets of blood. Hana eyed her pram on the opposite side of the table, conflicted between her baby and husband. If she got Logan safely to the door, she could go back for Phoenix. They shuffled around the table towards the door, Hana passing Michael first and keeping herself between him and Logan.

His face looked possessed as he drew back his fist, his face curled into a demonic snarl. Rage blinded him to the slender redhead between him and the half-brother who owned everything including his bastard son. Aroha cried out in fear. "Michael! No!"

Hana reacted, throwing the dregs from Aroha's mint tea into Michael's eyes and causing him to splutter and cough. She shoved Logan towards the doorway, dropped the empty mug on the table and seized the cake plate. She delivered a fantastic backhand into Michael's face with brute force, amazed the plate remained intact. Michael grunted and covered his face with his hands in self-defence as Hana risked a second swing, hearing the dull thud as the robust china clanged against his knuckles.

"Hana?" Logan's face channelled horror as the towel dripped onto the floor and his wife gulped and ran her hand over the floral design.

"I always loved this set," she said and hefted it with a flourish. Logan watched in amazement as Hana wedged the edge of the plate against Michael's throat and leaned in close. "Try that again and I'll hurt you worse!" she hissed.

The pained look on Michael's face spoke volumes but Hana hadn't finished. Logan continued to produce a red waterfall and recovered his face with the towel, stifling a snort of hilarity. He heard Hana get up into Michael's face and spit out the word, "Coward!" through gritted teeth.

Hana seized the pram handle on her way through and somehow acquired a sobbing Aroha. With pounding heart and shaking hands she guided her entourage towards the lift, leaving a bright red trail guaranteed to upset Leslie. In the bedroom she pushed Logan into the bathroom, parked Phoenix by the dresser and plonked Aroha back in the armchair by the window.

As her anger dissipated and her energy levels plummeted earthwards, Hana eyed the bed with a desperate gaze. "I'll be bloody glad when today's over," she sighed.

Chapter 30

"**I** can't believe this," Aroha sobbed. "How could I make this mistake again?" She clutched her stomach and bent herself double in the armchair. "I'm so stupid."

"Don't say that," Hana soothed. "It's not good for the baby to get so upset." Poor Aroha continued to cry. Michael had portrayed himself as the debonair doctor and then descended into the egotistical male stereotype and his girlfriend reeled from the shock. "I thought he was different to Kane," she howled. "But they're all the bloody same!"

"No, they aren't," Hana asserted, rocking the pram to keep Phoenix asleep. "Logan isn't."

"He was going to hit Logan!" Aroha sniffed. "That wasn't just inappropriate, it was unfair!"

Hana watched the distraught woman rock herself and mustered the energy to behave with compassion. Tiredness dragged at her feet as she fought to control the situation. Logan splashed around in the shower, washing the blood from his face and torso and Hana smiled in all the right places. Aroha lost everything in her flight from Kane, not only her baby son but her sanity and self-respect. "I'm done with all of them," she declared. "It's over!" Remembering her unborn child, Aroha sobbed at the cruel twist of fate which left her in exactly the same mess as two decades previously.

Hana checked on Logan, finding him naked and his clothes partly rinsed out in the shower tray. "You ok?" she asked.

"Yeah." He nodded, stuffing cotton wool into his nostrils.

"You shouldn't do that," Hana sighed and he raised his eyebrows in a half grin.

"Do you realise that you say that every time?"

Hana closed the door and leaned against it, watching her husband's reflection in the mirror.

"Stop checking me out," he said, turning so she could enjoy the full effect.

"Can if I want to," Hana leered, drawing a snort from him. She closed her eyes and leaned her head against the door. "What are we going to do?" she whispered.

"We?" Logan gave her a cynical look and Hana groaned.

"Fine, me then. What am I gonna do?"

Logan grabbed a towel and wrapped it around his waist. "What the hell happened?" he asked. "One minute I'm blinded by blood and the next, you're threatening Michael having thrown cake all over the table."

Hana gave the cotton wool walrus tusks a curious look, smiling indulgently but offering no explanation. Logan rolled his eyes. "I need my clothes; is she planning on staying in there all day?"

"Don't be mean," Hana sighed, pulling the door open.

Aroha saw Logan's muscular body partly clad in his towel and rose to leave. She wiped her hand across her eyes. "I should leave; I'm sorry. Do you think a taxi would come this far out?"

Hana shook her head. "I don't think so. How far do you need to go?"

"Auckland." Aroha bit her lip.

Logan stood in the doorway, drying his hair on a hand towel. "Stay here tonight," he said, his voice authoritative but unthreatening. "I'll get someone to drive you home tomorrow."

Hana nodded. "That's a great idea. Logan, do you know the keypad number for Barry's old room?"

He recalled it instantly; his mathematical brain impressing Hana and producing a smile of approval. She led Aroha down the hall, installing her in the spacious bedroom of a boy who died young. Barry Du Rose slipped into death as violently as he had lived his life, his organs shutting down one by one as he bled out inexplicably.

"It's a beautiful room," Aroha sniffed and Hana agreed. "Shame Barry Du Rose was such an arsehole."

"Oh." Hana's lips parted in amusement. "I didn't know him."

"But you've heard, right?" Aroha said, pulling open the drapes to reveal a room decorated in a classical theme. "I bet they're all too superstitious to use it," Aroha sniffed. She admired the pretty pale green colours with contrasting cream duvet cover and curtains. "At least I know Michael will stay away." Another round of tears sprang from her eyes.

"Think of your baby," Hana told her. She made Aroha a drink and settled her on the bed before excusing herself to return to her husband.

In the hallway outside she ran into Michael. "Don't touch me!" Hana snapped, distaste evident in her face. He put his hands up as though to defend himself and apologised.

"Please, I'm sorry; I don't know what came over me. You know I'm not like that. Can I see Logan and explain?"

"No way!" Hana exclaimed. "You aren't coming near my husband! Luckily for you, he didn't see your ridiculous behaviour. Why don't you devote your time to Aroha, who's now terrified of you, stupid little man!"

Michael groaned and rubbed his eyes. "I saw *'Tama'* written on his arm next to your baby and it hurt."

"What's your problem?" Hana raged. "You're like a spoiled brat who wants everything Logan has; it's pathetic."

"But Tama's my son!" Michael put his hands on his hips and towered over Hana. She saw the beginnings of bruising on his throat and forehead and took a step forward, seeing his cowardly demeanour return.

"And you gave him *nothing!*" she bit. "Logan loves Tama and always showed him a father's love. He belongs to us now so get over it. You just can't bear Logan to take something else you believe is yours. Do everyone a favour and grow up, Michael. You make me sick with your juvenile rivalry. Just go home!"

"You can't make me," Michael spat and Hana's green eyes flashed with the force of the dare.

"Can't I?" A wicked smile touched her lips as she accepted the dare. "I can call any of the stock men and they'll throw you out of here without asking why. Is that what you want?" Hana reached into her pocket for her mobile phone and Michael took a step back.

"You wouldn't."

"Wouldn't I?" Hana unlocked the screen and he relented with surprising speed.

"Don't! Please, don't."

Hana turned and stalked back to her bedroom, hearing Michael knocking on Barry's old bedroom door. She let herself into the room and leaned against the door with a sigh, dreading dinner time with a passion.

"Trouble?" Logan asked and Hana shook her head.

"Nothing I can't handle."

Logan pointed at his clean jeans and then wrinkled his nose. "I'm trying to pluck up the courage to put on a clean tee shirt." The walrus tusks still dangled from his nose, streaked with bright red blood.

"Maybe not yet," Hana said. "Wait awhile."

"You look knackered." Logan held his arms out to her and she nestled into his chest, feeling the soft black down against her cheek.

"I'm regretting bringing my father here," she muttered. "I should have guessed some disaster would befall us; it usually does."

"It's just a nosebleed," her husband reassured her, misunderstanding. "I think I lost pints with that one, I feel lightheaded."

"You need a hot, sugary drink." Hana flicked the kettle on to boil again and reached into the cabinet for a mug. Logan appeared behind her, putting his arms around her and pulling her backwards into his chest.

"What really happened?" he asked again, as she knew he would.

Hana sighed. "If I said you'd be better off not knowing, would you trust me and leave it alone?"

Logan put his head back and looked at the ceiling without answering. He felt under his nose to check the bleeding had stopped and sighed with relief when it had. Hana kept contact with him, managing to make him sugary coffee with his left arm laid heavily around her shoulder. She handed it to him, looking for an answer. Logan took the drink and then bowed his head regally. "Ok," he said slowly, staring into her green eyes. "I'm always asking you to trust me, so I guess it's fair." He smiled and withdrew the cotton wool sausages from his nose, flicking them into the dustbin.

Hana's body slumped as she felt the tension pass. Logan Du Rose stared at his beautiful, redheaded wife - certain he saw her slender fingers hold the edge of a cake plate violently to his brother's throat. He ran his thumb over her jaw line and behind her ear, watching her eyes close and her eyelashes flutter against her cheek. "You're gorgeous when you're mad," he whispered, slipping his other hand beneath her blouse and walking his fingers over her flesh, teasing her senses. Hana felt his lips brush hers and sensed her defenses weaken. Logan's grey eyes carried a hint of humour and his perfect teeth gripped his bottom lip lightly. "You're a powerful woman, Mrs Du Rose," he said with a smirk, "and I find that extremely sexy." He pushed his fingers into her bra, savouring the heaviness of her breast against his flesh.

"Good," Hana replied coyly. "But you're dripping blood on the floor."

They ate dinner in the formal dining room with the other hotel guests, avoiding the flash point of the private dining room. A subdued Aroha sat with Michael at a table for two near the door and Hana squeezed her shoulder as she passed. Robert was in his element, strutting through the dining room like a rooster and pulling out the ladies' chairs with a flourish. Leslie looked after Phoenix in her upstairs apartment so Hana had the evening off to play footsie with her husband under the table.

Logan looked dark under the eyes and the bridge of his nose swelled painfully from the broken blood vessels inside. His voice sounded like he had a cold and she squeezed his thigh under the table. None of the staff mentioned the blood bath in the family dining room or the scattered cake and Hana avoided their questioning gaze.

Robert and Elaine dressed for dinner, looking sweet in their formal evening wear. They chose from the menu like excited children and Hana found it endearing. "Ooh, let's have the salmon, Lainey." Robert clapped his hands together like a boy.

Hana felt choked that in a few short days they'd be gone, flying home to Blighty and a world she struggled to relate to. Logan chatted easily, explaining his plan for Reuben and Miriam's memorial garden.

"So, you didn't know he was your father until after he died?" Robert asked, his tone sad.

Logan nodded. "Yep. I was the product of a forty year affair. Must be some kind of record."

"Aye, son," Robert said, not fooled by Logan's bravado. "That's tragic on so many levels. You must be hurtin' in that big heart o' yourn."

Logan studied his plate and Hana watched her husband battle the familiar inward struggle. She reached a hand under the table and stroked his thigh again. Logan's fingers clasped hers and he swallowed, struggling more with Robert calling him *son*, than the loss of his *whakapapa*. It plucked at hidden strings and unbound something inside his heart.

"I'm so sorry for your loss," Elaine whispered, her eyes damp with tears. Hana felt a flush of affection for her aunt as their identical green eyes met.

"Thanks," Logan said, keen to move the conversation on. "The site we'll visit tomorrow is where Reuben's house used to be before the fire. The area's still quite charred. I bought it from my half-brother as they couldn't face building on the same ground; too many bad memories."

"I love the maze idea," Robert said, nodding enthusiastically. "That's my clever Hana. We can plan it out together later if you like?"

"Yes, thanks Dad." Hana felt grateful. It seemed an ironic tribute for a couple whose lives took such unfortunate twists and turns, going nowhere in the end.

"I'm excited about the centre of the maze," Elaine said, laying her cutlery down. "There's so many things we could do. The centre is such an important place because it's the prize for making it through and finding it."

"Yes, that's true," Hana said. "I never thought about it like that."

"The idea of a peaceful, gravelled area, with perhaps a bench seat and fountain would offer visitors the opportunity to sit and reflect. Maybe there could be a memorial stone or something appropriate?"

Robert cleared his throat, sounding nervous and directing his question towards Logan. "Perhaps you'd allow me as a former clergyman to say a blessing over the area, before you begin your revival of it?"

Hana's eyes flashed with pleasure at her father's thoughtfulness. She struggled not to jump up with excitement and clap her hands. Logan nodded with little hesitation. "That'd be great, yes please." He looked relieved as though asking God into the site would expunge the devastation of its past.

"The Māori *kaumatua* visited even before the fire investigators vacated," Hana said, pushing her plate away. "He banished the spirit of death and the *tapu*, returning it to a state of *noa*, or normality for the family."

Logan smiled at her understanding of his customs, his grey eyes appreciative. It was a kind thing the old man did, trudging through the ash and stench of burnt electrics and melted rubber on Christmas Eve. He was a gentle Māori named Arama, whose mana oozed from him in waves. Hana met him afterwards, receiving his *hongi* whilst painfully aware her nagging backache was finding a pattern and bite. He looked into her eyes deeply and smiled.

"Be well, *tamāhine*," he breathed and Hana wondered if he knew what she struggled to hide. Phoenix was born a few hours later in the midst of the tragedy.

The family parted outside the lift as Hana took her husband's hand. "Let's go up to Leslie's apartment and get Phoe," she said.

He pressed his lips against hers. "And miss the opportunity to spend half an hour with my wife *alone?*" he whispered, sounding sultry. He pushed her giggling along the corridor and into their bedroom.

"I need to get Phoe soon," Hana pleaded, wincing as Logan toyed with her full breasts.

"When are these gonna be all mine?" he grumbled, shifting his body over hers.

"You got me pregnant!" Hana exclaimed. "I didn't do it by myself."

"Ah, but I'm not totally sure what causes it. I think I need to get more practice in until I'm sure." Logan laughed, the slow rumble vibrating through Hana's chest wall.

"You're bad," she giggled, her words silenced by her husband's lips.

Ages later she pushed Logan away. "No more, Mr Du Rose. I'm getting my daughter and you're coming with me. Leslie has a habit of keeping me talking and I'm tired. I need my bed."

"You're in bed," Logan said, his voice sultry.

Hana ran her palms over his muscular back, feeling the bones in his spine through her fingers. "Yeah, that's an awesome idea. Thanks, babe. I'll just wait here while you go up to the apartment. Don't be long." Hana pushed him off her and rolled onto her side, snuggling into her pillow.

"You know that's not what I meant," Logan groaned. "Fine! I'll come with you."

Logan's feet were bare as they climbed the stairs to Leslie's refurbished apartment. The walls were a riot of gentle pastel colours interspersed with feature walls. The predominant shade was a soft mauve with white woodwork and ceilings, transforming the space from its former shabby chic to peaceful and comforting. Hana saw Logan ball his fists and regretted forcing him to accompany her. She knew he missed his mother with a tangible ache and visiting her former home wouldn't help. "Sorry," she whispered and he shrugged.

"It's just bricks, Hana. I know she's gone."

Leslie greeted Hana with hugs and kisses, eyeing Logan with deference and a nod of acknowledgement. "She ate well, my *mokopuna*." Leslie indicated the sleeping baby in the pram by the fireplace and Hana's eyes widened. Phoenix's stomach protruded from the blankets like a Father Christmas doll.

A movement in an adjoining room caught Hana's eye and she put her hand over her mouth to disguise the ready smirk. She glanced at her husband, feeling his body stiffen against hers. Alfred Du Rose strolled through the apartment in a pair of pyjamas and a dressing gown. He looked as though he still lived there and Hana wondered if he was lost.

Logan gritted his teeth and shook his head. "Yeah, his grief lasted a long time," he hissed under his breath.

Hana nudged him in the ribs as Leslie bent down over the pram, straightening Phoenix's blankets and stroking the soft pink cheek. Logan closed his eyes and ground his jaw, frowning as though pondering a massive problem. Hana sensed many emotions radiate from his unhappy core; embarrassment, anger and sadness. She reached for Logan's hand, entwining her fingers through his and feeling a flush of pleasure as he accepted the lifeline.

"Hana," Alfred said, his olive skin flushing red with embarrassment. "I didn't know…oh, never mind." He pulled his brown dressing gown more tightly around his waist and shifted on unsteady feet. His arm flailed towards Leslie as though in explanation but she refused to catch his eye.

Logan nodded to the man who parented him for forty years and it was a different greeting to the fond *hongi* and firm embrace of a year ago. Hana felt bereft for them both, wondering where the rot began and which man cultivated it first. She looked at Leslie and winced involuntarily, regretting that the older woman saw.

Leslie smiled and winked as though trying to communicate something to her, woman to woman. Then her brown eyes settled on her embarrassed lover. "Have you let that bath water out this time, Alfred Du Rose?" she demanded.

He nodded. "Aye, sorry about last time." He ran his hands through damp greying hair and looked unsure of himself. Leslie jerked her head towards Logan.

"There's more than just Hana here!" she said, speaking to the old man like a child.

"Ah, yep." Alfred moved slowly toward Logan and offered his hand to shake. "Good day, son."

Logan looked at the hand and then back at Alfred. It was a small offering, but he figured it was better than nothing. He accepted the proffered, arthritic fingers, shaking them and whipping a false smile onto his face. Hana ached for him so badly, she had to turn away to fiddle with the pram to hide her misery. "Thanks for looking after Phoe," she whispered to Leslie. "It was nice to be able to sit with Dad for an hour."

"Dinner's late finishing," Leslie smirked and Hana shot a frightened look over her shoulder. She turned back in time to see Leslie's veiled grin. "But I don't mind, ye know. I love that girl like she's my own."

Hana swallowed. "I know. I appreciate it so much. If I could just shake this tiredness, it would be easier."

"No matter. This old woman is here to help." Leslie enfolded her in a warm embrace which contrasted starkly with the formality of the men.

"Night," Hana whispered and Leslie ran the backs of her fingers down Hana's cheek.

"Night *kōtiro*."

They made their exit politely, trying not to make too much noise descending the wooden stairs. Back in their bedroom, Phoenix transferred from the pram to the travel cot without stirring. Hana swaddled her up, putting rolled up towels behind and in front of her to prevent her rolling onto her face. "Do you think Leslie drugs her?" Hana asked, staring at the comatose child. "She's overdue a feed." She ran a tentative finger over her swollen breast and saw Logan look at her with a sparkle in his eyes.

"What, so they can get a quick one in?" His tone was facetious.

Hana wrinkled her nose, trying to assess the level of Logan's distress. "We think they're appalling and Tama thinks we are. It must be the curse of the generations," Hana sighed. "I'm sorry though. I know it bothers you."

"My nose hurts," Logan complained, trying to distract her and pressing the bridge of his nose between his fingers.

"Enough to stop you discussing anything important?" Hana said with a smirk, slipping her blouse over her head. She peered down at her breasts as they fought to escape her bra. "I don't know if I can sleep with these."

"I can definitely sleep with them," Logan breathed, cupping them gently from behind and nibbling the soft skin of Hana's neck. The moment was ruined by the first of Phoenix's horrible wet farts and they dissolved into uncontrollable giggles.

"Boil up with pork and kumara," Logan sniggered, sniffing the air and covering his nose and mouth. "Leslie feeds her until she's got no choice but to sleep it off."

Hana shook her head. "I can't get rid of the image of Alfred in his paisley jim-jams and Leslie in a granny nightie, frolicking around above our heads."

"No! Don't create those images!" Logan groaned, collapsing onto the bad backwards.

Bright and early the next morning, Logan drove Hana, Robert and Elaine up to the site of Rueben's old house. "This is a trusty old vehicle," Robert commented, patting the side of Jack's red Jeep.

"It's older than me, I think," Logan joked. "It rattles a lot, but it's better now the new road is almost finished. We could only get as far as the bunkhouse before using a quad bike, but this road will take us right to the top of the mountain and the site for the new house."

"It sounds amazing, eh Hana?" Robert clapped his hands in glee.

"I hope Phoenix is okay." Hana worried, remembering the disgusted look on her daughter's face as she handed her over to Leslie again.

"The housekeeper seems to adore her," Elaine reassured, patting Hana's hand in the back seat.

"Yes, she does," Hana said, realising Leslie was the nearest thing to a doting grandmother Phoenix had.

The charred scent had left the area months since but the singed shrubbery around Reuben's old property still told a tale beneath its vigorous new growth. Weeds and grass had sprung up in the charred soil, cynically thriving in the charcoal remnants. "Shall we pray first?" Robert asked, heartened by Logan's nod as he put the handbrake on.

Hana's father prayed over the area and anointed the four corner posts marking the proposed maze site. The gathered group stood with bowed heads as the once-holy man blessed the site and asked for God's peace and grace to descend on it, touching anyone who worked or visited there in the future. "Amen," his deep, Scots accent intoned.

Hana eyed the tiny vial of oil between his fingers, her childhood memories stirred by the sight of something so familiar. Her gaze strayed to the steep bank behind her and she saw herself, heavily pregnant, slipping towards the fire site as she followed her sister-in-law, Liza. Hana recalled the flames, vibrant and treacherous against the night sky and Miriam's hair as she rushed into them, trailing out behind her as it ignited. Hana pushed her fingers either side of the bridge of her nose and shut her eyes and Logan saw. "What's wrong, babe," he asked, cradling her in his strong arms.

"How can you bear it here?" Hana hissed. "I can't stop myself being transported back to that awful night. How can you stand here so calmly, making plans?"

Logan shrugged. "It's part of the process, Hana. I'm a 'fixer' who lives to improve and enhance my surroundings and this is just another place to be fixed."

Robert smiled and patted Logan's shoulder in approval, smiling at his daughter with indulgence. "Your husband's right, hen," he whispered.

So Hana went along with it, trying not to look at the bank and focussing on Elaine's suggestions for suitable hedging. "Whatever you choose will take time to grow, possibly years, but it'll need to find the bush conditions favourable." Elaine waved her arms in animation and her Irish accent sounded more pronounced as she listed possible shrubs and bushes. Robert caught Hana staring at the rugged bank again and put his arm around her, looking at her with a question in his eyes.

Haltingly his daughter described her frightening descent and even more precarious climb back up the sharp, crumbling cliff. "Alfred helped me," she admitted, tears brimming beneath her eyelids. "He watched his wife commit suicide and then he walked me home. It feels surreal now." Hana wiped her eyes and sniffed.

"So what hold does the bank have over you?" Robert asked, taking Hana's hand in his. He led her to the bottom of the sharp incline and turned her to face him. "Is it just memories or is there something else?"

Hana stared at the craggy earth with narrowed green eyes. "Just memories, I think. But there's so much more, Dad. Logan's birth father lived here and he never knew. So much evil went on in this place and I can feel it." Hana wrapped her arms around herself and shivered. She lowered her voice. "I can't show Logan how much I hate it; he's trying so hard."

Robert nodded and stroked Hana's cheek. He took the oil from his pocket and removed the lid, dabbing his finger across the neck. He pressed a cross gently over her forehead. "May the peace of Christ be with you in this place, precious daughter," he breathed, his deep voice resonating in the air above Hana. Then he turned and flicked oil onto the bank. "I rebuke you, spirits of pain, depression and death in the name of Jesus Christ. Go! You are not welcome here."

Hana remembered what an awesome man of God her father was and regretted the awful memory which replaced the image of his great kindness. "Thanks, Dad," she sighed, pressing her face into his chest.

Robert smiled, closed his eyes and held his daughter for real instead of just in his head, relishing the preciousness of the moment and not realising how much it would haunt his nightmares in the days to come.

Chapter 31

Hana walked around Rangiriri Pa, absorbing the sacredness and abiding silence, despite its proximity to State Highway 1. The huge mound in the centre of the paddock was once part of the deep, five metre trenches, the Māori used to defend their redoubt from the English. It was an ingenious use of early trench warfare and confounded their enemy. Logan stood next to her, reading the decorative boards describing the war for visitors. "The Māori were war generals, far ahead of their time," he mused. "The battle for Rangiriri was one of the most significant of the New Zealand Wars and led to heavy losses for the British soldiers." Logan wrinkled his nose. "Unless you listen to their version, which is very different."

"Yeah, I can believe that," Hana said, smiling sideways at her husband. He bit his lip and narrowed his eyes, faking annoyance.

"You doubting me, *wahine?*"

Hana put her hand over her heart, feeling the tingling beat through her chest wall. "Would I?" She smirked and leaned over the information board, reading its factual description.

'The trenches were channelled between the Waikato River and Lake Waikare by hand and required the use of planks in order

to be crossed. A huge mound of earth rose up above the remains of the pa, betraying the position of the central redoubt which had towered above the ditches. Māori repelled eight British attacks from their stronghold, defeated finally by a misunderstanding over a white flag, which Māori intended for negotiation and the British claimed as surrender. The Māori king movement, Kiingitanga, had taken a significant hit that day.'

"I'm so glad we came," Robert said, his smile broad as he led Elaine across the damp grass. "Thank you for humouring an old man."

"It's fine." Logan smiled. "I haven't been here for years."

"It's great having that brochure rack in your hotel reception," Robert said, caressing the coloured pamphlet about Rangiriri in his fingers. He'd snagged it that morning after breakfast. "I'd never have known it was here otherwise and I'm so interested in history."

Logan nodded. "I love our New Zealand history, although many Kiwis seem more intent on discovering British roots. I always think that's a shame." He hefted Phoenix on his hip.

"Tell them about our family's involvement in the battle," Tama gushed with enthusiasm. "The Du Roses gave safe house to many of the fleeing Māori, including chief Wiremu Tamihana and Māori King Tāwhiao."

"Really?" Robert's eyes lit up with interest and the men wandered away, chatting about a shared passion.

"Logan's very ardent," Elaine said and Hana nodded.

"He learned about their history at his grandmother's knee. She was an important influence in his early life."

Elaine patted her hand. "I'm happy for you, my dear." Her green eyes strayed towards Logan's straight back and the sight of Phoenix twiddling one of his dark curls. "He adores you and your baby and that kind of devotion is very rare." She sounded wistful but before Hana could respond, she moved away.

Hana looked at the sky and contemplated fetching the picnic from the boot of the Honda, during a rare absence of meteorological discord. Her phone buzzed in her jeans pocket and she fished it out, reading the text from her brother. *'Just arrived. Are you through that funny gate thing at the top of the steps?'*

'*Yep*,' Hana replied.

"I can feel their spirits clamouring for my attention," Hana said softly as Mark puffed over to her and he stared at her, a strange look in his eyes.

"Whose?"

"The warriors and soldiers who died here," Hana said, her voice sounding dreamy.

"Weirdo!" Mark chuckled and kissed her on the cheek. "Just gonna say hi to Mum and Dad. I'll thank your husband for letting me spend a few days with them at your place too. I'm excited to see this hotel of yours."

Hana nodded and smiled, her gaze faraway. She placed her fingers into the space at the bottom of her ribs and ran them upwards in an arc. When she opened her mouth to speak, Mark was already striding over to Logan, his hand outstretched in greeting. "It hurts," she whispered, her words ending in a sigh. No one earthly heard but the *tangata whenua* groaned in dismay.

A little girl ran around on the delicate mounds of earth and Hana looked across in irritation. The signs clearly stated the area was *tapu*, sacred. They asked politely that visitors refrain from smoking, eating or walking on the area which represented the graves of the fallen, now buried in their trenches by time and weather. The child was attached to a group of tourists and they stomped around, behaving as though the signage didn't apply to them. It was just another thing to look at and photograph on their whistle-stop coach tour of New Zealand.

Hana put her hand up to get their attention and Logan saw, his brow creasing in irritation at their ignorance. He watched his wife's face change from mild discomfort to agony in a heartbeat, as the nagging indigestion exploded and revealed its true nature. It burst into flames in her chest wall and caused her to let out a loud gasp as breath exhaled, but would not return. Something was stuck somewhere, a bodily malfunction with no obvious cause. Hana suffocated in her own frame, the constricting pain squeezing air out without replacing it. She sank to her knees as a tingling ache began in her armpits, panicking and grabbing at her chest. The small explosion in her eardrums unleashed a darkness which reached for her. Nothing made sense.

"Take her!" Logan handed Phoenix roughly to a surprised Tama and ran towards his wife as though in slow motion. He hurled himself to his knees and pulled Hana into a sitting position, his arms around her ribs. Her green eyes stared at him, begging him to help and he floundered, not understanding.

Mark reached them and saw Hana's lips adopt a familiar grey hue and his face paled in agony. "No, no, no! Hana, Hana!" He kneeled next to Logan and wrenched Hana from him. "Get off!" he shouted. "You don't understand!" He hadn't been there for Judith, but he would be there for his sister. Mark dragged her from Logan's arms and laid her on her back, his fingers grappling for a pulse in her neck. "It's faint!" he shouted, his eyes finding Tama's. "Ring for an ambulance."

The last thing Hana remembered before her brain shut down was trying to turn on her side to alleviate the awful pain. Some part of her still believed it was indigestion, but Mark's terrified green eyes sent a thrill of inevitability as a painful tingle snaked up the front of her neck and into her jaw. A wise woman once told her before Bodie's birth not to fear pain, because her brain would override her consciousness before it became unbearable.

As the pain rendered Hana's lungs empty and stopped her heart, it wasn't the slow fade she imagined but more like a light bulb blowing. One minute, she saw the stricken face of her husband and the next moment, nothing.

Dear Reader,

I would love it if you could leave a review at your usual retailer.

I find the opinions of readers helpful and constructive. Reviews are the Holy Grail to an author as they cause our work to sink or swim. It is the bench mark for other readers and can determine whether our work will be successful and reach many or none. It doesn't have to be an essay or a literary criticism.

A few words about what you liked would be most appreciated.

The shortest review I ever received for my work was, 'Great,' accompanied by five stars and the longest was a whole video from a gorgeous woman in the USA. My favourite to date has to be the lady who said, '*I read until my eyes fell out.*' I keep looking at that one because it makes me laugh.

You can review on my website, ktbowes.com.

Go to the book's buy page where you can follow through to your own retailer and leave a review for me.

And hey, let me know when you've done it. I'd love to hear from you.

About the Author

K T Bowes is a bestselling teen and women's author.

Her novel, *A Trail of Lies*, was the winner of the genre award for Author's Cave in 2014.

Phoenix Du Rose was considered for the prestigious Ngaio Marsh awards for 2021 and *Her Quiet Legacy* in 2022.

K T Bowes is an Englishwoman in exile in New Zealand, swapping rugged cosmopolitan for mountain ranges and terrifying rivers. She loves Māori culture and has learned to weave flax using traditional methods. Her other passion is Rongoa Māori, which involves creating medicines from native plants. She is a student of Te Reo Māori.

You can find her hanging out on social media in the following places.

Check in and say hello. Maybe suggest she gets back to writing and stops watching cat videos.

FACEBOOK

https://www.facebook.com/NZauthorKTBowes/

TWITTER

https://twitter.com/ktboweswrites

INSTAGRAM

https://www.instagram.com/k_t_bowes

Also by this Author

The Hana Du Rose Mysteries Series:
Logan Du Rose
About Hana
Hana Du Rose
Du Rose Legacy
The New Du Rose Matriarch
One Heartbeat
The Du Rose Prophecy
Du Rose Sons
Du Rose Family Ties
Du Rose Vendetta
Phoenix Du Rose
Wiremu Du Rose

The Calculated Risk Series:
The Actuary
The Actuary's Wife
The Actuary in Trouble
The Heart of The Actuary

Troubled series for teens:
Free from the Tracks
Sophia's Dilemma
A Trail of Lies
Gone Phishing

Escaping the Back Country NZ Series:
Pirongia's Secret
Deleilah

Standalone novels:
Artifact
Demons on Her Shoulder
All Saints
Her Quiet Legacy

Humorous Cozy Mystery Series from New Zealand
Dead Straight
Bad Hair Day
Side Parting